THE LIGHTHOUSE DINER

The Lighthouse Diner

DAVID MAJOR

Contact Author:
www.davidmajorbooks.com
david@davidmajorbooks.com

ISBN: 978-0-9655533-6-0 (Paperback)
ISBN: 978-0-9655533-7-7 (eBook)
Library of Congress Control Number: 2023921725

Cover Credits: Melanie Conrad

First printing edition 2024

Published by Davidson Publishing
Glen Allen, VA

THE LIGHTHOUSE DINER

CHAPTER 1

I'm not the sharpest tool in the shed and that might sound fitting for a guy from Princeton, West Virginia. People figure the way we talk is because we're dumb hillbillies. But you can't be but so dull and get by living here. There are no jobs, no money, not much hope. But at least I know I'm not bright and that's a lot to know. So, when it comes to important stuff, I get help. I go online, I research. I ask smart people what they'd do about something.

And that's what had me sitting at the desk of Mr. Thomas Perkins, Branch Manager at First Community Bank. It was a Monday, the 15th of June, and I had just deposited $38,416.88 — my inheritance from Mom. About a month back she lost her battle with Alzheimer's.

He was talking to me about what to do with the money, and I was thinking a new F150, maybe even an F250 diesel. Not a brand new one, but a late model new to me. Thomas had other ideas.

"Age," he requested.

"What?" I asked.

"Your age?"

"Oh, 28."

He typed in the number. "Insurance would be roughly $2,400 per year." He was clicking away on his keyboard. "And personal property tax . . ."

Maybe an F150 with that turbo-charged six cylinder. Heard a lot of good things about them.

"Personal property tax about $300. Maybe less," he added.

My new truck dream was fading. I hadn't even picked out the color yet.

Out of nowhere another banker stormed in and dropped a stack of papers on the desk. "We need to talk about this," he barked and stormed out.

I turned in my seat to watch him leave, wondering why he thought he could interrupt us like that without so much as an 'Excuse me.' Maybe it was because he was wearin' a coat and tie, while I was wearin' an old T-shirt with a tear on the sleeve and a coffee-stain circle on the shoulder. Or maybe it was because he had his head up his butt.

Mr. Perkins picked up the papers, glanced through a few pages, and then placed them on the corner of his desk. The corner near me. "Sorry about that."

I nodded.

"You have a truck," he said, "not too old. A new truck would drop in value as you drove it off the lot. You'd have higher insurance, taxes. The roads here will start tearing it up. It's totally up to you, but I would invest the money, let it grow. It will be here when your truck dies."

That was the usual way, drive it till the wheels come off. I had to admit he had a good point. He started explaining some of the ways to invest my money.

I was trying to pay attention, failing miserably.

"Mr. Perkins?" It was Mr. Head-Up-His-Butt from the next office. *Geez, this guy is rude.*

Mr. Perkins was already standing up. "I'm *so* sorry," he begged, "I'll be right back. When regional folks come through and say jump, we ask how high."

He hurried out the door.

I was pissed but decided to let it go. I was pulling out my phone but stopped dead cold. My heartbeat quickened. There, on the desk, the address on the stack of papers. I knew that address! It's where my friend Jeff lived. Tree Fork is up Route 19, halfway to Beckley. Route 42 crosses it, coming from nowhere and going nowhere. My friend, my best friend Jeff, lived off Route 42. He lived and worked at Jim's Junk Yard. Jim was his dad's name.

What the hell?

I could hear Mr. Perkins and Mr. Butthead talking in the next office. My hand slowly reached for the top page and turned it over. At the top of the second page, stamped in bold capital letters — FORECLOSURE. Somehow my brain started working overtime. Words were jumping out at me: Market value $180,000, assessed value, same number ... principal balance $38,000 ... acreage 67.

Raised voices were still coming from the next office, mostly from Mr. Butthead.

I glanced at the third page. Property taxes ... mortgage insurance ... Eviction Notice: DELIVERED. They were kicking out my friend! Next page: Title ... deed ... late fees ... Auction. No Sale. Then another Auction. No Sale.

I hated what I was reading, but I had to keep going. Next page — no time to read any more. The voices got quieter. I flipped the pages back just in time.

Mr. Perkins came back in with, "Sorry about that."

"Must be end of month quotas," I said.

I was guessing they couldn't sell the junkyard. Go figure.

"Something like that," he replied. "Where were we?"

"What to do with my money," I answered.

"Right."

I pointed to the stack of papers. "Why don't I buy this?"

He reacted by sliding the stack back over to his side of the desk. "Chad," he began, "the truck would be a better decision than this property. And besides, you don't have enough money. Or a job. Just trying to be straight with you here."

He moved the papers to the bookcase behind him, then turned back to his keyboard.

"Mr. Perkins, the junkyard belongs to my friend. Hell, his dad started the business. It wouldn't be right to kick him out."

His business card was in front of me on the desk. I picked it up and grabbed one of the many pens lying around. On the back I wrote $32,000 and slid it over to him. "There. Now you can meet your quota, right?"

Thomas picked it up and rubbed his chin. I could tell he was actually thinking about it, so I pushed. "Run it by the regional guy. Ya never know."

He didn't answer. But he did get up and walk to the next office. And that gave me a minute to think.

What the hell am I doing? Am I really this stupid? I thought and thought about it. The only answer I could figure was it doesn't take long living here before you get tired of other people pulling the strings. And in this case, they were abusing my friend.

Mr. Perkins returned with Mr. Butthead, who went straight to the chair behind the desk, leaving nowhere for Mr. Perkins to sit.

Awkward.

Mr. Perkins did the introductions. "Mr. Blanchard, this is Chad Davis." *No Mr. Davis?*

"Chad, this is Mr. Blanchard."

Not because I wanted to, but because of the way I was raised, I stood and shook his hand. He stayed seated.

Mr. Perkins handed Mr. Butthead the papers and he leafed through them. As if he needed to. He knew exactly what was in there. He rubbed his chin.

Geez, I could read them like a book. Butthead was obviously holding a weak hand.

I decided to mess with him. "Anything in there about the sacred Indian burial grounds?" I casually asked. "I mean, you know, in the deed and all."

Butthead looked at me sternly. "There is nothing in here about Indians. What Indians?"

"I'm not sure," I replied. "Iroquois, I think. You'd have to ask Jeff — you know, the guy you're kicking off the property. His dad was thinking about selling the place years back, but there was something about a federal restriction."

His expression didn't change so I kept pulling stuff out of my ass. "It was either Iroquois or Cherokee. Both bury their dead with the head toward the east. And some of the pottery —"

He cut me off. "And where is this alleged burial ground?" he demanded.

"Smack dab in the middle of the junkyard."

I took a breath and started to speak but Butthead cut me off again. "And how did you know this file was about that property?" He glared at Mr. Perkins as he spoke.

"Because *you* dropped the papers in front of me," I replied.

Then I held up my hand to signal for him *not* to interrupt me again.

"Mr. Perkins snatched them up as you left, but I had already seen the address. I know that address and I know Jeff and I know he's so poor he can't pay attention. And I figure you can't give the property away 'cause no one around these parts is gonna mess with sacred burial grounds. Or, for that matter, buy the side of a cliff. Have you guys even *seen* this property? Hell, I'm doing you a favor!"

Now Butthead glared at me, as if he expected me to back down. I'm Irish. We don't. I stood up, put my hands on the desk, and leaned in. I was done playing.

"I'm going to buy me a new truck," I said. "The offer stands 'til I pick out the color."

I turned and left. I went out to the lobby, made a $200 withdrawal, then headed for the door. As my hand was pushing the handle, I heard Mr. Perkins calling, "Chad!" He was at his office door, waving me back. Mr. Butthead was walking into the other office.

Forty-five minutes later, I was the proud owner of a junkyard.

I drove north headed for Tree Fork. The sun was out, the clouds puffy white against a blue backdrop. June is a great month in West Virginia. The nights are cool enough for warm blankets, and the days get up into the 60s and 70s. I stopped on the way for beer, ice, and chips. I couldn't wait to tell Jeff about the dumbest thing I ever did. Not just dumb, the granddaddy of all things stupid.

Something to be said for that, right?

I was happy for Jeff but the $32,000 was *gone*. As my head was screaming "stupid!" my heart was at peace.

Jeff was my best friend, grades 1–12. We grew up on the same street four houses apart. We played together, got in trouble together, sometimes fought with each other, but never mad for long.

In high school we joined the football team. Coach put us on defense as linebackers in a 5-2 formation. You couldn't run against us, couldn't short pass against us. It threw off the other team's game and we usually won — if our offense could score. So we were the popular jocks. Now, ten years later, we still talk about the *glory days*.

After football season our senior year, Jeff quit school and went to work full time at his dad's junkyard. I pushed through until June and then went to work at the coal mines. Five years later, Jeff's mom and dad moved to Florida and left Jeff to run the business. And the mortgage.

At Route 42, I entered the "town" of Tree Fork. It had a gas station, a convenience store, and a few boarded-up office buildings. It didn't have a post office, but it did have a liquor store, a necessity. I turned right and headed east. On the left was a Dollar General, some mobile homes, then a church, then a mobile home, then what looked like an abandoned Waffle House.

And then Jeff's place. It was the last thing on the street. From back at the intersection everything on the right was steep uphill, no structures. But the land on the left side was flat by West Virginia standards. At Jeff's place the flat ran out. I turned in and down a very steep drop-off. From there, a sea of junk cars about two football fields wide and three football fields long. The office and shop were off to the right where it leveled off a bit.

As I stepped out of my truck, I stopped to look over my domain.

Acres full of junk cars. Then it hit me that the cars didn't belong to me. And that Jeff was now living in my house.

Hadn't thought about that. This could get awkward.

The office door faced the street. On each side were two flower pots with nothing in them. No "open" sign or hours of operation. Just "Beware of Dog" hand painted on a piece of plywood.

I walked in and could tell I caught him off guard. He had been crying. He looked away, trying to hide it. Moving boxes were everywhere.

"You okay?" I asked.

"I was better, but I got over it," he replied, sniffing. "Sup?"

"Going somewhere?" I asked, oh so happy with myself.

I looked in one of the boxes and pulled out one of his many trophies, this one for wrestling. Jeff was wicked strong. I put it back on its shelf, matching where the dust was missing.

"You don't have to move," I said. "I bought the junkyard."

"You *what?*" he yelled. He was mad.

I told him the whole story about Thomas Perkins and Mr. Butthead. I left out all the dollar amounts. He just kept staring at me. "You frickin' dumbass!"

"You're welcome?" I asked.

"Chad, this property is worthless! This business is worthless! Dude, you fried your nest egg!"

He was right. I looked out the window at my nine-year-old truck. Coulda shoulda bought a new one. But then I turned around.

"On the bright side, you don't have to move. You make enough to pay utilities, right?"

He looked at me in disbelief. "Where are you gonna live?"

I thought about it. No job, no money, lived in Mom's trailer. Trailer was paid for but there was rental for the lot.

"Wait a minute," Jeff said. "Now I'm bein' stupid. You have a house. This one. This is *your* house now. *Where am I gonna live?*"

"I'm not kicking you out," I said. "But we gotta come up with something. I wonder if between the two of us we could put together half a brain."

"Doubtful."

I turned to walk out. "Forgot to bring in the beer. We're gonna celebrate. And have ourselves one of them company meetings."

By the time I got back with the beer, Jeff had cleared his desk, found a cooler, and pulled out a chair. One of them foldable kind with webbing. He held up his arms. "Welcome home to Hillbilly Palace!" Then in a normal voice, "This is gonna get awkward."

I put the beer on the desk and looked him straight in the eye. "Yep. But I have a good feeling about this."

CHAPTER 2

After two beers each, Jeff and I had come up with some ideas. The first being that we might need more beer. Second, the property had a well and septic so that was covered. The property had power and TV thanks to the West Virginia State Flower—a satellite dish. If, of course, you could afford the service connection, which he couldn't.

Uphill toward and parallel to Route 42, we would carve a flat spot for my truck to park. Uphill again, a flat spot for mom's trailer. For the digging, Jeff 'knew a guy' and for the hookups Jeff also 'knew a guy.' There was still plenty of room between my trailer site and the road. So with no rent or utilities, I just had to come up with money for gas and food and stuff like that.

Once I got a job I could start dating again and maybe even get that new truck. I was thinking red for the color.

Neither of us wanted to talk about Jeff paying me rent. I was happy enough keeping him from being kicked out of his house, so it seemed wrong to turn around and start charging him to live there.

But it was also wrong for him to live there for free. So I came up with an idea. "Open a savings account and make your monthly payments to that, or as much as you can. We'll figure out what to do with it later."

He agreed.

With that settled we drifted into high school football stories.

We could pretty much run through every play of every game.

"Remember when …" he began as the door opened and in walked a young girl. She was about 24, I guessed, not pretty but not hard to look at either. About five-foot-and-no-change tall. She had long brown hair that rested on her shoulders, brown eyes, thick eyebrows, and a pointed chin. She was dressed in dark slacks and a white blouse. And looked familiar.

Jeff was pointing at her and saying, "I know … I know. Bishop! Billy Bishop's baby sister!" He turned to me. "Remember Billy? Offense left guard, a year ahead of us?"

I didn't.

She wasn't smiling. "I'm Beverly Bishop … Bev." She didn't offer to shake hands so we didn't either. Never know what to do when it's a girl.

"How's Billy?" Jeff asked.

"He's fine," she replied. "Married, three kids. Billy Junior, we call him Junior. Betty Jean, we call her Jean. And Billy Jo, we call her Toots."

Between Billy and Bev were two sisters, Brenda and Blair.

She knew about my mom and expressed her sympathy.

So finally, Jeff asked if she was looking for a car part.

"No," she answered. "A job. I've been babysitting and working part-time jobs since high school, but I'm always looking for a real job. I've been going door to door down in Princeton for the past few days." Today, she was on her way up to Beckley.

"Ever consider Charleston or maybe Roanoke?" Jeff asked.

She shook her head. "I want to be near Princeton. Come to think of it, Beckley is probably too far." Her shoulders dropped.

"Why?" Jeff asked. "Family?"

She shook her head again. "I'm pregnant. The father lives in Princeton."

"Oh." Jeff looked over to me. "I hadn't noticed."

I had noticed but like hell I was going to say anything.

"You're not a good liar," she replied, and at that she smiled for the first time. "So, are you guys hiring?"

"Well, actually," I said, "as of this morning I own the land, Jeff owns the cars." That didn't explain it so I told her about my morning at the bank, except for the dollar amounts.

Her only response was, "How'd you come up with the Indian story?"

"Yeah," Jeff echoed. "I was gonna ask about that."

"Your dad," I replied.

He crooked his head to the side. "Wut?" At this point he got up and slid his chair over to Bev. She accepted.

I continued. "The camping trips with your dad. Remember? Campfires at night, marshmallows, ghost stories, some local history. Stuff like that. I remember thinking how cool it was that some Indians buried their dead with the heads toward the east and some to the west."

"Indians didn't live here," Bev said. "At least not by the time settlers came along. West Virginia has no federally recognized tribal land. Indians that do live here came from elsewhere."

"Oops," I said. "Although I doubt my story had anything to do with them accepting my offer. But wow, you know stuff."

"I do," she said, "and I deserve a job that pays well. It's just so frustrating."

I felt bad for her, and I had the same problem except for being pregnant.

"So neither of you know anyone hiring?"

We both shook our heads. From the look on her face, you could tell the wheels were spinning and that she had come to a dead end.

"Bye," she said, standing up. She was halfway out the door but stopped and asked, "Who owns the old Waffle House?"

I shrugged my shoulders. "Dunno."

Jeff chuckled from behind me. "Chad, you are the dumbest," he grinned. "You do. It's dad's original office for the junkyard."

"His office was in a Waffle House?" I asked.

"I don't know what it was," Jeff answered. "It was here when he bought the place. His office was up there, then he built the shop down here, but ended up spending all his time down here so he added this office room. Then we added the loft for me to live in. Did you happen to notice that the sign for the junkyard is up there?"

I didn't answer but Bev chimed in. "I didn't notice either. Can we go inside?"

I could tell Jeff wanted to say no but reached in a desk drawer and pulled out a big ring of keys. We walked through the steep drop-off and back up to the old office. It took about twenty key choices to get the door open.

We walked in single file and looked around. The place smelled musty but not too bad. And it did look like a Waffle House. Longways were windows on the left wall, facing the street. On the right was a long bar and on the far wall were the restrooms. Even had some bar stools bunched up in the back corner. They weren't the kind that screwed to the floor, but instead had legs.

"I remember those," Jeff said. "I used to spin around on the seats. Dad's desk was here as you come in and the rest was mostly parts, like tires and batteries. Tires and batteries come off first on a wrecked car."

"What about the back half of the building?" Bev asked. "Maybe your dad kept some of the old stuff."

"Never been in the back room," Jeff said. He walked in first.

Bev followed in. "Oh my," she said. "Oh my!"

Inside were all the missing parts: grills, grill vents, booths, tables, pots, pans, boxes of dishes, and even a walk-in cooler.

Jeff was opening the door to the cooler. "I wonder is this thing works. If not —"

"— you know a guy." I finished his sentence.

Bev turned to me and asked if I had a tape measure. I said I did — in the truck.

"Get it?" she asked. "Please?"

When I got back, her and Jeff were standing face to face talking. They turned to me.

"Bev here wants to open a Waffle House," Jeff said.

"A diner," she corrected, "and I know it's a bad idea."

"I'm familiar with those," I nodded.

"I know it sounds dumb, but I would like to see what's here, what's missing, where to find the missing stuff, look up the legal stuff. You know, permits, things like —"

"Okay, okay," I said. "No harm trying. Not sure a diner in the middle of nowhere is going to work but whatever. But you strike me as smarter than that. Up to now, that is."

We both smiled, so my little dig was okay.

Her smile faded. She looked down and took a deep breath and asked, "Know what bugs me?"

Jeff and I knew not to answer.

"All this time I've been begging! Begging people to give me a job, begging for a decent salary, for them not to fire me when the baby comes. I'm so … very … tired of it!"

Her eyes got watery. "If I could get this to work, I wouldn't have to beg anymore! Sorry," she added, "hormones out of whack."

I knew what she was talking about and it hit a nerve. That feeling like you're a puppet and some jerk is jerking the strings up and down and you're just bobbing around all spastic like. I guess I have a problem with authority.

Just like back at the bank with Mr. Butthead fixin' to kick Jeff off his property. Sometimes it gets to be too much.

I heard the words slipping through my teeth.

"The diner is yours. Rent free."

Jeff rolled his eyes.

"And whatever help you need from me," I added.

Jeff rolled his eyes the other way. "And me," he whimpered.

She looked at me, then Jeff, and mouthed 'thank you' without saying it.

Then, she pulled a small spiral notebook out of her purse and started writing. For the next two hours she inventoried every pot, pan, plate, utensil, measurement, and created a to-do list three pages long. Finally, she stuffed the notebook back in her purse, thanked us again, and left.

Jeff and I just stood there for a minute.

He sighed. "Looks like we're gonna take a stab at makin'

chicken salad out of chicken feathers. What the hell you thinkin' just givin' it to her?"

I shrugged. "I dunno. I mean, I don't need the place, didn't even know I owned it. I guess … I mean … things are tough, ya know? She's bright, she's pregnant. Jobs are scarce, and along comes an opportunity. Who am I to get in the way of that?"

He put his hand on my shoulder and smiled. "You're a good man, Chad. Stupid, but good."

CHAPTER 3

Three days later we had a pad carved out of the hill for my trailer and another one for my truck. The dirt was pushed into the deep bowl between the new pads and diner, but you could hardly tell. And the pads had gravel too, worth more by itself than the $250 I paid for the whole job. The 'I know a guy' did it all as a side job. The backhoe wasn't his and neither was the gravel. Standard hillbilly economics — we were happy, the guy was happy, and the equipment owner was none the wiser. Plumbing and electrical would follow by a similar arrangement.

Meanwhile, I started on the diner. By the third morning I had painted the soiled ceiling tiles, washed down the walls and windows, and mopped the floor real good. The bathrooms took a solid day. I pulled one of the booths out from the back room and wiped it down. Each booth had a bench seat, a table, and another bench seat. The seats were green vinyl. I was shoving them into the corner to be the first table on the left as you come in the door. The "front door" was on the side of the building facing the junkyard.

Jeff was walking up from the office. He didn't really walk as much as ambled. He had a slight limp, thanks to football. Always wearin' shorts, all year, no matter how cold. And work boots, all year, no matter how hot. In cold weather he adds a shirt or jacket. Just over six feet tall, he's about 240 pounds. He's not buff or nothin', doesn't work out, and has a bit of a beer belly. But mostly what I like about him is he doesn't swagger like a badass. Doesn't need to.

He walked in and we fist bumped. "Wudup?" he asked.

"Check it out," was my answer, giving the table my best Vanna White reveal.

He nodded approval. "Kinda makin' me hungry just lookin' at it," he grinned. "Haven't had breakfast."

As Jeff was saying that, a red Toyota Corolla pulled in. It was Bev. She parked on the side, next to the front door. The trunk lid popped up. When he saw Bev was wrestling with a large cardboard box, he ran out to help her.

Bev came in, now wearing a summer dress instead of slacks. She was carrying a three-ring notebook, papers in it about an inch thick. "Oh good, a table. Jeff, put the box here."

He did. "Dude, there's some good, good smellin' stuff in this box."

He slid into the right-hand side of the booth, his back to the empty room. I could smell it too, like home cookin'. I peeked in the box and found Tupperware bowls, sandwich bags, and plastic-covered plates.

I pulled out the goodies and sat next to Jeff.

"Go ahead and start eating," Bev said as she settled into the left side of the table, her back to the wall. "I guess we'll start with the menu. I was going to start with permits and regulations, and — are you guys listening to me?"

"Wud?" Jeff asked, his mouth stuffed full of cornbread.

She shook her head and opened the notebook. "I have good news and bad news. First …"

Jeff started sipping soup straight out of the Tupperware bowl, plastic spoon sitting on the table. "Dude, try this."

"In a minute," I said, waving him off. I had a bowl of chili. "This is awesome."

"Biscuits!" Jeff exclaimed. "Chad, look at this! Fried chicken biscuits!"

We sampled barbeque, lima beans, brownies, and my favorite, cabbage and corned beef. Best. Food. Ever.

"This mince pie," Jeff said, "it'll make ya smack your granny."

"My Grammy made that pie," Bev retorted. She let us eat but wiggled her pen between her fingers the whole time. "Let me know when you guys are ready to talk about my diner."

"I'm sorry," I said. "I think all these are perfect. Can't find this stuff at a McDonald's or anywhere. Last time I had cabbage and corned beef was … Mom."

I thought for a minute that maybe Mom got me here, like it was meant to be. But Bev would soon nix that idea.

"Chad," she began, "everything in this book is laid out as me running a diner. I have to be honest — it won't work."

"Why?" I asked.

"Start-up money," she answered.

"How much?" I was thinking about the $6,000 I had left but knew it would dwindle fast.

She was smart. I wasn't. So I paid attention.

"Six thousand. Or more, probably more."

She let that sink in. It did.

"But," she continued, "there is a lot of information in here and maybe some of it will be helpful. Your best bet might be to fix it up and rent it to somebody. Let them put their money into it. And maybe hire me, who knows?"

"For way less than what you deserve," I countered.

"Well," she said, "there's that." She continued. "Let's keep going. Permits, health inspections, check. Here's the big thing: Mumma said she would help. She knows all about this stuff. There is so much to know about, I had no idea. She doesn't think this was a Waffle House, but obviously it *was* a diner. Probably went under when I-77 was built. Lots of coal mines up around Beckley, and lots of people down in Princeton looking for work. She thinks most of the meals will be take-out, in the morning. Early in the morning."

"How early?" Jeff asked.

"4:30 a.m.," she replied. "That means get up before 3 a.m. to get started on the biscuits. Mumma volunteered to be the one to get in first, but we would have to be here by 4:30."

"Okay, now I see why this won't work," Jeff noted.

"You do what ya gotta do," I countered.

But I was getting depressed.

Bev pulled out two sheets of paper and handed one to each of us. "This is a list, thanks to Mumma, of what we still need. The way restaurants go out of business, there's probably local sources for most of it."

"That's … encouraging," I muttered.

That restaurants go out of business, I didn't say.

"There's a food truck down the hill here," Jeff offered. "It might have a few of these."

"Mumma said it all comes down to traffic on Route 19. When the EPA closed down the mines, that closed down the railroad, and that closed down the machine shops, and that closed down — well, most everything else."

"Nice thing about living in a Third World country," Jeff said, thoughtfully. "When the bottom drops out, we don't have far to fall."

"I feel so blessed," I shrugged.

"Back to Route 19," Bev said. "Mumma and I talked about it at length. So yesterday morning I stood out at the corner of Route 19 and 42 and counted cars."

"And your conclusion is?" I asked.

"Inconclusive. But I don't think Route 19 is going to keep us in business. On the bright side I made a dollar. Some guy in a dump truck thought I was panhandling and gave me a dollar. Funny thing, there was a homeless guy on the opposite corner doing just that. From what I could tell he wasn't doing half bad."

"Oh yeah," Jeff said. "Thaaat guy. I think he sleeps in a van down near the bottom of the yard."

"And you let him?" Bev exclaimed, her eyes wide open. "What about that 'Beware of Dog' sign? Do you even *have* a dog?"

"Oh yeah, I think they're friends. And if Bear approves, you're good. Seriously, he does *not* approve some people, so they have to leave. He decides."

"Haven't seen him," Bev said. "Hope I'm approved."

"We'll soon find out," Jeff said. "That must be him scratching at the door. Chad, could you scoot out and let him in? He must've smelled the food. This breed has a nose on him."

I got up and let Bear in, a 150-pound Great Pyrenees. We knew each other, so I just gave him a pat on the head as he passed by. Did not have to bend down to do so.

Bev turned in her seat and, "Oh, my God! He is massive!"

"Bev," Jeff said, "this is Sir Barks A Lot, a/k/a Fluffy Butt, a/k/a Teddy Bear. We just call him Bear. Bear, meet Bev."

Bev extended a hand, nervously. Bear sniffed approvingly.

"Watch this," Jeff said. He picked up a crumbling biscuit and placed it flat on his hand and held it out. Bear gobbled it up, leaving only some drool. "Softest mouth ever." He wiped his hand on his shirt.

Bev took a plate and picked through the containers. "I've read about this breed. Bred by shepherds in the Pyrenees mountains. At first, considered a peasant's dog but declared the Royal Dog of France by King — can't remember his name."

She placed the plate on the seat next to her and held on to the edge to keep it from slipping. The very edge.

"How *do* you know stuff?" I asked as I sat back down.

"I read something, I remember it," she answered.

"Novel idea," Jeff noted, just short of sarcastic.

"Where did you — wait, Louis! Just came to me. King Louis the 14th. So where did you find him?"

"The usual way, on my doorstep," Jeff answered. "Before you ask, yes, I put up posters and asked all around. But my guess is somebody or somebody's neighbor couldn't put up with the barking. This breed barks. *A lot.*"

Bear finished with the plate, turned and walked back to the door.

I got up and let him out, sat back down and picked up a brownie.

"I guess he's done with us," Bev shrugged.

"Oh, yeah," Jeff said, "he's goin' back to guard his chickens."

"Chickens," Bev repeated.

"Right. Pyrs are bred to guard livestock. So I got him chickens. He loves it. Spends most his time there."

"Even at night?"

"Especially at night. He's nocturnal. I put a collar on him — *once*. Tried to pull him up the hill to come in and he nipped at me. Didn't break the skin but put me in my place."

"What about when it gets cold?" Bev frowned.

"I ran an extension cord down there, hooked up a heater coil for the water, and a heat lamp for the hen house."

"For the dog, not the chickens," Bev countered.

"Right. Built him a doghouse, never uses it. At 20 degrees he doesn't even curl up and tuck his tail in. Just lays out flat. One morning after it snowed, I couldn't find him 'til he sat up from under the snow."

"Under?" Bev challenged.

"Well, halfway. He blends in."

"How many chickens?"

"About 20."

"You must eat a lot of eggs."

"The trailer you passed comin' in? A lady lives there, name's Erma. Nice lady. She goes down there, checks on the water and feed, collects the eggs. Leaves me some."

"What does she do with the eggs?" Bev was pondering. "We could use fresh eggs if we got this diner going."

"She feeds hungry children around here."

"Wouldn't be right to take the eggs then."

Jeff stroked his long, shaggy beard. "Hell, you could take the eggs and hire her to cook 'em. That'd be fair. If she fit through the door, that is."

"So she's big?" I offered.

Jeff shrugged. "She licks the plate clean."

"Speaking of which," Bev said, "I'm guessing you two approve the menu."

Jeff was at the soup again, this time with a spoon. "Hey! There's beef in here!"

"Bev," I said. "I'd open a diner just so I could eat here."

"Okay," she said, "Let's keep talking like it's going to happen. I know it won't but I'm in the moment. It gives me hope."

I nodded. "My thoughts exactly."

"The biggest roadblock is lack of traffic. I-77 has it all."

"Roadblock!" Jeff exclaimed. "Right. One time there was a wreck on I-77 and traffic was routed to Route 19. It was a solid row of cars. Chad, you want the rest of that brownie?"

I slid the brownie to him. "How about one of those blue interstate exit signs? Could we get on one of those?"

Bev flipped through some pages in her notebook and tapped her pen on the page. "Other than maybe thousands of dollars to make the sign, there are restrictions. Has to be an up-and-running diner, open at least six days a week, 12 hours a day, and seating for at least 24 people."

"I wonder if this booth would count as four people or six people?" Now I was pondering.

Jeff lifted the empty cardboard box off the table and tossed it on the floor behind us. "Guess that depends on whether Erma was one of 'em."

"And restrooms," Bev added.

"We got restrooms," Jeff said. "That would add two more seats, right?"

Bev tried to give him a stern look but couldn't help but smile. She was very pretty when she smiled.

"The ladies room here has two stalls," I said. "I know 'cause I cleaned them."

"It just dawned on me," Jeff said, "that I have never been in that restroom."

"How many are in the men's room?" Bev asked.

"One toilet and one urinal," Jeff reported, "and a sink if those two are occupied."

He laughed. I laughed. Bev rolled her eyes.

Bev brought us back to business. "Anyway, the signs. Might be something you could tell a prospective renter."

"How about a billboard?" I asked, hopefully.

"You can't," she replied. "You actually have to go through an agency that has an agreement with the highway department. Or something like that. I stopped reading about it and just skimmed. The cost alone would nix that option. What you *can* do is put a sign on your own property, like the big pole you got here.

"Jeff, why *is* it so tall?"

"Dunno," Jeff answered, switching over to the chili. "Always been there. Ya notice the light on top?"

"No," we both answered.

"I know. It's way up there. No on-off switch that I can find. The light broke off its mount and just hangs there by the wires and sways in the wind. Doesn't even point down. Won't burn out, stays on all the time."

"You should fix that," I said. "Wait, no. I should fix that, it's *my* problem now. Crap!"

"We're gonna keep runnin' into questions like that," Jeff said. "The sign says, 'Jim's Junk Yard' and that's *my* business, but the post is — whaddaya call it?" He turned to Bev.

"Permanent fixture, conveys with the property. Jim is your dad's name?"

"Yeah. So, you can put a sign on your own property, right?" Jeff asked.

Bev nodded, skeptically.

"Why not put a sign on that hill?" He was pointing toward the back. "Bet you could see a sign from I-77 up there."

I wasn't following what he was saying so I got up and walked out the door to get a better look.

Jeff and Bev followed me out.

Down past the junkyard was a hollow, and then a mountain range. We couldn't see the interstate but knew it was off to the left.

Jeff walked up and put his hand on my shoulder. "You don't know who owns that hill, do ya?"

"No," I said. He just waited. Then it finally dawned on me. "Me?"

It took several whole minutes for him to stop laughing and catch his breath. "Chad, you are three pickles short of a quart."

I *owned* that hill. Could not wrap my head around it.

At least Bev wasn't laughing.

"Question is," she pondered, "could you read a sign up there, from I-77?"

"We need to know," Jeff said. "This is important."

Bev stepped forward, ahead of us. "What if we hang a towel or a tablecloth up there and see what it looks like from the interstate? Give us some perspective."

"Let's do it now," Jeff said. "Climb that hill."

I turned to him and tested out my poker face. "That's *my* hill. You'd be trespassing."

Even got a chuckle out of Bev on that one.

We didn't know how long it would take so we were gonna call Bev when we got to the top. Except she didn't have a phone. Never had. She would stay and fuss with stuff in the diner.

We gathered up some rope, a large towel, and water. We set out on our adventure and I gave myself permission that we were on to something. That this could work.

I was feeling something totally new for me — hope.

Past the junk cars was what used to be a fence.

"What's with the fence?" I asked, climbing over it.

"Dad put it up years ago," Jeff said, following behind me.

"Used to have a lot of theft, mostly at night."

"But no fence across the front," I added.

"Naw, he'd see them comin' from off the road. They were sneakin' in through the woods."

"Not much of a fence," I noted.

"True, they could still get in. But the fence made it hard to get stuff out. Car parts can be heavy."

We went about 200 yards more down a gentle slope full of brush and small trees. We zig-zagged our way to the bottom and came to a small stream. Next to the stream was a well-worn dirt path. I looked both ways and asked, "And this goes ... where?"

"That way goes a few miles and ends," Jeff said, pointing to the right. "And that way goes under Route 19, then under I-77, and to more ATV trails. Really big thing, you know, all the trails around here. And those monster side-by-side Razors. Wow!"

"Vaguely," was all I could think of to say. He looked at me sadly, and I knew what he was thinking.

"Buddy, you missed a lot the last eight years. Your mom and all."

I nodded. "Wait. Route 19 is right down the road from the diner, then the interstate is on down further. But where we're going the interstate is closer?"

"Right," he replied. "The interstate comes through the pass next to your hill and then it heads west. It crosses 19 and 19 comes in close to us."

"Okay," I said. "Let's get up this hill."

It was steep, full of brush and trees, and loaded with protruding rocks. We had to use our hands as much as our feet. We finally crested the top but couldn't see anything for all the undergrowth. We turned left and walked to find the interstate. The crest started to go downhill. We still couldn't see the road, but we did start hearing tractor-trailers when they made that machine gun sound of their compression-release engine brakes.

We found a tall oak tree that was climbable and it gave us a peek. The view was disappointing. The road was a long way away and a long way down. We tied the towel to an upper branch as best as we could.

Coming back was easier, thanks to gravity. But sometimes too helpful. We ended up sliding down on our butts much of the time. Almost to the bottom we heard a crash and then some screaming. At the trail we heard it coming from our left so we turned and ran that way.

We came around a bend to two ATVs, one upright and the other one on its side. The rider was underneath. He was screaming and I knew that scream. Something was broken. His friend was trying to pull him out. Wrong thing to do.

"Stop!" I yelled. "You're making it worse!" They were just kids.

Jeff came up from behind me and lifted the ATV off the kid. Not just lifted it, more like flipped it off. The poor kid's leg was obviously broken. It made an "L" turn below the knee. Fortunately, there was no blood. Jeff tried to calm the kid.

I pulled out my phone, had four solid bars, dialed 9-1-1.

The dispatcher answered and I started babbling. "Need an ambulance! Kid with a broken leg! In Tree Fork! On Route 42, off 19! Jim's Junk Yard!"

The dispatcher was calm, professional, and obviously used to excited callers. She asked questions, took a few seconds to make a radio call, said something about a lighthouse, a code 10-52 and some other stuff, but came right back to me and asked more questions. She tried to calm me down and I wasn't even the guy with the broken leg! She wanted the names of the kids so I gave my phone to the friend.

"How's he doing?" I asked Jeff. The kid was screaming names of people to call, yelling about his leg and cussing up a storm.

Jeff answered, ever so calmly, "We need to get up to the office to show first responders where to find us. Can you watch him?"

In my head I said *no* but "yes" came out. Jeff rushed over to the upright ATV, mounted and started it, and turned uphill. A dirt rooster-tail spit off the rear wheels. No clue how he got through the fence.

I tried to calm the kid, *promised* him it would be all right, told him the ambulance would be there soon. The minutes seemed like hours. *Shouldn't I at least hear a siren?*

Oh yeah, this was Tree Fork.

Later, a horn blowing nonstop. I knew that horn — Jeff's little wrecker and daily driver. The sound of the horn was joined by the cracking of tree limbs. Uphill above us but off to the side, Jeff's wrecker was coming down full throttle, in reverse! Half out of control, I could tell he was dodging the bigger trees, but anything vertical and small was disappearing under the thick rear bumper. He blasted through trees and brush and fence 50 feet down from us, then jumped out and ran over.

I was so glad he was back. He did a steal-second-base slide up to the kid and resumed his comforting care. "Ambulance is on the way … don't worry … hang in there."

While he was away everything was in slow motion. Now everything was fast forward. A guy came running down the new, wide path. He was a volunteer EMT and picked up the accident on his scanner. He took over. A siren, at first distant, got closer.

Standing next to me, Jeff said, "I told Bev to stand out front, tell them about the new path, bring a stretcher, not a gurney. "You okay?"

I said yes, didn't mean it.

Two fire department guys came down. They carefully got the

kid's leg stabilized and put him on the stretcher. They carried him down the path and turned up the hill.

Jeff rolled the ATV back on its wheels. It wasn't damaged much. The other kid gave me back my phone. I asked him if he wanted to take his friend's ATV up the hill or ride up in Jeff's wrecker.

"I'd feel better taking the ATV," he replied.

Smart kid.

CHAPTER 4

Jeff got his wrecker up the hill same as he came down: hell-bent and pedal to the metal. I made the mistake of riding shotgun. The ride was great fun but I kept bumping my head on the roof. I wasn't wearing a seatbelt. There wasn't one.

The parents arrived shortly. They were camping close by. The mom and dad of the injured kid scooted off to Princeton with the ambulance. They were grateful but obviously preoccupied with all the drama. The other couple started loading the ATVs on a trailer and Jeff pitched in to help.

I went into the diner and found Bev in the backroom cleaning shelves. The room still had piles of stuff stacked all around but looking better. It smelled like Lysol.

"Everything okay out there?" she asked.

"I guess," I replied. "They're loading up the ATVs."

"Good. How'd it go with the towel?"

"Not so good. Couldn't see much and I was surprised how far it is to the interstate."

Her shoulders sagged. "I was afraid of that." She started wiping the next shelf but stopped. "Look, Chad, if this is a bad idea — *and it is* — I don't want to pull you down. Wouldn't be right."

"Bev, here's where I am on all this. I'm countin' on you to make the right decision 'cause I don't count on myself. You say this diner is not gonna work, but here you are cleaning shelves. So what gives?"

She shrugged. "I dunno. I'm looking forward to being around Mumma and not having to beg somebody for a job. I'm gonna be out of a job anyway come five or six months."

I didn't know what to say, so I didn't say anything.

She left the rag on the shelf, turned, and walked over to a stainless-steel table, leaned against it and crossed her arms.

After a moment she said. "A few years back I was visiting my sister in Roanoke. We were downtown and there was this building. The sides were mirrors, so they reflected the image of the sky. I was outside, heard a thud, and looked up in time to see a bird falling down, spinning like a maple tree helicopter. It must have been fooled by the mirrors. I could tell a wing was broken and it would die. But the bird didn't know it would die. The only thing it knew was that it needed to fly, so it kept trying, flapping the good wing."

She shook her head back and forth. "Poor thing just kept doing its best, but all it could do was flutter in circles." She looked over at me, expression both mad and sad. "I feel like that bird."

I could feel a lump in my throat and goose bumps on my arms. I guess caring for Mom with the Alzheimer's had made me actually give a damn about people suffering.

I walked over to the shelves, picked up the cleaning rag, and started wiping down the next shelf. "We need to get this place cleaned up — so we can get this diner open."

Bev and I were pushing more booth seats and tables from the back when Jeff came in. The windows along the front gave a clear view of the family leaving with the ATVs. They waved, we waved.

"That does it!" Jeff exclaimed. "I'm gettin' out of the junkyard business! Hear me out!"

Jeff slipped into what would forever be his seat — first booth, seat facing the door.

Bev and I slipped in on the other bench.

"So I was talkin' to the dad about the trails. The hills are crawlin' with trails and not just here. Up Route 52 out of Bluefield, down into Tennessee. People come from everywhere — *and I mean everywhere* — to spend all day tearin' up ATVs. Bet you could make a fortune just sellin' drive belts … or even tires for that matter!"

"And there is nowhere else they can go to for this stuff?" I asked.

"And it's seasonal," Bev added.

"You two are lickin' the red off my lollipop!" he countered.

"Here's the thing. My junk cars are so picked over, there's nothin' left on 'em but the speedometer needles. So I sell 'em for scrap metal. So I'm figurin' — change from junkyard to ATV service. Hell, put a sign down at the trail with an arrow pointing up that says 'ATV Repair.'"

"And one that says 'Diner,'" Bev added.

We looked at each other, very pleased with ourselves.

"Well, ain't we sittin' in amen corner!" Jeff beamed.

"What we're doing," I said, "is burnin' daylight. Jeff, let's head out and see if that towel is still there. Bev, you comin'?"

"Naw," Bev shrugged. "But I'll be here when you get back so don't take any side trips."

"Yes ma'am," I said.

We got on the interstate heading north. When we got even with my hill, I pulled over. The towel was still there, a long way out and a long way up. But anybody on the northbound side would already be past the exit. We needed to know what it looked like for southbounders. So I pulled back onto the road, got off at the next exit, and came back.

It was even more disappointing. As I-77 came through the gap, it curved to the right. By the time we came to my hill and the towel, we were almost past it. I pulled over and we got out. We walked in front of my truck and leaned on the guardrail. The towel was just a small speck of white.

"Well, there it is," Jeff pointed.

"Yeah," I nodded. "By the time I noticed it I was up even with it. Bummer."

"Can you imagine how hard it would be to get a sign up there?" Jeff sighed.

I shook my head. "We keep runnin' into problems."

"Speakin' of which," Jeff smiled. A deputy car was pulling up behind my truck, lights flashing.

"We're not speeding," Jeff offered, "currently."

The deputy got out and came over. We were relieved that it was Greg Lawrence, just another guy from high school. Nice guy, trim and fit and all things law enforcement. He came over and fist-bumped, and asked, "Car trouble?"

We pointed to the towel and explained about the sign.

"Yeah," he said. "I heard about the diner."

"Whaaat?" I was floored. "How?"

"Oh, yeah," he explained. "Deputy Connor has a cousin and her mom has a friend, forgot her name. Anyway, the friend was always — and I mean *always* — winning blue ribbons at the county fair for the cakes and pies she made. The cousin's mom said the friend was going to bake pies to help her granddaughter open a diner at the lighthouse. Or something like that."

None of the cousin-friend-mom connections surprised me. Country folk telegraph gets the word out person-to-person. So I had to ask. "What lighthouse?"

"That one." He pointed up.

"Where?"

"That's my sign light," Jeff said. "What the hell?"

"Watch it blink," Greg said. "Like a lighthouse."

"That's my sign," Jeff repeated. "It's not blinkin'. It's just … hangin'. Why would anyone give it a name?"

Greg explained. "You would be amazed how many people break down and don't know where they are or even which direction they're headed. But they can see the light blinking. If they see it in front of them, they're southbound. Behind them, northbound. It helps. That light has been there a long time. Funny thing, you wouldn't believe how many times cars stop exactly right here."

He turned to leave. "When the diner opens, save me a piece of pie."

"Copy that," I said.

"Check it out," Jeff said, looking over the guardrail. "It's a *long* way down."

I came over and looked over the side. "What are we lookin' at?"

"The ATV trail. Runs under the interstate here. And check this out … on the guardrail. A reflector tape. And there's one on the northbound side too. Why would the highway department mark where the ATV trail runs?"

"No clue," I replied. "You never noticed your light? I mean, coming down the interstate at night?"

He shook his head. "Never thought to look."

It didn't take long to get back to the diner. As we turned into the junkyard, there was a second red Toyota Corolla on the side of the diner. Once inside, Bev's mom greeted us with a handshake.

"I'm Edith," she said, "Edith Bishop."

She was medium height, a little plump, with short brown, wavy hair. Her thin lips didn't smile, but her brown eyes did as if she just offered you a cookie. If a warm hug had a face, it would be hers. I liked her right away.

And on the table, another cardboard box.

"I'm sorry for your loss," she began. "I knew your mother and she was a fine lady. A good Christian."

I nodded and thanked her. Everyone spoke highly of Mom. But I couldn't stop looking at the cardboard box.

"Y'all hungry?" she asked. "Bev already fed you this morning."

Jeff nodded. "Yes ma'am, Bev did feed us ... but now that seems like a long time ago."

We took off our baseball caps. Jeff slipped into his side of our booth, facing the door. I sat next to him. Miss Bishop stood at the end of the table pulling out plastic containers.

"This round of menu items are salads. You would have both single serve and bulk containers, ready to go. You got potato salad, pasta salad, egg salad."

She kept pulling out containers, and I kept hoping plates would come out. I was ready to dig in.

"Here's tuna salad," she said. "Depending on what sells and

doesn't, you make accordingly. Here's some plates and stuff. And I figured you boys would be hungry, so I brought some sliced ham with brown-sugar glaze."

I tried to be calm and polite and move slow.

"Help yourself," she said. "Don't be shy. But save room for ..."

She carefully lifted the last thing out of the box, a lattice-crust apple pie. "Bev's Grammy made this. The crust is made from flour and lard, not shortening. The apples are off trees just out her back door."

She made room for the pie and sat the box down on the floor. Bev came in from the back room, slipped into her side. We dished out salad samples.

I tried not to talk with my mouth full but had to tell Miss Bishop, "We just heard about this pie!" I started telling them about the towel, the deputy, the blue-ribbon pies, and the blinkin' light.

Jeff helped with telling the story so we could take turns eating and talking.

"So the name of the diner should be Lighthouse Diner?" Bev asked. "In West Virginia? But there are no lighthouses in West Virginia."

"True," Miss Bishop nodded. "But lots of people like lighthouses. And everyone knows what they are.

"You boys approve the salads?"

Jeff answered, "I have never, ever, anywhere had food this good.

"Like Chad was sayin', I'd open a diner just to eat here."

"Good," she said. "So we have a building, a menu, a list of equipment, and a name. A name that lends itself to artwork on the menus, maybe placemats and containers. You know, a name on a to-go cup takes your name out into the world. Good advertising."

"After talkin' with the deputy," I said, "I don't think we could keep this place a secret. Miss Bishop, I'm thinking the success of this diner depends on you. Is this asking too much?"

"I'm happy to help," she replied. "But let's not get ahead of ourselves. Chad, the diner could fail. Leave you with less than you started with. I love my daughter, but I want to be straight with you. You could get a job, and *you* don't have to stay here like Bev wants to do. You could — and maybe should — search for a job ... anywhere, even out of state. Globally even."

I thought to myself how much I appreciate smart people like her, but leaving my property was not in the cards.

She continued. "And Bev here, she has options. She can move back home anytime."

"What about —" I didn't know the name of the baby's father.

"Rusty," Miss Bishop said. Saying his name made her voice sound like she was chewing rocks.

"I know him!" Jeff piped in. "And ... that's all I'm gonna say about that. Till Bev leaves, anyway."

"Say it," Bev dared.

"Oh no," he countered. "Mumma didn't raise no fools. She drowned the dumb ones."

"She missed one," Bev retorted.

"Children!" Miss Bishop scolded.

"He started it," Bev frowned.

I could not tell if she was kidding.

She leaned across the table toward Jeff. "He's my baby's father.

Wouldn't be right to move away from him."

Jeff leaned back. "Okay."

"Miss Bishop?" I asked. "Any way we could start small? Work our way up to a full-service diner?"

"I don't really know," she answered. "But probably not. Best chance of making a go of it would be jump in the deep end."

Jeff took his turn. "I'd be the last to offer advice," he began.

"No," Bev piped in. "You'd be the first."

Miss Bishop gave her daughter a look. Bev retreated to the back of her seat.

"Really," Jeff continued. "You need to think about this because once you work for yourself long enough, you're feral. After that, you get a job and a boss says he wants you to show up at 8:00, you'd be like, 'You talkin' to me?'

"Chad, you'd gladly put in sixteen hours a day workin' for yourself but resent workin' half that much for someone else."

"I agree," Miss Bishop said. "And speaking of hours, when will you be open?"

"24-7," Jeff answered, shoveling pasta salad.

The rest of us ignored his reply.

"At least through lunch," I offered.

"As long as possible," Bev said. "To get as much business as possible."

Miss Bishop nodded. "Yes, but you'll need some down time. 2 p.m.?"

"3:00?" Jeff offered.

"4:00," Bev said. "We'll see how much traffic we get and

change it accordingly."

"Same for days," Jeff suggested. "Start with seven days a week and see what's what."

"Sounds good for now," Miss Bishop agreed. "Except I don't work on Sundays. And Bev and I both don't like the idea of serving liquor. And that said, I will leave you kids to talk about it. Love you, Bev."

"Love you, Mumma."

The three of us sat there, thoughts rummaging around in our heads. I think Jeff was feeling a little uncomfortable after his tiff with Bev. He tapped me on the arm to let him out of our only booth, so I got up.

"I gotta check on the chickens, feed Bear … lock up the shop … and call it a night. You two talk amongst yourselves. 'Nite." He left. I sat back down.

I couldn't see Bev's eyes, but I knew the wheels were spinning. She was pulled up into a ball in her corner.

"I don't want to leave yet," she said. "Will you stay?"

"Of course," I answered. "I don't want to leave either. I like it here. It's quiet and peaceful. It's bigger in here than Mom's trailer and the lights are nice and bright. I'll be so glad to get it here."

We fell into a natural, comfortable silence.

After a while, I spoke up, "Jeff didn't mean nothin'."

"I know," she shrugged. "I'm not mad at … well … maybe a little. He means well."

"One of the many things I like about him," I said, "is that he says what the rest of us are thinkin'."

She nodded, and that was the end of that topic.

We fell into another period of silence. I managed to pick through and empty every container of salad, and then ate another piece of pie.

Finally, Bev started collecting the containers and plates. "Princeton is just down the street, but it seems a long way from here," she said quietly.

I was thinking the same thing. I lived in Princeton too.

"Want some more pie?" she asked. "Two slices left."

I was just about to say 'no' when a bright light reflected off the wall above Bev's head. It was the headlights of a very large RV camper. As big as a tour bus, it inched past us and spanned all four windows. As it stopped, we heard the loud hiss of air brakes like tractor-trailers make. The headlights went dark.

We looked at each other wide-eyed, jaws dropped.

Bev said what I was thinking.

"What the fuck?"

CHAPTER 5

We could barely make out the driver, moving to the passenger side. Campers open to the passenger side. Bev slid from her corner to the edge but stayed seated. I stood to greet our visitor.

I was expecting an old man. Instead, it was a woman, tall and broad shouldered but not at all fat. She had shoulder-length brown hair and a genuine smile. But her most prominent feature were her large, brown, piercing eyes. I look people in the eye but with her I got an eerie feeling she could pull a Jedi mind trick on me. These are not the droids you're looking for.

"Oh, hi!" she said, looking around. "Remodeling?"

"Something like that," I answered. "Sorry for the mess."

Did I just say that? I'm not sorry for the mess. Maybe she made me say that.

She stepped forward hand extended. "I'm Doctor … um … my name is Carolyn." I shook her soft but firm hand.

Bev stood up. "I'm Bev. Nice to meet you." They shook hands too.

"What can we do for you?" I asked.

"Well," she said, still looking around at all the scattered booth pieces. "It's so bright in here. Kind of reminds me of that *Nighthawks* painting."

"By Edward Hopper," Bev offered.

"That's the one, two people sitting in a bar at night. You two looked very comfortable in here, so I felt it was safe. The light coming out of these windows practically lights up the road."

"Come sit a spell," Bev said, this time taking Jeff's side of the booth.

Carolyn hesitated for a second but then took a seat across from Bev. I sat next to Bev.

"Want some pie?" Bev asked.

"No, but thank you," Carolyn replied. "I'm not lost, but maybe looking for a little local knowledge."

"A small piece then," Bev smiled, pulling a plate over next to the pie dish. "We're doing a test run of our menu items and need feedback."

"The crust is made from flour and lard," I added. "And apparently that's a good thing."

"So it's *homemade* pie," Carolyn said. "Can't remember the last time I had … probably at Grandma's house."

"My Grammy made this pie," Bev said while sliding it over along with a plastic fork.

Carolyn took the first bite and closed her eyes in appreciation. "This is so good," she exclaimed. "I just *knew* it was a good idea to pull off at this exit."

"Speaking of which," I pointed out, "you pulled off the interstate on an exit with no signs about gas or food or hotels."

Carolyn was chewing her next bite. "Yeah, that might sound a bit odd, but —"

Just then the door swung open and in stormed another lady, this one short, skinny, with wild brown hair and a toothy grin.

"Hi!" she shouted. "I'm Vicki!"

Before I could even get up, she was next to me with hand extended. We shook but I wasn't ready for such a strong squeeze.

"I'm Chad, this is Bev," I said. "Nice to meet you, Chad!"

She leaned over me to Bev. "Nice to meet you, Bev!" Then stood up straight at the end of the booth, hands on her hips. "So how are you guys doing?"

She wore cutoff jeans and a very large tank top. Tats ran down both arms, traditional on one, blackwork on the other.

Both women seemed to be about the same age — older than me, younger than my mom.

"Good," I replied.

She turned to explore the room. "Hey!" she yelled. "Nice place!"

Carolyn was now finishing the last bite of her pie. She paused to explain, "She's harmless."

"I love her." Bev smiled, turning in her seat to watch Vicki.

"As do I," Carolyn said.

"Like, your partner?"

"Yes."

"I'm happy for you," Bev said. "So hard to find a good mate."

After a minute Vicki was back, carrying one of the bar stools from the far corner. She put it at the end of the booth, then sat on it and spun in circles. "So what are we talking about?"

"Vicki, come sit next to me," Carolyn said. "This pie is to die for."

"Okay!" She hopped off the bar stool, turned and pointed to it, and said to it, "I'll be right back!" Then she sat next to Carolyn.

Since the last piece of pie was still in the dish, I slid the whole thing over to Vicki. Bev passed over a fork. Vicki's response to the pie was the same as Carolyn's. Only louder.

Carolyn said, "They were asking why we pulled off an exit with no signs as to facilities."

"Oh that," Vicki said with her mouth full of apple. "She has superpowers. Happens all the time. I love you, pie," she said to it.

"Actually, in this case, there *was* a sign," Carolyn said. "The lighthouse light."

"No, not again," I whined. "Not the lighthouse light."

I had to go through the whole story about the conversation with the deputy.

Carolyn shrugged. "Still, it was a light I could see, and it was moving. And it brought me here to you guys. I have a very good feeling about this."

I could sense the Jedi mind trick again. Then I noticed movement outside. It was Jeff and Bear coming up out of the bowl.

"As do I," Bev was nodding. They were definitely on the same page.

"But first," I teased, "you must be deemed worthy by our welcoming committee."

Carolyn cocked her head to the side and gave me a smirk as if to say, bring it on.

The door opened and in walked Jeff and Bear.

Vicki spun around in her seat. "Noooo wayyy!!" She slid off the bench and dropped to the floor facing Bear, legs spread eagle and arms wide open. Bear, an ancient breed of incredible perception, strolled up to her, sniffed her face, and accepted her affection. She patted his head, rubbed under his chin, stroked his long, full mane.

"Jeff, this is Vicki," I announced, "and Carolyn."

Normally, someone older would be Mister or Miss, but in this case all I had were first names. "Carolyn, Vicki, this is Jeff … and Bear."

Vicki and Bear took up all the room between Carolyn and Jeff, so they just exchanged waves.

"I think they are deemed worthy," Bev concluded.

Jeff's face was a big question mark.

"You're not gonna believe this, Jeff," I said. "They came off the interstate because of the lighthouse light and — what?"

Jeff had his hand up as if to say "stop." The expression on his face turned serious. *Real* serious. Slowly, he moved behind Vicki to study Bear's face. He looked over to Carolyn, their eyes locked as if communicating. Carolyn slowly slid over to the edge of the seat to get a better view of Bear.

While Vicki stroked his head, Carolyn was also studying Bear *real* careful. Then looked up at Jeff again.

I couldn't figure out what the hell was goin' on but something was. I turned to Bev for a clue, but she just shrugged.

Jeff was still staring at Bear and murmured, "He *knows*." Then he looked back at Carolyn. She nodded. Her eyes got watery.

"Knows?" Bev asked, softly. She passed a napkin to Carolyn.

Carolyn accepted the napkin, dabbed the corners of her eyes, and replied, "Bear knows … that Vicki … is ill."

Jeff stood up, slid the bar stool over next to me, and we all sat watching Vicki lovin' on Bear. The silence embraced us all like a hug.

After a few minutes Jeff got off the bar stool and crouched down behind Vicki.

"I want to show you somethin', Vicki," he said softly over her shoulder. "Trust me?"

Vicki nodded and kept rubbing Bear. Bear sat down.

"I want to show you a Pyr Paw," he said. "Put your hands down on your lap, and Bear is gonna raise his left paw and tap you on the arm to tell you he wants more rubbin'."

Vicki rubbed Bear some more, but then slowly lowered her arms. Right away he raised his left paw and tapped her arm.

"Bear loves me!" Vicki squealed, rubbing him briskly now. "He loves me!"

Carolyn turned to face me. "See? A lighthouse is a symbol of comfort and safe passage for weary travelers. And pie."

She looked back at her mate. "And therapy."

We all just sat quietly and watched Vicki and Bear. Bear would lower his head for head pats, raise and turn his head one way and then the other for ear rubs, then raise his head for some chin rubs. Vicki was ecstatic.

Jeff stood back up and sat on the bar stool. "So what brings you to Tree Fork?"

"Local knowledge," I answered. "Carolyn is looking for … directions?"

"It was looking like we would land in Princeton tonight," she answered. "Maybe find a Walmart to park in. But sometimes the streets in small towns get a little tricky, so I wanted to pull over and plan out my route. I saw the light blinking and it brought me here."

"Why not just park here for the night?" Jeff asked. He got up and walked over to the windows. "Maybe back up a few feet." He waved his hand to the right. "No, wait … up a few feet." He waved his hand to the left. "No, wait … back a few feet. No, up … no —" He motioned right, left, right.

"Guys, I'm not gonna stop 'til someone laughs."

"LOL," I complied.

"Could we?" Carolyn asked. "That would be so great!"

Bev grinned. "Of course you can."

Jeff walked back to the booth. "You're almost flat, but I'm sure your levelers can fix that."

"Yes," Carolyn nodded.

"Gas or diesel?" he asked.

"Diesel."

"So the generator is diesel."

"Yes, but we don't have to run it if it's a nuisance."

"Not at all. I *love* the sound of a diesel. And the smell."

"Then it's settled!" Bev exclaimed. "Right, Chad? He actually owns the property."

"Of course," I replied.

"This calls for a celebration!" Bev cheered. She was beside herself. It was nice to see.

"This calls for wine," Carolyn added, "now that I don't have to drive any further. And I have just the thing in the camper. Do you guys drink wine?"

"Does Boones Farm count?" Jeff asked.

Carolyn hesitated.

"Then no, but willin' to learn."

"Perfect!" Carolyn smiled. "Vicki, honey, I'm going to the camper. Need anything?"

"I got everything I need right here," she replied.

Carolyn edged past Vicki, stopped to kiss her on the head, and as she was leaving asked over her shoulder, "You got wine glasses?"

"Would red Solo cups work?" I asked.

"Even better!" And out the door she went.

It didn't take long for her to return carrying a large canvas bag with a Disney logo on the side. "I didn't want to take time doing all the prep stuff in the camper, so I'll need some help."

She slid back into her seat and started unloading the bag.

"Chad," she began, "could you open this bottle? Here's a corkscrew. Bev, here's a cutting board, cheese, knife. And Jeff, since you're up could you rinse off these grapes? Oh, and here's a colander. Let's see what else … a sleeve of crackers … some more plates. Somebody be thinking about a toast. Sorry to be so bossy. Guess I'm used to giving orders."

"You have made my day," Bev beamed, still beside herself. "What kind of cheese is this?"

"This one is Muenster," Carolyn said. "It's my favorite, but the wine goes better with the cheddar. And this is my favorite wine, a Petite Shiraz. Pricey but worth it. It's a little bold, maybe."

She pulled out one more thing — a can of ginger ale. "And here is your wine, honey. It's chilled from the fridge."

"Chad, you can pour Bev some wine, but just one finger, okay?"

"A fancy wine," I noted. "You *do* know you're dinin' with a bunch of hillbillies, right?"

"I have less expensive wine in the camper." She winked. "I only pull this one out for special occasions."

"How did you know I was pregnant?" quizzed Bev. "Am I showing that much?"

"No," answered Carolyn, "but your face has the glow."

When Jeff returned with the grapes, he picked up the wine bottle and stepped back directly behind Vicki. He got Carolyn's attention, pointed to the bottle, and then to Vicki. Carolyn gently shook her head, so he knew to pour just four cups. One of them just a finger high.

It's times like this that I realize other people are thinkin' about stuff way over my head.

Carolyn lifted her cup first. "Anyone have a toast?"

"I do, I do!" Vicki yelled. "To big, white bears! I love you, Bear!"

The rest of us raised our cups. "Here, here!"

"Yum," Jeff said. "This tastes like *more*."

"Me next," Bev chimed. "To love. I just love you guys."

Carolyn nodded. "Noted, logged, appreciated."

"I toast —" Jeff boasted, "— the sweet aroma of diesel. To that, Chad."

My mind was racing but coming up with nothing clever. "I got nuthin'."

"Then my toast will be for the both of us," Carolyn smiled. "To lighthouses … beacons of hope in the night."

We raised our cups once more, except for Jeff. He was walking out the door, didn't say why. He returned a few seconds later, a worried look on his face. "The light," he blurted. "It's been on, day and night, all my life. I noticed things looked different out there and — the light is burnt out."

"Lights do that," Bev offered.

"Yeah, but still, right as Carolyn is toasting it? Kind of a bad omen." He sounded kinda nervous.

"Maybe not," Carolyn explained. "And Jeff, I am all about the paranormal. I already know you have a sixth sense, as do I. So I see it as confirmation that the light got me here. Its mission is now completed, and the rest is up to us."

I had no idea what she was talking about.

"What, too deep?" she asked.

"No, no, I get it," Jeff said. "That makes it better —"

A loud crash from outside interrupted his reply. He rushed out and before the door closed behind him, he was coming back in.

"It was the light," he reported. "It fell to the ground. It was hanging by the wires anyway. I guess one came loose and then the other one couldn't hold the weight by itself. Soooo — how do we put a good spin on that one?"

"Easy," Carolyn said. "The light wanted us to know that the rest is up to us, but we shouldn't have to 'hang in there' by ourselves."

"That's a stretch," Jeff grimaced.

I raised my cup. "I have a toast now. To hangin' in there."

"Weak," Bev countered. But it did prompt another sip.

We talked and laughed into the night. I never talked to rich people before, but we got along like long-lost cousins. It felt so good to have conversations and laughter in the diner.

Bear concluded the party by up and leavin'. Vicki was disappointed but accepted the fact that he had to check on his chickens. At that point Carolyn and Vicki retired to their camper.

The drive back to my trailer in Princeton was long and lonely.

CHAPTER 6

I slept in late the next morning. I would've slept even longer if not for a bad dream. It was fading fast as I woke but had something to do with robotic-looking men taking the booths and tables out of the diner. They were all wearing white jumpsuits, they were faceless and looked alike, and none of them would tell me why they were taking my stuff. It was so real I was physically angry. And the message was loud and clear to me.

Chad, you can't win. You try and try, but life keeps knocking you down.

Bottom line—The diner was a hopelessly bad idea.

I got up and showered, put on shorts and a T-shirt. I didn't bother to shave, usually sported a heavy stubble. I headed out. Might as well get with Bev and get it over with. Forget the diner, get on with gettin' by.

When I got to Tree Fork, I was surprised to see the camper still there. Turning in, I was even more surprised to see Carolyn and Vicki on my trailer pad. They looked like they were in a living room, minus the walls. For a rug, they had a large camper pad over the rough gravel. For chairs, two folding chairs side by side with a small folding table in between. On the table a coffee cup, water bottle, and cell phone. They both wore shorts and V-neck T-shirts. Carolyn had on bedroom slippers, and Vicki wore running shoes. At Vicki's feet, a big, white familiar Bear.

I parked on the lower pad and walked up. "Now don't you two look comfy," I smiled, glad to see them.

"We're stayin'!" Vicki exclaimed. "Never leaving!"

"As long as you like," I beamed, honestly. "You two are a hoot."

"We really do hope to stay a few days," Carolyn said. "If it's okay with you."

"It is totally okay with me," I replied, "if you don't mind a campsite overlookin' a junkyard."

"Let me ask you something," Carolyn offered. "Do roses have thorns? Or do thorn bushes have roses?"

I didn't have a response, but she didn't seem to want one anyway.

"I'm not looking at the cars," she continued. "I'm looking at this beautiful mountain range. This ridge here, and the taller mountains behind it. The air is fresh, it's quiet. We're not squeezed in cheek to cheek with a hundred other campers. I'm telling you, Chad, you have a gold mine here."

"Guess I take the mountains for granted," I admitted. "Lived here all my life, ya know. But the cars, well …"

"Jeff was up here earlier," Carolyn said. "Told us all about you buying the land."

"And Mr. Butthead," Vicki chirped. "Ha! Cracked me up!"

Just then an old pickup truck turned down into the deep bowl, passed us, went down to Jeff's office, and parked. Bear got up and trotted down the hill.

"Hey!" Vicki yelled. "There goes my Bear rug!"

Two men got out. One white, one black. Both old. They were

regulars. Bear knew them and gave each a compulsory sniff. The black guy gave him a treat. The two men went into the office. Bear stood there, looking back our way.

"Vicki," I said, "I think Bear wants to show you his chickens if you want to."

"I do, I do!" she yelled. And with that she ran off down the hill. "Lead the way, Bear!"

"You want to know about Vicki," Carolyn noted, ever so perceptive. "Come, sit with me."

"Yes," I admitted, "But I really do think Bear was waiting for her." I came over and sat down.

"I know he was," she replied.

"Vicki has it rough sometimes. As you probably guessed, she has PTSD, along with injuries I can't get into right now. Last night she slept so well. No nightmares. Just blissful, uninterrupted, medicinal … sleep.

"This is paradise, Chad. It's therapy. The whole camping thing is about therapy — change of scenery, keeping her active, exploring, seeing new things. And this place fits right in."

"I get that," I nodded. "I know a little about illness. You are welcome to stay as long as you want."

She was looking at me directly, but I tried not to look her in the eye. "What's troubling you, Chad?"

"I had a nightmare of my own this morning," I began sheepishly. "About the diner. Robots taking out all the booths and stuff. I think it was my subconscious telling me to give up on the diner idea. I don't have the start-up money anyway so it's really a no-brainer. Which is what I have — no brain."

"What if you *did* have the start-up money?"

"I think that's what the dream was tryin' to tell me, Carolyn. Can't believe how comfortable I feel just blurtin' out all this personal stuff. Thing is, in West Virginia, you have to be careful how high you climb 'cause that's how far you're gonna fall."

I held up my left-hand palm up. "Job." And then my right. "Diner. The diner could maybe make money, but probably not. The job would be steady employment, maybe even insurance."

"No-brainer," she responded immediately.

"Job?" I guessed.

"Diner," she said with confidence.

"Carolyn, I'm all ears for diner."

"Okay," she started, while readjusting in her seat. "Diner first. You open the doors, work hard, do your best, but it's tough. Your diner will have ups and downs. And when things get rough, what do you do? You consider your options, come up with ideas, make decisions, right?"

I nodded.

"The fallacy of your thinking is that you're not holding this sacred "job" to the same standards. The company that hires you has the same challenges trying to make it work. Difference is, *they* make the decisions as to what to do when things get tough. And the boss you end up working for, know who he reports to?"

"Who?"

"Mr. Butthead."

It sunk in. "Carolyn, you just made my decision." I reached over and offered a fist bump. "Thank you."

We fist bumped, and I could feel the relief like an elephant moving off my chest.

"You're very welcome." She smiled. "Now, I have a favor to ask of you."

"Name it."

"I want to rent this campsite on a permanent, long-term lease."

At first, I didn't get what she was saying so I stalled for time. "This is my pad. Go get your own," I grinned.

"I just love you." She smiled, touching my arm.

I put my hand on hers and smiled. "Noted, logged, appreciated."

"Ha!" She laughed, pushing back in her chair. "Good one!"

"Carolyn, just to be straight with you, you can park whenever you want. This pad was for my trailer, and the other to park my truck."

"I want that pad too," she said, now grinning ear to ear. "This one for my camper, that one for a picnic table and a firepit."

"Okay, you can have these two, and I'll dig two more for me. Still plenty of room between me and the road. These two cost me $250 so I'd have to charge you for that."

She laughed out loud. "I pay $10K for a six-month lease for a campsite in Naples, Florida. Another $9K for a five-month lease in upstate New York. And a few little places month to month."

"Okayyy." My head was spinning. "And why?"

"Because we like to freestyle. The nice places fill up, especially for a rig like ours. And that means planning ahead and a schedule. A commitment. Of course, those places have amenities—concrete slabs, pool, pizza delivery to your door, stuff like that.

"And frankly, Chad, same sex couples aren't always treated well, so it's nice to know who you're dealing with."

"I am sorry about that, I really am."

"I know," she nodded. "So here's the thing. We have family in Cleveland, where I'm from, and Charleston, South Carolina, where Vicki grew up. This is about dead center in the middle, an easy drive to either. So here would be both a waypoint *and* a destination."

"In all fairness to you," I admitted, "— and I'm tryin' real hard to wrap my head around all this — you wouldn't want to stay here come winter. Some days you'd have a hard time just gettin' that rig in here."

"Thus the term 'freestyle,'" she countered with a grin. "Tell you what. I'll pay $8K for a one-year lease, starting today, and we'll see how it works out. And I'll pay for the concrete pad and hookups."

"I'm okay with it on my end," I said. "I'm just not comfortable that it's fair to you."

"Then we have a deal."

She extended her hand, and to my surprise we shook on it.

As we did, Bev pulled in. She drove over to us and parked behind my truck. She walked up carrying a grocery bag. Her hair was in a ponytail, and she wore a bright orange sundress.

"Oh, good," she exclaimed. "You're still here! I was telling Mumma about you guys and she whipped up some biscuits."

I gave her Vicki's seat and passed the bag to Carolyn.

"You're too sweet," Carolyn said.

"And how are you feeling?" to Bev.

"Great! Tired, but pushin' through. I go to bed tired and wake up tired."

"Have you had your prenatal exam?"

"No ma'am," Bev admitted as she looked down at her feet.

"I'm an OB/GYN doctor," Carolyn said. "I don't have any

equipment in my camper, but I do have some literature. And we can listen to your baby's heartbeat. Okay?"

"Heartbeat?" Bev exclaimed. "Carolyn, that would be wonderful! Yes!"

"Well, okay then," Carolyn said, reaching into the bag. She pulled out a biscuit and handed the bag back to Bev.

"Somebody say somethin' about biscuits?" Jeff was walking up from the office.

Vicki was walking up as well, not far behind.

Jeff did a nosedive into the grocery bag. "A fried-chicken biscuit! I love these!"

"Just help yourself," Bev scolded.

Vicki arrived, exclaiming, "Bear showed me his chickens!"

"Biscuit?" Bev offered.

"Oh, no," she replied. "But save me one for later. It's time for my run!"

"Vicki, honey," Carolyn said, "I'm concerned about you jogging on these roads. They're narrow and there's no shoulder."

"I need my run!" Vicki protested.

"Vicki," I said, "see that gap in the trees down there past all the cars? On the left, at the bottom. There's an ATV trail down there."

"Perfect," Carolyn said. "This place gets better and better. Mmm, this biscuit is delicious."

"But watch out for tree roots," Jeff mumbled, his mouth stuffed full of biscuit. "It's an ATV trail, not a jogging trail. And turn left. There's more to see."

"Okay!" Vicki yelled. "Outta here!" And off she went.

Carolyn watched Vicki until she disappeared from sight, then asked Bev, "You going to have a biscuit?"

"Oh, no," Bev answered. "My belly's a little queasy this morning."

"Morning sickness," Carolyn concluded, still enjoying her biscuit.

"I guess so. I hate throwin' up. It's gross."

"TMI," Jeff objected.

"So how do you guys like my campsite?" Carolyn asked.

"It's a great campsite," Jeff replied. "Yours? Whaaat?"

Carolyn explained about all the other leased campsites and the agreement she just made with me. Including all the mind- blowing dollar figures.

"Wow," Jeff said. "I mean *wow*. So instead of a site overlooking a pool, you want this site overlooking my cars?"

I tried to explain. "Jeff, do you see a rose bush or a thorn bush, or — Carolyn, how's it go?"

Jeff interjected. "Does a rose bush have thorns or a thorn bush have roses."

I nodded. "Yeah, that."

He looked out over the junkyard. "The cars are the roses to me. See? Some are red."

"Deep," Bev noted. She didn't mean it.

"Jeff," Carolyn continued, "I would like to enter into a contract with you as well."

She had his full attention.

"This pad," she began, "I want a concrete slab, level but

crowned for runoff. Steps down to the lower pad. Another slab down there. Some ground cover on either side of the steps. And hook ups, of course."

"Fifty amp." Jeff nodded.

"Right. And two more pads up from here for Chad."

Jeff looked around, then shook his head. "No."

"What?" I blurted out. Things were going so swell.

Jeff had a better idea. "Dig this pad down level with the lower pad, so no steps between you and your picnic table. And a retainer wall of some sort on the high side."

He walked and looked around. "Your RV is longer than Chad's mobile home, so we would have to dig back further. You know, these two pads are perfect for Chad, and closer to my office. We should dig you a new pad uphill from here. Still plenty of room between here and the road. You'd be up higher, too. Have a better view of my cars," he grinned.

"And the mountain range," Carolyn added, grinning too. "I like it. And you could push the dirt over into this drop-off area. I would need it more level to turn my camper around to back in."

"True 'dat," Jeff said. "But the thing is, we got these pads done cheap with a borrowed backhoe and some leftover gravel."

"Get bids for what you can't do yourself," Carolyn said. "Add a fair rate for your labor, and tack on a 10% overhead."

Jeff walked back over to Carolyn and extended his hand.

"This handshake is your contract."

Carolyn shook his hand. "I trust this handshake more than a paper contract. And I am dead serious, based on past experience."

"Same here," Jeff nodded.

With that done, Carolyn picked up her coffee cup and stood up. "Out of coffee. Bev, come with me to my camper? We can talk about prenatal care."

Bev stood up. "Let's go!"

And that left Jeff and me looking out over his cars and my mountain range. I sat in Vicki's chair. He sat in Carolyn's.

"By the way, Jeff, is there anything else I own I don't know about?"

"See this mountain range behind us, across the road? Runs parallel to your range —"

"I own that too?"

"Naw, just pullin' your leg. Mr. Tropicana owns it — that and the range behind it. That's why there isn't much traffic from that direction. His house is the only thing back that way."

"Who's Mr. Tropicana?"

"Rich guy that lives in a big — and I mean *big* house and a 10-car garage. Rich like, he sells his boat when the old one gets wet. Nice guy, though. He calls me to do oil changes and stuff."

"How'd he make his money?"

"Story goes he was a stock market analyst that lived in Richmond, Virginia. His house overlooked train tracks below. Sittin' on his porch in the evening, he noticed that the Tropicana cars were refrigerated. Thing is, orange juice has a short shelf life and it's sort of a luxury, so subject to the economy. Then he noticed how the number of cars varied from time to time. So he started countin' 'em. He took his car count and put it in one of his forecast formulas and used it to buy and sell stocks. And got rich."

"No way," I countered. "Totally not buyin' it."

"Makes for a good story though, right? Anyway, his wife is from around here, so he built a big house and moved in one day, and his wife died the day after. That part is true."

"That's sad," I said. "Money can't buy happiness."

"Speaking of which, what'd you pay for my land?"

"Thirty-two grand."

He nodded. "I think I owed thirty-eight."

"You did. And I would sell it back to you for what I paid.— cash or payments or whatever."

"No," he said. "Didn't have it then, don't have it now. I'm good. But just think, four years rentin' this little piece gets you your money back."

"I know. But the first year goes to the diner."

"So you're makin' a go of it. Final answer?"

"Final answer." I repeated Carolyn's story about working for myself or working for Mr. Butthead.

"She is one smart lady," Jeff said. "Can't believe the difference in West Virginia money and elsewhere. Geez, what a difference."

He pulled out his phone and did some tapping and swiping. "She's payin' you $22 per day, except she won't be usin' it every day. But a good deal, for both of you."

"You'll do well with your deal with her," I said. "I know you'll be fair, but still make a boatload of money."

"Oh, hell yeah. If I wasn't straight with her, she'd know."

He shook his head. "The idea about makin' the two pads into one was her idea."

"No," I blurted.

"Oh yeah. Laid it out so I would come up with the idea myself. And put it up the hill. She had it all figured."

"I do not know *how* you know that," I said. "It's like the two of you talk without words. It's kinda spooky."

He just shrugged.

Another truck pulled in, this one with a middle-aged guy and a teenager.

"Another customer," Jeff said, standing up. "Later."

And that left me sitting there alone, admiring my mountain with newfound appreciation. And my mind drifting back to Mom.

And watching her die …

CHAPTER 7

At nineteen years old, my mom, Lessie Ann Davis, gave birth to my sister Judy. Nineteen years later, she had me. Nineteen years after me, Mom started mixing up her words.

I don't know what it was like for her raising my sister. We didn't talk about that. Mom never married — unless you count her love and devotion for Fellowship Baptist Church. Especially the choir. She loved the choir. About the time I came along, my sister married and moved to Omaha, Nebraska.

My earliest memories of Mom were her hugs, tousling my hair, and telling me she loved me. I do remember when she got promoted to manager at the Hobby Lobby. That was a big deal. That's when we moved from an apartment to a real house and I first met Jeff. She was a good mom. It never occurred to me I was missing a father.

I didn't notice Mom's decline. At nineteen, everything was all about me. I had a job at the coal mines. I bought a truck — used — with payments that would run for five years. Best of all, I had a steady girlfriend — Brandi Hotchkiss. Brandi was smokin' hot, stacked, and fun. By West Virginia standards, I was upper class. I moved in with Brandi and became even less aware of Mom's condition.

But others noticed.

A year later Mom lost her job, and she wasn't vested for a pension. That got my attention.

I first suggested we find her a roommate, someone to help with the mortgage and just be there with her. She said she was not "livin' with a damn stranger."

I think it was the only time I ever heard her curse.

It was her idea to sell the house and buy a small one- bedroom mobile home within walking distance to groceries and a Goodwill store. She later decided to sell her car and pay off my truck. Her plan was to count on her lifelong church family for rides to church and choir practice. Except that the church shuttle bus only came on Sunday. And her lifelong choir friends became less and less available. So, my truck that she paid off filled in for her rides to choir practice.

But then Mom got more and more frustrated that she couldn't remember her friends' names, so she quit choir. It wasn't long after that, she stopped goin' to church.

My visits became more frequent. I sometimes found the oven left on or the TV remote in the fridge. She was forever losing her glasses.

At the relatively young age of 59, a trip to the doctor confirmed her illness — Alzheimer's. The doctor's signature activated my sister as power of attorney. But Judy didn't come to Princeton. I mailed the paperwork and Mom's checkbook.

Reluctantly, I moved in with Mom and slept on the living room sofa. That's when I discovered five-year expired cans of soup, smelly underwear in the dresser, and Mom's reluctance to bathe.

Early each morning I would fix breakfast for her, pack a lunch and label it, and put out a fresh change of clothes. When I got home — bone tired — I had to deal with reorganized placement of food, dishes, and clothes. *And findin' her damn glasses.*

I needed help.

I called some of her lifelong church friends. That netted one casserole. I called Judy, but she vetoed the cost of hired help. Mom's only income was a disability check. Her neighbors were of no help, not that I trusted any of them. I knew I couldn't quit my job, but it was getting more dangerous leaving her alone.

Fate decided to step in and move things along. I was woken up in the middle of the night to the smell of poop. Mom had come down with diarrhea. In her confusion she managed to spread it all over herself, her bed, and into the bathroom.

Modesty had long since been checked off as a luxury. I began cleaning her and getting her comfortable, but she kept adding more poop faster than I could keep up. I was exhausted and miserable, and my efforts were hampered by trying to see through my tears.

At 3 a.m., I called Jeff and asked for help. He replied, "On it" and clicked off.

By 4 a.m., Jeff and I were making progress. I called work to tell them I would be late. At 7 a.m., Mom was clean and sleeping peacefully. Jeff left with a load of laundry.

I called work again and said I would not be coming in that day — or ever.

At first, things got better. I could keep Mom safe, dressed in clean clothes, and fed. I took her on walks, to Walmart, and out for drives. I could even step out for a much-needed visit to see Brandi.

As each day melted into the next, and the next, and the next, the life in Mom's eyes faded. As did the money. Judy would pay for food, the lot rent, and my phone bill, but little else. She balked about everything and even deducted my beer off a grocery receipt. I threatened to drop Mom off at a nursing home, but Judy called my bluff.

Not surprising, Brandi got tired of it all. She didn't like visiting, said Mom made her uncomfortable. So she left me. Probably a good thing, really.

One of the things about Alzheimer's is that the parent and child trade places—not something that is supposed to happen when the parent is 61 and the child is 23.

As endless months toggled into years, Mom's mobile home got smaller and smaller, especially in the winter. The sofa I slept on is what Mom sat on during the day. She stared at the TV whether it was on or not. She liked to watch the birds perched on the bird feeder outside the window. The weather affected her condition, and a full moon got her agitated, fussy, and even mean.

I rarely knew the date, so it was a pleasant surprise to open my phone one day and see greetings on my 25th birthday.

I talked and texted with as many friends as I could. That put me in a good mood.

But at noon, when I brought the TV tray over to Mom, she looked at me in fear. She didn't know me.

"Mom, it's me. Chad," I said.

She shook her head violently, afraid of me.

I backed away and went to the kitchen. After a few minutes I came back. "I'm Chad," I said. "I brought you some lunch." Then I set it down.

From then on, I greeted her with, "Hi, I'm Chad. I'm here to …"

There was one way to pull Mom out of her empty, silent stare. I could call up a song like "Onward Christian Soldiers." She would come to life and belt out *every* word. And when the song ended, she'd drift away again. So I would play hymns with the volume up, and she would sing every word. It was a miracle.

I did it as long and as often as I could stand it. She liked Willie Nelson, John Prine, Patsy Cline, and Loretta Lynn. I could also throw in Toby Keith and Garth Brooks with no complaints.

One day I got out Mom's old six-string guitar. I plucked the top string, and that earned a smile from her. I kept plucking strings and it made her happy. I got tired of hearing the same notes over and over, so I pulled the beginners lesson book out of the case. Learning to play chords was much better.

It turned into a daily ritual, because it gave Mom joy, and I could go for hours without getting bored. Eventually my fingertips hardened and the chords came naturally. I must have inherited her ear for music because it got to where I could strum what I wanted to hear. It pleased Mom when I sang to her, even if I had to hum when I forgot the lyrics.

I guess every prisoner dreams of escape. I became obsessed with *anything* and *everything* written about the Appalachian Trail.

It passes through Pearisburg, and that's only a half-hour drive down Route 460. When Jeff and I were little, his dad would take us on hikes and we'd camp at trail shelters. As a kid it was just a fun trip. As a prisoner I ached for the freedom to wake up in one place and walk to another place. And then the next day walk to another place. And do that day after day, week after week, and maybe even month after month.

That freedom was just down the road. At Pearisburg I could get on the trail and walk 1,554 miles to Mount Katahdin, Maine. Or go south 635 miles to Springer Mountain, Georgia.

I read stories of people who had hiked the trail. I studied trail guides. I researched all the hiking gear that I could never afford. I dreamed of living in a world with no walls.

Out of desperation I also read magazines, trash novels, and even a few classics. For some books I had to keep looking up words, but that was okay. Hell, that was more English than I'd learned in high school.

I spent the next two years in a box 40' long by 15' wide. Not because I wanted to. Not because I'm a good person. I simply had no choice. I resented Mom, hated the disease, felt abandoned by God. If there even was one …

My one reprieve was Jeff. He would come over and sometimes bring beer and pizza. He would sit with me and talk. He was my connection to the outside world. He made me laugh.

Hell yeah, I would do anything for him.

Oddly, the end was the least worst. Gone was the false hope, the denial, the relentless piecemeal loss of a loved one. The soul-sucking drain of helplessness. Of choices that had no right answers.

The end isn't death. The end is when a loved one finally, mercifully, stops dying. Also, the end was busy. Meals were served as a puree, like different colors of apple sauce. And that takes time. Mom had to be changed, bathed, turned, and checked on. There was stuff to do.

Best of all, the end is when hospice came in to help. First, all the living room furniture was, literally, kicked to the curb. In came a hospital bed that lifted upward for changing and lifted just the head for feeding. And it had side rails. In came a bed tray and all kinds of supplies.

I moved into the bedroom after first pulling up all the carpet and disinfecting everything. Best of all, daily help came in the form of a visiting social worker. Her name was Sarah, and she was there to walk with Mom to the light. Sarah was about 5' 2", a little over 100 pounds, about my age. She had short, strawberry blond hair and bangs down to her soft, hazel eyes. She wore round, wire-rimmed glasses that wouldn't stay up on her button of a nose. She would push up her glasses with her index and middle finger. She had a permanent smile over a pointed chin.

When Sarah came, I was dismissed for a few hours. Mom was hers. She bathed Mom, rubbed her, talked to her, sang to her, and fed her. I was free to go if I wanted, which I sometimes did to run to the store. But mostly I just stayed and watched Sarah. Through her eyes I learned that Mom was still there, still receptive to love, still worthy of the best I could give. Sarah gave my life — and Mom's — peace.

Sarah was there when Mom took her last breath on Mother's Day. That day held no relevance for me. A birthday, a Tuesday, or a holiday had long since lost meaning. There were only days, nights, and nights with full moons.

I didn't know Mom had a life insurance policy. When Judy got the check, she didn't split it with me. She sent me the whole thing. Fair enough, but now what?

How do I take care of myself? I already blew the money.

The sound of Carolyn's footsteps was a much-needed interruption.

CHAPTER 8

"Has Vicki come back?" she asked.

"No," I replied.

Carolyn looked out over the cars, and paced back and forth. "She should've been back by now."

She sounded worried, so I offered, "Want me to look for her?"

"Would you? Please?"

"Sure." I stood up and jogged down the hill. Didn't want her to think I would just walk. Good thing I was wearing tennis shoes. I wondered what she was worried about. There wasn't any real danger I could think of.

Even out of sight I kept jogging. I expected to see Vicki down on the trail. But she wasn't there. I turned left and kept jogging, and I got more and more worried the farther I went.

The trail runs under Route 19. I had never noticed from the many times driving up on the road. I kept jogging, and I picked up my pace. Another mile and still no Vicki.

I started to dread that something tragic had happened. Our new friends, or just Carolyn, would hate us forever.

Then I stopped. The trail split three ways — straight, left, and right. I looked down each way. Maybe straight was the best choice. But if I went that way, she could be coming back from one of the other two.

I hate multiple choices.

"Think!" I yelled.

"Think about what?" Vicki replied, her voice coming from behind a patch of rhododendron. The leaves parted and she stepped onto the trail about twenty yards ahead.

"I am *so* glad to see you!" I exclaimed. "Are you okay?"

"Oh yeah," she replied. "I had to pee. You out jogging too?"

"I was looking for you. Carolyn was worried."

"Poo! She always worries about me. She's the best."

"I think you were takin' longer than usual."

We started walking back.

"Oh, that. I got lost. The trails! They go everywhere! Don't you love it?" she gushed.

"I've never been down these. But I like what I've seen today"

Heavy footsteps pounded down the trail. It was Jeff, running in his work boots.

Seeing us he stopped and put his hands on his knees, panting. He is strong, fast even, but he is a big guy. He was still out of breath when we reached him.

"Don't suppose," he said, gulping in air, "you coulda … thought … to bring your phone."

"Oops," I replied.

"Yeah … didn't think so."

He pulled out his phone and hit some buttons. "Four bars. Good signal … down here."

He handed the phone to Vicki.

When we got back, Carolyn and Vicki hugged. All was right

with the world. Carolyn had more chairs out so we could all sit around and talk about Vicki's adventure.

"I got lost!" she began. "Carolyn, we have *got* to get one of those ATVs! They are the bomb!"

"Oh good," Carolyn said. "More ways to get hurt."

"No, no!" Vicki replied. "I mean … the teenagers go bustin' through, sure! But there's kids and old people and … there was this one family. Dad was on the kind you straddle … you know… steer with handlebars. Then along comes mom in a two-seater, like a dune buggy on steroids. Got a kid in the passenger seat. Behind her was this cute little kid on a three-wheeler. I'm tellin' you, Carolyn, it looks fun! And the trails go everywhere!"

"And get lost," Carolyn added.

"So what! We'd figure it out. You gotta try it! Pleeeeze!"

Carolyn smiled. "Okay."

"Yea!" Vicki screamed, jumping up and waving her arms. "Let's go get one now! I gotta shower and change clothes!"

"Vicki?" Jeff asked. "How'd you get unlost?"

"Oh yeah, I got help. From the homeless guy. He lives down there. I was walking down the trail and he pops outta the woods and says, 'Hi, my name is Marvin. I think you're going the wrong way.'"

"So *that's* his name," Jeff noted.

"Yeah! He's smelly. He's a vet, like me! Messed up, like me! He walked me back to the right trail. Nice man. See ya! Outta here!" She turned and trotted off.

"Carolyn," Jeff explained, "Vicki would've been just fine without any help."

"And the homeless man is okay?" she asked.

"Yes."

"And you know this *how*?"

Jeff shrugged. "Cuz Bear is okay with him."

"You really getting an ATV?" I asked.

Carolyn was watching Vicki jog up the hill to the camper.

She turned and smiled. "Like I have a choice?"

Later, I drove Carolyn and Vicki to Princeton and helped them pick out a Polaris Ranger 1000. It came with a GPS to help them from getting lost. They also bought helmets, goggles, and gloves. I was floored that someone could just go out and spend $20,000 on a whim. And a trailer — if they ever wanted to tow it behind the RV. Otherwise, Jeff was going to clear out a space in his shop to park it.

On the way back Carolyn wanted to talk about the diner.

"I will write my rent check payable to Lighthouse Diner," she began. "You and Bev get a business license in that name, as partners. Open a checking account and deposit the check. Make sure everything is expensed to the business. That means gas, phones, utilities, insurance, almost everything from a grocery store or hardware store."

"Sounds like a lot of record keeping," I worried.

"It is. But expenses deduct from income."

"Income! Hope we have some of that."

"Me too," she replied. "We'll get together with Bev and talk about it. After Vicki and I go for a ride."

"Trail ridin'!" Vicki yelled from the back seat. "Don't wait up!"

All that afternoon and the next day they went trail ridin'

I don't know who loved it more. Not only did they love the rides. They met like-minded adventurous folks and made new friends.

Meanwhile, Bev and I went to town to get our license and open a checking account. First expense — the latest iPhone for Bev. It was her first phone, and it was worth more than her car.

Sadly, Carolyn and Vicki had to leave the next morning. Bev actually cried as the big camper pulled away. She kept watching it get smaller and smaller as if keeping it in sight would somehow bring it back. After one last sniffle and a long, deep breath, she turned to face me.

"I'm going to miss them," she whimpered. "I just love 'em."

I nodded. "Me too."

She looked back down the empty road. "*That* is what a relationship is supposed to be," she added. "And the money. I've never had so much hope as I do now."

"Me too. And fear."

She turned to me and nodded. "We've got work to do."

"I know. And don't get mad or nuthin' but I'm takin' the afternoon off."

She shrugged. "I'm not your boss."

"I know. I promise, come tomorrow I'll be full throttle."

She put her hand on my arm. "I trust you, partner. Wanna share what you're up to?"

"I'll tell you *all* about it when I get back."

My mission was to get a taste of freedom. I drove to Walmart and loaded up bags of energy bars, candy, peanut butter, bread, apples, water bottles, trash bags, and ice. I didn't even look at the prices. I have never, ever bought anything without checking the price. Then I drove down the road a piece to where the Appalachian Trail crossed at Pearisburg.

It was a warm, cloudless day in late June. I pulled the cooler out and set it on the ground, dropped the tailgate, and set the bags of goodies next to me. My trail magic station was open for hikers.

An hour went by. Then another. I got fidgety. What the hell was I expecting — a parade?

North Bounders — called NoBos — start at Springer Mountain, Georgia, around mid-March. That puts most of them through Pearisburg around mid-May. So most had already passed through, or quit. About three out of four drop out.

Finally, a hiker appeared and was coming my way. I waved.

"Trail magic!" I yelled.

The guy was tall, thin, bearded, and carried a huge backpack. His hiking poles seemed to be doing as much of the walking as his legs.

"Apples! Energy bars! Peanut butter! Water! What's your pleasure! I'm Chad, what's yours?"

I must have sounded like a carnival vendor.

"Thanks," he replied, leaning on his poles. "Love you guys, really do. But I just reprovisioned in town, so I'm good. But thanks."

He started to shuffle around me. "My buddy is coming along behind me. He might want something. Thanks again."

And on he went. I just stood there, a little embarrassed. Disappointed. I so badly wanted to be a part of the club. It took another forty minutes for his buddy to appear. This guy was short, also thin and also bearded.

"Trail magic," I stated, this time leaving off the menu. He

actually stopped and took off his pack.

"Thanks," he said, smiling. "Got water?"

"I do!" I said, delighted. I pulled a cold bottle out of the cooler. He drank it down.

"Another?" I asked. He nodded. I pulled out another. "I'm Chad. What's your trail name?"

"I'm Slip," he said. "My buddy is Trip. Guess it's obvious. He's always tripping on tree roots and I'm always slipping on wet leaves. So we're Trip and Slip."

"Right, good names. I've heard 'hike your own hike,' but your buddy is forty minutes ahead. Is that normal?" I was a sponge for information.

"Oh, hell yeah. He's been as much as a day or two ahead. Don't get me wrong, we almost always end up in the same place each night. And sometimes I get ahead of him. When your body says go, you go. When it says *whoa*, you stop. Hike your own hike."

"That is so cool. Can't tell you how much I appreciate what you're sayin'."

"You a hiker?"

"No. Guess I'm a wannabe."

"Well, if you ever do, you just got your trail name."

He raised a pole and tapped it on my right shoulder, then my left. "I dub thee Wanna Be."

"Cool," was all I could come up with.

"How about an energy bar?" he asked.

"Sure. How'd you know I had energy bars?"

"Trip called me. Said to say he was sorry not to stop for a bit. And asked if he could have one too."

"Tell him Wanna Be said no problem."

He took the bars and put on his pack.

"So I should hike the trail, right?" I ventured.

"Definitely," he replied.

As he walked away I just couldn't help but ask. "Why?"

He did a 180 and rested on his poles. "Because it's the most miserable adventure you will ever love." He smiled, turned, and walked away.

I could've stayed and waited for the next hiker, but I got all I wanted and then some. I scooted back to Tree Fork and found Jeff behind my trailer pad with a Ditch Witch. The trench was not straight at all. A bulldozer was up the hill pushing dirt around.

When Jeff saw me, he turned off the trencher and came over. "Um," I pointed at his trench. "Need some help keepin' your digger straight?"

Jeff looked up the hill, then turned back to me. "Naw. I'm diggin' around this here dogwood tree. Can't chance killin' it."

I looked at him, the tree, him. "That's a dang big dogwood."

"Dad planted it," he said. "Way long time ago. Called it his fishin' tree. You know, when a dogwood blooms, it's time to go crappie fishin'."

"He needed a tree to know that?"

"No, but he liked it, so I'm not chancin' losin' it."

Then wiping sweat off his face with his T-shirt, he asked, "So how was your trip?"

"Great!" I answered. "I got a trail name — Wanna Be."

"Wanna be what?" he probed.

"Wanna be hiking, of course."

"Oh, right."

"I met two guys, Trip and Slip, two buddies. But get this, Slip was forty minutes behind Trip."

Jeff shrugged. "So slippin' takes longer than trippin'."

"Slip said they usually end up at the same place each day but can sometimes be days apart. That kinda blew my mind."

"You're really into this."

"Oh yeah, even more now," I grinned. "Next time I want to hike to a shelter and camp. You know, mingle with my peeps."

"Right."

"Wanna come?"

"Noooo. I don't wanna have to dig a hole when I need to 'drop the kids off at the pool.'"

"Well," I shrugged, "a man's gotta doo-doo what a man's gotta doo-doo."

He just stood there and gawked, then asked, "You just come up with that?"

"Yeah, just did. Good?"

"No." He looked behind me.

I turned to see Bev walking our way and typing on her phone.

"She hasn't been off that thing since she got it," Jeff noted.

"Just get here?" she asked, strolling up next to me.

I told her about my trail magic, the hikers, my trail name. Her response: "Got the receipt?"

"Receipt?"

"From Walmart."

"In one of the bags, I guess."

She turned, went to my truck, and came back with the receipt. "Ice counts; diners use ice. Apples, yes. Energy bars, maybe not. Peanut butter, dunno. Bread! Bread counts." She shook the paper at me. "You gotta keep track of this stuff. We need receipts!"

I couldn't tell if she was really mad or just tryin' to be heard over the bulldozer.

"Got it!" I answered. "I'll do better."

"Speakin' of food," Jeff asked, "what's for dinner tonight?"

"Oh!" she exclaimed. "I'm your wife now?"

"No-no," Jeff stuttered. "I just thought you might be doin' taste trials or —"

"Tonight's dinner," she interrupted, "is … let's see. She read from the receipt: "Energy bars, apples, and peanut butter sandwiches. And water."

Jeff and I held up our hands in defeat, laughed, and peace was restored.

Bev faced Jeff. "You tell him about my idea yet?"

Jeff shook his head.

She faced me. "What if we moved *my* trailer here … and I pay rent to you? It will save me the trip driving back and forth from Princeton."

"Sounds like a great idea," I said.

"It's Mumma that thought of it, not only for me but for her. Come winter she would have to drive here in the dark on icy roads. It'd be better if after her and Dad have dinner, she could drive up and spend the night with me. Then next morning just walk to the diner instead of chipping ice off her windshield."

"Totally great idea," I confirmed.

I waved to Jeff. "Sir! Could we get another pad in here!"

"What about *my* fee?" he scowled.

"For what?"

"For havin' to put up with her!"

He was definitely pleased with himself.

Bev and I looked at each other and smiled.

"I have an idea myself," I said, "and this is serious, so hear me out. So, I own the land and Jeff owns the business that's on the land. But it's headed toward bein' a trailer park, or an ATV repair center, or maybe campsites for the trail riders. Bev runs the diner, and we're partners, and Jeff does stuff to help with the diner.

"Thing is, everything is so mixed together. We're all just workin' together. I think we should have an understanding of what already is — the three of us are partners. Equal."

"Agreed," Bev said quickly.

"Ditto," Jeff replied. "Seriously."

I put my hand out, palm down. "Partners."

Bev slapped her hand on mine. "Partners."

Jeff followed with his hand on Bev's. "Partners."

"Geronimo!" Jeff exclaimed while pulling out his knife and flickin' out the blade. "Now we mix blood to consummate the agreement." He placed the blade on his arm.

I pulled out my Buck knife from its sheath. It was a straight knife, so no need to flick out the blade. I mimicked Jeff's actions. We both looked expectantly to Bev.

Bev's eyes got huge. She looked at me and then Jeff, back and forth. I couldn't keep a snicker from slippin' out.

Jeff coughed.

Neither of us could keep from laughing.

"What!" Bev yelled. "What? What the heck?" She punched me in the arm. Then she punched Jeff. Then she grimaced and shook her fist because hitting him hurt her wrist.

"How did …!" she shrieked, "did you guys rehearse this or something?"

We shook our heads.

Jeff stopped laughing and turned serious.

"Oh crap, now we have to tell her the code word."

I stopped laughing. "Well, she *is* a partner."

"Might come in handy," Jeff noted, "in front of diner customers."

"What?" demanded Bev, arms crossed.

"Okay, okay," I said, holding up my hands. "We came up with it in third grade. When one of us says 'Geronimo,' it's code for heads up — follow my lead. Or it could just be a warnin', like the teacher is comin' up behind you."

"Or," Jeff added, "it could mean shut up because the person you're talkin' about is comin' around a corner. But heck, I don't think we've used it for — what — eight years?"

He slid his knife back in his pocket.

I nodded. The eight years I spent caring for Mom.

I returned my knife to its sheath and smiled. "On the bright side, you don't have to cut yourself."

"Noted, logged, appreciated," she replied.

"Hey," I complained, "You're quoting Carolyn."

"Just wanted to see if you're paying attention. I brought fixins for pork chops, potato salad, corn on the cob, and dinner rolls tonight. Now you two behave, I might share some."

Jeff usually has a good poker face, but he couldn't keep it straight.

"Was kinda hopin' for lobster," he sputtered.

Bev looked at him and smiled. "Get back over to that ditch digger thing and get busy!"

He saluted and trotted off.

"And you," she announced. "I have a list for you."

I smiled. This diner idea was going to work.

CHAPTER 9

A few hours later we all met at the diner and started working on dinner. Jeff and I were in the back room peeling taters and Bev was in front working on the pork chops. It was nice just being together and raggin' on each other and carryin' on. Life was good.

Till Bev came to the door.

"Guys," she said. "Listen up. Drop what you're doing. Get up. Don't come to the door."

She was halfway in the doorway, looking out the front, then back at us. "On my phone, news clips, story about a guy raping women. Light gray van, no windows. Pretends to be in a wheelchair struggling with something. Woman comes by, sees him, offers to help. He's not disabled. He rapes them, leaves 'em on a deserted road alive but injured.

"*He is here*, outside."

"Call 9-1-1," Jeff said, "and get in here!"

"No," Bev said, stubbornly. "He'll get away. I'm going to bait him. You guys slip out the back and get ready to nab him. But *not* 'til he makes a move."

"No!" Jeff demanded, standing up. "It's too dangerous. You're pregnant. You'll get hurt. Get in here!"

"I know what's coming, so I'll know what to do," she retorted while still glancing out front. "Look, the van is next to the door, facing in. Look under the van to see his feet. Sneak up to the front of the van when he's at the back. You'll hear him and me and know what's going on. Hurry!"

"No!" Jeff roared, angrily. "You have no idea. You've never been in a fight."

She glared back, just as angry. "And *you've* never been raped!"

Time froze. Bev and Jeff were like statues in a stare down, motionless. As the reality sank in, Jeff kinda just melted.

"Oh," he whispered.

Bev pointed to the back door. "Get out and get ready!"

Jeff and I scrambled out the door. We ran to the side of the diner and peaked around the corner. We could see the guy's feet at the side of the van, and the wheels of the wheelchair behind the van.

His feet went to the back and that gave us time to crawl to the front of the van. We could plainly see his feet come to the wheelchair, turn around, and lift to the foot pads. The guy was not a cripple.

Bev's feet came along the driver's side. "Are you okay?" she asked sweetly, her voice dripping with innocent kindness.

"Oh, I don't mean to be a bother," came the reply. "This here box has been rattlin' around in the van, so I decided to pull over and get it situated. Then I'll be on my way. Is the diner open?"

"No, it ain't," Bev replied. "I'm just here, by myself, fixin' to get it ready. Can I help you? With the box?"

"Well," the guy said. "That'd be awfully kind of you. Maybe it'll fit in the side door."

Bev's feet and the wheels came around to the side of the van. First one of Bev's feet went up, then the other.

"There's room in here," she began. "We could put it —"

The guy's feet hit the ground. The wheelchair went rolling backwards. "What we can do, bitch, is have ourselves a little fun!"

Jeff and I were up and running. The guy was halfway into the side door. Jeff grabbed his belt with one hand, his hair with the other, and lifted him up and out. Then he threw the guy on the ground, face down, and jumped on his back.

The guy started yelling. "Get off me, asshole! I didn't do nuthin'! Lemme go! Let go of me!"

Jeff held his arms down. I jumped on his legs, couldn't hold 'em down.

"Bev!" Jeff yelled. "You okay?"

"I'm fine!"

"Find me some rope!"

Bear came running up, barking nonstop.

"Get your dog away from me!" the guy yelled. "I'll sue your ass! Get off me!"

"How 'bout zip ties?" Bev yelled. "Lots of zip ties in here!"

"Even better!" I hollered.

Bev brought out the zip ties. I had to let his legs kick while I put one on each wrist. Jeff pulled the two wrists together and I zipped them together tight. Then we tied his ankles. Then I daisy-chained a few together and tied his legs together just above the knees.

Bear was barking. Bev was crying. Jeff was screaming at the guy. "He *will* bite you if you keep jerkin' around!"

"Untie me!" the guy yelled. "I didn't do nuthin'! You'll be in big trouble! I got friends! You will regret this! Let me go!"

I didn't like the idea of this guy having friends. That scared me.

But it gave me an idea.

"Hey Geronimo," I remarked casually to Jeff. "Kill him … or call the sheriff?"

"Kill him," was Jeff's immediate answer.

I turned to Bev. "What's your vote?" I asked, not calling her by name.

"Um, not sure."

"I'm for callin' the sheriff," I announced. "I mean, if we kill him, what would we do with the van?"

"Do you even *know me*?" Jeff asked. "I can have this van in a thousand pieces in two hours."

He got off the guy and went over to Bear. "Easy, Bear. Not yet."

Bear was still agitated but not barking as much. The guy had stopped yelling.

"We could hide the body easy enough," Bev offered, now catching on. "But wait, if his phone has one of them 'find my friends' app, somebody might know he's here."

"True," I agreed. "And callin' the sheriff might earn us some points. He's been on our case ever since, well — you know."

I could tell the guy was buying it.

"Make the call," I stated.

"This is West Virginia," Jeff countered. "Kill him."

"I'm making the call," Bev said.

The first car to arrive was Deputy Lawrence. He came to a screeching stop with lights flashing and siren blaring. He jumped out, drew his gun, and ran up to the guy — which was kinda overkill since the guy was hogtied.

"Everybody okay?" he asked.

"Fine," Jeff replied.

"Good," I added.

"Except for the lights and siren," Bev complained, still on the phone with her mom. "Now you got Bear barking again."

Deputy Lawrence holstered his gun, patted the guy down, pulled out a wallet and a small pocketknife. He keyed his mic and read the driver's license info to the dispatcher. Then he turned the guy over, took his picture, and sent the picture somewhere.

An unmarked car pulled in, lights flashing but no siren. The officer had on street clothes. He stayed right beside the guy while Deputy Lawrence went to his car, turned off the siren, and keyed stuff into his computer.

Next thing we knew, a State Trooper pulled in. Then an ambulance, another deputy, and then the Sheriff.

Sheriff James Bailey was your classic, hefty, gruff-looking sheriff. He first put his handcuffs on the guy and recited the Miranda Rights. The others clipped off the zip ties and took him away. Everyone bunched together in small group conversations.

Sheriff Bailey took us off to the side, away from everyone, and faced the three of us. Bear butted in between him and Bev and sat down, facing the sheriff. Sheriff Bailey took off his hat, handed it to Jeff, then — with some difficulty — got down on one knee and petted Bear. Bear accepted his attention.

"First," he said, looking up at me, "Chad, I'm sorry for your loss. Your mom was a fine lady. And I'm proud of the way you took care of her. You're a good man."

"Thank you," I said.

He nodded, kept rubbing Bear, and gave a respectful pause. "Second, what happened to the lighthouse light?"

"It broke," Jeff replied.

"Hope you can get it fixed. I almost missed the exit, so used to it bein' there." With some effort he got back up, put his hat back on, adjusted it just right. "Third, whose idea was it to capture this guy?"

Bev raised her hand meekly but didn't need to. Jeff and I had both backed up a step. Sheriff Bailey stared at her. "And what made you think that was a good idea?"

"Well," Bev began, "I was sure it was him. Light gray van, no windows, the wheelchair ruse, remote locations —"

"None of which, by the way" the sheriff interrupted, "were in West Virginia."

"No, but in several states. He didn't stay in just one."

"What states?" he quizzed.

"Illinois, Indiana, Tennessee."

"None of which border West Virginia."

"I got a quick glance at the wheelchair, but him not in it. But then he was. It had to be him."

"That was enough to risk your life?"

Bev looked down and pushed gravel with her foot. "I felt bad for all those girls he hurt," she mumbled.

"Look at me," he said softly, compassionately. "You know anyone personally been raped?"

She shook her head, looked away.

He studied her, didn't look away. "I got three daughters," he began. "If I'd caught him, they'd never find the body. So … I get it."

She looked up at him, her eyes watered.

"Let's move on to number four," he said, looking at me, then Jeff. His glare was like daggers. "You two. If there was a law against stupid, I'd have you two in cuffs. Bev here risked her own life. You two, you risked her life. Totally different. Understand me?"

We nodded vigorously.

"Why?" he demanded.

We both shrugged. I raised a hand, "She seemed confident about it bein' him."

Jeff started to say something, but the sheriff cut him off. "So you two boneheads let her put her life in jeopardy?"

We had no answer.

"Either one of you know someone been raped?"

"No," Jeff muttered.

I just shook my head.

Sheriff Bailey's eyes went back and forth looking at me, then Jeff, then me. Reminded me of one of those clocks that the eyes go back and forth in sync with the tail.

"Either of you own a gun?" he asked.

"No," I answered.

Finally, an easy question.

"Dad's Glock," Jeff answered. "It's somewhere in the house. Not sure where."

That reply earned a good long glare from the sheriff.

Then, "Either of you have a knife?"

I lifted my T-shirt up over the handle of my Buck knife.

"Hell," I admitted. "Forgot I had it. It — it's always on my hip."

Jeff pulled out his knife but didn't flick it open. Then put it back in his pocket.

"Either of you think you'd have to use it?"

I shook my head. "Never thought about it."

Jeff spoke up. "Knew I had mine. Knew Chad had his. Didn't know if the guy had one. Figured he did. That's why I made sure I kept his hands pinned."

Sheriff Bailey seemed okay with our answers. "Number…" "Five," Bev offered.

"Number five. Any way you can get this dog inside? I know this breed don't take orders too well."

"We'll get it done," Jeff confirmed.

"Number six," he continued. "Good job, all three of you. I'm so very proud of you. But understand, you won't hear me say that in public."

He let that sink in. "Number seven is all about politics. A sheriff spends half his time doin' his job, and half his time gettin' reelected. This puts my next reelection in the bag. So I'll have more time for gettin' work done. I want you to know — you will see me shamelessly tootin' my own horn as to how I cuffed a Federal criminal."

"I took a picture of that," Bev nodded. She showed him her phone.

He looked at it and nodded. "I called the reporter from Princeton Times and he's on the way. I'd appreciate you gettin' that to him."

"Absolutely." Now Bev grinned. "And we would shamelessly appreciate any mention of our diner."

Then the sheriff smiled. "I'll see what I can do. What number we on?"

"Eight," Bev filled in again.

"No, we're still on seven. Politics. The FBI is comin' and they will take over jurisdiction. They will drill you like I did, but worse. Just hang in there. They'll bring in forensics, go through the van. They might want your clothes. Jeff, there's blood on your shirt and some scrapes on your elbows."

Jeff looked at his arms. "He put up a fight, so —"

Sheriff Bailey nodded. "Whatever you do, don't lie. If that Glock is sittin' on the bedside table, say so."

Jeff's expression gave him away. "Yes sir."

"If they ask if any of you know someone been raped and you answer 'no' — don't look to the side when you answer, like you did me. Keep lookin' 'em in the eye."

He studied each of us one by one. "And if you answer 'yes' — you are not legally obligated to say who. Decide on your answer now before bein' asked again. You didn't hear that from me."

We all nodded vigorously.

More flashing lights rolled in. Now the street was blocked by all the cars.

"Gonna be a long night," the sheriff said while turning to leave. "Hang in there."

He left. The three of us walked Bear down to the office. We went in, Bear followed. Then we turned right around and walked out. Bear started barking his head off. You could hear him all the way back to the diner.

Miss Bishop came running down the hill. She hugged Bev and wouldn't let go. She cried. Bev cried. We all went inside.

It was now a safe place from all the activity.

"You know your dad would be here but he's at a job site and there's no cell signal out there. I left him a text. I grabbed some coffee on the way out of the house. Does the coffeemaker work?"

"Dunno," Bev said.

"Miss Bishop," I asked. "Should we give you some space?"

"Maybe a few minutes," she replied.

Jeff and I walked out. Everyone seemed to be busy but not really doin' anything. No one went near the van. The wheelchair was still off to the side.

"You really thought about us both having knives?" I asked.

"Oh yeah," Jeff replied. "Everything just kinda slowed down. I was very aware how tight I had his belt, how to plant my feet, how I wanted him comin' out of the van, then makin' sure I had a good grip on his wrists, keepin' his arms spread so he couldn't get up on his elbows. Thinkin' ahead — what if this, what if that? Everything in slow motion. Was it like that for you?"

"I was terrified," I admitted.

"Wasn't at all like football," he conceded.

I agreed. "Not at all. That was just a game. Big difference."

Sheriff Bailey strolled back over. "Just so you know — got confirmation this is the guy we thought it was. Works for a company that builds medical office buildings. They bring in their own crews and put 'em up in cheap hotels. And that's why he kept poppin' up in different states. Worked during the day, trolled for women at night. He had just finished today, down near the hospital in Bluefield."

"Thank ya, Sheriff Bailey," Jeff replied.

"One more thing. He keeps goin' on and on about you guys killin' him. Know anything about that?"

"I know by now," Jeff acknowledged, "that we can't lie to you."

Sheriff Bailey smiled, tapped his hat, and turned to leave. "Have a good evening."

After a long while, Miss Bishop stepped out. "Boys," she called as she walked toward the back of the diner. We followed. Once distanced from everyone she turned and faced us. "I think the three of you have a good thing going here. I have never seen Bev so happy." She paused, searching for words. "I don't want tonight to spoil it. I think this will eventually make you three even tighter."

We nodded, didn't utter a word.

"What happened to Bev in the past will stay in the past. Bev doesn't want to talk about it. Doesn't want you two bringing it up. But I'm sure you're wondering, and I want you know, it wasn't anyone in the family. Not her brothers, dad … cousins. Certainly not Rusty — otherwise, he'd be dead. Just a random guy, not someone you know or know of. For her, therapy is letting it just melt back into the past. We good?" Her eyes were teary.

"We're good," I assured her.

"Good," Jeff agreed.

She turned and went back in the diner.

"Now what?" I wondered.

"Now we go back and deal with the elephant in the room," Jeff sighed.

"Awkward. How?"

"Dunno."

We went in. Bev was seated in the corner booth with her back to the wall and her legs pulled up to her chest. Flashing lights from outside reflected off her face. Her eyes were swollen.

"Coffee?" Miss Bishop asked. "I got it working."

"Yes."

"Yes."

We grabbed the mugs off the bar and turned to watch the lights.

"I had to park at the church and walk over," Miss Bishop explained. "The street is blocked with all the cars."

Silence returned and engulfed the room.

After a few minutes — what seemed like forever — Jeff set his mug down. So I did the same. Then he walked over to Bev, I followed. He stood there a second. Bev turned her head in our direction but didn't look at us directly.

Jeff put his hand on the table, palm down. "Partners," he whispered.

I put my hand on his. "Partners."

Bev looked at our hands, took a deep breath, and put her hand on top of mine. "Partners."

"FBI!" This guy suddenly busted in and held up his credentials, just like in the movies. "Special Agent Floyd McIntosh. You the kids that apprehended the alleged rapist?"

I would've figured he'd be dressed like *Men In Black*, but instead he had on jeans, a sport shirt, and a windbreaker with the FBI logo. He was medium height, medium build, no hair anywhere.

"We are," I answered.

"And you are …?" he asked Miss Bishop.

"Bev's mom," she replied.

"You can leave," he announced.

"Not leaving," she replied flatly. "Coffee?"

His expression didn't change, but he answered, "Yes, ma'am, that'd be fine. Thank you."

"I'd like to speak to each of you individually," he explained with authority.

Jeff and I took our mugs. "We'll be outside."

The interviews went fine, thanks to the prep from Sheriff Bailey. We skimmed past the questions about Bev being so adamant about catching the guy. After all, we're just a bunch of dumb hillbillies.

The van was closed up. The wheelchair was tagged. The cars pulled out. They took Jeff's shirt. He was a little peeved that they didn't want to hire him to tow the van away.

Miss Bishop took Bev home. The pork chops and taters were tossed. Jeff and I had energy bars and apples for dinner.

I didn't bother going home. I slept on the floor in Jeff's office with Bear lying next to me.

CHAPTER 10

June melted into July and gave us longer days to get stuff done. Jeff got my trailer and Bev's trailer moved in and hooked up to power, water, and sewer. It was so nice not havin' to drive back and forth to Princeton. The three of us were like a little commune. Bev even took to fixin' dinners, not that we expected her to. We ate in the diner together every night and talked and laughed into the wee hours. Jeff and Bev picked at each other constantly but there were no hard feelings, usually.

There was no doubt by then that Bev was pregnant. She had two sundresses that fit fine, so she just alternated between the two. Carolyn was right about pregnant women having a glow, and it really did on Bev. She looked older, but in a good way. Jeff noticed too. And I noticed him watching her closer. I didn't say anything though.

By August the wide, deep, concrete camper pad for Carolyn and Vicki was finished. It took a lot of railroad ties for the retainer wall. All the dirt from the pads filled the deep bowl comin' off the road.

At Carolyn's request — and financing — another large pad was dug downhill from Jeff's shop. She had two couples in mind. His only concern was the capacity of his well and septic tank. He figured, eventually, he would have to connect to county utilities, and it would be expensive. The diner was up next to the road and on the grid. So he asked us to use the diner restrooms as much as possible.

Not a problem.

Jeff started selling his cars for scrap and the improvement was amazing. He put in a row of new fence posts about a third of the way in on the diner side, and moved the chain link fence to the new posts. That gave room for a trail from the back of the diner to the trail at the bottom of the hollow. ATV trails are easy to clear because ruts, bumps, inclines, and drop-offs are a good thing. He also repaired the rest of the fence around the perimeter.

Bev painted a nice sign that said "Lighthouse Diner" with a lighthouse logo. I made a quick poster that said, "Opening Soon." Jeff and I nailed the signs to a large tree down at the bottom.

No sooner than we had walked back up, an ATV rider drove up. "Diner open yet?" he asked.

"Not yet," Jeff replied.

"We just put a 'Opening Soon' sign up," I added. "Did it come off the tree?"

"Oh, no," he answered. "Just didn't know how long it'd been there." And off he went.

An hour later, another rider. Same conversation.

Next morning, I was coming out of my trailer when the sweet smell of biscuits drew me to the diner. Jeff was coming out of his shop and smellin' it too.

"Breakfast!" he exclaimed.

We walked in and found Bev in the back room, pulling biscuits out of the oven. She wore an apron over her sundress.

"Made our first sale!" she cheered, her voice almost singing.

"Really?" I asked. "How'd that happen?"

"Well, I was in here trying to do biscuits like Mumma does. I can never get the dough just right. I heard trail riders comin' up so I went to the back door. It was two kids on three-wheelers. They asked if I was open and I said 'no,' but I could whip up some biscuits. Guess what they wanted?"

"Hamburgers," Jeff answered.

"How'd you know? Anyway, they passed on the biscuits and left. But I left the back door open and sure enough two more ATVs show up — a dad and a kid in one, a mom and a kid in the other. The mom and dad settled for biscuits and coffee. Guess what the kids wanted?"

I jumped in, "Hamburgers."

"Right! They settled for peanut butter and jelly sandwiches. I didn't have a menu to go by so I came up with $12 for the tab. They gave me three fives. Can you believe it?"

"We gotta jump on this!" Jeff exclaimed. "Chad, you go into town and — no, Bev you go into town and get hot dogs, hamburger, buns, condiments. You know what to get. Chad, bring my grill up here and then meet me down the hill. Help me pull seats out of a short bus. But first, get that 'Opening Soon' sign up here and set it on the back door 'til Bev gets back!"

Bev giggled with excitement. "We're in business and not even open yet!"

Jeff and I were still settin' up bus seats when the next ATVs arrived. They seemed to come in waves. The riders paid with cash and Paypal and Venmo, but some only had credit cards. For them we wrote IOUs. We were giddy about money coming in and didn't want to slow the flow. Bev was mad at herself for not being set up for credit cards yet.

Bear was barking from his side of the fence, but his tail was wagging. We brought him in the front door, through the diner and out the back door. He mingled with the riders and scored handouts. We took in over $300 that day.

That evening over dinner we talked about our new income source.

"I talked to one of the riders," I began, "and she said the trail ends about two miles east of here."

"In layman's terms, please," Bev said.

"Down to the trail, turn right," Jeff filled in. "Wasn't there when I was a kid. Goes about as far as where Mr. Tropicana lives."

"Who?" Bev asked.

"Walker Bryson," Jeff said. "We call him Mr. Tropicana, but that's another story."

"Going the other way ... west," I continued. "Goes under 19, then under I-77, and on to where most of the trails are, around Bluefield. A lot of those trails are gnarly, which is what most riders like. But this trail is a pleasant ride through the woods and lots of people like it for that."

"And they get here about lunchtime," Bev noted.

"Exactly," I replied. "Mostly, but you had some riders early."

"And here I've been working on getting people in the *front door*." She leaned back and stared out the window.

We all fell silent for a minute, until Jeff commented, "The mouse is runnin' but the wheel ain't spinnin'."

I looked over and Jeff was smiling at me. "Care to share?"

I blinked, came out of my spell, and sighed. "It's like ... with Mom ... time went by sooo slow. Now I'm in one of those videos like ... whadda you call it? Time-lapse? A house goes up in a few minutes. Geez, everything is happening warp speed. It was just … what day did I buy the land?"

Jeff shrugged. "Dunno."

"June 15th, a Tuesday," Bev replied.

Jeff looked at her, amused, "What time did you walk in?"

"2:46 p.m.," she said with authority.

Jeff looked her in the eyes and she looked back. Then they locked in a stare down until Bev started giggling.

"Almost had you!" Bev claimed.

"It probably was 2:46 p.m., if that's what you thought first," Jeff conceded.

"It was … actually." She smiled. She had our full attention. "The clock in your office … like the chant 'two-four-six-eight, who do we appreciate.'"

"You're scary smart," I noted.

Jeff nodded. "Smart as a tree full of owls."

She shrugged. "Thanks guys."

Jeff turned to me. "Know what you mean about life in fast-forward. One day I'm packin' my stuff, then all of a sudden you show up … then Bev … at 2:46 p.m.," he grinned. "Then Carolyn and Vicki, and then I get busier than a funeral home fan in August. Wonder how long it's gonna be like this …"

I thought about it. "Probably the same 'til you get the cars out of here."

"True," Bev agreed. "Two things I'm getting used to living here — the smell of oil and Bear barking. So I close all the windows and turn on the AC."

Jeff and I gaped at each other, then back at her. "You have air conditioning?"

I finally got to meet Erma, the lady that helped with the chickens. She was making her way down from the street with a large straw basket in one hand and a hefty-looking bag over her other shoulder. She greeted me with a smile.

"You must be Chad," she began, adjusting the heavy bag. She was short but not at all fat like Jeff had said. He was just pulling my leg. Her silky-smooth black skin gave her a younger look than what her bent-over posture was saying. She wore a green cotton shirt and baggy jeans.

"Can I help you?" I asked. "Here, let me take that bag. It looks heavy."

"Now don't you go a-spoilin' me," she murmured with a smile. "I might get used to it." But she handed it over.

"I don't think it will hurt nuthin'," I said.

We had a pleasant conversation as we walked down to the chickens. I was impressed how content and happy she seemed just bein' where she was and what she was doing. The world needs more people like her.

It was a Wednesday. We were planning to open come Monday, August 17th. We were sitting down for dinner — fried chicken, mashed taters with gravy, and biscuits.

"Bev," I wondered, "okay if I use your diner for a party? I was thinkin' Saturday. I haven't seen my high school friends for years. Might even help get the word out."

"Make it BYOB," Jeff added, as he poured gravy over everything.

Then to Bev, "Thanks for dinner. If I was doin' any better, I'd be two people!"

"I'll pick up some chips and soft drinks," Bev added, inspecting her biscuit with a sigh. "Still can't get the dough right."

"Don't lose the receipt," Jeff commanded. "The bookkeeper here is verrry —"

Bev's look stopped him.

"Jeff," I asked, "can you help get the word out?"

"Sure."

"Y'all have fun," Bev said. "I was takin' the night off anyway. I'm spending some quality time with my phone."

I was anxious about the party. I mopped the floor real good and cleaned the restrooms. I even made a laundry run to Princeton. Back in high school, I was popular. Were things still the same? Or had everyone changed while I cared for Mom? Whatever, this was my chance to get a life. Maybe even meet a pretty girl.

We set the time for the party to start at 8 p.m. so nobody showed up 'til after 9:30. First to come in was Clyde Evans. He played the tuba in band. He was heavy back then but trim now. He wore jeans, a T-shirt, and a baseball hat on backwards.

"Clyde!" I greeted. "How's it been?" His fist bump was halfhearted.

"Got any beer?" he asked. He was standing right in front of me, facing me, but not looking at me.

"It's BYOB," I replied. "But the gas station down the road sells beer."

"No car," he muttered.

"How'd you get here?" I had to ask.

"Pinky," he replied.

"Where's he?" I had to ask.

"Outside."

"Why outside?"

"Waitin' for Gator."

I wanted to ask why but gave up. "Guess I could take you."

"No matter. Got no money."

"Okay, you can have one of mine. In the cooler over on the bench seat."

He didn't reply. Just turned and walked to the bench, took out a beer, and sat there with his back to me. As far as I could tell that beer had his full attention.

The door opened again and in walked a guy I didn't know. He saw me, then Clyde. "Hey Clyde, where'd you get the beer?" he asked.

"Right here," Clyde said, then handed him a beer out of my cooler. The guy sat across from Clyde and didn't say another word.

In burst Brandi, still smokin' hot, strands of long, wavy hair catching in her cleavage. "Well hi, sweetie!" She embraced me in a bearhug and kissed me on the lips. Then she stepped back with her hands on my shoulders.

"You are looking *good*," she cooed, eyeing me up and down.

She grabbed my belt. "Everything still work down there?"

I started to wonder if she was going to take me right there.

"Been hearin' about your diner," she beamed. "Sounds like you broke out in money. Maybe we should get back together."

I didn't have a clue what to say so it was a relief to see the door opening again. In walked a very big guy. He had to duck to get through the door. He wore bib overalls and no shirt. His beard hid his neck. Couldn't tell if he was grinnin' or not.

Brandi let go of my belt but kept her other hand on my shoulder.

"Hey Bo! Get over here!" she cried. He walked up and shook my hand. "Bo, this is my old fling, Chad. Chad, this is Bo."

"Nice to meet you," he said. "Nice place you have here. Brandi here's been tellin' me about you."

"Hoping to open come Monday," I replied. I was looking straight up at him. In my head I could hear the lyrics *"gimme three steps, mister, gimme three steps toward the door."*

But then a smile appeared from behind all the hair on his face. "You're a little out of the way, but you'll do well. Just keep pluggin' away at it. Be good to your employees. Sell at a fair price. You do, word gets around."

"That's why *he's* so successful," Brandi chirped, leaving my shoulder and hugging his arm.

"What'd you do?" I asked.

"Oh, I run a machine shop up in Beckley."

"Tough business?" I asked.

"Sometimes. In a poor economy folks gotta fix the old stuff. When things get good, they buy new equipment. So I have to wait for it to break. Eventually, it does."

"I'll keep you in mind," I said, "in case the diner doesn't work out."

"Wouldn't hire you," he grinned. "Once you run your own business, you don't wanna punch a clock for someone else. But you'll do fine."

He reached in his pocket and pulled out a massive wallet. "Here's my card. Send me some buy-one-get-one-free coupons, good for Mondays only. Friday is payday, and some of the yo-yos that work for me blow it on Saturday night's bar tab."

"That would work for both of us," I nodded.

"Yep." He turned to Brandi. "Honey, that call I was on comin' in … I gotta get back to the shop and handle a problem. You comin' or stayin' here?"

"I'm with you," she said like a cat purring.

Bo extended his hand. "It was nice to meet you."

As they left, Brandi looked back and mouthed "call me" as she held her hand to her ear.

What an airhead.

The rest of the night was a blur of endless insanity. A guy lit up a cigarette. I told him to put it out. He argued it was a private party. I agreed and said it was my party, my place, my rules.

So he dropped his cigarette on my nice clean floor, stomped it out, and left.

People started milling around behind the counter. Didn't occur to me that anyone would do that. Had to shuffle them out.

No one talked to me, or to each other. At least not in a conversation. Just mindless chatter. I found people in the back room playing hide-and-seek in the walk-in freezer. And leaving the door open! Had to chase them out.

I finally found Jeff out back sitting on one of the bus seats and talkin' with some guys I didn't know. So he would be no help.

As I was turning to leave, a young girl walked up. She looked to be about Bev's age, blond and petite.

"Has anyone seen Bev?" she asked.

"She's in her trailer," I said, pointing. "The one on the right."

"Okay." She hurried off and around the corner.

I went back inside, and for the rest of the night I was yellin' "Stop that!" and "put that down!" and "leave that alone!" Last to leave were a guy and girl coming out of the ladies room, zipping up their pants.

Next morning, I knew there would be hell to pay so I was worried to see the front door to the diner propped open. *Might as well get it over with,* I said to myself.

Bev was behind the bar writing on a notepad. The place was a disaster.

"I'm *so* sorry," I blurted, honestly.

"Must have been some party," she said. "Wanna hear what's missing?" But she wasn't mad.

"Bev —"

"It's not your fault. Don't feel bad about it."

"Thank you. I mean noted, logged, appreciated." We both smiled. "So, what's the damage?"

She picked up her notepad. "Nine knives, six forks, two coffee mugs … another one broken, and a spatula of all things. I mean really, a spatula? Two salt and pepper sets … the list goes on. And that's just the front. Guess what wasn't stolen?"

I looked around, couldn't guess.

"The most valuable — at least most precious to me — thing in the place." She pointed. "Grammy's glass cake stand. Would have broken my heart if that was missing."

"If pie was in it, the pie would be missing," I guessed.

"Haven't tallied the back room, except that the walk-in freezer was turned off."

"I did check that the door was shut," I said, "after making sure everyone was out of there. But —"

"But someone turned it off," she said. "Probably lots of spoilage."

"God," I said, shaking my head. "It was like babysitting a kindergarten class. I had no idea … and … I gotta poop."

"Just a sec," she said. She reached under the counter, pulled out a roll of toilet paper, and tossed it to me. "The ladies' room didn't have any. I doubt the men's room does either."

"Thanks," I said, catching the roll. "That would've been ugly."

She smiled. "I had to find out the hard way."

When I came out of the restroom, Jeff was coming in the front door. He looked around and shook his head. "Anyone hurt when the bomb went off?"

Bev spoke up. "And where were you when all this —"

A truck was pulling in, a F350 dually. A guy got out, slammed the door, and marched into the diner.

Jeff turned to face him. "Help you?"

"Where's Trish?" he demanded.

Bev froze.

"Where is she?" He stepped toward Bev.

Jeff stepped in front of him. "What'd she look like?"

"Bev knows," he scowled, looking past Jeff to Bev.

"Oh," Jeff retorted. "Small girl? Long blond hair? Sleeveless white blouse? Haven't seen her."

"Where. Is. She?" he roared. "Her car is here!"

Jeff got up in his face. "Pick a number, one through four."

"Why?" The guy snorted.

"So I know which window to throw you through."

Bev pulled out her phone. "9-1-1." Her finger paused above the screen.

The guy glared at Bev, then me, then Jeff. He turned and stomped away. "I'll be back!"

We watched him peel out of the parking lot.

"Whew!" Bev sighed.

"So glad you showed up, Jeff," I admitted. "Not sure I could have turned him away."

"You could," Jeff shrugged. "Guys like that are all hat and no cattle."

"She's at my place," Bev said.

"Figured that," Jeff nodded.

"How'd you figure?" I asked.

Jeff looked over at Bev. "Girl comes up to us last night, scared, askin' for Bev. This morning there's an extra car here. Let me guess. Abusive husband?"

"Abusive boyfriend," Bev replied.

"Boyfriend with a wedding ring," Jeff corrected.

"Abusive, *married* boyfriend," Bev conceded.

"She's safe here," I suggested.

Bev shook her head sadly. "No. He'll call. Tell her he misses her. Promise he won't hurt her — again."

"You took pictures, I hope," Jeff asked, softly.

"Yes, I did," Bev replied. "But she'll go back. So sad."

"This is not going to end well," Jeff concluded.

The sound of an ATV, and Bear barking, ended the conversation. Bev went to the back door to take the trail rider's order. I got busy cleaning the diner. Jeff left to shuffle his junk cars around.

Come Monday I was up and dressed by 4 a.m., feelin' proud of myself, 'til I looked out and saw the lights on up at the diner.

Bev was at the counter, looking at her phone and writing on her notepad.

"Order up!" she barked. "I just love sayin' that! We're getting some online orders for pickup. No walk-ins yet."

"Put me to work," I volunteered.

"Nuthin' much to do yet. Me and Mumma got it covered.

Fix yourself some coffee and we'll holler when we need you."

I could have stayed in bed.

Jeff strolled in about six. He plopped down in his seat — first table, booth facing the door. I came off my barstool and sat across from him.

Bev walked up with a pot of coffee, a mug, and a menu. "Morning, sir. You dining in with us this morning?"

He looked her up and down. "Well now, don't you clean up all pretty. Hair all done up and nice dress. The apron is a nice touch, too. And I'm bein' serious, Bev. But don't get used to it."

She curtsied. "Thank you. Since you're bein' so nice, I'll bring you some breakfast."

He glanced at the menu and held it up. "I'll have eggs Benedict."

She snapped up the menu. "And we're back to the old Jeff. Sausage biscuit for you." She walked away.

"Sausage and *egg* biscuit?" he called to her.

"Whatever!" from the back room.

He turned to me. "Maybe we *should* serve eggs Benedict."

"Never had one," I said. "Aren't they hard to make?"

"Dunno. How's it goin' this mornin'?"

"Slow. Just a few take-outs. No sit-downs, no trail riders."

He looked over my shoulder. "Looks like our first customer might be comin'."

I didn't turn to look, didn't want to be impolite. Or look desperate. But I could smell him as he passed by. It was Marvin, the homeless guy. His clothes would gag a washing machine. He wore stained khaki pants that covered his shoes, a sagging coat with the liner poking out from the sleeves, and a wide- brimmed hat on top of his long, shaggy, gray-and-white hair. The big hat hid his eyes. A full beard covered the rest of his face.

Jeff nodded but he didn't respond. Marvin went to the last booth and sat with his back to the wall.

"I don't think we're gonna need smelly homeless people in our diner," I complained.

Jeff shrugged.

"This is your specialty," I said. "Will you take care of it? But don't throw him out a window."

Jeff looked at me blankly, got up, and walked down to him. They talked, both nodded. Jeff went into the back room and talked to Bev and Miss Bishop. Marvin sat there, staring out the window. Jeff came out, poured a cup of coffee, and took it to him.

Then he came back and sat down. "Settled."

"Good job," I said. "That'll teach him not to come in here again."

"He served same time as Dad, same division. And he helped Vicki, right? I told him he's welcome any morning 'til it starts fillin' up. And I'll pay for his breakfast."

"I guess you're right," I admitted, feeling guilty. "It's the right thing to do. The diner should serve him for free."

"Yeah. That's what Bev and Miss Bishop said too."

"Well, if that's the worst that could happen —"

"Don't jinx us," Jeff warned.

Then Rusty pulled in.

CHAPTER 11

If you knew Bev, you would never picture her with a guy like Rusty. A little short, real thin, blond hair and pale complexion. His jeans sat halfway down his butt with the crotch around his knees. He sorta waddled his way in. He ignored us, sat on a barstool, and treated us to his butt crack.

Bev came out from the back. "Hi Rusty."

"You look nice," he commented.

"Breakfast?"

"Sure. Whatever."

"Coffee?"

"Got any chocolate milk?"

"Yes." She went to the back room. We heard her and her mom talking. It didn't sound friendly. She came back with the milk and took his order. "By the way, I've picked out the names I have in mind for the baby. If it's a girl —"

"Don't care what you'd name a girl," he snorted.

She ignored his remark. "If it's a girl, I'll name her Carol, after my doctor friend, Carolyn. And since I'm due in December, Carol like a Christmas carol. How cool is that?"

"Wut ev."

"And if it's a boy, Victor … after Vicki."

"That them lesbos you been talkin' about?"

"Those women love each other. And they care for each other the way couples are *supposed* to. Don't be a jerk, jerk."

I leaned into Jeff and whispered, "Pick a number, one through four."

"I'd love to throw him out a window." Jeff nodded. "Then go out and throw him back in. What did she *see* in this guy? He was born tired and raised lazy."

Their conversation went on with Bev being pleasant and Rusty being a nitwit. After she brought out his breakfast, she busied herself behind the bar.

Finally, Rusty pushed his plate forward and got up to leave.

Bev handed him his tab.

"I gotta pay?" he smirked, as if insulted.

"Well, yeah," Bev answered.

"I ain't payin'," he said flatly. "Least you can do is feed me." He balled up the receipt and threw it in her face.

"Hey!" she cried. "That hurt."

Jeff went ballistic. He jumped up, grabbed Rusty, turned him upside down, and held him by his ankles.

"Chad," he yelled, "see if any money drops out."

No money fell out, but Jeff's grip on the pant legs pulled Rusty's pants down, exposing shiny white butt cheeks.

"You're pullin' his pants off!" I hollered.

Miss Bishop came running out. Bev ran out from behind the counter. Jeff let him down gently. "Oops."

Rusty tried to cover himself with one hand and pull his pants up with the other. Bev started yelling at Jeff. Rusty was yelling at Bev. Miss Bishop was trying to calm her daughter.

Jeff just stood there.

Rusty scrambled to his feet and waddled out.

Bev followed him out. "Rusty!" He got in his truck. "Rusty!" He drove off.

She came back in loaded for bear. "Jeff, just who do you think you are? You big, obnoxious … you … you. Just get out! And stay out!"

"Hey, wait a minute!" I begged. "Your diner is sitting on my land and —"

Miss Bishop put her hand gently on my shoulder.

Jeff went out. Bev went after him, fussing at him across the lot.

"Oh, God," I moaned. "This is bad." I turned to Miss Bishop — and she was smiling! I looked into her angelic eyes.

"She hates him!" I exclaimed. "Why are you smiling?"

"I know my daughter," she said calmly. "Don't worry, Chad."

"She hates my friend," I whined defensively. "My only friend."

"Know what's the opposite of hate?" she asked.

"Yeah, love."

"Love and hate are bedfellows. Both are an active relationship with another person. The opposite of love is apathy."

"Kinda goin' over my head," I admitted.

"Then let me spell it out," she began, kindly. "Bev and Rusty aren't in a relationship — not even before she got pregnant. Okay? But she feels sorry for anyone picked on. Or anyone weak. She's mad at Jeff, sure, but only because she loves hating him."

I looked at her blankly.

"Just be patient," she advised. "Don't overreact. I promise it will all work out."

Bev walked in and could see me and Miss Bishop were in a serious conversation.

"Everything all right in here?"

"Well," I said, "things can't get any worse."

"No, don't say that. You'll jinx us."

Just then a late-model red Mercedes with a New York license plate pulled in.

I rolled my eyes. "Uh- oh."

An attractive lady who looked to be in her mid-forties got out. She was dressed like a model, hair all done up, designer jeans, a silky, long-sleeve blouse with slits down the sleeves, and shiny bracelets. She looked around like she was waitin' for someone and maybe havin' second thoughts about a Waffle House in the middle of nowhere.

But she came in.

She acknowledged each of us, then took the third booth with her back to Marvin. Bev handed her a menu and promised to come back to take her order. But the lady just glanced at the menu and asked, "Can I get a BLT? Maybe some chips?"

"Sure," Bev replied. "Something to drink?"

"Just water. Thanks so much."

I settled back in my seat. Seemed I didn't jinx us after all.

But then a black Chevy Impala, also with a New York license plate, pulled in and parked next to the Mercedes. A true *Men-In-Black* character got out — dark suit, white shirt, thin tie, and shades.

The lady noticed him right away. She grabbed her handbag and started to slide out of the seat. But Marvin was standing in her way.

"Excuse me, ma'am," he said. "My name is Marvin. I can see that the man coming in is someone you fear. If you let me sit next to you, he will have to touch me to get to you, and that will be assault. I promise he will not want to assault me."

She looked up at Marvin and nodded vigorously. He sat down and gave instructions. "Bev, you and your mom go in the back and call 9-1-1. Report a 10-31 and a 10-32."

Then Marvin looked at me. "Chad, stay put, don't engage. It'll only make matters worse."

The guy marched in, glanced at me, kept walking toward the lady. "Let's go," he demanded.

Then he pointed to Marvin. "You, get up. Out."

Marvin looked up at him, showed no fear. "You touch me, that's assault."

"Up!" he growled.

"You're ex-military so that would be a veteran assaulting a veteran," Marvin warned him.

The man put his hand on his hip, which pushed back his suit jacket and exposed a gun. "I got no time for this. Peyton, slip out past this guy. Now!"

"Like hell," she retorted.

"You're going back one way or the other. Front seat, back seat, or in the trunk — your choice. This 'ol coot won't stop me. Do you really want harm to come to this *hillbilly* on your account?"

I have never, ever sooo loved the sound of a siren. Deputy Lawrence came in hot, screeching to a stop behind the black sedan.

Dust engulfed his car. He jumped out, gun drawn like before, and stormed in. "Hands up where I can see them!"

We all reached for the sky — well, except the Man-In-Black. He had one hand up and held his coat open with the other to show his gun.

"Concealed-carry permit," he stated.

Deputy Lawrence pulled the gun out and set it on the counter. "Maybe where you come from. You're in West Virginia now! The rest of you can lower your hands. Any more weapons?"

The guy did not reply.

"Ankle holster, left leg," Marvin said.

Deputy Lawrence took that gun, cuffed him, patted him down, and said, "Sir, this is not an arrest. Just precautionary restraint 'til we get things figured out."

Jeff came rushing in, I pulled him aside. Bear ran up to the door, barking nonstop. Then, as before and just a few minutes apart, an unmarked car, a State Trooper, an ambulance, and another deputy arrived. Then Sheriff Bailey came in grinnin' ear to ear.

He stopped at the first booth and leaned into me and Jeff. "You boys are gonna keep me reelected for the next twenty years."

"Probably not an arrest this time," I informed him.

"By the time I put my spin on it, tomorrow's paper is gonna read, 'Sheriff Bailey Stops Kidnapper Ring from Abduction Attempt.'"

He patted the table. "Thanks, boys."

Jeff, not wanting to push his luck with Bev, left and took Bear down the hill. Marvin moved back to his booth. Don't know if he was self-conscious about bein' smelly or just wanted his space.

Eventually, the Man-In-Black was released and one by one the flashing lights drove away.

I joined Bev and Miss Bishop at the lady's booth.

Introductions were done. Her name was Peyton Carter.

"I appreciate your help," she began, "and I am so very sorry for putting you in harm's way. I've been driving for three days straight. Thought I got away."

"Harm's way?" Miss Bishop asked.

"I don't know for sure, but things are getting ugly. My husband — Richard Carter — is very aggressive. He's arrogant, egotistical and lately … abusive. When I married him, he wasn't like that at all. But now …"

She looked out the window and sighed. "You nice folks have done more than enough. I don't want to burden you any longer. I've lost my appetite, and I'm so tired. Haven't slept in days. Maybe you could point me to an out-of-the-way motel."

"You wouldn't get there," came Marvin's voice. "They're following you."

"Oh, I'm sure," she sighed again, turning in her seat to face him. "He has all kinds of techy stuff and lots of money."

"But why run?" I asked. "Can't you divorce him?"

"Oh sure," she replied. "I filed papers, but he won't settle for anything but me walking away with nothing. And the way he intimidates lawyers — after a while you'd think they're working for him. And that's not right. I put him through law school. I've been a good wife. Until he started …"

"Do you have relatives?" Miss Bishop asked.

"One sister. That's where I was headed. But after all this, it would put her in jeopardy. I should just go back and sign his papers."

She turned and looked out the window.

We let her think in silence.

"I have some cash," she continued. "All my credit cards are closed down. Using them would just give me away. But if I could get some rest and sneak out of here. Wherever here is."

"He's got your car bugged," Marvin commented.

She turned to face him again. "You sure? How do you know?"

"You came from the wrong way, from the east. Nobody much comes from that way. That's what got my attention. You came around the bend, saw the diner, and pulled in. The guy following you had his turn signal on as he was coming around the bend before seeing the diner. He knew exactly where to find you."

"Oh," she gasped. "Oh my."

"Chad," Bev said. "Get Jeff up here. Get him to find the transmitter thing. Miss Carter, can I borrow your keys?"

"Might be more than one," Marvin said while getting up to leave. "Most likely more than one. Ma'am, I wish you luck, I really do, but you're up against a heavy hitter. Take it from someone that spends *all* his time hiding. You got to offload everything — your car, your clothes, *everything* if you decide to run. Now these folks here are good people. They'll help you get a head start."

"Thank you for everything," she smiled shakily, taking his hand in hers. "I am so grateful."

"People like that don't scare me," he replied. "Them I can see." And out he went.

"Well," I offered, "at least now we know things can't possibly get any —"

"Don't jinx us," Bev demanded.

"Again," Miss Bishop added.

"I was just kidding." I shrugged. "I wasn't going to finish sayin' — Uh oh."

A large black sedan pulled in next to Miss Carter's car. And it had a New York license plate.

"Crap," I pouted.

I texted Jeff to come back up to the diner.

A middle-aged gentleman got out wearing khaki pants, a white shirt, and a blue blazer. A lady got out too. She looked nice.

She wore a pretty white dress and a pearl necklace. They didn't look dangerous. Marvin was watching them too, and I could see him just outside the door. He looked back at me, gave a thumbs up, and walked off.

They came in and since the four of us were the only people in the place, walked over.

"Good morning," the man said, pleasantly. "My name is Parker. Walter Parker. This is my wife, Penny."

We each gave our names.

"We're the parents of the kid injured down the hill," Miss Parker began. "It was pretty unnerving, and we left without saying thank you. Are you the man that helped him?"

"One of them," I replied, "but not the main one. My friend Jeff was. I felt like I was just watching."

"The two of you saved my son's life," she continued. "He had some internal bleeding, broken ribs, and stayed in the ICU a few days. It's a good thing you came along when you did. But he's going to be okay. We got him home and he's recovering just fine. We are so grateful."

"Would you like to stay for lunch?" Bev asked.

"Oh, no thanks. But we will next June. We come down every year for a week and ride the trails. There's a group of us actually. Our son should be able to ride by then, but I doubt we'll let him out of our sight."

"We're just passing through today," Mr. Parker said while pulling out his wallet. He handed me two business cards. "I would like to offer our services to show our appreciation."

"Pro bono," Miss Parker added with a smile. "My husband and I are both lawyers."

"Eventually you will be sued by someone slipping and hurting themselves," Mr. Parker said.

"Or serving coffee too hot," Miss Parker frowned.

"Hope you never need us," Mr. Parker added. "But it would mean so much if you would call us for anything."

"I'll give Jeff this card," I said, "and he and I appreciate your offer. As for my card … well … I would like to pass it to this lady we just met, Peyton Carter." I nodded her way. "She is also from New York, by the way."

"What is your legal issue, Peyton?" Miss Parker asked.

Miss Carter sat up straighter. "Divorce, but I just met these overly nice folks and they have already done more than enough, and the paperwork is up in New York City, and —"

"What is your husband's name?" Mr. Parker asked.

"Richard Carter."

The Parkers looked at each other.

"Small world. We know him," Miss Parker commented. "We

know *of* him. He's what you might call —"

"He's a piece of work," Mr. Parker finished.

"Then you know he's not someone you want to mess with," Miss Carter sighed.

"On the contrary," Miss Parker grinned. "He is not going to be happy hearing from us."

"We kick ass," Mr. Parker boasted. "Here, here is my card." "Peyton, dear," Miss Parker said, "come sit with us in the car and let's get some details. Chad, you keep your card. Richard Carter will be paying our fees."

Jeff held the door open as they went out. Mr. and Miss Parker stopped and talked to him. Miss Parker gave him a big hug.

He came on in and I gave him his card. We explained everything and gave him the car keys. Jeff drove it down to his shop

Bev pulled out her phone. "All this excitement and it's not even ten o'clock yet. Mumma, can you and Chad run things so I can stay with Miss Carter? I think she'd sleep better if I stayed with her. I've got plenty to do on my phone."

"I was thinking the same thing," Miss Bishop said. "What about Trish?"

"Gone," Bev said, with a shrug. "Yesterday afternoon. Said she was runnin' out to pick up a few things." There was nothing more she could say.

I pulled out my wallet to add the Parkers' business card. "That reminds me," I said, "got a business card from a guy at the party. Runs a machine shop. Said to send a flyer or something. Offer a two-for-one coupon, good for Mondays only."

Bev took the card. "Bo Schmitz. You met Bo Schmitz?"

I nodded. "The only good thing about the party. Wasn't sure about him at first, but he ended up giving me encouragement and advice. Really nice guy."

"That's him," Bev said. "Big as a Yeti but nice, and very smart. Owns a machine shop and a bunch of stuff up in Beckley — a strip mall, a factory of some sort, and some land. He's well liked by his employees."

"If they didn't," I asked, "who would they tell?"

"Good point."

A little later everyone came back and Mr. and Miss Parker said their goodbyes. Bev took Miss Carter to her trailer and Jeff met them there with Bear. Somehow Bear knew the girls were his new flock.

Around dinnertime I ran down to Princeton and got a bucket of chicken. We ate in Bev's trailer and then sat around talkin'.

I guess Bev and Jeff's spat got put on hold.

Miss Carter slept 'til nine that night.

You could tell she was embarrassed. She went on and on how beholden she was for our kindness. She was hungry but "not a big fan" of leftover fried chicken. Bev heated up a can of tomato soup.

"If it wasn't for you guys, I'd be in that big black car," she shuddered. "Probably in the trunk."

"You're not out of the woods yet," Bev said. "We were just talking about what Marvin said."

"Oh yeah, Marvin. Where did you find him? He knew about the tracking device, the ankle gun. And yet, he's homeless, right?"

"Today was the first day we met him," Bev answered.

"We knew *of* him," Jeff added, "but hadn't met him 'til this mornin'."

"He was amazing," Miss Carter said. "And I believe what he said about ditching everything. There could be a listening device in my clothes even."

We all looked at each other. Bev made a zipper-across-her- lips gesture, and she and Miss Carter got up and went to the bedroom. Minutes later, Miss Carter came out barefoot and in a tattered house robe. Bev came out with a large trash bag in her hand. She tossed the bag and Miss Carter's handbag out the door.

That bag would later be headed for a dump twelve miles on the other side of Princeton.

"All that and I still wonder if we're safe," Bev admitted.

"I know," I agreed. "The technology these days. It's crazy."

"Well," Miss Carter added, "the Parkers said I'd get the divorce and a good settlement, but my husband would manage to drag it out. How long, they weren't sure. So … all I have to do is go off grid for a while and I agree with that Marvin guy. I need to be *completely* off grid."

"Miss Carter, you don't strike me as an off-grid kind of a lady," Jeff noted. "No offense."

"None taken, but how about Peyton instead of Miss Carter? I'm not that much older — or maybe I am. Anyway, a few hundred years ago we didn't even have a grid. Now we can't get off of it. But I wasn't always so prissy. I grew up on a farm. And when I got out of college, I thru-hiked the Appalachian Trail."

"Oh!" I blurted. "We have so much to talk about."

"And not near enough time," Bev added. "Miss Carter —"

"Peyton."

"Peyton, here's our plan — the best we can come up with. Leave tonight in my car and take my driver's license. You'll be legal. The car is in my name and the tags match."

"Except I'm twice as old as you," She smiled.

"You have a young look," I added my two cents, "and you two look similar, 'cept your hair is longer."

Bev held up a pair of scissors. "Snip, snip."

"Oh my!" Peyton exclaimed. Her head was shaking "no" but she was smiling. "I'm not taking your license, but I *will* let you cut my hair. Might as well get real about all this."

Bev circled around her and began cutting at chin length. "What about my car … and the GPS?" Peyton wondered, watching her hair fall to the floor.

"I found the transmitter and turned it off," Jeff said. "Our plan is to take it down to the truck stop and put it on somebody's truck. Give that transmitter a nice long ride. We have to assume there's another transmitter somewhere. Hell, the damn car even knows where it is. So we need to tow it away."

"Why not just drive it?" Peyton asked.

"Because, first, I'd like to take the engine out. Thing is, your car doesn't have a VIN label. Might mean it's stolen. Don't know for sure. There's a VIN on the engine but I'd have to remove it to get to it. If there is a VIN, and turns out the car is stolen, it might be evidence against your husband. If the VIN is scratched out, that's bad. Might be advance planning that your husband could run you off a cliff or somethin' — set it on fire. No way to —"

"My husband doesn't need to steal a car." Peyton shivered. "As desperate as I am, I have to accept your help. And I know in my heart I will repay you. That said, you got anything other than this housecoat I could wear? I'm buck naked under this thing."

"Activate Peyton Extrication Plan," Bev announced.

Jeff and I went to the shop and removed the engine. Didn't take long. The VIN was scratched out, as we feared.

Meanwhile, Bev and Peyton removed all of Bev's stuff from her car, loaded it with water, food, and stuff like soap and toothpaste. For clothes, Peyton was larger than Bev and smaller than me, so she ended up with things from both of us. Flip-flops for shoes. Fortunately, Peyton had about three thousand in cash. That and a pair of sunglasses were the only things she would leave with that she came with.

An hour later, I left in Bev's car, Bev took my truck, and Jeff and Peyton headed down the ATV trail in Carolyn's Polaris to where it crossed under Route 19.

I stopped at the gas station just down the road. First, I filled up at the gas pump. Then I moved over to the vacuum machine. With all the doors and trunk open, the idea was that for anyone watching, it was just me.

Then I drove north on Route 19 and pulled off where it crossed over the ATV trail. I crawled over to the passenger side, opened the door, and slid out. I stayed low on my hands and knees and looked around where the underbrush began. Peyton popped out from the bushes. As she made it to the car door, she whispered, "Thank you All of you."

I nodded. "One question. What was your trail name?"

"Fakahwee," she whispered.

She slipped in, crawled over to the driver's seat, and drove off. I watched Bev's car disappear into the darkness, wondering if we would ever see Peyton — or Bev's car — again. I slid down the hill to where Jeff was waiting on the Polaris.

We drove it back home, parked it in his shop, then hooked

Peyton's Mercedes to Jeff's wrecker. We took the license plates off and towed it to Princeton and left it in the Walmart parking lot. Jeff left me there. I hid in some bushes at the entrance, then he drove to Love's Truck Stop. His mission was to put that transmitter on a southbound truck.

Peyton had driving directions written by me that took her off Route 19 and down a narrow country road. It meandered more than it went anywhere. But it would get her to Route 52, and that would take her to I-64. And safety. At a particular sharp bend in the road, she would see headlights flash, and that would be Bev.

Bev would wait — we figured a half hour — to see if the guy in the black sedan came through after Peyton passed. If it did, she would call 9-1-1.

There was no black sedan, so Bev drove to Walmart and picked me up. I hadn't seen any interest in the Mercedes. We got back home about the same time as Jeff. We left lights on in Jeff's place and my trailer. Bev's trailer had a bedroom at each end and a comfortable couch in the living area, so we all had a place to sleep in her trailer. We brought Bear in, turned off all the lights, and went to bed. We hoped a black sedan wouldn't pull in.

After a sleepless night, we had one last task. It was a shame to ditch all of Peyton's nice clothes. Bev was especially sad to see Peyton's handbag go, but it was obviously a liability. But some of the stuff was too valuable—diamond rings, earrings, necklaces, bracelets, a pendant, and some scarfs that looked innocent enough. It all went into a bag, and the bag was placed into a metal box. Then that box was put into a large toolbox, and that was buried. We were hyper-paranoid.

Peyton said she would be back someday for the jewelry.

We could only hope.

By that time Jeff and Bev were friends again. You could tell by how much they picked at each other. The three of us entered the diner a little after six. Marvin was in his booth having breakfast. We waved, he nodded. Him being there made us feel safer.

Miss Bishop was behind the counter. "Just so you know," she tattled, "our morning customer is very picky. Coffee — black, hot. Bacon — crispy, not chewy. Scrambled eggs — a little runny. And toast — lightly buttered and cut on the diagonal."

"Well," I said, "if that's the worst we have to deal with —"

Three heads spun to face me with a glare.

"Just kidding," I grinned, holding up my hands.

But then Deputy Lawrence drove up and parked next to the door.

"See what you did?" Jeff grumbled.

Greg came in smiling. "Things look a little less hectic this morning," he announced.

"Much better," I agreed. "And thanks for your help yesterday. You got here fast."

"I was just down the road. Heading here, actually."

"Comin' for breakfast?" Bev asked.

"Comin' for pie," Greg grinned. "Forgot to get one after all the excitement."

"Cut you a piece?" Miss Bishop asked. "For here, or to go?"

Greg shook his head. "The *whole* pie. Word's out that Miss Baker's Blue Ribbon County Fair Apple Pie can be purchased here. That's what they're calling it — Miss Baker's Blue Ribbon County Fair Apple Pie. And that's why I'm here early. How much?"

He reached for his wallet.

Bev had to think about that. "Um … $2.50 per slice … six slices. That's fifteen, I guess. Hadn't ever thought of pricing it for the whole thing."

Greg put a twenty on the counter. "You could sell them for this much *all day long*."

"We don't even have a to-go box for the thing," Miss Bishop fretted. "But I'll figure something out."

She picked up the entire cake stand and took it to the back.

Greg leaned against the counter, looked over at Marvin.

"Got yourself a regular."

"Yeah, our best customer."

Greg nodded. "You guys wouldn't know anything about an abandoned red Mercedes, would you?"

"Like the one here yesterday?" I asked.

"Verrry much like the one yesterday. But no VIN, no plates." He chuckled. "No motor."

Jeff and I shrugged.

"The sheriff got a junk car guy to haul it off. He's working on the paperwork to get it designated as a dumped vehicle so the state can get some money for it. Of course, the junk car guys can get a salvage title for it and sell it. Nuthin' wrong with it … 'cept it's missing an engine."

He shrugged. "Oh well."

Miss Bishop came out with the pie. "This is the pie tote I use. Just drop it off next time you come through."

"Thank you kindly," Greg said. "The way things are going around here, it won't be long before I get a call to come here again."

He turned to leave but stopped. "Oh, the sheriff did want me to ask. Did that lady get away okay?"

Jeff nodded. "As far as we know, yes."

"Without being followed," Bev added.

He nodded and left.

Jeff crossed his arms. "As far as we know. God, I hope she's okay."

"We did all we could," Bev said. "I just hope they don't decide to take it out on us. It's so scary. What if that guy comes after us?"

"You needn't worry," Marvin affirmed, somehow now standing next to us. We faced him and waited for more. His expression seemed to say it was obvious. Explaining it would be a burden.

"Marvin," Miss Bishop said with authority, "is my daughter in danger?"

Apparently, her question got to him. He sighed. "You did get a visitor last night … about two this morning. Parked in the church lot, as I thought he might. That's what I would have done. We had a nice chat."

We all stood there, waiting for more. He offered none.

"Did he pull his gun on you?" Bev pleaded, fear on her face.

Marvin looked at her as if annoyed. "Started to, but I didn't flinch. Told him Peyton was gone, if that's what he wanted to know. After that, we talked about … our past. Not a bad guy after all. We shook hands and he left."

That said, Marvin stepped past us to leave.

"Thank you," we all said in unison, and out he went.

"See you tomorrow!" Bev said, hopefully. Her phone chimed and she looked at it. "Take out order."

"Good," Miss Bishop said. "Let me get my order pad."

Bev shook her head. "Just one thing. Apple pie."

"The whole thing?" Miss Bishop guessed.

"Yep."

"We have one more. I'll figure out how to pack it. But your Grammy isn't going to be able to crank them out like this. She was just trying to help out."

Bev nodded. "We should go over and help her."

Miss Bishop shook her head. "I have a better idea. How about you and your partner going over there. Figure out how to make pies here."

"She's right," I said. "Your mom and her mom are doing more than enough."

Bev nodded. "Mumma, I'm sorry. I don't mean to take you for granted." Her phone chimed again. "Another pie order."

"We're all out," Miss Bishop shook her head.

"How about biscuits?" Jeff asked, sheepishly. "Any biscuits left?"

Bev looked at him and grinned. "We're all out of biscuits. But we do have eggs Benedict."

Jeff was at a loss for a comeback.

"Haha," Bev said. "Gotcha."

For the rest of the week "gotcha" was the victory cry of a successful practical joke. I would've thought Jeff would be the obvious winner of their little game. But Bev exposed a mischievous, devious side. On one occasion she put salt in Jeff's coffee. Another time she put a plastic bug on top of his scrambled eggs. Most of his "gotchas" were comments.

I asked for a truce when I found plastic cling wrap stretched across the toilet bowl in the men's room.

Also, for the rest of the week, we realized that hoping for customers didn't do any good. It was our first week, so we shouldn't have worried about it. But deep down we were wishing for a miracle. On Friday it rained all day, and trail-rider business was zero.

The next day, Saturday, was warm and sunny. The trail riders came in droves and we ran out of hamburgers. Twice. Biscuit sales were zero.

Sunday, the one day Miss Bishop didn't work, we had to be up at 3 a.m. to open the diner and start cooking. We had stayed up late the night before, so it was rough. Bev burned two batches of biscuits before getting a good one. We didn't have the usual customers on their way to work, but we did get a few local folks. No sit-down customers. Another good day for trail riders, though.

The nice thing about trail riders is that they're friendly. They aren't on the way to work, so they're in a good mood. Sometimes they would hang out with us after eating. They came in batches, so in between time the three of us just chilled. Bev and Jeff would rag on each other, but it was all in good fun. Mostly.

For Sunday night dinner we cooked hamburgers. We congratulated ourselves for living through the first week, in spite of the drama with Peyton. And Jeff was pleased with how many junk cars he sent away for scrap.

And, of course, we wondered how Trish — the girl with the abusive, married boyfriend — was doing.

The sun sank behind the mountains and slowly dimmed the color out of the trees. Then darkness fell. But we just kept talking and laughing. With Bev there, Jeff and I didn't talk about football as much. And we had to be civil. But it was okay. It was better having her there.

The next morning, I woke up hopeful. Maybe there would be more customers this week. Late August was perfect weather for trail riders. Miss Bishop and Bev were already at the diner, of course. They had the cookin' chores covered so that left cleanin' for me. The take-out orders were disappointing.

Jeff strolled in just after sunup. It was already getting warm. I sat with him at the counter and Bev brought us breakfast. She stood behind the counter and we talked about stuff on her to-do list. She was starting to say something, but then her jaw dropped.

"Oh, my God!" She ran out the door.

"Now what?" Jeff asked.

CHAPTER 12

The answer was Carolyn and Vicki's huge RV pulling in. Jeff and I got up and walked out to greet them. Bev was frantically running up to the RV and waving. Carolyn and Vicki's rig was followed by another, equally huge RV. Bev had to keep moving out of the way for them to maneuver.

Jeff directed the second RV down the hill. Carolyn expertly backed her RV into their new campsite pad. As she came to a stop, the door opened and out popped Vicki. She was holding something white, fluffy, and wiggly.

I caught up with Bev to meet the new Great Pyrenees puppy. He had a sweet face and silky, thick fur. I was trying to find a place to pet him that his teeth couldn't reach. Vicki giggled as he squirmed in her arms. Bev hugged Vicki and the puppy in one embrace.

Carolyn appeared at the door, phone in hand, taking pictures. "Isn't he adorable?" she squealed. She came down the steps and hugged me, then handed me her phone. "Here, take our picture!"

I clicked and clicked as they stood in endless poses.

The puppy barked. "Uh-oh," I said. Sure enough, Bear came tearing up the hill. Vicki sat the puppy down and held the leash.

Bear ran up and sniffed the puppy nose to nose, then he went in circles sniffing from nose to tail. The puppy stood on its hind legs to reach Bear's head. Bear ducked and the puppy's paws landed on his head. The puppy kept leaping and Bear kept ducking, sometimes raising a paw.

"What's his name?" I asked, handing Carolyn back her phone. She started taking even more pictures.

"Working on it!" Vicki exclaimed. "Maybe Moose. He's a boy, by the way."

"Or Barkley," Carolyn responded.

"Or Pooh Bear!" Vicki added. "Except you already have a Bear, so probably not."

"Beaujolais," Carolyn offered, "for a touch of class."

"Or Digger," Vicki said. "You should see our carpets. What he doesn't chew, he claws. He is tearing up the camper!"

"What do you think, Bev?" Carolyn asked.

The puppy barked.

"I think he just named himself," she chuckled.

Vicki squealed. "Yes! He just named himself! Carolyn?"

Carolyn nodded. "I was leaning toward that name, but wanted to make sure it was something you liked."

"Not like … *love*!" Vicki yelled. "Barkley! You sweet, sweet boy! You like your name?"

Of course, Barkley barked. Then he walked under and around Bear while getting the leash tangled.

"This is just too much!" Bev cried. "I'm so happy you're here!"

Vicki got down next to Barkley to untangle the leash. "We'll see what you say after your whoopin'," she said, standing up. "For taking on that rapist guy."

She turned to me. "And you. You goin' along with it. Drop and give me ten!"

Not quite knowing if she was serious, I complied. Ten pushups.

"Really," Carolyn added, giving each of us a frown. "I mean … really."

"Please don't be mad," Bev begged. "You two mean so much to me."

"I know," Vicki said, giving up on the leash. Barkley was in and out of Bear's legs. "You're special to us, too. We have to fuss a little bit to get it out of our system. Stuff like that …" she paused, "it pushes a button."

It was the first time I heard Vicki speak in a calm voice. I was thinking, though, wait 'til they hear about Peyton. Obviously not a good time to bring it up. My guess was this is how women work through things.

Then it was Carolyn's turn. She hugged Bev, then held her at arm's length.

"We love you so much, Bev. You're such a sweet, special person."

"Noted, logged, appreciated," Bev offered, hopefully.

"Nice try," Carolyn smiled. "Now promise me you will never … ever —"

"Uh-oh," I interrupted, watching a certain car pull in. "Might want to put off that promise for a minute."

Bev turned around. "Oh dear."

It was Trish. She jumped out and ran to Bev. "Bev! I'm so sorry! I didn't know where else to go!" Her lip was bleeding and there was a scar on her cheek. Her blouse had a rip on the sleeve. She embraced Bev and sobbed.

Carolyn took over. She put her fingers on Trish's wrist, held her chin up to look at her pupils, asked her question after question.

The F350 dually pulled in, and out stepped the married boyfriend.

He stomped right over to us. Bear started barking loudly at him. Vicki handed Barkley's leash to me. The guy tried to step past Bear, but Bear stood his ground.

Vicki walked up to him. "Hey, jerk, get outta here! Now!"

He made the mistake of pulling out a knife. "Who the hell do you think —"

The knife went flying off to the side. The hand that was holding the knife got yanked behind his back. Vicki kicked a leg out from under him, and he went ass over teakettle to the ground while yelling in pain. Vicki jerked his arm and he yelled again. She stepped back from him. It was just her and Bear as a wall between him and the rest of us.

Carolyn, more concerned about Trish, asked Bev, "Take her to your trailer?"

Bev nodded and off they went.

Vicki retrieved the guy's knife and walked back to him. He sat up and started to say something. She held up her finger. "I don't negotiate," she said with a cool calm. "The reason I didn't break any bones is so you could walk back to your truck and drive away. You come at me, I *will* start breaking bones."

She handed him his knife. He took it and limped back to his truck.

I don't think I breathed again until the truck pulled out.

"Whew!" Vicki smiled and was back to her old self. "Now feel better! Lucky for you, Chad! Took care of some of the whoopin' I had in mind for *you*… you helping Bev with the rapist guy."

She took Barkley's leash and headed over to Bev's trailer. Bear followed, did three circles in front of Bev's door, and laid down.

Miss Bishop came, stepped over Bear, and walked in.

I walked back over to the diner in case a customer would appear. *Fat chance.* So I busied myself wiping down the counter. As hard as I scrubbed, I couldn't stop thinking how useless I was in a fight. I didn't have Jeff's strength or Vicki's technique or Marvin's experience or the bravery of any of them. I was just a total wuss. *When the hell did that happen?*

After a while Deputy Lawrence pulled in, no siren or lights. Or gun drawn this time. He walked in and greeted me. "Might as well just stay here at the diner — save me the drivin' time." He sat on a bar stool while I poured him a coffee.

"The sheriff is on the way … and an ambulance. You know this Chuck guy that came here looking for a fight?" he asked.

I shook my head. "I like his truck, but not the way he treats women. Chuck who?"

"Chuck Chandler. Local guy. No priors. Just an ordinary guy … on paper." He glanced around the diner. "Me and the homeless guy are your only customers?"

"Yep," I admitted. "We get more customers from the back door than the front door."

"How's that?"

"The trail riders comin' up from down the hill."

"A trail comes this far?"

"This far and then a few miles further. Then just stops."

"Next time I'm ridin' I'll have to check it out. Might as well get a biscuit while I'm here."

"Comin' up."

He had to take the biscuit to go. The sheriff decided to meet at the ER in Princeton. Then they would pay Chuck a visit.

Miss Bishop and Bev walked in. Bev asked to borrow my truck. She and Carolyn wanted to follow the ambulance.

I handed over my keys. "Good luck 'splainin' why your car ain't here."

"Yeah," Bev admitted. "Not lookin' forward to that conversation."

"Guess you don't want to take Trish's car," I said in jest.

"She was lucky it got her here. Might as well park it down with the other junk cars."

"The sheriff will meet you at the hospital," I said. "To get a statement, right?"

Bev nodded. "I laid it on her heavy. After taking pictures of her injuries, I told her to file a complaint or get out of my house."

"Nice bluff," I said.

"Yeah, I know. But I was so mad, I meant it when I said it. Now I feel just awful. I think ... we think ..."

She couldn't finish. She just turned and left. I watched her kick rocks all the way across the lot.

Miss Bishop watched too, her arms crossed. A tear rolled down her cheek. She wiped it off and sniffled. Her eyes told of a hundred heartaches.

"Carolyn thinks Trish might be pregnant," she said, then paused. "Or was ..."

"Miss Bishop ... if you'd like to go home ..."

She shook her head vigorously. "My husband's at work. I don't want to wallow around in an empty house. Instead, I'm going to pull out everything we got in here and cook it. We are going to have Carolyn and Vicki and the dogs running around, and their friends, and there is going to be love in this diner. Damn it, the outside world can just go to hell. To hell! We will all come together and there will be love!"

And that was that, and I was dismissed. "Now run on down and see what the friends are up to. I've got work to do."

I did as instructed. As I got down to the other RV, the ambulance was coming in with its siren blaring. That got Jeff running around from the far side of the camper.

"What's goin' on?" he exclaimed, starting up the hill. "Somebody hurt?"

"The ambulance is for Bev's friend, Trish," I filled him in. "Carolyn and Bev are with her, they got it covered. They're taking her to the ER. You didn't hear all the ruckus?"

"Last thing I seen was everybody up there takin' pictures. They get a puppy?"

"Yeah, a Pyr. But you missed the fight."

I told him about Chuck, the knife flyin' through the air, and Vicki takin' him down.

"Sorry I missed that. Really sorry I wasn't there to help."

"Maybe for the best. Vicki took him down clean — and son, it was over before it was even on!"

"Call a Marine!" Jeff sang, taking my cue. Gotta love Toby Keith songs.

"Yep. Good thing Vicki stepped in. I was afraid Bear was gonna bite him."

"Naw," Jeff said, waving his hand. "A Pyr won't start a fight …
but he *will* end it."

"Good to know. Now can we talk about what y'all are talking
about? I'm a little overloaded with drama."

"Sure thing."

Jeff turned to take me down to the side of the RV.

"Chad, this here is JB Smith. JB, this is Chad Davis."

I shook his hand. He was about Carolyn's age, I figured.
Average height and weight. Had silver hair and a tanned face — a
handsome white guy with a hint of Asian around the eyes. The
Hawaiian shirt, colorful shorts, and flip-flops would tag him as a
tourist. *Only thing missing was the camera.*

"JB has been tellin' me how to build a campground," Jeff
explained.

"No, an RV resort," JB smiled politely.

"Right," Jeff said, "much better. Help me 'splain it to Chad
here, what you was tellin' me."

JB turned to me. "I could give you a hundred grand, turn this
hill into a resort, run it for four years, and then give it back to you
with all the improvements — roads, concrete pads, utilities, and
everything up and running."

I did the math. A hundred divided by four was twenty-five… so
he's talking twenty-five thousand a year. "I could live on that," I
nodded.

"But it wouldn't be fair," he smiled, "to you. It's worth far
more. And I'm not up for building a resort. Been there, done that."

"He built houses for a living," Jeff added. "Subdivisions,
actually. He knows stuff. JB, tell Chad the 'how' part."

"First," JB said, "I like this pad. It's everything Carolyn told me and then some. It's at the crest before the hill starts sloping down. The view is great. It's just off the interstate but you can't hear it. A good place to watch the leaves turn in the fall. We like to start in Vermont around the middle of September. Then we head south in sync with leaves turning —" He interrupted himself. "When is the best time to be here?"

"Depends on the year," I answered, "but sometime in October."

"Right. I thought so. Anyway, I'd like to make an offer similar to Carolyn's, with a few changes."

"Chad, hang in there," Jeff said.

JB continued, turning to face all the junk cars below and pointing with his head. "All the cars — gone."

Jeff nodded. "Right. Still workin' on that."

"Okay, now … a road down the right side, one down the middle, and one on the left, all asphalt. Spread out, all facing the mountain. Each one looking over the one below it, so everyone has a view.

"Good drainage is important, *very* important. Soft, low- running lights lining the roads. Concrete pads. Picnic tables under shelters or gazebos. Every year add plants, flowers, ground cover.

"Go easy on signage. It just adds clutter. By the way, how is the water here? Is it drinkable?"

"I told JB I didn't know," Jeff said to me. "My water is well water. The diner is from off the street, but I've never tasted it 'cept with coffee. Do you know?"

"Same here. Just with coffee," I replied. "I don't know."

"It's very important," JB said. "Most people drink bottled water, but you still have to shower in it. And cook with it."

"We'll have to pour a glass from up there," I suggested. "Geez, I never would've thought about that."

"There's a lot we don't have a clue about," Jeff admitted. "But JB has offered to get us started."

"And front the money needed," JB added, his expression now dead serious. "Surveying, grading, design, drainage, utilities, …"

"Sounds too good to be true," I blurted, but it came out way too skeptical.

JB continued. "And all the site rental money comes back to me, until I'm paid back."

"Now *that* sounds … more realistic," I hesitated. "Honestly, I'm not sure what we would live on in the meantime."

"On what *really* makes the money." JB smiled. "Care to guess?"

I shrugged.

"I think the cheese just slid off his cracker," Jeff observed.

"Kinda did," I agreed.

JB began reeling them off one after another. "Maid cleaning service. Laundry service. RV exterior washing. RV repair service. Grocery delivery service. Propane refills. Golf cart rentals. ATV rentals. ATV repairs. Meals delivered. And —" he paused, "—on top of the fees?"

I held out my hands, palms up, not having a clue.

"Tips. People with money love to tip. It quells the guilt. It's all … symbiotic."

I squinted at Jeff.

"We can look that word up later," he offered.

JB continued. "People with money don't mind paying for good

service. And from talking to Carolyn — hell, just from talking to you two — I know you are real. That is, honest, caring, and kind. The challenge will be finding like-minded individuals as help. That will be hard. Very hard."

I pictured Clyde's dull face from back at my party, drinking my beer. I nodded. "I can't think of *anyone* I'd trust ... in your RV."

"Finding good people is the hardest part," JB repeated. "And I'm not knocking West Virginia hillbillies. We built our business in Philadelphia with millions of people to choose from. We'd keep one in a hundred. Literally. But once you do find that one in a hundred, I just can't describe how great it is."

I pushed in an imaginary stack of poker chips. "All in," I grinned.

"JB! You down here?" It was Vicki, coming around the front of the camper with Erma at her side.

"JB! This is Erma. Erma, my friend JB!"

They shook hands.

"Erma is on her way down to get eggs! We're all having dinner tonight. Attendance is mandatory!"

JB nodded in compliance. Erma continued down the hill. Slowly.

"Need any help?" I called to her.

She waved. "No thanks!"

We all watched her walk down the hill a bit, then Jeff turned to Vicki. "Tell me about the knife thing. Wish I had seen that."

Vicki walked past me and handed him a straight knife that looked like mine because ... it was mine. I felt my right hip. It wasn't there.

"Here!" she ordered. "Hold it loose. Don't want to hurt you."

He did. She hit his grip with both hands. The three of us watched the sun reflect off the blade as it spun end over end.

Jeff picked it up. "That was so cool! Do it again."

She did — same result. JB backed up a few steps. Jeff picked it up. "Slower this time."

Vicki showed how one hand hit the inside of his wrist, and the other the back of his hand. She did it in slow motion but even in slow motion it didn't look possible.

"Let me try." Vicki held the knife and Jeff lightly hit her wrist. It didn't go end over end, but it did fall to the ground. I think Vicki dropped it, mostly.

"You did it!" Vicki squealed. "Nice!"

"What's it feel like if the guy is holdin' it tight?" Jeff asked.

"Feels even better!" she announced. "But you have to hit it *hard*!"

"So cool," he smiled. He gave me back my knife.

"Enough of that!" Vicki ordered, walking up to the camper door. "Got to work off some steam! Still have some anger in me about that redneck. Got fire in my belly!"

She banged on the door. "B! It's V! Get your ass out here!"

"Not coming out," came a muffled voice from inside. "Busy!"

Vicki banged on the door. "Get out here, you hussy!"

"Doing dishes," was the reply.

JB, amused, with arms crossed, "She doesn't do dishes."

Vicki banged again. "Beatrice! B-E-A-T-R-I-C-E! Find out what you mean to me! B-E-A-T-R-I-C-E! Take care of V-I-C!"

JB shook his head. "This is their routine. Never changes."

From inside the RV, "Sock it to me! Sock it to me! Sock it to me!"

Vicki backed down a step and the door flung open. The lady filled the door space and then some. A silky, colorful muumuu draped over a beautiful, large black woman. She was as tall as me, about 5' 11." But her wavy hairstyle made her look even taller.

Like her husband JB, she had Asian features in her otherwise large, dark eyes. Her chubby cheeks, super-white teeth, and large earrings gave a movie star vibe.

She raised a hand for Vicki's help and in a singsong voice belted out, "What you want! Baby I got it!" She gingerly came down the steps, one at a time. Vicki and her hugged. As they did, she caught sight of Jeff and me.

"Oh my!" she exclaimed, coming toward us. "You got me cabana boys! Two of them!" She looked back at Vicki, grinning. "I didn't get you anything! I feel so guilty!"

She came up to me first and cupped my face. "This one is pretty! What's your name?"

"Chad."

"My name is B!" she exclaimed. "But you can call me B!"

Then she turned to Jeff. "But wait! I like this one too! Oh V, you shouldn't have! What's your name?" "I'm Jeff, B."

"He knows my name!" she said, delighted. "I like this one too! Can I keep them both? But wait, here's another one!"

She sauntered over to her husband and kissed him.

"What to do," she said softly. "This one kisses good. A little old, though."

Jeff cleared his throat. "Well, Miss B, as much as I want to be your cabana boy, I have to admit — the new broom sweeps clean but the old one knows the corners."

She smiled, giggled, and nodded. "This one *does* know how to get in the corners."

"You done, woman?" Vicki protested. "I'm taking you ridin'."

"I'm not riding — wait, you're really troubled, aren't you? What's the matter, dear?"

"She was in a knife fight," I said. "Wasn't much of a fight, though."

"V! Dear! I'm so sorry!"

"I'm okay, B. But I need to go riding or running, one or the other."

"We'll go riding. Let me change first. Jeff, Chad, it was nice to meet you both. I already heard all about you so I didn't think introductions were necessary."

I grinned. "It was nice to meet you."

"I'll bring the Polaris down," Jeff offered.

"Thanks," Vicki said, helping her friend back up the steps.

Dinner turned out to be the best in my life — as far back as I can remember. Carolyn, Bev, and Trish had returned in high spirits. Trish was *not* pregnant, and her injuries would heal.

Another plus — the sheriff used a facetime call to Bev's phone to go through Chuck's place and retrieve Trish's belongings. All of which barely filled a kitchen trash bag.

Dinner was fried chicken, mashed potatoes and gravy, coleslaw, green beans cooked with bacon, mac and cheese, deviled eggs, and biscuits of course. A choice of sweet tea or homemade lemonade, and for dessert Miss Baker's Blue Ribbon County Fair Apple Pie and ice cream. I will forever cherish that evening full of friendship and belly laughs.

We had the tables and benches turned to run the length of the diner. Everyone was talking at the same time and laughter filled the room. One-on-one conversations developed. Mr. Bishop had come in from Princeton. He was an amiable, soft-spoken guy. Turned out he and Jeff were both Chicago Cubs fans.

Miss Bishop stayed close to Trish, mothering her — or smothering her — I'm not sure which. Trish would now be staying at Bev's. And Miss Bishop was already planning to stay for the night.

Erma and Bev talked about apple pies. Miss B and Vicki cackled endlessly. Carolyn and JB got into a long discussion about RV batteries.

I found myself listening more than talking. I think I was a little out of practice.

Erma was first to leave. Retired, she had more than a full- time job feeding hungry children in the area. She had deliveries to make so she took all the leftovers.

JB and Miss B peeled off. Miss B was unable to resist another comment about JB "gettin' in the corners."

Mr. Bishop kissed his wife and bid everyone goodnight as Miss Bishop, Bev, and Trish left to get Trish settled in.

Vicki decided to take Barkley for a walk down to the trail so Bear went too. Jeff decided to join in as well.

That left me and Carolyn. She was coming out of the back.

"There's room in there for a washer and dryer," she commented.

"For the RV resort *and* for the four of you."

"Good idea," I said. "Not sure what they cost."

"This is a good example of the sad fact that people with money spend less than people without," she claimed, sitting across from me. "I know you think it's cheaper to run clothes down to the laundromat, but eventually a quality washer and dryer will make money. It won't take long."

"As usual," I said, "you know stuff."

"Get good ones, new, commercial grade. You'll be glad you did."

I nodded, reluctantly.

"So how are you doing so far?" she asked.

"Glad you asked," I responded, sitting up straighter in my seat. "It's kinda like rowing a boat that's sinking and hoping I can reach the shore in time."

She nodded. Didn't reply.

"Not much coming through the front door. Most of our business comes from the back door, feeding the trail riders. Although we could make a killin' selling pies if we could make 'em fast enough. The diner and resort are exciting but overwhelming —"

I stopped and then wondered, "You and I ended up here the last ones talking on purpose, right?"

She nodded. "Are you glad it's you making decisions instead of Mr. Butthead?"

"Oh heck yeah," I agreed. "Hadn't thought of that. But the biggest thing is you and your friends coming along. We would be lost without your help."

"*Our help?* Let's review. You cared for your mother. You saved your best friend from eviction. You gave Bev a chance with the diner. You gave Vicki and I safe harbor — and therapy for Vicki that you can't begin to know. Then, the three of you feed a homeless guy, take down a rapist, help an abused wife escape, and now give refuge for Trish."

"About that," I started. "I have to know — you *have* to be straight with me, Carolyn. You still want to come in here and mingle with all these West Virginia rednecks? I mean, come on. Vicki in a knife fight? And from what JB was sayin', we'll need to bring in local hillbillies to help with stuff. From the looks of it, we'll be bringing in more battered women."

"Vicki and I can take care of ourselves. And if things come up regarding prejudice, racism, or abuse, we're more than up for a fight. And did JB mention anything about a front gate?"

"No. Who are they running from?"

"Their kids. But you'll have to hear it from them."

"Wow. What a strange world we live in."

"True. And speaking of which, there's Marvin. Certainly has abilities for a homeless guy, and obviously has a military background."

"True. Glad he's on our side."

"And a good thing the sheriff is on your side too. That's another mystery. He had to know you towed Peyton's car to Walmart."

"Right."

"The sheriff found the car and called the junk car people."

"Right."

"The sheriff had to know it was Peyton's car. Had to know you left it. Had to know you took out the engine. But didn't ask you any questions?" Carolyn paused.

"Questions he already knew the answers to," I finished. "Never really gave it much thought —"

"He likes you."

"Come to think of it, the deputy did have one question the next day. He asked if Peyton got away."

Carolyn nodded. "And that's all the sheriff wanted to know." "So now everybody's happy," I concluded. "Except for the boyfriend, the husband, and the rapist."

"Question is — Chad, are *you* happy?"

"I wanna be."

Carolyn reached over and squeezed my hand. Her hand made me feel good but also confused. And I was tired of feeling that way.

"I thought all you rich people were snobs," I kidded.

She smiled. "I thought all you hillbillies played the banjo."

"Good one!" I grinned. "How come I can talk to you like this?"

"Because you know you can trust me."

"True. But how come I know I can trust you and I don't really *know* you?"

"You trust me intuitively, without facts."

"Facts," I repeated. "Facts are good."

She nodded.

"Okay," I said, still searching, "how do you know you can trust *me*? Or better yet, why do you even like *me* ... us?"

She leaned back, taking her hand from mine. "The night we met was special. It was the end of a long day. Vicki was jumpy, I was tired. Not that we couldn't push through. If the diner had been full of gruff-looking men, I would've just kept going. But I could tell you and Bev were harmless, just seeing you through the window.

"Even so, I asked Vicki to hang back a minute. Then meeting you — your demeanor was pleasant, your voices relaxed, unstrained. Your hospitality was genuine. "I liked *you*. Immediately, intuitively."

I turned and stared out the window, thinking.

"What are you thinking," she asked, "thinking *right now*?"

"Oh," I shrugged, "I don't know … I feel like I've outgrown my high school friends. And now I've met you and Vicki, and Miss Bishop, Erma, Miss B and JB … all of 'em *special*, you know? Wish I could find someone for *me*, my age, someone as special as all of you."

"You will," she nodded, confidently. "Just follow your heart. Obviously, you are prone to making decisions with your heart, such as buying this land and helping Bev with the diner."

"In conclusion, I'm doomed to making colossal, dumb decisions."

"Oooh," Carolyn cooed. "Those are my favorite kind."

CHAPTER 13

I didn't need my phone to wake me up the next morning. It was still dark and cool enough to want to stay under covers, but I was up at five and looking forward to the day. The sun wouldn't be up until 6:30 a.m., and even then, it had to climb over the mountains. For some places late August might be warm, but in West Virginia the nights get a little chilly. I knew it would warm up in a few hours, though, so I put on shorts and a T-shirt. Halfway across the lot I could smell the biscuits.

Coming in the diner, I noticed all the tables pushed back to the windows. Trish appeared from the back room, so I took a seat at the counter. Her lip was swollen and the cut in her cheek had a bruise. I recognized Bev's bright orange sundress. It was a little big on Trish. She wore an apron that helped hold the dress snug.

"Hi Chad," she said cheerfully. "Bev has mornin' sickness so I'm her replacement. Coffee?"

"Yes, thank you," I replied. "But I'm here to work."

"Not much goin' on," she said, looking under the counter. "Miss Bishop! Where are the … never mind. Found 'em!" She pulled out a coffee mug.

Miss Bishop emerged from the back room, flour dust on her apron.

"Good morning, Chad."

"G'morning, Miss Bishop."

She handed me a phone. "This is Bev's," she said. "Help me with this, will you? This app here is for take-out orders." She pulled out an order pad and a pencil.

"Gladly," I said, happy to have something to do.

"We got a few orders already," she announced. "I think business is picking up."

"Sounds good."

"We even got a call this morning, and the lady — uh oh, biscuits are ready." Off she went.

Trish came and poured coffee. Spilled some. Looked around for a dish towel. "Miss Bishop! Where do we keep the — never mind! Found them!"

The phone chimed. Eight sausage, egg, and cheese biscuits.

I wrote it down and yelled, "Order up!" This was fun.

Trish took the order and scampered to the back.

"And maybe one for me!" I called.

A few minutes later Trish came back with my biscuit — bacon instead of sausage, no cheese, the egg more off the biscuit than on.

"Perfect," I reported. "Maybe a napkin?"

She looked under the counter. "Got it."

Miss Bishop soon came out with a paper bag full of biscuits. She placed it under the glass dome of the pie plate. The dome fogged up right away.

"So this lady called —" she started, "asked if she needed to make reservations for lunch. Can you believe it? Reservations! I said no, come anytime."

"That would be a hoot," I chuckled. "A waiting line for a table, that is."

"We'll get there, but I'm going to cut back on my time here 'til it does."

I agreed. "It's only fair. But we'll have to cut your pay."

She smiled. "Nothing from nothing leaves nothing."

She reached over and squeezed my hand just like Carolyn did the night before. "I would pay to work here. The time with my daughter ... it means so much to me. And now Trish here too."

She looked over and smiled at Trish.

"I'd pay too," Trish offered, "if I had any money."

I didn't know what to say, so it was a relief that the phone chimed again. I wrote it down. "Order up!"

Trish grabbed the order and scurried to the back room. After a moment I heard, "Miss Bishop! Where do we keep — never mind! Found it!"

Miss Bishop smiled. I smiled. Life was good.

The orders kept coming, spread out thin but enough to give hope.

Around 6:30 a.m., the sun started adding color to the trees.

Marvin walked in. Trish watched him pass by, then looked at me.

I smiled. "He likes his coffee black. Miss Bishop knows his order."

Vicki came in and heard me. "I'll have what he's having!" she announced. She had Barkley on his leash.

"G'morning," I said. "Just unhook Barkley if you want. He'll be okay in here."

"Sounds good. Morning Trish! Morning Edith!" Barkley proceeded to sniff every inch of the diner.

Vicki sat with Marvin. It was a quiet, private conversation. Barkley took to Marvin. Marvin took to Barkley.

A little later, Jeff strolled in and sat with me. Then Bev came in. She was now sporting a belly that took out all the guesswork.

Jeff turned around and before I could warn him, said, "Good morning, Chubby." She cupped her hand over her mouth, turned, and ran out. I guess the smell of bacon got to her.

Trish tossed off her apron and ran after her.

"Trish!" Jeff called out to her. "Tell her I'm sorry!" He turned to me. "Oooh," he grimaced, "I feel bad about that."

"Morning sickness," I nodded. He ate his breakfast quickly and left.

A little later, Vicki left with Barkley in tow. Then Marvin left. Trish came back in. A to-go customer came and went. Miss Bishop and I watched him leave.

"Other than Marvin, and Peyton, have we had *any* sit-down customers?" I asked.

Miss Bishop shrugged. "A few. Mostly just the trail riders coming in from out back. By the way, Jeff has an idea for grilling the hamburgers. He's rigging a firepit out of a truck hub. He figured firewood would be cheaper than propane for the grill. Smart idea, I think."

The Smiths walked in. Same people as the day before but dressed totally different. JB wore khaki pants, a white long- sleeve, button-down shirt with the cuffs rolled up. Miss B had on a dark-pink pantsuit with a white blouse. Her hair was all done up.

I got up and shook their hands. "We're kinda full," I kidded, "but we'll see what we can do."

Miss B responded by cupping my cheek in her hand.

Trish was behind me. She quickly went to the second booth and wiped the table, which was already clean. But, as she did, moved the table to leave more room for the far seat. She offered that to Miss B. It was obvious, but also subtle. I was impressed.

"Coffee?" Trish asked. She handed them menus.

"Tea, thank you," JB replied.

"Water, please," Miss B replied. "Not cold, no ice."

"Oh yeah," JB added, "and a glass of tap water." He looked at me. "Join us, Chad."

I pulled over a barstool and sat at the end of the table "You guys are all dressed up. Going somewhere?"

JB looked down at his shirt. "No, why?"

"We didn't know if there was a dress code," Miss B smiled.

"You might be setting the bar too high," I grinned, looking down at my own clothes. "You guys sleep okay?"

"Yes. It's so quiet here," Miss B replied.

"Except for Bear barking," I added.

"I don't mind him. It's yip dogs I don't like."

"I don't think we heard him from in the camper," JB noted.

"He can't hear," Miss B whispered.

"Heard that," from JB.

Trish came with the water. "The tea will be a few minutes. Should I take your order? Wait, did I come back too soon? Need more time to look at the menu? I'm not sure."

Miss B looked up with a gentle smile. "You're fine. Pancakes and some bacon on the side."

JB ordered scrambled eggs and a biscuit. They waited patiently as she wrote … and wrote … and wrote, then walked away still writing.

I rolled my eyes. They smiled. They both took a sip of the water and approved.

"Glad you approve." I meant it. "I do have one question about your site, though. Why is it so wide?"

"We need it wide enough for two campers," JB replied. "We have friends, Lou and Debbie. Ingram, Lou and Debbie Ingram."

"Very dear friends," Miss B added. "We camp with them more often than by ourselves. Usually on a group site. We back in and they drive in so the doors face each other, the awnings overlap, and we have total shade in between."

"Thing is," JB continued, "people walk by and say hi, maybe strike up a conversation. Most are sincere. Campers are the nicest people. But you can tell they start to wonder who is with whom."

"Forgot to mention. Lou is black, Debbie is white," Miss B continued. "So we appear to be a black couple and a white couple."

"Oh, right," JB said. "When it's just the four of us, we talk and laugh and joke around. You forget black and white. I guess that's the biggest motivation for us to work with you guys."

"I can't begin to know what you see in *this* place," I ventured.

"I need to be straight with you," JB explained. "There's six or seven couples we know that want a site at a place like this. We have even talked about finding a piece of land and making our own campground. But these people move around so owning land jointly is unrealistic. You already have the land, so all we have to do is build the type of place we want. But the thing is, what we want isn't typical. And also, I can't promise what the other couples will do."

"What's so different?" I asked.

Miss B spoke up, "Most campgrounds put you in side by side, all squeezed in. No view. Usually a theme going on, so you end up with a big, obnoxious neon cactus sign."

"Or fake totem poles." JB rolled his eyes.

"Or cartoon statues." Miss B grimaced. "We don't need a pool, a playground, or a bandstand. Just a view. And some services. And owners I call friends." She smiled at me with those big, beautiful eyes.

"You had me at 'cabana boy.'" I smiled back. "So, you want to build a spread-out campground, right?"

"Right," she nodded.

"Hell, I'd just go over to Pipestem. I hear they even have a golf course."

"I know," JB replied, "and full hookups even, which is unusual for a state park. And the rates are great and they have Wi-Fi. We love it over there. It's exactly the kind of place we like to meet the other couples I'm talking about. But *here*, the view is better, and this would be *our* campground. Not exclusively ours, but smaller and more intimate. Easier to schedule so we can cluster near each other."

"Would we hold sites for you and your friends?" I ventured.

"I gave that some thought," he replied. "Give us time to see how many sites we fill word of mouth. You know, our friends have friends, and they have friends, and so forth. See how it sorts out, and go from there. I can't give you a guarantee, but I think it will work out for you."

"If you were me, would *you* do this?" I asked.

"Yes."

"Then I'm up for this. It sounds like a no-brainer, which is frankly the only thing that bothers me. I'm more of a colossal dumb-decision type of guy."

Trish came with the tea. The cup must have been full because she was very nervous about keeping it from spilling. We all leaned back as she placed it on the table.

"Breakfast will be here in just a minute," she announced.

"What about the trail riders?" I asked JB. "We met a really nice couple that wants to camp here next June."

JB shrugged. "A little annoying, but it does add some excitement. Carolyn and Vicki want us to get one of those dune buggies and go riding with them."

Miss B waved. "Not for me. Vicki took me yesterday and my boobs were bouncing all over the place. It was painful."

"Okay." JB agreed. "We'll stick to cornhole tossing."

Miss B nodded her approval.

"And a gate," I pressed.

"Yeah," JB nodded. "It's more a symbol of exclusivity. You know ... like a gated community. And security, of course.

"But the technology is just plain fun. You have an inside and an outside box for code entry. You also get an app for your phone. You and I get a permanent code and visiting customers get a temporary code. So the gate does its job ... but doesn't get in the way."

"Sweet," I exclaimed, and decided to press further. "And your kids get codes?"

Miss B shook her head vigorously. Hard no.

JB readjusted himself in his seat. "You've been talking to

Carolyn."

"I got the impression it wasn't a secret," I replied.

"It's not. My first wife is white, and our kids are white.

Beatrice's first husband is black, and their kids are black. And they hate each other. They're all prejudiced. And they don't approve of us. So I get a hard time from her kids, and she gets a hard time from my kids."

"And an even harder time with our own kids," Miss B added.

"We're all but done with them. I love my kids, but their behavior is unacceptable."

"I'm so sorry," I sighed. "Can't think of a thing to say that's helpful or encouraging."

She smiled, reached over, and squeezed my hand just like Carolyn and Miss Bishop did. "That's awfully sweet of you. I guess all we can do is hope for the best."

"You're too nice," I objected. "Makes me mad just hearing about it. I don't think I could take the high road."

She leaned in. "Oh, we have yelled and threatened … and we've cried and … I mean, what else can we do? What would you do?"

I looked at them and noticed again a likeness in their eyes. "Well, you two have a common … what'd you call it … ancestry?"

"Korean," JB filled in. "We both have a Korean grandmother."

I leaned forward. "Tell 'em you did one of them DNA things and come to find out *you're* related. That would make *them* related!"

"I like it!" Miss B beamed. "Wouldn't do any good, but it would rattle them."

"We're *all* related," JB stated, "if you go back far enough."

"True," I grouched. "I guess I'm feelin' spiteful. And that's not right. See? I'd have a hard time bein' nice about it."

"Feeling our pain?" Miss B asked.

"Yeah, I am. Have you ever had them all in the same room?"

"Once," JB shook his head. "It was awful."

"The hatred was unprecedented," Miss B whispered.

Trish walked up with their breakfast. "Here ya go! Can I get you anything else?"

"Maybe a fork?" Miss B requested, apologetically.

"Oh no!" Trish exclaimed. "Right. Just a sec!"

It was kinda funny watching Trish. But also kinda sad. With forks delivered, JB and Miss B dug in.

I was thinking. Thinking hard. Feeling angry.

"Do you have a sister?" I asked Miss B.

She was in the middle of a bite of pancakes. She swallowed before answering. "Yes. A younger sister. Lives in New York."

"Since y'all are eating, I'll ramble on with a solution just for the fun of it."

They nodded, continued chewing.

"Okay," I began, mischievously. "So … JB here had an affair, years ago, with your sister, and a child was born. The child is JB's love child and your niece. That makes her a half-sister to JB's kids … and a cousin to Miss B's kids. Here in West Virginia, this kinda family tree is very common," I grinned.

Miss B was tickled. "Love it! That would get their goat."

"Yeah, but you get off easy." JB grinned. "I'm stuck with having an affair."

"Not really," Miss B mocked. "Now I find out my sister is a

slut. And I *can't* believe you cheated on me."

"Not since it happened *before* we met," countered JB, "which it would have."

"So you cheated on your first wife," I noted.

"Oh," JB said. "That's worse." He shrugged. "Oh well."

"I like both ideas," Miss B chuckled softly. "And you know what? JB and I have been through counseling trying to deal with this. We have been going through gut-wrenching, soul-searching sessions trying to work through this. And here, in a few minutes, you make it all so clear. This isn't our problem. *It's their problem.* They should be in counseling!

"Thank you, Jesus! I feel like an elephant just got off my chest."

JB was nodding. "You're right, honey. Chad's first idea is a physical possibility, and that would mean our children are blood relatives. But it wouldn't make a damn bit of difference. It is their problem! Hallelujah!"

He looked at me. "Thank you, Chad."

"I got goosebumps!" Miss B exclaimed. "And by the way, these pancakes are the best ever."

JB smiled playfully at her. "Honey, let's use Chad's second idea, except you have an affair with my brother."

"You don't have a brother," she countered. "Oh yeah." He nodded. "There's that."

"You two are gonna run this thing into the ground, aren't you?" I guessed.

Miss B grinned. "I can't wait to call my slut sister. It's going to be a fun call."

"Tell her I still think of her fondly," JB added.

I laughed, then spoke my mind. "I know I'm not that bright about things. But it seems like, if you keep taking abuse and not taking up for yourself, it's like you take it because you deserve it. And that's not right."

Miss B set down her fork, leaned back, and crossed her arms. Her eyes had a thousand-yard stare. "One time, a while back," she began, "we had just met Lou and Debbie. We hit it off with them right away. We were camping down in the Florida Panhandle. Remember, JB? There was a get-together at the campground. Burgers and bonfire thing of some sort. We had already been through some 'who is with whom' situations and decided — God only knows why — to go as a white couple and a black couple." Her chin dropped to her chest.

JB laid down his fork. "Debbie and I went as the white couple. We mingled in with the crowd. Beatrice and Lou followed, holding hands just for the fun of it. At first it was kind of our own little joke, and Debbie and I got into a conversation with some people. I mean, nice people and all.

"But then I look over and Lou and Beatrice are standing next to a picnic table." His voice started to quiver. "The picnic table had all the condiments … plates … and cups! Stuff everyone needs, right? So there *should* be people around.

"But nooooo. No one within 50 feet of them! I looked around and all the white faces were smiling and talking and *so* cordial. And just wandered away from Lou and Beatrice. Debbie started to cry. I mean, dropped to her knees, bowed her head, hands to her face, and sobbed. It was so sad. I helped her up. People turned away in polite indifference. We walked over to Beatrice and Lou. Like, let's get the hell out of here. And then …"

"Cue the trumpets!" Miss B exclaimed. "That's the day Debbie became my bestie. Can I tell him the rest?" she pleaded.

JB gestured "yes" with his hand, then picked up his fork.

Miss B took a deep breath. "We were walking off and Debbie turns to me and says BB — she calls me BB. She says, 'BB, I hope you can forgive me for what I am about to do because I love you and I hope my actions don't ruin your opinion of me.'

"Well, I didn't know what she was talking about, but I told her I loved her and always would."

JB was trying to stab scrambled eggs while watching Miss B, and murmured, "This is good." I wasn't sure if he meant the eggs or what she was saying.

"Anyway, Debbie spins around and walks into the crowd. Now, Debbie is small. I mean, she is a peanut. That's what we call her, Peanut. People are standing around with either a plate or a cup or both. First lady — Debbie tips over her drink, beer goes down the lady's pants. Debbie goes 'Oops!' and keeps going, tipping over drinks and plates! And people are trying to avoid her but she's on a mission so she just keeps bumping into people, all the while apologizing. Meanwhile, food and beer is going everywhere!

"And no one can stop her because she is just a little peanut and who is going to mess with a little white peanut? Debbie gets more and more aggressive and keeps knocking plates and cups and people just start holding out their plate or cup for her to slap. Then they back away and nobody stands up to her. She doesn't stop until just about everyone has backed up into the shadows. The grounds looked like a red Solo cup graveyard." Miss B paused.

"Debbie did what I could never do. She went up against racism. Gosh, she was fabulous. I always wanted to do the same for her. And you know what? I can. I *can* go up against my racist family. I feel so empowered. Thank you, Counselor Chad."

"Great story," I replied.

Miss B took a deep breath, picked up her fork, looked at me long and hard, and asked, "So how did you avoid being racist?"

I shrugged. "Growin' up, there wasn't anyone below me to look down on."

They both nodded, but with a question mark on their faces.

"Didn't matter what color you were," I kept going. "If somebody had a ball and somebody had a bat, we'd be playin' baseball. Simple as that. Gettin' into high school, the school district got bigger, so there were kids there with money. Of course, those kids with money looked down on us that didn't have any. I didn't like that. Wasn't right. Not then, not now, not ever."

Trish walked up to top off their water, but they declined. Then Miss Bishop came over and reminded me that Bev and I had a date with Bev's grandmother to talk about apple pies.

I turned to JB and Miss B. "The diner's name is Lighthouse Diner. We should come up with a name for the campground that honors what Debbie did. Maybe 'Debbie's March' or something. Will you help me name the campground?"

They both nodded. I started to get up and leave. Miss B held up a hand and asked me to send Trish back.

"Sure," I said. "Need something?"

"No," she replied. "But when Trish is free, I want her to come to my RV for a manicure, pedicure, and makeover."

"Wow," I exclaimed. "Those are special things. Not sure what they are but I know they take a long time and cost a lot."

"My first job I was a beautician," she smiled. "It would give me a little practice and give Trish some confidence. She is a sweet child and needs to know she's special."

I nodded. "You rock, Miss B."

Walking out the diner, I headed across the lot where Jeff and Bev were pitching a baseball back and forth. It was nice to see them getting along … but pitching baseball???

Bev took off her glove, threw it to Jeff, and asked me, "Ready?"

Jeff walked off and Bev and I got in my truck. We headed to Tazewell, Virginia. Of course, Miss Baker didn't live in Tazewell. She lived off Route 460 in a hollow. On the side of a ridge, actually. Flat land in these parts is scarce.

Other than my little side trip to Pearisburg this was to me like a road trip. My years in Mom's trailer left me craving escape. It was just under an hour to Miss Baker's, and every mile was precious. I watched asphalt disappear under my hood and loved every minute.

On the way, I told Bev about the campground plans. She asked questions about zoning, insurance, site rates. I couldn't answer any of her questions.

"What's with the baseball lesson?" I asked.

"It was his idea," she answered. "Jeff said I didn't need Rusty to teach a son how to throw. And he said it didn't have to be a boy, either. A girl can play baseball, too. Jeff can be a jerk, but sometimes he comes up with something sweet. I can teach my kid to throw, boy or girl."

"As long as they're Chicago Cubs fans," I added. I glanced over to her. She was smiling. "I just want you two to get along."

She shrugged. "No comment."

"Tell me why you two bicker so much."

She hesitated, then said, "Ask me after I can drink again."

"Nope. Fess up."

She shook her head.

"Don't make me release the flyin' monkeys," I warned.

She took a deep breath. I watched more road disappear under the hood while I waited.

Finally, "You know, growing up, I heard about you and Jeff from my brother before I saw you. Then, when I was old enough to go to the home games … it was exciting to watch you and him. You two would high five, and the team would pat you on the shoulder. And when you took off your helmets … I mean, you're both … you know … not hard to look at. You were gone before I got to high school, but kids still talked about you.

"So … I don't want to sound resentful, or jealous. But you two are a little bit intimidating. With you it's not so bad. You gave me the diner, and you have worries like me. Like … are we gonna make it? Pay our bills? Make the right decisions?

"But with Jeff, he's like bulletproof or something. So when he makes a dig — and I know he's just kidding — but when he does, it makes me want to dig back, ya know?

"It's weird, but when we went after the rapist guy, I knew he would keep me safe. Just knew it. But at the same time, it rubs me that someone can be that strong, that capable, that reliable. I know he doesn't know how special he is, but it still makes me feel small. See? I can't explain this sober."

"I'm guessin' this isn't something I can share with Jeff," I offered.

"Not a word!" she commanded. "Not one word!"

She presented me with her pinky finger, so I had to submit to a pinky swear.

A hollow is the low spot between two mountains, and more often than not a creek runs down the middle. It's the only place to put a road, except the creek was there first. So the road has to go to the side. We pulled off the road at Miss Baker's house and got out. There was barely enough room between the road and the creek. A footbridge crossed it. It was made up of a side-by-side row of telephone poles across the water, and two-by-eights crosswise on top of the poles. It didn't look safe.

Bev crossed ahead of me. "Don't worry, it'll hold."

"It'll hold you," I grumbled.

She turned around. "Come on."

I walked across after her, stepping carefully.

"This is about the third or fourth bridge I've seen here," Bev explained. "Storms come through and wash it out. Daddy comes over and puts in a new one."

We walked up the path to a two-story house with a large front porch. A chimney ran up each side, and I could tell it was only one room deep front to back.

"A log cabin," I commented.

"What gave it away?" Bev asked.

"For one thing, the windows. They're inset about a foot, so the walls must be, what … a foot thick? The front is covered in siding. Are the logs covered up on the inside?"

"No. The walls inside are big long logs with chinking in between. The ceiling on the first floor is what you're walking on upstairs. You can tell where someone is walking above you because dust sprinkles down between the cracks. Small price to pay for charm, right?"

I nodded. "Can't wait to see it."

We didn't go to the front door. The path didn't go that way and the lawn showed no sign of foot traffic. Front doors are for guests, not family. We walked around the left side to the back and came up on a one-story kitchen addition. Apple trees dotted the hillside up to the skyline of the mountaintop.

Bev knocked as we walked in. Miss Baker was at the sink. She was short, round, energetic, and happy to see us. She dried her hands on her flower-print apron and gave Bev a big hug. If wrinkles only go where smiles have been, she must have done a lot of smiling in her life.

"You're late!" she admonished playfully, as if time meant anything to her. "So glad you're here. Nice to meet you, Chad."

A beagle puppy waggled over to me. "Missy! Get down! Stop that! Bev, how's that baby? Chad, would you like something to eat? Haven't got much, but you're welcome to what we got. Missy! Get off that chair!" Miss Baker was endless with questions and commands.

"Let's get started," she began. Bev had a notebook, and I thought we were there to write down cups of this and teaspoons of that … throw it in the oven. *How hard could it be?*

I was so very wrong.

"First, apples," she announced. "Follow me." She handed me a canvas bag. We went outside and I noticed all the rotten apples lying under the trees. It had once been an active tree farm. I was about to be schooled in apple harvesting. Miss Baker grabbed an apple picker from the side of the house, which was basically a long old rusty pole with fangs and a basket under the fangs.

"It's a shame all these apples go to waste," she whined. "But nobody wants to work for how little you make selling 'em."

"In other words," Bev explained to me, "Grammy don't want no strangers around her house."

"Now Bev," Miss Baker responded. But she didn't deny it.

"This here is a Granny Smith tree," she was saying. "It's the most common apple for pies. It's tart and stays firm when cooked. Can't have apples too soft. Now see here?" She lifted the pole with fangs and snagged an apple. She tugged on it gently. "This one don't want to let go, so it's not ready. This one … see? It came off. It's ready."

She kept pulling on apples and I collected them from the basket. Then she moved to another tree.

"This here is a Braeburn. It's my secret apple. Not as firm but sweet and spicy and smells good. Got to smell good to win a ribbon."

"So … you need different apples," I commented, trying to sound like I was learning something.

"You need different apples to pollinate," she corrected. "Even the ones that self-pollinate do better. So there's different varieties in here. But these two I use for my pies."

She picked a few Braeburn apples and green Granny Smiths and I helped, but I had to get her approval for them to go in the bag. Meanwhile, the ground was slippery with mushy apples, and bees were everywhere. I was glad to get back in the house, and I figured the rest would be easy. *Wrong.*

The apples had to be peeled, cored, and sliced to a certain thickness. Then each had to be notched on the side where the core was for the right look. Half-moon slices with no notch look store bought. Not a good thing. Notched shows they're homemade.

"Makes a difference," Miss Baker said authoritatively. "You taste with your eyes too, you know. A sundae without a cherry on top don't taste as good."

Making the crust sounded like a chemistry class — and I flunked chemistry. I knew she used lard and flour. What I didn't know was that the water had to be very, very cold. Same for the lard. Something to do with the fat. I thought lard was fat. But there are different fats in lard.

Did it have to be so confusing? Fortunately, Bev was nodding the whole time.

For the pie filling there was cinnamon, caster sugar, and a touch of molasses. Molasses because sugar was scarce during the Depression so molasses was used as a substitute. It is the old way to make pies so it is the right way. Go figure.

"Sauer's Apple Pie Spice," Miss Baker instructed, "not McCormick."

"Why Sauer's?" I made the mistake of asking. She looked at me as if I had asked a dumb question.

"Cuz Sauer's was started in the 1800s in Richmond," she answered.

"1887," Bev added.

"And it's still run by the Sauer family, I think. Anyway, Richmond is a nice place. They make Duke's mayonnaise, you know."

I nodded. "Well, there you go. Sauer's it is then."

We made two pies. My mouth was watering before we even put 'em in the oven. I'm glad I didn't ask how long to leave them in. That would be too easy. You leave them in 'til they're done.

Like I'm supposed to know.

Bev was still nodding, so I figured we were okay.

Meanwhile, Miss Baker went up the path to the storage shed and came back with a stack of old wicker baskets. Bev and I spent an hour filling the baskets with apples. And Bev, bless her heart, worked as hard as I did. We scored two pies and apples for more. And didn't get stung.

Finally, I got a tour of the house. From the kitchen, there was a step down to a family room. It was a room added between the log cabin and the kitchen. It had a sofa, chair, and lamps. No television or computer desk, but a sewing machine with fabric lying around instead. The far wall was the outside of the log cabin.

Another awkward step down through that wall got us inside the log cabin part. The ceiling was low with exposed beams holding up the floor above. The walls weren't round logs. They were flat, hand-hewn logs twelve to eighteen inches tall with chinking in between. I was in awe.

"This part of the house," Miss Baker bragged, "not a nail or screw in it. It's all held together with pegs. Built by my late husband's great, great, great grandpappy."

"If these walls could talk," I said in admiration.

"If they could," answered Miss Baker, "they'd say 'it's awfully crowded in here.' Big families back then."

"So wall-to-wall beds," I guessed.

"Not sure when beds came along," she replied. "But I do remember something about Granddaddy Baker. Lived to 82 and died in the same bed he was born in."

The room inspired me. "I'm gonna build me one of these. Heck, I got the trees for it."

I looked back at Miss Baker. She was nodding.

"I think you should. You'll need some big trees, though."

176

"True," I nodded. "Be nice to live in something that didn't have wheels. I really like it in here."

"We should get back," Bev said, ending the tour.

Heading home, I was back to lovin' the feel of drivin' my truck. I figured I would someday take it for granted, but right then it felt so good. Now, if only we could turn apples into money.

"Bev?" I ventured to ask. "Are we gonna be able to make blue-ribbon pies?"

She answered right away. "I have good news, iffy news, and bad news. Good news is, I think we can make an acceptable blue-ribbon pie. Iffy news is, we don't have an apple orchard out our back door. And apples are seasonal. So … we will need to find a dependable supplier.

"And come to think of it, Grammy used to bake three or four pies for the fair and pick the one she liked the best. I mean, that's what it took to win. But all in all, I think we will do her proud."

"And the bad news?"

"Oh yeah, the bad news is you're going to be peeling apples for the rest of your life."

"Great."

"On that note, can I ask a personal question?"

"Sure." I hoped for an easy question.

"Did you ever miss not having a dad?"

"Easy question. I didn't know I was missing anything. Can't miss something you never had."

"Good point."

"And Mom took care of me, helped me with homework, got me to games on time. I hardly ever went hungry. So no, I didn't feel like something was missing. Does this have anything to do with throwin' ball with Jeff?"

"Kinda," she answered, meekly. "Rusty will never be a part of my life. I just feel like I owe it to him to be a part of my baby's life if he wants to. I assume I'll be raising my baby by myself. But like … my daddy is a rock, ya know? He's my rock. Mumma is … like a warm blanket. Was your mom a rock? And a warm blanket?"

I thought about it. "I honestly can't put it in a rock and blanket thing. Mom was all I had, and I didn't need any more than that. But now that I think about it, the way things are going, your kid will be raised by a village. We're like our own little family, you know?"

"I was thinking about that too," she said as her phone chimed. She answered it. "Lighthouse Diner, may I help you? Yes … yes … got it. Thank you for your order. Bye."

"Can you believe it?" she asked me. "We started cooking hamburgers for the trail riders, and now people are ordering them to go. Biscuits and hamburgers are all we sell, hardly anything off the menu."

She called her mom and gave her the order.

"I know I should've just left my phone with Mumma, but I love it so much and I use it constantly. Anyway," she continued, "I agree that my baby will be surrounded by you and Jeff and Trish, and hopefully Carolyn and Vicki, as much as possible. I have a good feeling about all that."

A few miles passed in silence. With Bev it was never awkward.

"I do need to tell you something about Rusty," she began. "He's not as bad as you think. I mean, he is what he is, but he wasn't always like that. When we were kids he was sweet and kind and stupid. Kinda happy-go-lucky … like Jeff, 'cept without the muscles. It wasn't 'til high school that he started thinking he was supposed to act like an asshole.

"We broke up senior year but kept running into each other after graduation. We'd date some now and then. Can't explain why. I'm not a party girl, but I guess it was nice to go out every once in a while. Can't believe I got pregnant. I guess every now and then I see the person he used to be."

I shook my head. "The outside is all I see. Like Rusty throwin' that paper at you. Just sayin'."

"I don't deny anything you say about him. And I know he's not fit to be my baby's dad. But you didn't see his face when he threw that paper at me. He was smiling when he threw it, but when it hit me his jaw dropped and he looked horrified. I know he meant to miss. He wouldn't hurt a fly. All in all, he is a good person."

Her phone chimed. "Lighthouse Diner, may I help you? Yes … oh hi, Deputy Lawrence. Are you calling for an apple … no … no … *what? Where?"*

She listened … and listened. Her face went white. "Okay!

Yes! Meet you there!"

She clicked off. "It's Jeff! He's hurt! Hurt *bad*! Head to Bluefield Hospital!"

CHAPTER 14

My foot mashed down on the gas pedal. I had two lanes and used both. The road was mostly straight and had few cars on it. I had to look as far as I could see because I kept getting there so fast. The lines down the middle looked like dots.

Bev didn't need me to ask. "They found him behind a warehouse in Bluefield. He's the one that dialed 9-1-1. He's hurt *bad*, conscious but incoherent. Looks like it was a fight. Deputy Lawrence is there. Said he didn't know who to call but remembered to look up the diner number, so it came to me. He said they're loading him on the stretcher.

"I'm calling Mumma. Should I call Carolyn?"

I slowed down to around 80 mph. No sense killing ourselves, or someone else. "I don't know," I answered. "I need to just drive."

She called both. Her mom would stay put, for now. Carolyn would drive Miss Bishop's car and meet us there. I had to slow down even more as we got closer to Bluefield. Cars started getting in the way. Stoplights started catching me. It was frustrating. Bev yelled at everything that slowed us down.

Finally, we pulled into the hospital, parked, and rushed in. A lady behind a glass window challenged our entrance. She asked if we were family.

Bev and I looked at each other and Bev answered. "We're the

only family he's got!"

That got a door buzzer to sound off, and in we went.

Inside the ER, most of the beds were empty, but one in particular was surrounded by people wearing green scrubs. "Is that Jeff?" I asked to the backs of them. I didn't get a reply, but as they moved around, I could see Jeff. Right away I wished I hadn't. His face was covered in blood, and I couldn't tell if his right eye was still there. Tubes ran everywhere. His shirt and shorts were torn to hell. Monitors bleeped and clicked and buzzed.

I couldn't tell what they were doing … I couldn't tell if he was breathing … I couldn't tell if any of this was real.

My stomach ached and started pushing up to my throat. I turned away and ran, but there was nowhere to throw up. So I ended up spewing against the wall a few feet away. I tried to keep the vomit in one place, but I just kept heaving and heaving. I was miserable and embarrassed.

"We're just in the way in here," came Bev's voice, her hand on my shoulder. "Let's go out in the waiting room."

I was bent over, partly because of the knot in my stomach, partly because of the embarrassment. I watched the square tiles pass under my feet.

"It's okay, happens all the time," from a kind voice off to the side.

A buzzer sounded and double doors parted to let us out. Rows of empty seats waited. Bev guided me to one. Jeff's face flashed on a giant screen in my head. Sadness and fear swallowed me to the core. My heart ached and my stomach burned. I waited … and waited … in a blankness of despair.

Bev must have walked off without me noticing. I was now

staring down at carpet instead of tile. Her feet walked up and she handed me a can of ginger ale. It really helped with the taste in my mouth. She offered no conversation, and that was fine with me.

I concentrated on the pattern of the carpet between my feet, decoding where the random colors kept repeating themselves. It gave my brain something to do.

Carolyn's voice reached my ears, but my brain was too busy with the carpet pattern. She and Bev whispered, and Bev sobbed as they hugged. I could feel Carolyn's hand on my shoulder, and then a "Be right back" comment. The doors buzzed and Carolyn entered the ER. I returned to my task of staring at the carpet. I was perfectly fine feeling numb. But after a while boredom set in, and I needed to face reality.

Then Carolyn's shoes covered the carpet pattern. I looked up and she was looking at me with compassion.

"Jeff is going to make it," she began. "He lost a lot of blood and has some broken bones that will need to heal. But he is young and strong, and everything will be fine. I promise."

I looked over to Bev and she had her hand over her mouth. "Broken bones?"

"Let's not get into all the details just yet," Carolyn said. "I talked to the doctors long enough to know he will recover, so let's just start with that. Okay?"

"Thank you, Carolyn," I managed.

Bev nodded. "Thank you. When can we see him?"

"The doctors will let us know. Right now the ER isn't too busy, so he's fine where he is. It's not private, but all the equipment needed is close at hand."

She sat next to me so I was in between her and Bev. As if I was the one that needed support. I went back to staring at the carpet. I was following the little flecks in the random pattern, which weren't random at all, when another pair of shoes covered them. The shoes were black — *really shiny* black — and for a second I marveled at how perfect they looked. My stare followed up the crisp blue slacks, the thick, wide black belt, and past the bulging belly to the face of Sheriff Bailey.

"A minute," he said to me and to Bev. Then a nod to Carolyn.

"She's with us," Bev said with authority. "This is Carolyn, our doctor."

Carolyn introduced herself. Sheriff Bailey introduced himself

"Either of you know what Jeff was doing in Bluefield?" he asked.

I shook my head.

"He said something about a tow job," Bev replied. "We were pitching ball and he got a call. I remember he shook his head at how weird it was to get a tow job that far. But he said he wouldn't turn down a job. Something like that."

Her phone chimed. She looked at it and said, "It's my Mumma."

"Answer it," he instructed.

She did, listened, and looked back at him. "She says there's a deputy at Jeff's place. What's this all about?"

"Trust me," Sheriff Bailey answered. "Is the dog bothering him?"

"I don't know." She asked her mom. "Mumma doesn't know."

"Ask your mom to take a biscuit down to the deputy. For the dog," he added. "I'll pay for it."

Bev passed the information to her mom and hung up.

"Sheriff Bailey, what's going on?"

"Either of you know if Jeff's gun is still on the nightstand?"

I shook my head. Bev shrugged, "Wouldn't know."

Sheriff Bailey nodded. "Most likely is. But I can't enter his house without his permission. The deputy is there to confirm that no one enters the premises. Just keeping everything nice and airtight legal. Does the name Mark Miller ring a bell?"

Bev and I shook our heads.

"How about Ricky Miller, his brother?"

We shook our heads. "Who are they?" I asked.

He ignored my question. "Did Jeff have a beef with anyone, to your knowledge?"

"No!" Bev exclaimed, standing up. "And you know it! What's going on, sir!"

Sheriff Bailey raised his hands chest high and smiled. "Just doing my job. And again, trust me." He nodded and turned away.

Carolyn got up and walked away too. She entered the ER again. A few minutes passed and she returned. She kneeled down right in front of us.

"Thought that name sounded familiar," she whispered. "Mark Miller is — or was — in the ER, and is now in the OR. I remember hearing his name. His injuries are severe and life threatening.

"His brother, Ricky, is on one of the other beds in the ER, but I don't know his condition. There's a deputy in there with him, and I don't know what that's all about. I can't think of any kind of argument that would lead to this much violence."

"Jeff doesn't get in fights," I protested. "Mostly, no one is big enough to take him on. And if someone is stupid enough to start raggin' on him, he just walks away. He doesn't need to prove anything. He wouldn't hurt a fly."

Carolyn stood back up and sat down next to Bev.

We waited. Two hours later the doctor came out and the three of us jumped up. He looked happy with himself, so that was good.

"We got Jeff up in a private room. You can see him now, but keep it short. He needs his rest."

Carolyn stepped forward. "Thank you, doctor. Just to prepare us, a quick rundown of his injuries might be helpful."

The doctor nodded as he shifted from one foot to the other. "Twelve stiches over his right eye, six more on his left cheek. It was like a sewing class in there. His hip, both legs. We cleaned the wounds, but infection is something to watch. Let's see ... three cracked ribs, a broken finger. We thought a leg was cracked, but it turned out to be an old wound that healed."

"Football," I confirmed.

"Right. A stretched-out ligament in that leg, and ... bruises. And, um ... the gunshot wounds."

"What!" Bev screamed, both hands to her mouth. "Why would someone want to shoot him! *Who!*"

The doctor nodded, his expression calm. "One in his right buttock, one skimmed his right calf muscle. Neither too serious. He was more concerned about the two that hit his right boot."

I nodded. "Red Wing. He *loves* those boots."

He smiled. "I think the boots will be fine as well. And, there was a bullet lodged in the heel of the boot. Really, other than blood loss, his vitals stayed stable the whole time."

"We won't be long," Bev said. She was holding Carolyn's arm

as we went to see Jeff.

Sheriff Bailey was standing in front of Jeff's room. We collected around him.

"I'll be in the background, out of your way, but I will have a few questions," he said flatly. He opened the door for us.

Jeff looked better, except for spots shaved on his head and beard. I managed to look at him and not get sick. It helped that the sheets and bandages were white instead of red. His head was bandaged, his right eye covered.

It seemed I should be the first to speak to him so I picked his left side, the side with the good eye. I couldn't find anywhere that wasn't covered in bandages or tubes, so I just whispered in his ear. Hell, even his ear was bandaged.

"Hey bro, it's Chad."

His good eye opened and he smiled at me. He started to motion with his left hand but then stiffened from the pain it caused.

"Easy, Jeff. We're here, buddy. Just checking on you."

He nodded. Looked around, moving his head ever so slightly.

Bev and Carolyn were on his right. Neither spoke, but their expressions said volumes.

He looked back at me. "She has to leave," he announced. I was confused. "Who?"

"Bev."

"Bev? Bev who?"

He looked back at her. "This," he said, his eye taking in all the tubes and wires, "was for Rusty."

"He did this?" she blurted, frightened.

"No, *for* him. Bunch of thugs came after me sayin' they didn't like me messin' with one of their —" He closed his eye, his face got calm. Seemed like he was sleeping.

We stood still and let him rest. Bev ran out, came back in a few minutes later.

As she entered, Jeff woke up.

He watched her move next to me. "Go," he commanded.

She didn't. She held up her phone. "Rusty doesn't have a phone, but I talked to one of his friends. Rusty wasn't pushin' it. He didn't have —"

"Just go," Jeff repeated.

"No." Bev objected.

"Bev, I'm gonna miss you, I really am," he said, now more awake. "But I don't like the company you keep. You lie down with dogs, you get up with fleas. Now go."

"No. Please, no," she begged.

"Go."

"No!"

"Give me one good reason why not," he ordered. "One."

Her lower lip quivered and a tear trickled down her cheek.

"Because …," she sniffled. "Because I love you, Jeff. Damn it! Don't do this to me!"

His good eye stared at her. It was hard to know what he was thinking, so I looked over to Carolyn. She was smiling.

"Oh crap, Bev," his one eye watery. "I love you, too."

Bev started crying and she leaned over to touch him but couldn't find anywhere safe. "Can I kiss you?" she whispered.

"Oh yeah," he replied.

She found a place on his neck below his bandaged ear and kissed him passionately.

"Go easy," Jeff said, "the children are watching."

"I did *not* see that coming," I admitted, watching them.

Carolyn found a tissue box and was wiping her eyes.

"Of course," I smiled at her, "not a surprise for you."

"Oh, hell no," she replied, now blowing her nose. "This was festering the day I first met you."

She leaned in over Jeff. "Jeff, I'm going back to the campground, now that I know you will be okay."

Bev walked around the bed to hug her. They shared the tissue box.

"Come to think of it," I wondered, "how'd you come and go from the ER? Did you tell 'em you were a doctor?"

"I told them I was Jeff's GP," she grinned. "It was a little dicey, since I didn't know his last name."

"Oh no!" from Bev. "I … I don't either!"

Carolyn smiled and put her hand on Bev's shoulder. "Might want to find out before sending out the wedding invitations."

She waved, turned, and stepped out.

Bev was smiling with a look of fear at the same time. "I love this man, and I don't even know his last name!"

And then it hit me. I started to laugh, and laugh hard. And cry, at the same time. I just let it all go, the tears washing away the stress of Jeff's injuries.

Bev was desperately trying to remember Jeff's last name. "McDonald? Something like that? I'm having a brain fart!"

"McCormick," I filled in, catching my breath. "Like the spice company. I am sooo telling your Grandma."

Jeff's one eye tried to watch the two of us. Bev giggled and turned ten shades of red. I couldn't stop laughing.

Even Sheriff Bailey got in on it. He took his hat off and asked Bev, "May I have a word with Mr. McCormick?" It was too funny.

The sheriff had work to do so I backed away.

"Jeff," he began, leaning in. "I have a few questions and will try to be as brief as possible. Are you up for this?"

"Yes," Jeff replied.

"Good. Is your dad's gun sitting on the night table?"

"Yes."

"Do you give me permission to enter your premises and retrieve your gun, regarding this case?"

"Yes."

"Is the door locked?"

"Doesn't have one."

"Can you describe the two guys you fought?"

"Two? What about the other three?"

The sheriff stood up straight, studied Jeff, then excused himself and walked out.

After a moment, Jeff asked, "What's with my last name?"

Bev was tenderly stroking his right arm in between bandages. She shook her head. "Not now. It would make you laugh and hurt your ribs."

Jeff gave a measured nod, then looked up. "Know what's weird? You know … in the movies, like when a bunch of dudes come up on Bruce Lee, and they surround him … right? They start talkin' smack. Then the fight starts and Bruce Lee picks 'em off one at a time … like they're waiting their turn or somethin'."

He paused to watch Bev caress his arm. She pulled the cover off his hand and held it with both of hers. Then he looked back up at the ceiling.

"So … these guys come at me," he continued, "like all at once. They're talkin' trash and I'm wonderin' what the hell they're talkin' about … and it wasn't like Bruce Lee at all. They just come up and start hittin' me."

He sighed, and I could tell it hurt.

Sheriff Bailey returned. I stepped out of his way. "Jeff," he advised, "stop as needed, okay?"

A slow nod from Jeff.

"We know where you were. We don't know why you were there."

"Got a call to tow a car."

"Make and model?"

"Um … Lexus … light grey … no, silver with pimped out rims. Out-of-state license plates."

"What state?"

"Dunno. Just not West Virginia. And now with a broken headlight. Wasn't broken when it came in."

"The car wasn't there when you drove in?"

"Naw. The lot was empty. I was wonderin' if I had the right place. But then it drove in and five dudes got out."

"What did they look like?"

"Uh, first guy was tall and thin. Had a 7/8" lug wrench. Blue handle."

"What'd he *look* like?"

Jeff closed his eye. "Can't really picture his face."

"You remember the size of the wrench, but not his face?"

Jeff seemed confused. "He warn't hittin' me with his face."

The sheriff held up his phone. "This him?"

Jeff looked at the picture for a good bit. "That's him."

The sheriff swiped to another picture.

"That's the second guy. Had a knife." Jeff looked over to me and grinned. "Chad, I did Vicki's wrist slap on him. Worked like a charm."

"Third guy," Sheriff Bailey continued.

"Shorter than the first two, dressed gothic, had a bat … and now has a broken nose."

"Fourth guy."

"Young kid. Real young. Had a small knife. I think he did most of the stabbin'. Jeans and T-shirt, long hair."

"Fifth."

"He was the driver, definitely the leader. Dressed like a pimp. Wore a thin, flashy jacket."

Sheriff Bailey held up his phone.

"Oh God," Jeff moaned. "That's him. Who the hell is he?"

"Can I see?" Bev asked.

Sheriff Bailey shook his head and pocketed the phone. "I will need more details, but for now, how did you manage to survive? I'm especially interested in the first guy."

"Right," Jeff said immediately. "The guy with the wrench …."

at first I was just tryin' to block all the hits. I kept askin' what they wanted. But real quick they had me down on the ground and I was startin' to feel like I was a goner. My right eye was full of blood and I couldn't see much, but my hand landed on a foot. So I grabbed it and pulled, and he fell. It was the first guy. I kept pullin' … managed to stand up. It hurt like hell. Everything hurt.

"I dragged him and started swingin' him in circles. I kept backin' up and swingin' him, and that kept the others from gettin' to me. That was nice. I started to get tired, so I threw him as far as I could.

"The second dude you showed me came after me with a knife. I wrist slapped it out of his hand, and that gave me a grip on his arm. So I swung him around like I did the first guy. Threw him too. But then the third guy got me in the ribs with a bat. Hurt like hell. I punched him in the face. Like, I was tired of playin' around. Just wanted it over.

"I think that's when I broke a finger. But it was my left hand and I'm right-handed. I picked up the wrench and the little guy started runnin' back to the car. The pimp started runnin' too, but he pulled out a gun and started shootin'. He was holdin' it sideways and wasn't really aiming. And I think he musta limp-wristed it because it jammed. I threw the wrench at him and hit the car instead. Him and the kid drove off. The third guy got up, looked at me, and ran after the car."

Jeff stopped and closed his eye. He slowly shook his head.

"I might've tried to drive, but the first two guys weren't movin'. So that's when I called 9-1-1. Are they okay?"

The sheriff didn't answer his question. "Do I need to tell any of you not to repeat this story? To *anyone*?"

We all said as one, "No."

The sheriff turned to leave. "Get some rest, Jeff."

"You going to arrest that guy? The pimp?" Bev demanded.

"Bev," he replied, "I'm unable to comment on an ongoing investigation. That will be my answer to all your questions. So you have to trust me, okay?"

"Okay."

"Good. Now ... a deputy will be posted at the door until Jeff is released, okay?"

"Why?" Bev blurted.

"I'm *unable* to comment on an ongoing investigation." He turned and left.

Jeff sighed. I watched his hand squeeze Bev's hand. Bev lowered her head and wept softly.

Minutes passed.

Hours passed.

It wasn't the same as when I sat at Mom's bedside. With Mom, I was waiting for her to die. It's much better waiting for someone to get well.

A nurse came in and checked the numbers on the machines. Then the bag hanging on its hook. She clicked on the computer more than anything.

Then a doctor came in. "You can stay if you like," he offered, pulling the covers down.

"When can he come home?" I asked.

"Probably day after tomorrow," he replied. "Just want to make sure there's no infection ... and get him in for a CT."

"How long for him to get better?" Bev pressed.

He thought for a few seconds. "As long as the wounds heal … his ribs will probably take the longest … about three weeks or so. Hard to say."

Bev and I decided to take a break.

We walked down to the cafeteria for a sandwich. We picked a quiet corner and ate in silence.

"I might as well leave for now," I decided. "Get the apples out of the sun."

She nodded, her mind a hundred miles from apples.

"If your mom wants to come, should I agree?"

She shrugged. "I can't think too good right now. I'd leave it up to her."

I nodded. "My mind's kinda blown, too. Mostly about the fight, but please tell me what just happened between you and my best friend."

"Funny you want to talk about *that* instead of the fight."

She sighed.

"This is more … you know, important … sorta," I insisted.

"Yeah, like how did I hook up with a guy I met just two months ago?"

"Two months of arguing," I added. "Yeah, how did that happen?"

She looked at me eye to eye, her expression dead serious. "If I tell you why I love *him*, will you please tell me why he would ever want *me*?"

"Easy question," I said. "You first."

"Well, when he told me to leave, I understood why. I agreed why. It's what I would've said. But then, I thought about living the rest of my life not fussin' with him, not hearing his voice, not seein' his smile. Missin' out on all those hillbilly anecdotes he comes up with. God, Chad, it scared me to death!"

"So … you can't live without him callin' you Chubby."

"There. You got it. You're not so dumb after all." She smiled. "Your turn. Be honest."

"Easy. You're a good person. A genuinely good person. It's rare. If I had to count all the truly good people I know, I wouldn't run out of fingers."

"That's good. Rings true. Now the hard question. Chad, how could he possibly love my baby? How could he possibly love Rusty's baby … especially after all this?"

"Another easy question," I replied, as I collected cartons on my tray. I looked her in the eye. "Jeff is adopted. To Jeff, his mom and dad are his mom and dad. He doesn't see it any other way because it isn't. He knows what a loving family is, and I'm sure he knows how to be in one." I smiled. "We good?"

"Perfect," she replied. "Now I'm happy again. I mean, you know, except for the fight."

"Yeah. Like, is that deputy gonna come home with us? And… should we be worried about the pimp? Or, should we worry about friends of the two guys here in the hospital?"

"I wonder if we're in danger." She looked truly worried.

"We should ask the sheriff," I decided.

"If he gives me any more of that 'still under investigation' crap, I'm gonna have to show my ass and demand some answers."

She stood up. "Will you get my tray? I want to get back to Jeff."

I nodded, and she walked off.

When there's a tragedy, loved ones spring into action and start bakin' casseroles. Or whatever they can do to busy themselves. The next day Miss Bishop put her planned semi-retirement on hold and opened the diner as usual. Trish and I were right there with her. Bev slept in, came in and picked up a biscuit to go, and took my truck to the hospital.

The Smiths were out in the field taking measurements and hammering stakes in the ground.

They wouldn't say why, but Carolyn and Vicki unhooked their camper and left. Said they would be back in a few days.

I could tell Bear was out of sorts, especially when Deputy Lawrence showed up with Jeff's wrecker. After breakfast orders petered out, I was fixin' to get ready to go and check on Jeff. I needed to get a new pair of shorts and a shirt for him to come home in. What he wore coming to the ER was bloody and torn from knife stabs. Even his socks had blood from wounds running down his legs. Besides, all those clothes were bagged and carried away as evidence.

The apartment over Jeff's shop was one room with one window. There was a kitchen, a table, a bed, and a bathroom. No walls, not even for the bathroom. The floor was unpainted plywood. I found what I needed out of a three-drawer dresser.

Bluefield is about an hour's drive from Tree Fork. I could have shaved fifteen minutes off by taking the interstate. But I was afraid to drive his wrecker too fast. It had a three-speed stick shift, no power steering, and the clutch pedal took all my strength. No wonder Jeff was so strong. The cab was full of car parts, fast-food bags, napkins, wrappers, papers, junk, junk, and more junk.

So I took Route 19.

Entering his room, I found him sleeping with Bev seated next to him and stroking his arm. I sat on the other side and watched them. It was endearing how Bev cared for him. I was happy for him. And her.

"His color is better," she whispered.

"You're gonna rub all the skin off his arm," I kidded.

"Make her stop," Jeff smiled without opening his eye. "She's botherin' me."

Bev's face glowed with delight, and she leaned down and kissed his hand.

"Same 'ol Jeff," she purred, "still pickin' on me. I love you, Jeff."

Jeff opened his eye and looked at me with a shit-eatin' grin under all the bandages. "Lost count how many times she sez that."

"I'm happy for you both," I said, honestly. "Didn't see it comin', don't understand it, but it looks real from here. When I get you away from her, you're gonna 'splain it to me."

"Simple," Jeff grinned, while glancing over to Bev. "I traded boobs for brains."

"I'm going to hurt you," Bev kidded, "if I can find a place that isn't already hurting."

"I know one place." His grin widened.

"I know that place," Bev hinted.

Couldn't believe my ears. I shook my head. "Noooo. No, you did not just say that. You didn't —"

Their mischievous grins gave them away.

"Already, Bev? How'd you keep from killin' him?"

"Very carefully," she confirmed.

"Very," Jeff added.

"TMI," I objected.

"And we're engaged," Bev announced, her grin melting into a gentle smile.

Jeff was watching her. "And it's a good thing," he added, "since the corn done got planted before the fence was built."

They both looked at me, I think for approval. "Bro, she's outta your league."

"I know," Jeff agreed, happily. "She's a spittin' image of herself."

"This is good stuff," I said, nodding.

We just sat there for a minute, letting it all sink in.

Finally, Jeff had to get better situated in the bed, and that meant figuring out how to do it without hurtin'. Bev helped keep the covers straight. Once settled, he turned a bit to face me.

"Seriously," he began, "I do want to 'splain something. You know … since you're so clueless and all."

I nodded in agreement.

"I knew I had feelins' for Bev. I mean … and I'm bein' serious … I never figured she felt the same way about me. I'm okay with me bein' me, but she can do better, right? So I just kept clownin' around … happy with the way things were. I liked her so much it was hard to want for more, ya know?

"But when she told me she loved me … and … and the look on her face … and … it just opened up a floodgate. Like, if she's dumb enough to want me, it took all the doubts I had … had in myself. So I told her I loved her, too. I knew she would be everything a woman can be for a man, and I would be happy to be everything she needed from me. For the rest of our lives."

He paused.

"You should do 'serious' more often," I remarked. "You wear it well. Really. So when and how did you pop the question? You *have* to tell me."

"Can I tell him?" Jeff asked, glancing over to Bev.

She rolled her eyes, then slowly flipped her hand over, palm up. "Whatever."

He looked back to me. "Earlier this morning, just after we ... you know ... how do I put it?"

Bev scowled. "Very carefully."

"Well ... after we ... *took Granny to Cracker Barrel* ... she got off me, carefully, and looked around for her clothes. But then she stopped, stood up straight, mostly naked, and asked 'Think this bod will work for you for the rest of your life?'"

"Hundred dollars if you guess what he said," Bev challenged.

I thought about it. "He said, 'Works for me.'"

She shook her head side to side.

I guessed again. "Okay, but just this once."

She shook her head again.

Jeff chimed in. "I told her that bod would look good in a weddin' dress."

"So ... Bev McCormick ..." I tried it on for size, "and little McCormicks running around."

"Bite me," Bev kidded.

"Bev, your language," I chided. "You're turnin' into a Jeff."

"And this concludes *all* conversation about me and Jeff and sex.

I let it go this far just to get it over and done with. Got it?"

"Yes, ma'am."

"Anyway," Jeff concluded, "If a woman asks if her bod will be enough for you for the rest of your life, marry her."

"Does she need to know my last name?" I asked. Bev tossed a box of tissues at me, missed.

"So … you guys moving in together?"

"We were just talking about it," Bev answered. "I'm moving in with Jeff. Won't take much to do, just my clothes, and I don't have a lot of them."

"My closet is half empty," Jeff added.

"Most of the furniture came with the trailer," Bev said, "and it's Mumma's anyway. Everything is yard sale stuff."

"That will leave your place for Trish and your mom," I guessed. "Or maybe rent some day. I keep wondering how our checking account is holding up."

"I've been workin' on that," she replied. She poked and swiped on her phone. "Up to now, we make way more out the back door than the front."

"I got money from workin' for Carolyn," Jeff offered. "It might cover the hospital bill."

"I wonder how long trail ridin' season lasts," I pondered.

Bev leaned back in her chair, looked out the window, and sighed. "Yeah, come winter … and I'm due in December." She kept staring out the window. "It's looking like a long, lean winter comin'."

I searched through the empty shell of my brain looking for options. It sucks being dull. We needed more customers, more ideas, more money. I couldn't think of a thing to do about it. It would all be up to a pregnant 24-year-old who came out of nowhere.

"I should do a website for Jeff's ATV business," Bev said, still looking out the window.

"And hand out business cards to the riders," Jeff added, his eye closed.

Bev turned back to us. "Yeah. Put cards in the take-out bags. Never know …"

"I wonder if people would want off-season storage," Jeff pondered.

"And winterize them," Bev added.

"Right. And oil changes. 'Coming to a shop near you, on sale now, prices vary, quantities limited, void where prohibited.'"

Jeff's eye was still closed, but he was smiling, "And then a de-winterization service, same conditions.

"Chad, jump in anytime."

"Wish I could," I said. "I got nothin'."

"Then maybe you should get busy peeling apples," Bev suggested. Her lips were smiling but her eyes weren't.

CHAPTER 15

The next day started like the last. Bev took my truck and later on I took Jeff's wrecker to visit him. He looked better but was getting restless. The doctor said he would be released, but paperwork had to be done and paperwork takes time. After a few hours, Bev suggested I should go back home and peel apples.

"Gonna have to hold off on the apples for a bit," Sheriff Bailey announced. He was standing in the doorway.

For all the nice things he had said to us, I still couldn't help but cringe a little when first seein' Sheriff Bailey. He is large and in charge. It's not just the big belt or the big belly. It's that you can't bullshit the guy.

From behind him a nurse walked in. She started unhooking Jeff from the tubes and wires.

"I've been in touch with the hospital since yesterday," the sheriff said. "Jeff can be released. Chad, I see your truck is outside."

I nodded. "Yes sir."

"Inspection sticker is expired. I know your plate is kinda full right now, but don't let it go too long."

"Yes sir."

"And Jeff's tow truck is out there," he said.

"Yes sir."

He stepped back to give room for the nurse to walk from one side of the bed to the other. "As soon as she's done, we can leave. The bill has been paid, so that's done. I'll take Jeff in my cruiser and meet you at the diner. From there, we all go to the residence of Walker Bryson."

"Who's he?" Bev asked, alarmed.

"Someone you need to meet. Other than that, I can't divulge information regarding an ongoing investigation." He stared Bev down as he said it.

"This is gonna be epic!" Jeff said, cheerfully.

"Who paid the bill?" Bev asked the sheriff.

"Ongoing investigation, Bev," he retorted.

"My guess is Carolyn," I ventured.

"She didn't need to do that," Bev said. "We should pay her back." Jeff agreed.

The biggest problem of moving Jeff was getting him seated on his left butt cheek because the other side had the bullet wound. He leaned over on his left in the wheelchair while leaving the hospital, and then the same in the cruiser. We dropped his wrecker and my truck off at the diner and hopped in the cruiser with the sheriff. I sat in front and Bev sat in back with Jeff. Then we continued east on Route 42.

I had never been that way. The narrow road was between a cliff wall on the right and a steep drop on the left. In less than a mile two brick pillars appeared on the right. We turned up a driveway that climbed the side of the mountain.

"Must be hell when it snows," I commented. It was so steep our seats were like recliners.

"Nope," the sheriff said. "Whole driveway is heated. Snow and ice just melts away."

"Wow," I said, "that musta cost a bundle."

The road kept climbing until it reached the crest and an English Tudor-style mansion. It had to be half a football field wide and two stories tall. The walls were gray stone and beige stucco.

"Oh my God!" Bev exclaimed. "A castle!"

Sheriff Bailey followed the circular driveway around to the front door and stopped. With some effort he turned in his seat.

"From here," he stated, "I am not involved in this situation. Everything from here on is between you and Walker. Do not ask for my advice, and only tell me what I might ask about. Walker is a good man, and he has my trust and respect. Understand?"

We all said "yes" but I really didn't understand. The sheriff handed me his card.

"I'll be in the area. Call me when you're done. I will take you back to the diner."

Jeff could walk, slowly, and we made our way to the front door. In my head I could hear the lyrics to "Hotel California."

The door opened before we even knocked, and a middle- aged dude welcomed us in. He had a short haircut, combed perfectly. His eyes were brown, his nose had a slight beak, and his smile didn't show his teeth. No facial hair. He was slim, wore a white shirt, khaki slacks, and brown penny loafers. He didn't introduce himself, just waved us in.

As we walked in a girl rolled up in a wheelchair. She was movie-star gorgeous with long blond hair, blue eyes, and super white teeth. She wore a sheer white blouse and very short shorts.

"Hi y'all!" she squealed. "Welcome!"

I stepped forward, hand extended, to keep her from having to roll any closer.

"I'm Chad," I said. "Chad Davis."

"I'm Piper," she said, shaking my hand. Then she stood up.

Duh, she wasn't disabled. The wheelchair was for Jeff.

I tried to hide my embarrassment while looking back to Jeff and Bev. "See that? I healed her. Now she can walk!"

Bev rolled her eyes out loud. "Now that she can walk, maybe we can use the wheelchair for Jeff. Hi Piper, I'm Bev. This is Jeff."

Piper and Bev pulled the wheelchair behind Jeff.

We were standing in a room as big as the whole diner, and the ceiling was two stories up. And it wasn't even a room. It was just the foyer. Two curved sets of stairs led to the second floor.

Large, wide halls went right, left, and straight under the stairs. Piper led us that way.

"Gramps is waiting back here," she said. Bev followed while pushing Jeff. I brought up the rear.

At the back, on the right, a large room full of chairs and sofas, and a huge stone fireplace. And two men — one middle-aged and the other an old guy. They both stood to greet us.

The old guy turned out to be Walker Bryson. Most noticeable was his wide, friendly smile. He had bushy gray eyebrows — the only hair on his head. He wore an old, heavy, unbuttoned brown sweater over a white button-down shirt.

"Come in, come in," he waved. "Find a seat. Make yourself comfortable." He shook our hands. "And this ... is Paul Miller."

Mr. Miller wore a dark suit, had a preacher vibe. A very large man, his full head of dark brown hair parted on the side. His nose was noticeably large, and his mouth looked like he forgot to put his teeth in.

"Isn't Miller the name of the two guys in the hospital?" Bev asked.

I was thinking the same thing.

"Yes," Mr. Bryson replied. "He's their father."

"How are they?" Jeff asked. The tone in his voice was calm and casual, telling me that he was not concerned for his safety.

Still, I edged over a step to come between Jeff and Mr. Miller.

"The younger brother, Ricky, will be fine. Just some bruises. My oldest, Mark, will be paralyzed from the waist down for the rest of his life. When you threw him ... he hit the corner of a dumpster and it 'bout broke him in half. He has a cracked pelvis and his spine is broken. It breaks my heart, but I'm not here to blame you."

"Still, I'm sorry," Jeff responded. "I wasn't tryin' to —"

"Why *are* you here, sir?" Bev asked, facing a man twice her size.

Mr. Miller's chin dropped to his chest. Talking to the floor, he said, "It was bound to happen sooner or later. They were always trouble growing up." He looked up at us all. "I did my best. Took them camping, taught 'em to fish, made them keep their grades up. But they were always getting into trouble. Then got into drugs. Drugs from that Snake boy."

"That's the pimp?" Bev asked, crossing her arms.

"Yes."

"He needs to be arrested," she concluded.

"That's why we're all here," Mr. Bryson said, calmly. "It's going to take a little while. But first ... does anyone want something to drink?"

The three of us shook our heads, but then Jeff asked, "A beer? Any brand."

"I think we have some Corona," Piper said. "And limes."

"Thank you," Jeff replied.

"Make it two," Bev added.

"Three," I joined in.

"Maybe a little swig of whiskey," Mr. Bryson added. "Paul?" But Mr. Miller declined.

As Piper walked out, I couldn't help but watch.

"Please, everyone, have a seat. There's much to talk about." His chair was a large, ox blood leather wingback. Next to it, a small three-legged table. From the table he picked up a spiral notebook, then reading glasses from under his sweater.

Bev and I shared a sofa, Jeff right next to us. Mr. Miller sat on another sofa.

"I just met Paul yesterday," Mr. Bryson began, "so some background information first." He leaned back in his chair. "I'm originally from Baltimore, born and raised. I've done very well for myself. Some say from counting Tropicana freight cars. More on that later.

"I always promised my wife, Betty, that upon retirement we would move here. She was born and raised in Bluefield. You kids know Erma, down the street. She was Betty's roommate at Bluefield College, and they have been best friends ever since. More about Erma later.

"Anyway, Betty missed her friends and family, and these mountains. And I have to say I'm very glad to be here, and I can see why she wanted to come back." His smile faded. "And... of course, I feel close to Betty, living here. She's buried in a small plot out back that you can only see from the porch off my bedroom. I go out there every morning with my coffee and say, 'Good Morning.' And every night, with my whiskey, I say 'Good Night.' I guess that part doesn't really add anything helpful as to why we're here."

"I'm sorry for your loss," Bev murmured. "You're a sweet man."

"Thank you," he nodded, and his smile returned. He opened his notebook and put on his glasses. "We'll start with Snake. He moved here about nine months ago, rents a house up around Littlesburg. Started giving out drugs like candy and got some people hooked, and now has a growing drug business and some prostitutes on the side. Classic drug dealer playbook.

"Question is, why here? There's no money here. Not many people, either. We think he's from Cleveland; it's straight up I-77. Or maybe Detroit. We just don't know."

"So next step is arrest him," Bev interjected.

"Bev, James can arrest him. It would go to court and Snake would have a dozen people take the stand and swear he was with them. James will have played his hand, and we still won't know why he's here. I'm sorry it works that way, but that's why we're talking today. Okay?"

Bev crossed her arms. "Why did he beat up Jeff? Or try to kill him?" She reached across the sofa arm and held Jeff's hand.

"I don't think he planned to kill anyone," Mr. Bryson answered. "What I *think* is, it was all for street cred. And more important, for gang loyalty. If the four guys beat up Jeff, they would have to stick together and not tell on each other. And especially not rat out Snake, because he has the drugs. I think he shot at Jeff because he was scared. Maybe thought Jeff had a gun.

"But now, Snake has a problem. He got beat. It cost him some respect, he lost the Miller brothers ... and what he doesn't know is that he pissed off their dad, Paul, here."

Mr. Miller reflected, "I knew my sons were into something. But I didn't know what or with whom. At the hospital I pressed them for information and learned about this Snake guy. I was so mad I wanted to kill him. But then Sheriff Bailey pulled me aside and set me up with Walker. Obviously, the sheriff and Walker work together."

"And that information can't leave this room," Mr. Bryson said. "Everything said today goes nowhere. I think James made that clear as well."

We nodded.

Mr. Bryson continued. "Bottom line, Jeff, Snake is out to get you. Or just make it look like he tried. I don't know.

"Listen, I knew he was up to something, knew it had something to do with you, and I should have warned you. I am *so very sorry* I didn't. That's why I paid your hospital bill — not that it atones for your suffering. But I was hoping for more information, and since then I had a GPS tracker put on his car.

"So now I know more, and now I *am* warning you and doing something about it."

"Thank you for paying the hospital," Jeff said. "It *does* help, not that any of this is your fault. But how do you know all this stuff? You got spies or something?"

"Something better," Mr. Bryson explained. "I have two cleaning girls that come twice a week. They're from Guatemala. Sweet girls. They work hard and talk the whole time in Spanish. Thing is, I know Spanish, and they don't know it. It's sorta like eavesdropping, but very helpful.

"So one day I overheard them talking about a friend of mine, a lady down in Princeton. It was something my friend didn't want anyone to know. And yet, she talked to a friend about it in confidence, but didn't realize she was overheard. You might call it a form of systemic racism — the mindset of ignoring the hired help as if they weren't there. And it wasn't even my girls, it was another cleaning company. Shows how word gets around."

"I guess in all fairness," I offered, "your friend probably didn't think they could understand English that well. Like your girls don't think you know Spanish."

"You got a point there. Didn't really think of it like that. Either way, it gives me 'boots on the ground,' you might say. *And* it gives me a way to pass along rumors … for various purposes."

"Like the Tropicana rumor," Jeff grinned.

Mr. Bryson's smile broadened. "Gee, I don't know what you're talking about."

"So, hypothetically," Bev offered, "you *could* start a rumor that the Lighthouse biscuits are the best ever."

"I could," Mr. Bryson answered, "but that fact is already out there. And the pies. Especially the pies."

He adjusted his glasses and looked at his notebook. "We're getting out of order from the way I wrote it down. Let's add a little more background." He looked over the top of his glasses for approval.

We all leaned back in our seats.

Piper came in and passed out the beer: Coronas with lime wedges poking up. Then a glass to Mr. Bryson.

"This looks like water," he noticed.

"Because it is," she chirped, taking a seat.

He rolled his eyes, took a sip, sat it down. "Now, where —"

"More background," Bev answered.

"Right. So … it was very important, to Betty, that we do as much as possible to help people. People here. But you can't walk down Main Street and pass out cash. It doesn't work. So, you do what you can … knowing you can't do it all. Betty had a lot of ideas, and I try to follow them as best I can.

"I contribute, anonymously, to local charities. I've joined local clubs and business organizations. I work with school PTAs. For example, I'll buy uniforms for the high school band, help with school supplies, meals, and such, but it is very, very hard. You give a kid a warm coat and the next day it's on Craigslist for sale, for the dad to buy drugs. It is so hard to get past all the parasites of society.

"The point of all this is that Snake is a very big problem. He can do much more harm than I can do good. I can't ask him nicely to leave, and I can't threaten him. A threat would be a game to him — and end up helping him recruit more kids. He has to *want* to leave. That's what I've been working on."

He paused to look down at his notebook.

"Now you might ask," he continued, "how come I sit up here in this big house and Erma lives just down the road in that worn out trailer? Believe me, I would put her in a big new home. But she won't hear of it. She was a teacher her whole life, and she is hell-bent on feeding as many children as possible. She has a small group of women doing their best — and again, can't do it all. It's very disheartening, the need is so great.

"And get this, she'll come up to a house and there'll be the dad standing there. He'll say something like, 'The food doesn't come in unless you throw in a pack of cigarettes.' Erma doesn't budge, bless her heart. She's tough. Only thing she can do is go to the next family because there are always more families than food. Thing is, some folks come to *her* place to pick up food.

"If she lived someplace nice, it would only add more pressure for her to give more. She finally agreed to a new trailer with all new furniture and appliances. I had to spend an extra $15k to make it look old, and it'll have a vestibule-type thing on the front porch. That way, people only see what's in the vestibule, not the trailer. I think the only reason she agreed is because the old trailer finally became unlivable. Anyway, I'm moving her things out as we speak, and she will stay here the next couple of days."

He took another sip of water, frowned at the glass, and glanced at Piper. She smiled back.

"So one idea I had … was to put Snake in the old trailer and tow it to Alaska. Take his wallet and his gun. Break into his house and toss everything. Let him know that we have resources and really don't appreciate him being here. Of course, he would find his way back. But if we kept doing it — kidnapping him and hauling him away — he might get the point. But more than likely it will just piss him off. Still …"

"We could just shoot him," Mr. Miller offered.

He was dead serious.

"We *could*, if we were impious. Paul, neither of us could pull the trigger even if looking down the barrel of his gun."

Mr. Miller shrugged. "True, but I could if he was pointing it at one of my sons. So we need to get that point across to Snake."

His comment gave me an idea, so I spoke up.

"We could hang him."

Everyone looked at me like I was crazy. Except Jeff. He was grinning. So I pressed on. "What if he thought we were hanging him? I think I know a way he would believe it."

"Love it," Jeff grinned. "Church Camp initiation, right?"

"I'm listening," Mr. Bryson said.

"I'll show you. I'll need a strong, sturdy chair with armrests, some rope, a blindfold … and a small rotten branch that I can break over my knee. And a branch off a bush."

"On it!" Piper cried, jumping up. "Sounds like a MacGyver thing."

"It is," Jeff echoed. "You're gonna love this!"

It took half an hour to get everything ready. I insisted Mr. Bryson would *not* know what I was doing. He could judge for himself if my idea would work.

First, we sat him in a metal chair strong enough for Mr. Miller and me to lift him off the ground without breaking the armrests. We tested it. With Mr. Miller on one armrest and me on the other, we lifted Mr. Bryson off the floor a few inches, then let him down.

"Mr. Bryson," I announced, "you are now Snake, and we are going to hang you."

I showed him a 3/8" double-braided line tied in a hangman's noose. "If we do this for real, this would be one-inch-thick hemp instead."

I placed it over his head and snugged it loose around his neck. "Imagine this larger and scratchy."

"I like it," confirmed the man with the rope around his neck.

"Now the blindfold," I continued, motioning to Piper. She placed it over his eyes and tied it good. Then she kissed him on the head.

"I have an idea," Mr. Miller interjected. "A prayer … like, um…Dear Lord, forgive us for having to take the life of this scumbag, but after all this *is* West Virginia, and we don't take kindly to out-of-state foreigners coming in and hurting our children and … yada-yada. Amen. Or something like that."

"Nice touch," Mr. Bryson smiled.

"Now you hang," I announced.

Mr. Miller and I lifted Mr. Bryson a few inches. We didn't need to fake the effort. He was heavy.

"Up he goes," Piper cried. Then she kneeled down. "Up!" Then she bent lower. "Up!" Then she got lower and lower until her head was on the floor. "He's up there!"

Bev brushed some of the leaves of a bush on the top of his head.

At that point Piper stood up and held the noose, pulling it a little.

"Hang him!" Jeff yelled.

At that signal, Mr. Miller and I jerked the seat up a few inches. Bev snapped a piece of branch over her knee and Piper yelled while pulling gently on the noose. Mr. Bryson frantically grabbed the armrests. We sat the chair back down.

Mr. Bryson ripped the blindfold off his face. "That was perfect!" he exclaimed. "It felt like I was dropping, not going up! I heard Piper's voice from way down below me! And then the branch breaking! And falling! And the noose! Perfect!"

"We'll drop him further and make it a crash landing," I finished. "The noose will be scratchy, and tighter. He'll be tied to the chair."

"Add something in the prayer," Bev added, "about him being buried with the 'other' dudes that messed with us. Let him know this is how we deal with pond scum."

"This will work!" Mr. Bryson exclaimed. "We just need a way for him to escape, but I have an idea for a distraction! How did you come up with this idea?"

"Church Camp initiation on camping trips. We'd take the new kids off into the woods at night," I explained, "and all the other kids knew what to do 'cuz they'd been through it. Stood 'em on a backpack frame, blindfolded, and told 'em we were going to lift them up about five feet. We called it a 'leap of faith' ceremony.

"So we'd lift them up a few inches, and shake the backpack frame — so they'd have to balance themselves, ya know. All the other kids would get lower and lower and talk about how high he was. Someone would brush a branch on the kid's head, like he was way up. So when we told him to jump, him thinkin' it was a five-foot drop when it would only be a few inches. When they landed they'd fall, every time. Always good for a laugh. Probably lucky we didn't break any ankles."

Mr. Bryson was writing feverishly in his notebook. "One- inch hemp, you say?"

"Yep."

"Wait a minute," Jeff interrupted. "Anyone else gettin' the feeling we're talkin' about hittin' a hornet's nest with a short stick? I mean, even if I was *fully* recovered I wouldn't take on this dude."

"You know Marvin," Mr. Bryson answered, smiling.

"Yes," from me.

"He's Betty's younger brother. My brother-in-law. Probably my wife's biggest reason for coming here."

"Oh," from Jeff. "Well, that clears up everything! Your kin sleepin' in a van ... down in my junkyard ... instead of up here. Now don't that put a milk pail under a bull."

Mr. Bryson held up his hands. "Hear me out," he said. "Marvin came out of the military messed up. You probably know that. On top of that, he is phobic … something I don't understand. He has a bedroom upstairs that he has *never* slept in. Only on the coldest nights will he come and sleep here, somewhere in the garage. I have begged and pleaded with him. But Marvin has demons I can't see or understand. I tell Betty about it all the time. All I can do is be here when he chooses."

"This has somethin' to do with why there's good cell service down in the hollow," Jeff noted. He never ceases to amaze me.

"Yes," Mr. Bryson chuckled. "Cost me a bundle. But it ensures Marvin can call at any time, for any reason. I convinced him it was something Betty wanted."

"And he will go up against Snake?" Bev asked.

"Yes, he is more than capable. And he's fond of you kids. Not that fond of your food, though."

"What?" Bev exclaimed.

Mr. Bryson waved her off with a chuckle. "He's just that way about food. Marvin was a chef before going into the service. Thinks he knows more about cooking than God."

"If he has a connection to you, why does he let us feed him for free?" I asked.

Mr. Bryson rubbed his chin again. "I actually didn't know that. But he's a strange person. My guess is he figures you're feeding him because you like him, not because he's paying you. If you let him pay you, how would he know you liked him?"

"I get that," Jeff nodded.

Mr. Bryson pulled a phone from one of the big pockets in his sweater. He poked buttons. "Right now, Snake's car is in the shop, so I assume he will stay put until he gets the headlight fixed.

"In the meantime, James and his deputies will stay close. That gives us time to get ready. So … unless you want a tour of the place, you can call James to take you home."

"Tour," Bev piped up immediately. "Jeff, you in?"

"Not unless the place has elevators," he answered.

"It does," Piper replied. "Chad, you up for a tour?"

Of course I was. I'm not into big fancy houses, but I *did* want to watch Piper. She was fun to watch, comin' or goin'.

The kitchen could feed an army. The dining room could seat a hundred. Not really, but it looked that way. At first, I was in awe. But as we went room to room, it started to lose charm. Piper gave each room a name.

"This is the library." It had books.

"This is the billiards room." It had a pool table.

"This is the piano room." It had a grand piano.

"This is the indoor pool." It had an indoor pool.

"This is the gym." It had heavy stuff.

"This is the home theater." It had a popcorn machine. It also had an outdoor pool, a tennis court, and a flower garden.

I could tell Jeff and Bev were getting tired of it as well and I was starting to get annoyed at how entitled Piper seemed to act about everything. But then she changed my mind.

"Had enough?" she asked. "Obnoxious, isn't it?"

We nodded but dared not say it.

"This isn't what Gramps would have built for himself. It's what he wanted for Betty. He loved ... *loves* her so much, bless his heart. Notice the breakfast nook just off the kitchen?"

"Kinda distracted by the SubZero fridges and Wolf stoves," Jeff remarked.

"Little banquette seating in the corner," she said. "Windows down each wall, a laptop on the table, and a small TV on the wall. He sits on the wooden bench. That little room is how much of the house Gramps actually lives in. I kinda feel sorry for him."

By the time we got back to Mr. Bryson, he had two pages of notes and questions. Mr. Miller had already left to buy supplies. If nothing else, Mr. Bryson was all about the details.

Jeff and Bev were excited about the plans, but for me, I was scared to death. We were preparing for the assault of a drug dealer with a gun. My choice would be to run away.

There was one good thing, though. We all exchanged phone numbers, including with Piper. Yea, score!

CHAPTER 16

Sheriff Bailey took us back to the diner. Miss Bishop was gone. The diner was closed. Trish was gone. Carolyn and Vicki were still gone as well. JB was up next to the diner talking to a guy wearing a hard hat. We were dropped off at Jeff's place, and a deputy was waiting for us. He sat in his patrol car and lowered the window as we approached.

"Deputy Connor," he said, extending his hand. Given his size, I could see why he didn't get out. "I'll be here 'til relieved," he said, flatly.

"The diner is closed," I said, "but Bev's mom left us a crockpot of bar-b-que chicken. We'll bring ya a sandwich in a bit."

"Make it two, if ya don't mind. And a slice of one of them pies I've been hearin' about."

"Will do, 'cept the pies sell faster than we can make them."

First thing to do was show Jeff's place to Bev. Jeff had to climb the stairs one step at a time. I was wondering how Bev would react, it wasn't real homey. She wandered around, looking but not touching. I didn't blame her. No tellin' the last time anything was swept, cleaned, or washed. There was a faint smell of oil from the shop below.

Jeff was trying to get comfortable on the bed. We watched as Bev looked around, arms crossed. She didn't look too thrilled.

"The baby crib could go here," she spoke finally, pointing. "Keep the diapers under it, maybe." She looked sad. It got to me.

"Why not stay in your own place?" I asked.

Bev shrugged. "Well, Trish for one thing. She'd end up feelin' like a third wheel. And when Mumma wants to stay overnight ... you know ... that'd be four of us."

"Move Trish into my place," I offered. "I'll move in here."

Bev looked at me as if startled. Her hands went to her mouth. She didn't speak.

"You need the two bedrooms," I continued. "Move Trish into my place and when your mom visits, she can stay with Trish. Or with you if you want. Done and done."

"You're the best!" she cried. "Why are you so nice to me?"

"I like you. And now you're gonna be my best friend's wife."

Jeff looked at me with his one good eye. "Thanks, Bro."

I nodded. "What do you need outta here for the night?"

Jeff looked up at the ceiling, thinking. "Well, the sheriff took my gun ... so just my toothbrush, I guess. Oh, and Bear's food and bowls. I got a hunch he'll stick close to us tonight."

Getting Jeff down the steps was harder than getting him up. But he made it, and then over to Bev's. Her trailer smelled good, like bar-b-que, and it was a feast. I took two sandwiches to Deputy Connor and apologized about the pie. Then came back to Bev's.

As we started to eat, I had to ask, "So ... what did you two think of Piper?"

They looked at each other. Neither answered. So that told me what they were thinking loud and clear.

"She seems nice," Bev tried, faintly. She wiped the corner of her mouth. Jeff nodded eagerly, then stuffed a big bite in his mouth to keep from talking.

"You two are so busted," I declared. "You don't like her."

"We don't *know* her," Bev replied. "Just met her today, just like you."

"I know she's pretty," I stated. "Don't you?"

Jeff nodded and gave a thumbs up.

"She's gorgeous," Bev replied. She didn't offer anything more, so I let it drop.

"We all set for the hangin'?" Jeff asked.

"Far as I know," I replied.

"Wish I could be there," he complained.

"I'm afraid I'll pee in my pants just seein' the guy," I admitted.

"I know I would," he agreed. I doubted that.

Trish rolled in as we were scraping our plates into Bear's food bowl. We had to update her on Jeff moving in. And why.

"Where am I gonna live?" Trish complained. I would've thought she'd come up with something a little less selfish.

"You can stay at Chad's place," Bev answered. "Starting tonight, if you want." She looked over to me for consent, and I nodded.

With that said, Trish went into her bedroom and returned a few minutes later with all her belongings, still in a trash bag.

"Outta here," she said. "Thanks, Chad."

I paused until her footsteps faded away, then commented, "You're welcome, Trish."

"She's high," Bev explained.

"You sure?" I asked.

Bev nodded. "And that means she's been out with that married guy."

I looked at them, from one to the other. "I gave up my trailer to be nice to her. This bites." I was angry.

"Ain't right," Jeff agreed.

"I ain't gonna get my panties in a wad about it tonight," Bev responded, "but tomorrow we're gonna have a come-to-Jesus meeting."

"Who *are* you?" I asked. "And what did you do with my friend Bev?"

"Whaddaya mean?" she asked.

"I dunno. You used to be timid and proper and too nice. Now you're a girl version of Jeff."

It stumped her. She thought about it and then smiled. "See this gorgeous man sittin' here? Big … strong, he's the pick of the litter. And a good man, bigger than life and twice as handsome."

"I'm all that and a bag of chips," Jeff added.

"And know what? He picked me. Me! He thinks I'm pretty. And now, I *feel* pretty. Pretty and lucky. I am bitchn'!"

"You wear it well," I smiled. "Funny, though, you were pretty *before* he said so."

She shook her head. "Some things ain't true 'til you believe it. Now I do. Now I'm gonna be hard to live with. Praise the Lord!"

"Jeff," I grumbled, "you have created a monster."

He nodded politely, but obviously in pain. It had been a long day.

Bev noticed, too. "Time for your pill," she announced.

"Please," I kidded. "Don't beg me to stay. I know you want me to, but I got things to do. Really, I must go."

They smiled in appreciation.

"There might an extra toothbrush in the medicine cabinet," Jeff yawned. "Nite, Bro."

When I stepped into Jeff's apartment, I realized I was stepping into *my* apartment. I owned the land and the building. It had a well and septic, so I had that too. If I couldn't pay the electric bill, it wouldn't be a problem until winter. And even then, I could get a wood stove. I had acres of trees to keep me warm. It was a good start. As long as I could make enough to feed myself, I'd be okay.

In all the years I spent taking care of Mom, it didn't occur to me that when she died, there was no one to take care of me. Now, it weighed on me. I was living Plan A. I had no Plan B.

I should kick Trish to the curb and rent my trailer. But, somehow, that was not an option.

As I roamed around the room, I opened the medicine cabinet to check on that toothbrush. There were five of them, all new in their wrappers. I grinned. Jeff said there "might" be an extra. He knew damn well he was stocked for overnight company.

Well, maybe now it was time for *me* to have girls over. I wondered if Piper would spend the night. Probably not. Definitely not.

I peeked out the one window to see the patrol car parked below. I felt good about that. But I knew I wanted to talk to Carolyn when she got back. There was so much evil here that I had never known about. No matter about Vicki's combat training, they should consider leaving. And I would be obligated to give back the money she gave me. Money I had already spent.

All these bad thoughts kept banging around in my head, so I kicked off my shoes, dropped my shorts, and just plopped down on the bed. I pictured Piper's face. And that was the last thing I remembered.

The sound of footsteps creeped into my sleep. Who could that be? But first, where was I? Why did my trailer smell like oil? Oh, I'm not in my trailer. I'm in Jeff's apartment. Did I leave the light on?

I quickly went from sleep to scared shitless by a gun pointing at my face. Behind the barrel, an angry face glared at me.

"Where's Jeff?" he demanded. His thin, flashy jacket, like Jeff had said, confirmed I was going to die.

"Who?" I asked groggily, as if that was gonna fool him.

"Don't fuck with me, asshole! Where is he?" The gun came even closer.

My brain went into overdrive, but of course came up empty.

"Next trailer up the hill," I lied.

The gun waved. "Get up. Take me there. You run and I shoot you."

I got up and started down the steps. I tried to think. The next trailer up was *my* trailer, not Bev's. But he didn't know that. I would bang on the door knowing Trish was there, instead of Jeff. Would the pimp get mad and shoot me? What would he do about Trish?

Where the hell is the damn deputy??!

The steps came down to the office, dark except for the light from the stairway. The front door was already wide open. I headed for the door, dreading what would happen next and just wanting it to be over. The fear was worse than the outcome.

I guess the walk down the steps got the blood pumping enough to wake my brain. I remembered my knife. A plan came. I could knock on the trailer door, turn to my left, and he would still be looking at the door. Pull my knife, put it through his head. Probably take a bullet in the chest. Probably die, maybe not.

But I would try to save my friends. But … I didn't have my knife. It was upstairs … on the belt of my shorts.

Death was near, and my life flashed before me. In the small space of a split second, dozens of memories flashed by. I said goodbye to everyone that meant something to me. I wished them well, and said goodbye.

Jeff's office chair tumbled over, then the desk was pushed. I figured the pimp stumbled. I turned around and there was Marvin, fighting the pimp. Thank you, God, it was Marvin!

The pimp was quick. He flipped around like a just-caught fish but Marvin's moves were even quicker. The gun slid across the room. The pimp was on his back and a shotgun was pushed against his nose.

"One move and your face disappears," Marvin warned, calmly. Very calmly, actually.

The pimp lifted up and smirked. "Fuck you, asshole! I got more dudes comin'! Better get outta here while you can!"

That response was met with a hard poke on his forehead. The smirk was replaced by a figure-eight mark from the barrel of Marvin's shotgun.

"Flip over," Marvin instructed. The pimp didn't move. "Flip over or I'll shoot your nuts off."

The pimp complied. Marvin tied his hands behind his back and his ankles together. I looked back and forth between the pimp and Marvin. The pimp kept yelling threats. Marvin's expression was peaceful.

"Now what?" I begged.

"Now we wait," Marvin replied. He pulled out a phone and started typing. I leaned against Jeff's desk.

Marvin stood over the pimp. For the first time in my life I wished I had a dad growing up. How does a *real man* handle stuff like this? I had no clue. I'm a total wimp. Hell, the damn pimp was more a man than me.

We waited. Snake would fidget and fuss now and then, but a poke from Marvin's shotgun would put an end to it. Marvin's dominance over Snake was incredible.

We kept waiting. Then Jeff and Bev came to the door, Bev holding Bear's leash. Bear wasn't barking but he wasn't happy either. Marvin motioned me to go outside.

As I came out, I pressed my index finger to my lips. "What's going on?" Bev whispered. We stepped away from the door.

"It's Snake, and Marvin standing over him," I said, still shaking. "Snake came in and had a gun … and asked where Jeff was … and I said 'Jeff who?' and he didn't buy it and … and … so I told him he was at the next trailer up the hill and … he told me to take him there and … Jesus, I didn't know what to do."

"He came *into the apartment*?" Bev glared, her eyes huge.

I nodded.

"Where the hell is the damn deputy???" Jeff demanded.

"Dunno."

"And this is Snake's car," Jeff said, pointing. "He drove right up to the shop. How'd *that* fit in the plan?"

"He came *in* the apartment," Bev repeated.

"I was in bed, asleep. All of a sudden there's a gun pointing at me. The bore on that thing looked as big as a doorknob. Scared the *shit* outta me. Guys … I gotta be straight with you … he told me to take him to you."

"You were bringin' him to us???" Jeff asked.

"Well … no, I was takin' him to *my* trailer. I was hoping it would buy some time … or somethin'. Thought maybe Trish would be passed out so he'd have to bust the door in and maybe the noise would wake you guys. Jesus! I was putting everybody at risk! Anyways, we were on the way out when Marvin took him down."

"Chad," Bev demanded, grabbing my arm. "You saved our lives when you switched with us! Think about what would've happened if Jeff and I were up there!"

"We'd be dead, Bro," Jeff realized. He looked up at the night sky and breathed deep. "Dead."

As he said it, headlights were coming from Mr. Bryson's direction. A red Jaguar pulled in and Piper jumped out, still in the same clothes from earlier. She hurried over. She was a gorgeous woman, but not as much when worried.

"Everybody okay?" she asked.

"No!" I replied. "I had a gun pointed at my head!"

"I know," she replied. "Look, it wasn't supposed to go this way. The deputy runnin' off was out of nowhere."

"Wait," I said. "You *know* I had a gun pointed at me?"

"Yes. I know you had — hold on." She held up her index finger.

then put her hand up to her right ear. I hadn't noticed the earbud. "Yes," she said, looking away. "Sorry, I'll put it on mute. Okay, I won't put it on mute. Yes … I'm telling them now … Yes. … Okay, hurry up every chance you get."

She turned back and faced us.

"This whole thing is about getting Snake the hell out of here," Piper continued. "To get him to *want* to leave, okay? The thing with Jeff put the plan into motion, with the deputy on guard to keep things safe."

"Yeah," Jeff commented, "that idea went over like a frog in the punch bowl."

"Wasn't a deputy from this county," Piper explained. "The guy was borrowed from the next county over. And right now *he* is a person of interest."

She stopped to let that sink in, and to think.

"Let's talk about the *legal* way to handle this," she continued. "We're getting ready to make Snake think he is going to be hung, right? That's not exactly legal, and that's why Sheriff Bailey is up in front of the diner. Hypothetically, he doesn't know what's going on, but he's really up there in case Snake has any backup coming.

"Meanwhile, it's probably a good idea to keep Jeff and Bev out of sight. Okay?"

Bev nodded. "We're outta here."

She and Jeff turned to leave when the sound of a motor running came from down in the hollow. It was an ATV on the trail. It got our attention.

"Friend or foe?" from Jeff.

Piper smiled. "That's Gramps. He's got stuff for the hangin'."

"How'd he get on the trail?" I asked. "His house is on the other side of the road and past where the trail ends."

"You think the trail ends up that way, don't ya?" Piper answered with a question. "It don't."

"That's why the trail up that way is so smooth and perfect," Jeff said, thinking out loud.

"It's Uncle Marv's way to get up to the house," Piper said, "when he wants to. But that's not often. Please, please don't judge us. Gramps has begged him to come in out of the cold."

The sound of the ATV got closer. Piper turned to Jeff and Bev. "Time to go."

The two turned and together dragged Bear back to Bev's place. It was kinda sad to see Jeff sidelined.

Piper turned to me. "Chad, you are already knee-deep in all this, thanks to Snake. And we could use your help. So are you up for hangin' this guy?"

"I am so ready," I said. I was actually ready to hang him for real.

At first two headlights bounced up the trail, then Mr. Bryson came into view. It wasn't an ATV but a UTV, a four-wheeler with a small hauling bed on the back. He had to follow the trail up the outside of the fence, go around the diner, and come back down to us. I could tell he was talking on his phone hands-free. He stopped and got out. He was surprisingly agile.

"Chad, I am so sorry," he said. "I felt bad enough about Jeff, and now you get accosted. I am so very sorry."

"Well, at least I didn't get hurt," I said, halfheartedly.

"Don't downplay it," he said, authoritatively. "Emotional wounds cut deep and heal slowly. You have to care of yourself and take it seriously."

He turned and went into the office, and came out with two sandwich bags, a gun in one and a phone in the other. Without a word he hopped into his UTV and drove up to the diner.

Piper watched him head uphill, then turned to me. "There might be — hypothetically — someone up there that could match the gun to a recent shooting and a phone that has calls made to a missing deputy. And maybe some GPS stuff."

"I had that gun pointed at my head, Piper. I think we're past the fuckin' hypo crap," I objected.

"I agree," she replied, nodding.

A new car pulled in. It was Mr. Miller. Like Piper and Mr. Bryson, he was in the same clothes as when I last saw him. He walked up, cheerfully, rubbing his hands together in triumph.

"Snake in there?" he asked, eyeing the office.

"Yes," Piper answered. "But let's wait for Gramps so we're all on the same page."

He shrugged, disappointed. "Can't wait to hang him."

"I've got some enhancements to the plan," Piper began. "I think you'll like them. And I really think this is going to work."

I watched her face as she spoke. Geez, she was pretty.

And then I realized I was wearing a T-shirt and boxer shorts. I turned and went to back in. Snake was face down and Marvin had a foot on his butt. I walked as far away from Marvin and Snake as possible, then climbed up the steps.

When I got back, Mr. Bryson was returning and, of all things, he handed me Jeff's gun.

"Run this over to Jeff's," he instructed.

I did, then ran back.

Mr. Bryson had put on a black choir robe and a pointy black hood. It gave him a great imposing look. Piper also had on a black robe and hood. She was holding a clipboard. We entered the office.

Mr. Bryson walked up to Snake in full emperor character. "Turn him over," he commanded.

Marvin poked Snake with his shotgun. "Turn over." Snake didn't. Marvin set his gun aside, grabbed an arm and a leg, and flipped him over. Snake started cussing but stopped when Marvin retrieved his shotgun.

"Gag him," Mr. Bryson ordered, handing Marvin a bandana. "For some reason he thinks he is in charge. He is not. He will listen."

Once done, Marvin untied his ankles and stood him up.

"Bring him," Mr. Bryson instructed. With Marvin on one side and Mr. Miller on the other, they took him outside. Once there, Mr. Bryson turned and said simply, "Keys."

Marvin pulled the keys out of Snake's jacket and handed them over. Mr. Bryson gave them to me.

"Take his car over to the church parking lot. Leave the keys in the ignition. We will need to move it later, but I'm afraid the firetrucks will block us from doing so. Meet us in the trailer up the hill."

I followed his instructions and even I knew why. Mr. Bryson wasn't worried about firetrucks. The hanging tree was on the other side of the fence. It was expected that Snake would park in the church lot and sneak in from the road. But instead, he drove straight in and that put the car in the wrong place. The car had to be moved to make it easier for him to escape. Nice car, but it smelled like pot.

Once done, I rushed back and entered Erma's old trailer. I had never been in her trailer, even when it used to have furniture. Snake was seated on a mattress. Mr. Miller began pouring kerosene on the mattress. The kerosene had Snake's full attention. The smell filled the trailer.

Piper was standing at the door and at Mr. Bryson's signal she announced, "The committee members have arrived."

"Mr. Miller, state your case," Mr. Bryson said.

Mr. Miller sat the can down and walked around to face Snake.

"I am Paul Miller, father of Mark and Ricky Miller. Because of you, my oldest, Mark, has a cracked pelvis and his spine is broken. He will forever be paralyzed from the waist down. Ricky will heal, but he is forever poisoned by your evil influence. If you are not found guilty by the committee, I will kill you myself."

He stepped aside. It wasn't just an act.

"Noted," Mr. Bryson replied. "However, you are not a voting member." He pulled out a black cloth bag. "Place this over his head. Committee members will not be allowed to see his face."

Piper motioned for me to come outside.

"Phew," she whispered. "It's smelly in there. I wanted you to see my contribution. Watch this." She pulled out her phone.

"Committee member District One," Mr. Bryson announced from inside. Piper walked in, poked her phone, and a recording announced, "District One, innocent. Two wrongs don't make a right."

Piper poked her phone and walked back out. Once out, she changed into a pair of clog shoes.

"Committee member District Two," Mr. Bryson said.

Piper clomped back in, poked her phone, and a different voice announced, "District Two, guilty."

Piper poked her phone and clomped back out. Once out, she changed into a pair of flip-flops.

"Committee member District Three," Bryson announced.

Piper made exaggerated flapping sounds with her flip-flops and a new voice gave another "innocent" vote.

Next came bedroom slippers that gave a shush sound, and another "innocent" vote. Still a new voice.

Next was a pair of boots that gave a distinctive heel-to-toe step, followed by the same boots but with an uneven pace that sounded like a limp. Both of those were "guilty" votes, each a new voice.

For member number seven, Piper herself announced that the member was unable to attend due to an unfortunate case of "Grande malaise." That made it a tie. Go figure.

The smell of kerosene forced everyone out of the trailer. Mr. Bryson announced that in the event of a tie, he would make the deciding vote. After much deliberation, he voted "guilty." Snake was to be hung. You could tell Snake was nervous, the act was getting to him. Marvin and Mr. Miller had to practically drag him to the hangin' tree.

Piper and I held back. "How'd you like my little committee vote?" she whispered.

"Nice," I replied, softly.

"Yeah, Gramps liked it too. Said it would let Snake know there were others out there that don't like him either. Did the voices sound like a phone?"

"A little. Even so, he might have thought people were using recorded voices on purpose."

We made our way down the hill behind Erma's and then toward the church. Everyone gathered around a large tree. The underbrush was freshly cut. Mr. Bryson and Piper took off their hoods. A large broken limb lay on the ground. Next to it, a wooden chair with two pipes running crossways through the legs. Broken lumber was scattered around. It sure looked real, especially in the dark.

Marvin and Mr. Miller forced Snake on the chair and tied him down good, except they used shoestring knots. Then Mr. Miller headed back up to the trailer to set it on fire. Snake was yelling, but you couldn't understand what he was saying. I felt bad for him, and that made me mad at myself for feeling that way.

Mr. Bryson pulled out a piece of paper and a small flashlight, then adjusted his glasses.

"Let us pray," he began. "Dear Blessed Lord Almighty, we call upon you for your forgiveness and guidance. We are once again faced with an evil parasite eating away at our peaceful, innocent, God-fearing community. It is written: 'Thou shalt not kill,' but Lord, he is the devil, and his deeds perpetrate unbearable discord. We ask for your understanding, forgiveness, and to keep us as your faithful followers. In His name we pray, Amen."

We echoed, "Amen."

Marvin put the noose around Snake's neck and pulled it nice and snug. Snake's mumbling was now more begging than cussing.

"Okay," Mr. Bryson said, "hoist him up." He took the rope from Marvin and held it firm. Marvin and I got on our knees to get a good grip on the pipes. With a nod, we lifted up a few inches. With all the jerking from Snake, there's no way he knew what we were doing.

Piper kept saying "higher, higher, higher" as her head got lower, lower, lower to the ground. She was holding a small dead branch. Then we lifted up a few more inches. Peyton stood up and rubbed the branch on Snake's head. Mr. Bryson pulled up on the rope. We dropped Snake almost to the ground and Piper cracked the branch over her knee. Marvin and I spun the chair, tipped it forward, and let it land on the ground. Snake landed on his knees, and then his shoulder and face. He wasn't yelling but breathing really loud.

We all looked at each other and nodded. The hanging was truly believable!

"What happened?" Mr. Bryson roared.

"The branch broke!" Piper answered.

"How'd that happen?" Mr. Bryson yelled, angrily.

"I don't know! It never did before!" Piper explained.

"He dead?" Mr. Bryson asked bluntly.

Marvin gave Snake a poke. "Nope. Still breathing."

"Now what are we going to do!" Piper yelled. She sounded downright desperate.

"We could shoot him," Marvin offered, "with his own gun."

"No thanks," Mr. Bryson said. "Our luck a cop will just happen to be nearby."

It was time for my line. "You're gonna put him in the trailer and set it on fire anyway. Just put him in and light it up."

"I know, I know, but it's not humane!" Mr. Bryson exclaimed. "We're not animals, you know!"

We were all looking up the hill. Finally, light flickered from the trailer windows. The flames grew by the second.

"What the *hell* is that?" Mr. Bryson roared again.

"It's the trailer!" Piper cried. "On fire! How'd that happen?"

"Relay must've gone off early!" I yelled.

"Can't *anything* go right tonight?" Mr. Bryson grumbled.

"So we bury him here," Marvin offered.

Snake wasn't moving.

"We gotta get out of here!" from Mr. Bryson. He stepped toward his UTV. "Somebody sees us down here, we'll get arrested!" He kept walking downhill.

"What if he gets away!" Piper yelled.

Marvin stepped back into the shadows.

"Don't care!" Mr. Bryson answered, his voice further and further away. "We'll get him another day!"

That was his last line.

"Let's go!" Piper cried.

"Right!" I agreed. We ran up the hill. Looking back, we could see that Snake wasn't moving. We got to Piper's car, jumped in, and took off. Piper did a great job peeling out. She turned left and headed to the castle. Once there, she drove around the left side to the garages.

Mr. Bryson arrived soon after. A garage door opened as he approached. He drove in and parked his UTV. We followed inside and stood next to him.

"I think we got him," he said.

"Yeah," Piper agreed, "I can't think of anything that gave us away."

"It looked good to me," I added.

We talked about it and talked about it and waited and waited for Marvin's call. But Marvin doesn't talk much. Instead, Mr. Bryson got a text with a thumbs-up emoji.

"This is frustrating," he said. "I need details. But I can't call him. He would get *really* mad."

He poked and swiped his phone, then "Ah, this is better. Forgot about the GPS tracker. I-77, northbound. Snake's heading home! Wherever that is."

I called Jeff to give him and Bev the news. They were grateful, but Bev asked if I was up for helping her mom open the diner. It was four in the morning. Bev and Jeff both needed to rest.

I said "Yes." No way I could sleep anyway.

Piper took me to the diner. The trailer was still burning. No firetruck yet, but I could hear one coming. Pulling in, Piper parked and turned to me.

"We should go out to dinner sometime," she announced matter-of-factly. "My treat."

"Sounds great," I replied. Couldn't think what to say next.

She tilted her head and smiled. "Not good at this, are ya?"

"Guess not. You caught me off guard."

"Long night." She patted me on the leg. "Call me."

"Right." I got out and still didn't know what to say.

"Night." She put the car in gear.

"Night." I watched her leave.

CHAPTER 17

As Piper's car disappeared, Miss Bishop's car appeared from the other way. As she pulled in, a firetruck rolled up to the burning trailer. There wasn't much left burning, but it made a lot of smoke.

Miss Bishop got out, glanced at the trailer, then met me at the door.

"Come here, you," she said, and gave me a hug. Then she stepped back and looked me in the eyes. "You okay?"

"No, I'm not," I replied, glad to say it out loud.

"We'll talk all about it." She turned to unlock the diner.

There was work to be done, and work comes first, so conversation was hit or miss. But it was comforting to be mixing dough and cooking bacon. Now and then the smell of Erma's trailer crept in. A wet trailer smells worse than a burning one. But mostly, the diner smelled like biscuits, bacon, sausage, and coffee.

"I take it Jeff's apartment didn't work out," Miss Bishop ventured, peeking at biscuits in the oven.

"I don't know what they were thinkin'," I said. "Plywood floors, no door to the bathroom, not sure what heats it come winter."

"Probably thinking the trailer isn't hers." Miss Bishop wiped her hands on her apron. "It's mine."

"The apartment isn't Jeff's, come to think of it. It's mine."

She nodded and poured flour in a mixing bowl. "Either way, switching with them saved their lives. No thanks to that deputy."

"Can't wait to hear what *that's* all about," I said.

We both drifted into our own thoughts.

The griddle for the sausage and bacon was on the back wall of the diner. I was cookin' the bacon and sausage when Miss Bishop's phone chirped.

"Order up!" she exclaimed, coming from the back room with a load of biscuits. The order had come to Bev, and Bev texted the order to Miss Bishop.

"Might as well go and get Bev's phone," I suggested, "so she can get some sleep."

"You'll never pry it out of her hands. She loves that thing.

She'll probably get dressed and come on in."

Sure enough, Bev walked in a few minutes later. She looked tired, but upbeat. She showed Miss Bishop an order on her phone and got busy putting it together.

The two of them talked about wedding plans. No formal wedding, of course, just a small family get-together. It's not like anyone could afford bridesmaid dresses. The minister from Miss Bishop's church could do the ceremony — for a small contribution.

The conversation was interrupted when a customer came in. He wasn't unfriendly. But like most customers he was in a hurry to get his biscuits and go to work. They never talked much.

He left and Miss Bishop and Bev talked more about the wedding. But then an argument broke out and they went to the back room. From what I could make out, there was a problem with Bev wanting Carolyn and Vicki there, and the minister. Bev was enraged and Miss Bishop was equally firm. The argument ended with Bev storming out. She left her phone on the counter. Not wanting to get in the middle of it, I went out back and started peeling apples.

Miss Bishop continued taking orders, but it didn't keep her busy. I had to peel, core, slice, and notch the apples. If you have all the time in the world, it could be a relaxing thing to do all day. But if you just wanted to just get it done, it was painfully boring. After filling a bowl, I needed a break.

The sun wasn't up but I could see well enough to walk around. I checked out the stakes that marked where roads would go. It helped to think about what was coming instead of dwelling on what was happening. I returned to the diner and took my apples inside.

Miss Bishop glanced in the bowl, then gave me a look that said *you dummy*. "These won't work," she remarked, as if amused.

"What's wrong?" I asked.

"They're brown," she answered, pointing. I looked in the bowl. Some of the apples had turned a little brownish.

"I just cut them," I argued.

"By the time you get the crust ready, they'll be too far gone." She patted me on the head like I was a kid. "Maybe wait until Bev and you can work together."

I looked at my bowl of apples. "What a waste."

"Let's see what we can do." She took the bowl from me. "I have an idea."

She cooked the apples in brown sugar, cinnamon, and nutmeg. She started a new batch of biscuit mix but added applesauce to the mix. I kept expecting measuring cups and teaspoons to be used, but … nope. I don't think the diner even had them. She baked the biscuits as usual, and the sausage on the grill as usual, and ended up with a sausage apple biscuit.

"Mama used to make these on Sundays," she reminisced, "as a treat for going to church. Believe it or not, there was a time when I didn't like church."

They were messy, and the apples kept sliding out of the biscuit, but it was worth it. They were awesome. I downed two in two minutes.

"I have an idea," I said, licking my fingers. "We put some in with the orders as samples. Just being free will get attention. Besides, people don't know to order them yet. Whaddaya think?"

"Sounds great, and we can call them Miss Baker's Sausage Apple Biscuits."

"I wonder if we could get away with Miss Baker's Blue Ribbon County Fair Sausage Apple Biscuits."

"A bit long, I think. And not honest."

"True," I nodded. "I'm gonna start writing notes to go with the biscuits explaining that they're free samples, and to tell us what folks think of them."

She nodded. "Let's get busy."

As more orders came in, we added the extra biscuits.

Come sunrise Trish walked in, and that made for another heated conversation. When Miss Bishop learned that Trish came home high, all hell broke loose.

I decided to slip out. Walking around the front of the diner, I watched as trucks, trailers, and a crew of five or six pulled up to Erma's trailer. Or what was left of it. They started shoveling trash into black plastic bags for removal.

As I stood there and watched, Jeff hobbled up next to me.

It was still upsetting to see him covered in bandages. One thing different about him — he was wearing his dad's gun.

"Oh. My. God," he said, pointing to the burnt-down trailer.

I followed his finger, but I didn't see what he was talking about. "What?"

"Cordless sawzalls," he said in admiration. "Look at 'em go."

I nodded, shrugged, didn't share his enthusiasm. What *did* impress me was how quick they stripped down Erma's trailer to just the frame. Another truck pulled in with new tires. It looked like a race-car pit stop — old, burnt tires coming off, new tires going on.

Jeff was in heaven. "Cordless impact wrenches! Chad, run over and fetch me one."

"Sure thing," I lied. "Wait for me here."

The tire truck left, an escort car pulled in, then a Toter truck came and hooked up to the old trailer frame. In no time they pulled out, heading east. Good thing, because Erma's new trailer was coming from the other way. I don't think the two trailers could have passed on the narrow road. I'm guessing they knew that.

"I just love watchin' what money can do," Jeff said.

"Ditto," I said. "I wonder if Mr. Bryson is coordinating all this from his house."

"No. That guy, the one with the white hard hat. See? That's your straw boss right there."

Bev walked up from behind, lifted Jeff's left arm, and slid under it. "You boys having fun?"

"I'd pay money to watch this," I sighed.

"You okay?" she asked.

"Nice havin' this distraction," I shrugged. "Otherwise, I'd be thinkin' 'bout that gun pointin' at me."

Neither replied.

As the new trailer was being parked Sheriff Bailey's cruiser slipped past. He pulled up next to us and stopped. It took some effort for him to get out of the car, what with all the stuff on his big black belt.

"Enjoying the show?" he drawled, almost smiling.

"I'd pay money to watch this," I repeated.

"You okay?" he asked, just like Bev did.

"Not really." It seemed proper to answer his question with total honestly.

He nodded and put his hand on my shoulder. "Time will help. And some information."

As he leaned on the rear quarter panel, we gathered around. "You probably know Snake is out of West Virginia."

We nodded.

"Now, my office has come into possession of Snake's gun and cell phone. Ballistics match his gun to the bullet that came out of Jeff's boot. So we'll see where Snake stops and go from there. But all in all, I feel better about your safety."

"Sounds good," Bev said. "What about the deputy that left?"

"That," he replied, "is what's got me runnin' this morning.

At first I thought it was the deputy we borrowed from next county over. Thought that he got mixed up with Snake. Turns out he was called off by his sheriff, Sheriff Tate. I just paid him a visit and he tried to give me the 'good 'ol boy' attitude, like us sheriffs got to stick together. I'm so mad I could spit nails."

He crossed his arms and turned his head.

We waited.

"There's no jurisdiction over a sheriff, but I'm taking this straight to the state police," he continued. "See where it goes from there. What Tate doesn't know is that his number is on Snake's phone."

He turned to me. "Chad, it might come to you having to testify in court. If so, don't lie. You don't need to. All I'm asking is, y'all don't offer any information to anyone about anything. We all clear?"

"Yes sir," I replied.

"Got it," from Bev.

"Right," Jeff added.

The sheriff eyed Jeff up and down. "Mind if I look at your gun?"

Jeff nodded and handed it over. The sheriff took it and pulled back the slide. "Not chambered," he noted. "Your choice, of course."

"I know," Jeff said, apologetically. "Dad always said to chamber the first round. I just couldn't bring myself to do it. Kinda makes it too real that I even need a gun. Besides, I'm right-handed and right-eye dominant — and I currently got *no* right eye."

"I get that. Some advice?"

"Yes sir."

"First, clean the damn thing. It's dirty as hell. Then teach Bev how to use it. Then practice. Clean it again. Then put it away. Especially with the baby comin'. Don't take long before they can reach stuff."

"Jeff says *yes sir*," Bev mimicked.

It earned a grin from the sheriff. He handed back the gun. "Gotta run now."

After he left, we kept watching as Erma's new trailer got

parked. A little while later, Miss Bishop came out from the diner and got in her car. She waved as she pulled out.

As she weaved through the trucks, I asked Bev, "How's Trish?"

Bev scowled. "She's a hot mess. Mumma gave her hell worse than me. Don't think it'll do any good, though. It's scary, actually."

The Toter truck left and they started leveling the new trailer. The guy in the white hard hat was walking around, pointing and barking orders. The wheels that got the trailer there got removed.

"I'll tell ya what's scary," Jeff said, his voice serious. "Since Bev came into my life ... and I'm grateful ... right? Well, the day we met, she was probably standin' right here in front of an empty Waffle House ... and askin' herself if she should drive down the hill to my office. I mean, from up here ... I'm bettin' she hesitated comin' down to the office."

"Yep. I was standin' right here," Bev nodded. "And yeah, it looked sketchy."

"There was that deep gulley between here and the office," I added. "But ... you were on a mission that day."

"I remember," she said, turning to face that way. "I almost decided to leave."

"Why didn't you?" Jeff asked.

"That dogwood tree," she said while pointing to it. "Big tree, for a dogwood. Nothin' around it."

"So you took that as a sign?" Jeff pondered.

"Well ... sorta. It's a sacred tree, and all that. But I wasn't thinkin' of it that way. I guess it moved the needle enough for me to say 'what the hell' and give it a try."

"My dad planted that tree. It's like *he* brought you to me."

"That's really sweet," she purred, wriggling back under his arm.

Just then a truck pulled up with a small trailer attached, and on the trailer a brand-new golf cart. It turned in and headed down to the Smiths.

"I guess Miss B got tired of walkin' up the hill," I smiled.

"Maybe they'll come up for breakfast," Bev said, hopefully.

Another truck turned in, this one with fencing.

"A day late and a dollar short," Jeff complained. "Would've been nice to have a gate."

"Still," I said, "it's fun watching what money can do."

I turned to Bev. "Can you and Trish work on the pies? I need to move my stuff in and Jeff's stuff out."

"Sure," Bev said.

The door to my trailer was locked. Not sure how Trish thought she would get back in. I used my key to get in and I didn't plan to leave it for her.

The place was a mess — even messier than before. Clothes and stuff sittin' or thrown everywhere. And she'd only been there overnight. A lot of my clothes were tossed in a corner. I couldn't tell what was clean and what wasn't, so I just put everything in bags and drove down to the Lost Sock Laundromat in Princeton. Then I headed over to Walmart and splurged on a new set of sheets and a laundry basket.

I moved into my new apartment, then put Jeff's clothes in the bags and took them to Bev's trailer. I was done before noon. I decided to shower and change before handling my new sheets. It felt great to be clean and in clean clothes. It helped wash away the memory of the night before. The new sheets smelled fresh, and I couldn't resist lying down for a minute.

I fell asleep as my head hit the pillow.

When I woke up, I first had to figure out where I was. The fresh sheets reminded me I was in Jeff's apartment. I would probably always think of it as Jeff's apartment.

The next thought was: *Why did I wake up? Was someone coming up the steps?*

I listened. There was nothing but silence, and it was dark. I must have slept through the night. I sat up and looked at my phone. It was 9:38. *Wait, shouldn't it be light by now?* I looked again: 9:38, Friday, August 28. That meant it was p.m., not a.m.!

I stood up and stretched, then walked over and turned on the lights. So … I was up, rested, showered, and dressed with nowhere to go. I looked out the window. In the darkness I could see the outline of the diner. It was the only thing in view, but no lights on. Bummer, I was hungry.

I walked down the steps slowly, wondering if there would be someone with a gun waiting for me. There wasn't. I went outside. Bev's trailer was dark and quiet. So was mine. Everything was quiet and peaceful, the moon and stars well worth a long stare.

Walking across the lot, I came up to the new fencing and gate. The halfmoon gave enough light to examine how the wide gate would slide sideways on rollers when pulled by a very long bicycle chain. It was closed, and that was nice to see, but it came between me and the diner. There was also a regular gate on the fence behind the diner, so I could get in through the back door.

I turned on all the lights and wandered around. I took a minute to enjoy the fact that I owned all this stuff. It wasn't paying for itself, but for now, I was livin' the dream. I pictured myself showing it off to a cute girl.

But right now I was hungry so I walked behind the counter. "What to fix, what to fix?" I said out loud. "Maybe a hamburger? Eggs maybe? We got lots of eggs."

My conversation with myself was interrupted by headlights from a car that pulled in. I couldn't see who it was, and it scared me. *One of Snake's friends?*

I reached for my phone. *Call 9-1-1? Call Jeff?*

Then it occurred to me that the door to the diner was locked. *Or should be.* I froze.

The headlights turned off and the lights coming from the diner gave me a good look at the driver. It was a middle-aged woman, and a small kid in the back seat. She looked as concerned about me as I was about her. But she got out and opened the back door to get her kid. I walked around the bar and unlocked the door.

She walked in, holding hands with her son. She wasn't ugly, but masculine looking — no makeup, a square jaw, not a hint of a smile. She stood straight and stiff, looked around as if inspecting the place. I wasn't sure if she approved.

"I can't believe there's a restaurant open this late out in the middle of nowhere."

I couldn't help but smile. "Well, it's not open, really. I own the place and live down the hill here. I'm hungry and thinkin' about fixin' something to eat."

Her expression didn't change.

"Anyway, I was thinkin' hamburgers, so I'd be glad to throw on a few for you and your son. I'm Chad, by the way."

"We've had dinner," she said flatly, but her son was tugging on her arm. "I was just looking for a place to park for the night." She stood there as if that explained everything.

"There's hotels down in Princeton," I offered, "if that's the way you're headed."

I wondered why she didn't offer her name. Maybe just being careful?

"No. Just looking for a place to park for the night."

"Okayyy." I was getting a little frustrated. "I own the place, like I said, and you're welcome to park here." I looked at my watch. "A lady will be coming in around three in the morning … to start cookin' the biscuits. Her coming in would probably wake you up. But it's up to you."

She stood there, thinking. Her son kept tugging on her sleeve. She leaned down and he whispered. I heard the word "hungry."

"I'm going out back to start the grill," I said again. "Sure you don't want me to throw on some burgers for you?"

She hesitated, then, "Sure."

I started the grill outside, then came back in and pulled out the hamburgers, buns, tater chips, and some condiments. I set everything on the diner bar.

"Go ahead and get your buns ready. I'll be cookin' the burgers out back. Want something to drink?"

"Water will be fine," was her brief reply.

"Okay, plates and cups are under here behind the counter. Help yourself." I turned and went out.

When I returned with the burgers, the lady was seated at a booth with her son across the table. They each had a plate, a napkin, and a glass of water. Her son was gobbling down tater chips. It was obvious I wasn't invited to sit with them. I served the hamburger patties on a plate and took a seat at the counter.

We all ate in silence.

They finished eating before I did. The lady got up, came over and asked, "How much?"

I sat my burger down, finished chewing, then turned to her and replied. "I don't really know how to do a sale. I wasn't planning on chargin' anyway."

Her expression never changed. "I'm just homeless, not needy. How much?"

I pointed to a menu sitting on the bar top. "The prices are there on the menu, but I really don't know how to do credit cards. Just pay what you want."

I was kinda done with her.

She pulled a ten-dollar bill out of her purse and set it on the bar top. "I appreciate dinner, but I don't think I will stay here tonight. The lady coming in might be alarmed to see a strange car parked outside."

"You might be right," I said. I was grateful for her concern.

She and her son used the restrooms and then headed out the door. I followed to lock the door behind them, but then had a thought. I walked out and got her attention.

"Ma'am?" She turned around. "This fence right here is new, just went in today. The gate opens with a code, but I don't know how it works yet. But I will tomorrow. I could give you a code, and you could stay here, behind the diner … overnight, if you wanted."

She stepped toward the gate to get a better view, still no change in her expression. "Who lives in there?"

"Well, up here, on that slab right there," I said, pointing, "now and then a big RV sits there. Two ladies, very good friends of ours. That trailer there … my friends Jeff and Bev. It's Bev's mom that comes in early to open the diner. Next trailer is Trish. She's a friend of Bev's. Then my place. And further down the hill … can't really see it from here … is where the Smiths are. Really nice people. And we hope to fill it with more campers. But we're just gettin' started."

She nodded but didn't say anything.

"I'm just tryin' to help," I offered.

"I'll keep it in mind," she said, and walked to her car.

Nice talk, lady.

I wasn't hungry anymore, or sleepy. The night was warm with just a hint of a chill when a breeze rustled the trees. I locked the front door, turned off the lights, and walked out the back. I followed the stakes that JB placed for the trench diggers. The ground had a slight pitch at first. About a third of the way down, in the middle, was a set of four large boulders. There was something about them that pulled me closer.

With a running start, I scrambled up the closest boulder and got to the top. I sat and looked around. From there, the lot was much steeper. It would be harder to get campers down there, and the view got worse and worse the further down you went. I wondered what JB had in mind for that part of the lot. I tried to picture campers parked below me. It was so quiet I could occasionally hear trucks on I-77 far, far away.

From the silence came a voice. "Chad?"

I flinched. Then froze.

Was I going to die?

CHAPTER 18

"Didn't mean to scare you," Marvin said, apologetically.

First time I ever heard him speak with any emotion. He came out from behind one of the other boulders.

"Marvin!" I exclaimed. "Ya scared me to death."

"Sorry. It was that or wait for you to leave. I should've waited."

"No, no. It's okay. I'm just edgy, ya know?"

"I *do* know. But you'll be okay. Really."

I wished I knew what he was talking about. "I hope you're right."

He walked closer and raised his hands. "Getting hurt by others leaves small scars," he stated. "Hurting other people is what leaves big scars."

I nodded, now more aware of what haunted him. "I'm sorry."

He nodded, leaned back against the other boulder, crossed his arms.

"Thank you for saving my life," I said.

"Sorry it came down to that. Wasn't supposed to go that way. The deputy leavin' … that threw us off."

"Where were you?"

He pointed. "Just off the church parking lot. Walker was

watching Snake's GPS signal and we figured he'd pull in there. But then I heard the deputy's engine start up. He left and Snake came right in. I had to run like hell to get over here."

"Wow," I said.

"It was close," he added.

I nodded. "Too close."

We sat there and took in the night and the quiet.

After a while, I asked, "What took so long with Snake leavin'?"

Marvin snorted. "Oh, that. What a loser. He got his hands and legs untied in no time. Almost too quick. I was afraid he'd figure out he was being played. But the knot on the hood … over his head, gave him a problem. The string wasn't any bigger than a shoelace. He tried to pull it off his head and that made the knot tighter. So then he tried to untie the knot but got too impatient. Then he tried to tear the hood fabric. Got so agitated he wore himself out. Finally, he picked at the knot long enough to get it untied."

"Did he see the trailer burnin'?"

"Oh yeah. It was nothing but flames at that point."

"Then he ran?"

"Like a scalded dog."

"And he didn't see you?"

"Course not."

Just like me to ask a stupid question.

I looked up at the night sky and found the Big Dipper. "It's nice out here. Peaceful."

He didn't reply.

I followed the two stars on the Big Dipper that point to the

North Star. It was just above my mountain range. "Wait a minute," I said, holding up my hand as a guide. "The North Star is directly above the rock you're leaning on."

Marvin crossed his arms. "Just noticed that, did ya?"

"And these other two boulders," I said, looking around. "They're pretty much at a right angle. So they're lined up east and west."

"You're catching on," he said earnestly. "Anything else?"

I looked around. The four boulders were about the same size, like four Volkswagens poking out of the ground. They were about ten feet apart. They weren't exactly the same shape, but very close. And they were where the ground started sloping down more steeply. "Nope," I replied.

"You don't feel the energy here?"

"Um … no," I replied. "No … I don't. You?"

He nodded. "I do."

"Like … supernatural?"

"I just feel it. Can't explain it. So does Jeff's dog. He never walks through, always around the rocks. What's his name, by the way?"

"The dog? Bear."

"Perfect. That's what I call him — 'Ours Blanc,' French for White Bear. After all, he's French, right?"

"I guess so. You speak French?"

"And a little Spanish."

"Okay." That was all I could think to say.

I looked down at the boulder I was perched on. It was the south boulder. Then over to the one Marvin was leaning against. It was the north boulder, with the North Star just sitting above.

"When I was at the bank," I began, "makin' an offer on this land, I told them there was a sacred Indian burial site in the middle of the junkyard. Now here I am in the middle of what was a junkyard. I have no idea where I got that idea, but now it makes me wonder …"

Marvin turned to leave. "You're getting there. I'll leave you be to figure it out."

"How about a hint?" I begged.

He stopped, stood still for a moment, and looked up at the sky. "Okay," he said, without looking back. "You'll know you're there when you realize that some questions don't have answers."

Then he disappeared into the darkness.

Nice talk, Marvin.

I continued to watch the sky for hours. With the North Star perched over the boulder, I began to see how the rest of the stars were rotating around it, counterclockwise. I had never sat long enough to notice. It added to my wish to go hiking. Not just a want.

I needed some time in the open.

Did these compass rocks send me a message to stump Mr. Butthead? Would they even care who bought this property?

"Hey rocks," I asked out loud. "Did you send me a message to stump the banker guy?" No answer.

But I did hear car tires on the gravel in front of the diner. I looked at my watch. Must be Miss Bishop. I stood up, brushed off the back of my shorts, and came down off the boulder.

Nice talk, rocks.

"Oh, hi," Miss Bishop said as I entered the diner. She seemed pleased to see me. "I was wondering who left the back door open."

"Me," I said. "Reporting for duty."

We got right to work. I was catching on to cookin' without measuring anything. In no time we had biscuits, bacon, and sausage cookin'.

About an hour later Bev came in, cheerful as ever. "Good morning, everybody! Order up! Just got it as I was walking over."

The order was for two sausage and egg biscuits. Half an hour later, another order for two sausage and egg biscuits. Bev's phone didn't chime after that. With plenty of biscuits cooked, Miss Bishop was fixin' to leave.

"I'll be off tomorrow," she announced, hiking her purse strap over her shoulder. "Probably won't need me next week. We'll talk about it."

Bev nodded. "Thank you, Mumma. Love you."

"Love you too. Bye-bye, Chad."

Bev and I fixed ourselves breakfast and took our usual booth. It started to get light outside. The sun would be up soon, and then a while longer to crest the mountains.

"How'd you sleep last night?" she asked, dabbing her scrambled eggs.

"Heck," I replied, "I laid down around one or two in the afternoon and fell asleep. Woke up and thought it was morning."

"We figured you were takin' a nap or something. We would've checked on you but didn't want to bother you … or scare you."

"Appreciate that. Anyway, I got up around ten. Came over here and fixed me a hamburger." I told her about the homeless lady, and

Marvin.

"You've had a full day already," she said, munching down on toast.

"So what'd I miss yesterday?" I asked.

She rolled her eyes. "Me trying to get Trish to help out. She's such a diva. Even complained that she has to work and doesn't get paid."

"Where is she now?"

"Dunno, probably sleepin' in."

"Well, it is an honor to have her here," I mocked. "She even redecorated my trailer for me."

"Really?"

"Yeah, I'm not fussy about keepin' my place all nice … but she is a mess.

"I know what you mean. When we were little, she'd come for a sleepover. Next day Mumma would make me go through the house and pick up and put up."

"What else I miss?"

"The new gate went in. JB was showin' us how it works. Ya know, at first I thought it was dumb. But now, I really like it. Makes me feel safer. And like, with Trish livin' here, you never know who's gonna show up."

She pulled out her phone and tapped on it, grinning. "Watch this. Watch the gate."

All I had to do was lean over enough to see the gate outside.

It was sliding open. Then it stopped and closed again.

"Love it!" she gushed. "I'll put the app on your phone.

"And …" she continued, "I ordered to-go boxes for the pies. And I'm thinking of checking in with some local grocery stores about selling the pies. If, that is, we can get enough apples peeled."

She leaned in. "I'm having personnel problems with you and Trish. It's affecting production."

"Oops," I muttered.

Just then a truck pulled in. I got a glimpse of Jeff coming out to meet it.

"What's that about?" I asked.

"Dunno, but he seems very excited about it."

Her phone chimed. She looked at it, swiped, swiped again. "Well, well," she said. She looked up. "We have a standing order for Mondays. Twenty Sausage Apple Biscuits for Bo Schmitz … even gave his credit card number. He's going to give one to every employee that gets to work on time on Mondays. Now *that's* how you deal with personnel problems."

"Well, there ya go," I nodded. "I just need incentives."

She shook a fist at me. "I'll give ya —"

She stopped. Erma was walking across the front of the diner. She waved as she passed. She came in and walked up to us. Bev slid over to make room.

"Thank you, dear," she said, plopping down into the seat. "Go ahead and finish eating. I need a favor when you're done."

"I can finish later," I said.

"Oh no, no rush. I just need help with some boxes in my trunk. The moving company came yesterday and brought in most everything. I just have some personal, breakable things I wanted to handle myself."

"I'll bet you're looking forward to getting back in your home," Bev assumed.

"Oh, don't you know it. Walker, bless his heart. He means well. I stayed at his house, you know, while he was burning mine down." She chuckled. "His house is nice, but too big. I kept getting lost! And most of the time him and Piper were busy with getting that Snake boy to leave.

"Chad, I hear he gave you *quite* a scare."

"Yes ma'am. Very."

"I'm so sorry. So much evil in this world. I deal with it every day."

"Hope it was nice taking a break from it for a few days," Bev said.

Erma put her elbows on the table and rested her chin on her hands. "Walker put together a nice dinner for me and Piper last night. He tried, bless his heart … but it was an awful night. He had lobster flown in from Maine, even talked Marvin into doin' the cookin'. You probably didn't know … Marvin is an accomplished chef. Studied in France for two years, before … you know …

"We ate in the formal dining room, with formal place settings, and drank expensive wine." Her eyes watered.

I handed her my napkin. "Lobster flown in from Maine … sounds just *awful*."

She dabbed her eyes with my napkin. "All that money up there, all the stuff it can buy. But my friend Betty not there to enjoy it. It's so sad. They were such a happy couple. A team, really. Ended up Walker and I just sobbing. We lost our appetites … and all that food went to waste. Made it awkward for Piper, so she slipped out."

Erma pushed back in her seat and took a deep breath. "Sorry to get into all that, but I guess it helps to talk about it."

"Not at all." Bev put her arm around Erma's shoulders. "I'm so glad you shared that with us."

Erma blew her nose and put her hands on her lap. "My story does have a happy ending, if you'll indulge me."

"Please," Bev begged.

"Well, dinner was a bust. Walker and I were a mess. So we grabbed the wine and our wine glasses and went out to Betty's gravesite. We sat down on the grass next to her and talked to her — for hours. We talked and drank and laughed and cried. It ended up being a very special evening. Very special."

"Wow," was all I could think of to say.

My appetite was gone because of the lump in my throat. Same for Bev. She pushed her plate away.

"Didn't mean to spoil your breakfast," Erma said, apologetically.

"No worries," I said. "I'm so glad to be your neighbor."

"And we need to make a point of bringin' over leftovers," Bev decided. "No sense in anything going to waste."

Erma smiled. "Oh, you must come see my new trailer. I'll be *much* better at feeding the children."

That said, we walked over to her place. I lifted a box out of her trunk and she opened the door for us. I was expecting a fully furnished home.

The door was in the middle of the trailer. Erma went in first, then stepped aside. Then Bev, who exclaimed, "Oh my!" when she entered. I followed.

To the right, there was no furniture. Instead, a stainless-steel counter ran along the back wall with shelving above it. On the front wall there was nothing but storage racks floor to ceiling.

"Just put the box on the counter," Erma instructed.

Bev was walking around and looking at all the empty shelves and storage racks. Erma followed her. "Isn't it great? Now I can prep my food bags for the children. I got storage racks over here … lots of storage. And I can keep it all organized with bags and boxes on these shelves over the counter. Isn't this the best?"

"This isn't a living room," I proclaimed. "It's a food-processing plant."

Erma cupped her hands together. "It makes me so happy. As long as I can get food in here, I can give aid to those in need. And there is a *lot* of need out there."

Bev stopped gawking at everything just long enough to face Erma. "You. Are. Amazing. I feel so … uncharitable. Just worryin' about myself instead of others."

Erma waved her off. "Don't be. Come see my kitchen." It was to the left of the front door. And it didn't look like a typical kitchen. It had a floor-to-ceiling fridge and a floor-to-ceiling freezer. With them and an oversized stove there was very little room left for cabinets.

"This kitchen is all about function," Erma said, proudly.

"You are too much." I was moved.

"Oh, I do have a little piece of heaven back here," she grinned. Just past the kitchen was a door. Not a flat, cheap door. A six-panel cherry door. She opened it and exclaimed, "Ta-da!"

Her bedroom was wallpapered in a pink floral print. The floor was oak hardwood with a Persian rug that covered most it. The antique-looking dresser matched the mirror frame and bedside table.

The bed was a simple, single bed. No headboard. A large TV spanned the front wall.

"I told Walker not to put that thing in here," Erma grumbled, pointing to it. "I don't watch TV."

"Might come in handy," Bev offered. "Catch up on the weather now and then so you don't run out in a snowstorm."

"Maybe," Erma replied, half-heartedly. "Come see the best part — the bathroom. I gave Walker permission to do whatever he wanted and, of course, he overdid it."

I peeked in. The floor, the countertop, and the backsplash were white marble. The cabinets were bright white. The walls were an aqua color that somehow went well with the shaggy turquoise rug. On the back wall sat a large Jacuzzi tub. I hesitated walking in. I might get something dirty.

Bev pushed past me. "This is amazing, Erma! I'm *sooo* jealous, but happy for you."

Erma nodded. "My little piece of heaven. The floor is heated, and the water heater is oversized to fill the tub. I will spend some quality time in here."

"You deserve it," Bev smiled.

Erma shrugged. "It's very nice. No room for a washer and dryer, though. Just couldn't justify the space. I pass by laundromats when I'm out delivering, so it's not a bother."

Bev hugged her. "Erma, you are the most wonderful, most kind person."

"I'm the most blessed. And sometimes the most frustrated. Some of the children, when the husband is there, don't get fed because the husband will try to bargain for a pack of cigarettes or something. Their dad will say, 'No food comes in unless cigarettes or beer come in.' I have to just walk away when that happens. It's so sad."

We made our way back into the kitchen. I went out to retrieve more boxes. They were full of lamps and picture frames and fragile knick-knacks. We stayed and helped her hang the pictures.

On our way out, Bev stopped at the door. She turned to Erma. "The husbands that want cigarettes, what if you bribed them with a coupon for a free biscuit?"

"Make it a Miss Baker's Sausage Apple Biscuit," I added. "They're awesome."

"Might work," Erma replied. "But no, they'd want one *every* visit."

"Then we'll give them one every visit," Bev said. "Might even help get the word out."

"There's one family in particular," Erma said. "I desperately need to get them fed. I could try it with him and see if it works."

"I'll make up the coupons," Bev said, and we left.

The sun had come up and the hill across the street was in full color. Not in sunlight yet. The sun was still climbing up the back of the mountains. As we got to the diner, JB was with a guy working on the gate. Bev went in and I walked over to JB.

"Morning," I said. I shook JB's hand. He introduced me to Frank, but Frank's hands were too greasy for a handshake. The gate was open so I walked through.

"Frank is making adjustments on the chain tension," JB explained.

"Takes some tweaking to get it just right."

"Got a minute?" I asked.

"Sure. Frank is doing all the work. I'm just watching."

We walked down the hill to the boulders. I stood behind the south boulder where it lined up with the north boulder. "What do you have in mind for these rocks?" I asked.

"Well, I'm glad you asked. It gets steep past here. And not much of a view. I'll run the plumbing and electrical down there, but I'm thinking everything below us should be campsites for the trail riders. Maybe put a gate at the bottom for them to come straight in off the trail. So, everything up from here for the big RVs, and everything below us for the trail riders. Maybe even some tent sites down in the woods."

I nodded. "I like it. Perfect. And the rocks? What about the rocks?"

"Too big to dig up. It's a nice rock formation. Gives the place character, don't you think?"

"I do. Can you put something around them to keep all the construction away from them?"

"I could. Good thing you said something because the plans call for a pipe to run right through here."

"I don't want anything on them or around them," I replied sternly. Then I realized how I was coming across to him. He was looking at me as if concerned.

"Stand over here with me," I pointed. "See how this rock and that rock line up? Last night, I noticed that the North Star sits directly in line with these two rocks."

"You're sure it was the North Star, right? It's not a big star, you know."

"The Big Dipper was pointing at it."

"Wow! Okay, I'll come and look at it tonight."

"You're really excited about this," I said, flatly.

He smiled. "Gotta love a mystery."

"JB, I didn't mean to stir up this much … you know … interest. I just wanted to make sure no one digs here, or even around these rocks."

"I was about to say maybe we should get a metal detector over here, but —"

I cut in. "Then we'd want to dig. I don't want to dig here."

He nodded. "I respect that. You're right."

He looked back at the mountain ridge. "Might want to keep this under your hat. People get wind of this, they'll want to come and chip a piece of rock off as a souvenir."

By the time we got back up to the gate, Frank was gone. His bill was rolled up and stuck in the fence. JB took it out, folded it, and put it in his pocket. He shook my hand.

"Thank you, Chad."

"Comin' in for breakfast?" I asked, hopefully.

"No thanks. Lou and Peanut are coming in today. I have to help Beatrice get ready. Always a big deal when they show up."

As he walked down the hill, Jeff was coming up. He looked like the Jeff back in high school — no beard and no hair on his head. And no gun. I mimicked like I was stroking a long beard.

"You look better without the beard," I informed him.

He came over and we fist-bumped. "That's what Bev sez. Sleep okay?"

"I caught up, I guess. But now I've been awake since last night."

"You're nocturnal now, like Bear. He could have kept you company, but he's still stickin' close to me. I guess he'll get back to his chickens soon as I get better."

The truck from earlier was coming up from the shop. Jeff waved as it went by.

"What's that all about?" I asked.

He reached in his back pocket, pulled out a thick envelope.

"That was all about five thousand dollars," he grinned. "Let's get some breakfast and I'll tell you all about it."

As we walked into the diner, Bev was coming from the back room. "Still no orders," she said, sadly. "Chad, did you tell Jeff about the order from Bo?"

"No."

"Jeff, we got a standing order for Monday mornings. Twenty Apple Sausage biscuits. Bo is going to give them to employees that get to work on time."

"Nice," said Jeff. "Can I get some? Like three maybe? I can pay." He held up the envelope as he slipped into his booth facing the door.

"What's that?" she asked.

"Five grand, in cash."

"Three biscuits comin' up!" she exclaimed.

"And one for me?" I asked.

Jeff gobbled down one of the biscuits as we waited to hear the story. The stack of bills was out of the envelope and sitting next to the window. Bev slid in next to him.

"Hey there, big boy." She looked at the money. "Show you a good time?"

"Hell," I crowed, "for that much *I'll* show you a good time." That earned a glare with his good eye.

He finished chewing and sipped some coffee. "So, yesterday I finally found the junk car guy that got the Mercedes. He was *very* interested in a Mercedes engine that I just happened to have in the shop. Made him a deal — take the engine and all the junk cars I still got down the hill."

"Five grand for a used engine?" I asked.

"Oh, hell yeah. He's got the salvage title, so the car is legal. With the engine it's worth a bundle. Deal of a lifetime for him. That's how I got him to agree to gettin' my cars outta here. They're in the way, but I'm too banged up right now to get it done." He started in on the second biscuit.

"Score," I said. "Five thousand dollars."

"Of Peyton's money," Bev added.

"Oh yeah. There's that. Maybe we could deduct what your car is worth since, you know, she has your car."

"How much is my car worth?"

Jeff mumbled with his mouth full. "Couple hundred."

Bev leaned back and crossed her arms. "You two gonna make me the heavy about this? I'm as tempted as you are. Geez, I can't believe the money that flies around this place. Carolyn and Vicki, then the Smiths, and Mr. Bryson up the hill. And now Peyton's money just sittin' here."

Jeff paused. "You think about it, this fat wad of money represents the other world ... the friends you just said that have money. Good friends, but in a world we don't live in."

"And we've eaten more biscuits than we've sold today," I added.

"We should put that money in the bank and forget about it so we don't start pickin' at it —" Bev said. Just as she was saying it, her red car drove up and parked.

Peyton was inside, smiling. She waved. "— or not."

Bev slid off the seat and met Peyton at the door. They hugged and Bev made a big fuss about Peyton's new haircut. She must have had it fixed from our hack job. They were talking at the same time.

"So good to see you … are you okay … come sit … can't wait to tell you … you hungry? … love your new haircut."

Bev slid in next to Jeff, and Peyton slipped in across from them.

I looked out the window. "We're not expecting anybody to come lookin' for you, are we?" I asked as I sat down.

"Oh no, we're all good," she replied. "Thanks to you, Chad."

Jeff dropped his biscuit, but just for exaggeration. "Not another Chad-to-the-rescue story." He winced. "You're gonna give the guy a big head."

"Want some breakfast?" Bev asked.

"No, no thank you," Peyton replied. "Jeff, what happened to you?"

We gave her the rundown on Snake, the fight, Snake comin' in, the hanging, and especially, Marvin's help.

Then Bev reached across Jeff, picked up the stack of cash, and placed it in front of Peyton. Peyton looked at it, then looked at Bev. Jeff explained the sale of the engine.

"You could've gotten way more for the car," he concluded, "but not without a title."

"You're right. My husband knew it didn't have one. He won it in a poker game. He probably knew it was stolen but didn't care. That's how he rolled."

"And he's not chasing you anymore," I said, hopefully.

"No, and really … *you* deserve the money. You made it happen. I wouldn't have got a penny for it."

"Don't make it hard on us givin' you *your* money," Bev begged. "We could sure use it, but right is right and wrong is wrong. You know us, and how we roll."

Peyton hesitated, then carefully put the cash in the envelope. "Let me think about it." She looked at Bev. "What would you do with the money?"

Bev replied right away. "Put it in the bank."

Peyton looked at Jeff. "And *you*?"

He smiled. "I'd buy me a bitchin' new eye patch."

Peyton smiled, then turned to me. "And *you*?"

I thought about it and figured I would answer honestly. "I'd buy a commercial-grade washer and dryer."

"Keep the money," Bev insisted, "and tell us how Chad helped."

Peyton placed the envelope in her purse. "I'll keep thinking about this but thank you. All of you. But *especially* Chad."

She grinned at Jeff. He rolled his one eye.

"I see you two are out of the closet," she winked.

"Okay, now it's *my* turn to drop something," I said. "You knew they were a thing? Hell, *they* didn't know they were a thing."

"How's the song go?" she asked. "Stand just a little too close, stare just a little too long? It was so obvious."

Bev scooted up against Jeff and rested her head on his shoulder. He put his head on top of hers. They gave Peyton a short version of their engagement.

"Now tell us what Chad did," Jeff grinned, "so we can get it over with."

"Well, you drove me down the trail to the road. Chad pulled up in the car. It was so surreal, and I was scared to death. Chad slipped out from the passenger side and I slipped in. And as I got in, he asked me, 'What's your trail name?' I told him and drove off, didn't give it much thought.

"So I made it to I-64, and from there into Kentucky. I checked into a hotel and was satisfied I got away clean. Next day, I drove west all day and checked into another hotel. I felt safe. But then I thought: *Wait a minute. This isn't a hotel room, it's a jail cell! And I deserve better.*

"Not only that. I don't need my husband's money. I mean, it's *my* money too. But do I really want to be tied to him? I don't need him, and I can take care of myself! After all, I hiked the Appalachian Trail and that's sayin' something. So right then and there I called him up and told him I'd sign the divorce papers."

"That made him happy?" Bev asked. "He won't be chasing you?"

"I asked him about that, and he gave me some song and dance about tracking me like it didn't mean anything, but I think he was pissed about me having a mind of my own. And just to make sure, the Parkers sent him a copy of the pictures Bev took of me, and a signed affidavit that he assaulted me. If they don't hear from me every few months, and can't get in touch with me, they will take him to court."

"What if you just die first?" I asked.

"That's exactly what he asked. I told him if I die first, same thing — the affidavit goes to court. So he better hope I stay well. He didn't like that. Either way, I'm not going to live in fear. I can make money when I need to, but right now … I'm going hiking!"

"So what is your trail name?" Bev asked.

"Fakahwee."

"Oh yeah," Jeff exclaimed, "an ancient, now extinct tribe indigenous to West Virginia!"

"Don't make me hurt you," Bev kidded. "You know there are no tribal lands in West Virginia."

"Was too. Brave and proud, they were. And nomadic, but they kept getting lost. Right Chad?"

I nodded, knew what was coming from Jeff.

"Thus their war cry, *Where the Fak Ah We!*"

I was amused. Bev was too but tried not to show it. She looked at Jeff with a scowl, then at Peyton with a scowl, then Jeff, then Peyton.

Peyton grinned. "I earned the name. I took a wrong turn on the first day, on the approach trail no less."

"So you plan to go hiking?" Bev confirmed.

"Yes. After all, I know almost all the wrong turns."

"Kinda late to start now," I piped up, "At either end."

"Oh, I've done the trail. I've got nothing to prove. I plan to start here and hike north, then turn around when I hit cold weather. That is, unless I meet a group I like. I'll be hitting all the south bounders thru-hiking. If I run into a group I like, I'll just turn around and come back with them."

"You rock," Jeff said with admiration.

"You guys still have the jewelry I left?" she asked.

"Sure," I replied. "I can run and get 'em now if you like."

"Please, yes."

I dug up the toolbox, pulled out the metal box inside, and retrieved the plastic bag. By the time I got back the three of them were laughing and cackling like old friends. I sat next to Peyton and gave her the bag. She pulled out the scarves and draped them around her neck. Then she put the bag in her lap and rummaged through the jewelry. She pulled something out and hid it in her hand. She reached over and put it in Jeff's hand and closed his hand so Bev and I couldn't see it.

"Now," she ordered him, "do it right this time."

He peeked in his hand, then looked at her. "You sure?"

She nodded.

He turned to Bev, opened his hand and asked, "Bev, will you marry me?"

Bev looked down at the diamond ring, cupped her hand over her mouth, and started pumping tears. "No, No, No!" she cried. "I'd lose it! I'd sell it for rent money! I'd be a trainwreck worryin' about it! Oh, it is so beautiful! Peyton, please. Take it back, please!"

"Relax," Peyton said, ever so calmly. "It's fake. People with money don't buy real jewelry. They don't have to. It's one of the perks of being rich."

I could tell she was lying, and so could Jeff. As Bev stared at the ring, Jeff gave Peyton a slight nod, and I caught a glimpse of her giving him a wink in response. *It was real.*

Jeff took Bev's left hand and placed it on her quivering ring finger. Of course, it was a perfect fit. More tears ran down Bev's cheeks. "Dammit," she cried, "I can't see it anymore! My tears are making it blurry!"

Knowing Bev would come around and hug Peyton, I slipped

out of the booth. As Bev came and buried herself in Peyton's arms, Jeff mouthed "Thank you" to Peyton.

There were tears in her eyes, too.

After all the crying, Bev came back around to Jeff and hugged him. Then they took pictures of her hand. She texted them to her mom.

"The rest of this stuff," Peyton said while rummaging through the bag, "is just random jewelry. Bev, can you hang on to all this for me?" She pulled the scarfs off her neck and put them in the bag.

"Sure," Bev said, still staring at her ring.

"And I need a favor, Bev. Can I borrow your car for a few days?"

"You can *have* my car," Bev answered.

"You hangin' around a few days?" I asked.

"I'm waiting on a backpack. It's supposed to come in at the Princeton Post Office. In the meantime, I need to get provisions. Can you guys recommend a good hotel in Princeton?"

"You're not going anywhere," Bev said, happily. "You're stayin' right here with me and Jeff."

"Thought you might say that. Hoped you would say —"

We all saw it at the same time, a very large RV was slowing down and turning in.

Bev squealed. "It's Carolyn and Vicki!" She hopped up and ran out the door.

CHAPTER 19

Jeff and I smirked. I said it first, "That's *not* Carolyn and Vicki."

"Must be Lou and Debbie," Jeff nodded.

The RV stopped at the gate. I stood up and looked out the door. "There's Miss B comin' up the hill. Her golf cart is covered in balloons."

That got Jeff and Peyton up. We walked out to watch. Miss B waved at the RV, did a U-turn, and headed down the hill. The big RV followed.

Bev walked back to us. "They said to come down and say 'hi.' But first they want to get the camper set up."

"Might take a little while to get it just right," Jeff suggested. "Let's give 'em a few minutes."

Bev held up her ring and turned it to catch the light. "It's so pretty. Peyton, this is the most precious thing I've ever owned. Ever."

"Makes me happy seeing how much joy it gives you," Peyton said. Then she shook her head and smiled. "Can't believe you gave your car to a perfect stranger. You people are nuts!"

"True," Jeff agreed. "And have a problem with authority. People here get pushed around a lot by, you know, 'da man.' So we don't take kindly to men in suits bein' bossy."

Peyton nodded. "It's like another planet here." Then she noticed

Trish walking up.

Trish walked past us with her head down. "More of your rich friends coming in?" she mumbled with disdain. She walked into the diner.

Peyton turned to us with a question mark on her face. We shrugged. "Her name's Trish," Bev explained. "A friend of mine."

With her arms crossed, Peyton nodded, turned to face the campground and breathed in deeply. "It's *magic* out here," she sighed. "So peaceful … spiritual, really. Gives me hope my hike is a good idea."

I faced Bev. "Mommy, can I go hiking with Peyton? Please? For just a few days maybe?"

She answered with the stink eye. "Might as well. Can't get no work outta ya."

"Totally," Jeff agreed. "You're 'bout as useful as a back pocket on a T-shirt. Might wanna ask Peyton if she minds you holdin' her back, though."

"Oh, I'd love the company," Peyton gushed. "You guys will never know what you mean to me. You're giving and caring and sweet, and it is so very different from the toxic world I lived in." She kept gazing at the mountains and drew in another deep breath.

In my head I was flipping through pages of hiking gear I couldn't afford: tent, sleeping bag, backpack, other expensive goodies. Jeff was saying something was burning, but it didn't register until I looked over. Him and Bev were watching me.

"I smell it too," Bev said, smiling. "Earth to Chad, come in Chad."

"I was thinking about all the gear I would need," I said. "Not sure I can swing it."

"How far do you plan to hike?" Peyton asked.

"Hadn't thought about that. Couple days, maybe a week?

"We can share my cook stove, my water purification stuff, and my maps."

"I got a canvas backpack," Jeff offered.

"Ugh," Peyton replied. "Too heavy."

"Little, thin straps," he continued. "Put bra-strap dents in your shoulders."

"A blanket will do for a sleeping bag," Bev suggested. "The weather is warm."

"A tarp for a tent," Jeff added.

"But get a good sleeping pad," Peyton insisted. "You'll be glad you did."

"I hope to hike for real someday. Maybe a few things now will be a good thing. Hell, I wasn't expectin' Bev to let me go."

"Tell you what," Bev ordered, "get your butt inside and start peelin' apples. See how many pies we can turn out before you leave."

"I'll help," Peyton offered.

We all started back to the diner, but my phone rang so I held back to take the call. I knew it was Piper, and the conversation left me a little dazed.

As I walked in the diner, Trish was coming out. She had a scowl on her face again. Jeff was in his seat, on his phone. Peyton was peeling apples in the next booth.

I walked to the back to find Bev.

"Need your help." I started pacing back and forth. "Got a call from Piper. She asked me out."

"This might be a question for Jeff," she smiled.

"Might. Probably both of you." I stopped pacing. "Dinner at Greenbrier! And come back the next day. Did I miss something while takin' care of Mom? First date *overnight*? And why am I having doubts? She's hot … she's rich … she's … what the hell? I should go, right?"

"Wouldn't hurt," Bev smiled.

"Yeah, wouldn't hurt."

"You like her, right?" Bev was carving pieces off a block of frozen lard.

"How would I know? I just *met* her. And so far, she's amazing! You should've seen her playin' Snake. She was fearless. And she's smart. I like smart."

"You gonna keep lettin' him fish in the clouds?" Jeff drawled. He was standing in the doorway.

Bev looked up. "Figured he could take the long way 'round the barn 'til he figured it out for himself."

Jeff grinned and leaned against the door frame. "That might work for most folks. But with Chad here … well … you know."

I turned to face him. "You hear what we were talkin' about?"

"Enough to know you could get laid," he replied. "And you need to get laid."

"See?" Bev said. "It *is* a Jeff question."

"You'll need a tux," Jeff continued, "or at least a sport coat … collar shirt … tie."

"Dress slacks and a belt," Bev added.

Jeff took his turn, "Dress shoes and black socks. There's a dress code, you know. Any of that in your closet?"

"Nope," I answered.

"Notice the pictures of her up in the castle?" he continued.

"Nope."

Bev laughed. "He was too busy watchin' her butt."

"Yeah," Jeff agreed. "But if Chad *was* lookin' up, he'd have seen pictures of her all over the world. She likes to travel."

"She did say something about taking me to Greece someday. She has friends there."

"Yep," Jeff nodded. "I doubt she has many friends here."

"So I should *not* hook up with a good lookin' rich woman and travel the world?"

"Your decision," Bev smiled.

Jeff crossed his arms. "One to ten, how confident are you this diner will work?"

I looked around the room. "I'm fixin' to peel apples in a diner that's got no customers out front. I'd say barely hangin' on to a four."

"Well, if you end up with Piper, you will live in her world. You'll never know how your life would've turned out if you'd stayed here."

That said, he turned and limped back to his seat.

Even Bev stopped what she was doing. "Was that the first, second, or third ghost that visited Scrooge?"

"Dunno," I replied as my phone rang. "But he gave me my answer just in time."

I took the call and walked out back. After the call, I came back in.

Bev was busy with pie makin'. "So now, how we doin'?"

"I just told a beautiful, rich woman I'd rather stay here than travel the world."

She nodded. "If you had decided to go … and it worked out … I would've been happy for you. But for a minute there you scared me to death. The idea of you not bein' here …"

"I think you and Jeff could run this place just fine without me."

"Oh hell, we'd run it *better* without you in the way." She grinned. "Besides, now you know how it feels to be the girl. Your date wants to take you to dinner, expects sex, and you haven't a *thing* to wear."

As usual, I couldn't think of a comeback.

"Now get busy peelin' apples!" she commanded.

I sat down with Peyton and talked about what I really did want to do — walk for miles and miles in the mountains. It made peelin' apples less boring.

Although I liked Peyton, I didn't think of her as someone I'd hang with. At least not at first. She was older, refined, educated, and urban. All good things, but none compatible. But she was also down-to-earth and pleasant, and I was grateful to have her as my guide to the trail. We talked about provisions, equipment, accessories — and the weight of each piece.

I started callin' her Fakahwee, and she started callin' me WannaBe.

It bugged the crap outta Jeff and Bev — a plus.

We pumped out eighteen pies that day, and finished with eggs, bacon, biscuits, and coffee for dinner. Bev, Jeff, and Peyton kept talking, but I had been up since the night before. I left and headed over to my place, but laughter lulled me down the hill.

The two RVs faced each other and the two awnings covered the space in between, just like Miss B had said. Pink flamingo patio lights hung longways down the campers and crossways in between. The two couples sat in the middle talking and laughing and drinking. A propane firepit served as their campfire.

No one got up. I fist-bumped the newcomers and JB, and got a big hug from Miss B. Just as they said, Debbie was a peanut, like their name for her. Her face was cheerleader-grade cute. Her short, straight, strawberry hair was never still as she was always snapping her head back and forth to face whoever she was talking to, and she was always talking to somebody. She held a drink and a cigarette in one hand and pointed with the other, constantly. They could have named her Chipmunk. She was always moving — quickly.

Her husband Lou was the polar opposite. He was a black version of Frankenstein, minus the neck pegs. He moved slowly and mechanically. But there was a permanent smile on his face and he had a deep laugh. With each laugh he slapped a large hand on his knee. His other big hand was wrapped around a cup you could hardly see.

It was great to see friends so happy together. I wanted to stay, but I knew the magic of their party didn't include me. Still, I did have one task to take care of.

"Before I leave," I began, "have we come up with a name for the campground?"

"Not 'Debbie's March,'" Debbie quipped quickly. "JB was telling us about that. Can I veto that name?"

"It was my first choice," JB chided, pouting.

Miss B waved him off and laughed. "Don't worry, Chad. We have a list of names."

"We do?" JB asked.

"Well … did. The dog ate it."

"Did you see that dog!" Debbie yelled. "He is h-h-huge!"

"Dog?" Lou asked. "What dog?"

"You know *what* dog!" Debbie laughed. "Chad, what's your dog's name?"

"I don't have a dog," I answered, truthfully. That got a laugh out of all of them.

"Good one, Cabana Boy." Miss B raised her drink.

"Jeff has a dog," I conceded. "His name is Bear. Speaking of names …"

"Oh darn." Now Lou pouted. "We have to be serious for a minute."

"Okay," JB said, "I'll go first. Mountain View Campground."

Miss B put a finger in her mouth as if throwing up.

"Booooring," Lou drawled. "Lighthouse Campground. Like, Lighthouse Diner and Campground."

"Too safe," Debbie noted.

"Me next." Miss B raised her drink again. "Red Solo Cup Campground. Nice ring, right?"

Lou snickered. "Or Debbie's Red Solo Cup March Campground."

"Veto!" complained Debbie. "I really do *not* want to remember that day. Please, no. If anything, drop the Solo. It's redundant. Just Red Cup Campground."

"Okay," I turned to Debbie, "your turn."

"Um, Mountain View Campground."

"That's already one of the choices."

"Really?" she countered. "Who gave that one?"

JB smiled. "Me."

"Okay, then … Chad's Campground. Final answer. How's that?"

"We could vote on it," Miss B suggested.

"Vote on what?" Lou kidded.

That set them off again.

Their laughter was contagious. "I'm not gonna get a straight answer out of you guys tonight, am I?"

They collectively shook their heads.

I laughed and turned to leave. "I'll table it for now. Have a good night, y'all."

When I got to Jeff's apartment — as I would always call it — I was looking forward to a good night's sleep. I had been up for twenty-four hours, and that was long enough. I pulled off my clothes and got under my new sheets. I listened to the laughter from just down the hill. There would be calm conversation for a while, and then — a burst of laughter. Then calm conversation, then more laughter.

I figured sleep would slip in during the calm, but it didn't. If it was consistent, I might've had a chance, but it wasn't. They kept me awake for hours.

As if the noise wasn't enough, I couldn't help but think about my upcoming adventure. For the first time in my life, I was going on a vacation. Growing up, there was spring break, summer, and Christmas. None of them meant going anywhere for me. But it did mean pitching ball with Jeff and not going to school. That was reward enough.

But now I was taking off from work — even though I didn't have a job. And going somewhere special, although not Disney or a beach or far-away relatives. I couldn't help but daydream of walking down a path in the woods for miles and miles.

I don't know when I fell asleep, but it was daylight when I woke up. Good thing it was a Sunday. Weekends are slack for morning biscuits. I wouldn't be needed until lunch for the trail riders — if at all.

When I made it outside, Peyton was coming out of Bev's trailer. She smiled at me.

"Hey there, trail partner! You up for stocking up provisions today?"

"So ready!" I exclaimed as we walked up toward the diner. "Just as soon as I get some breakfast and find out what Bev's up to."

Walking inside, we found Jeff in the first booth, sitting on a pillow, leaning left. You could tell he was hurting, but his grin was reassuring. Peyton slid in across from him and I sat next to her.

"You two finally decide to join the living?" he asked, smiling.

"So Fakahwee is one of us now," I noted.

He nodded. "Oh yeah. After chewin' the fat with her last night, we dropped all manner of respect and politeness. She's part of the gang now, 'cept we still call her Peyton."

Bev walked in the from the back. "Morning! Breakfast anyone? We got biscuits ... since nobody else wants 'em today."

"No orders, then?" I guessed.

Bev shook her head. "Nope."

You could tell it made her sad.

After breakfast, Peyton and I drove to Princeton with the promise to stay in touch if Bev ran low on hamburger buns. First stop was Walmart for Ramen Noodles, dried fruit, nuts, granola bars, trail mix, tuna, and peanut butter. It was great not to have to think about what and how much to buy. Peyton had it all figured.

Then we drove to an outfitter store for some real hiking stuff. I bought a headlamp and a high-quality, lightweight sleeping pad. I looked at sleeping bags and tents but couldn't handle the cost. But we stopped in a thrift store and I scored a fairly nice backpack.

It took some getting used to the 'new' Peyton from the Peyton we first met. She was more carefree and happier. And her eagerness about hiking made me hanker to go even more.

We got back in time to help with the trail riders. The weather was perfect, not a cloud in the sky, and temps in the mid 80s. A perfect day for ridin' the trails and stoppin' in at the Lighthouse Diner for burgers. We made money and we made new friends.

Thank God for trail riders.

The next day, Monday, Jeff presented me with hiking poles made from a luggage rack off a Dodge Caravan and wrist straps from seatbelts. The poles weren't collapsible like Peyton's but way cool nonetheless. Bev, for her contribution, would follow us up to Daleville, Virginia, so I could drop off my truck. Then she would bring us back to Pearisburg to start our hike. That way we would be hiking toward my truck. No telling what day or what time we would get there.

We spent the afternoon peeling apples and making pies. I was getting more and more excited about my escape into the woods, but also feeling more and more guilt about it. Naturally, Jeff could sense what I was worryin' about. He brought it up as the four of us sat down for dinner that night. Peyton fixed the meal. She used leftover hamburger to make spaghetti. She and Bev brought out the plates, French bread, wine, and a bowl of the spaghetti.

"So Chad," Jeff began while adjusting his weight on his pillow. "You're probably frettin' about leavin' us high and dry back here in Tree Fork ... with crops that need tendin' ... fields that need plowin'. You know, tryin' to make ends meet."

Bev sat next to him, beaming.

I extended a hand, palm up, inviting her to add to his dig. "Well?" I asked.

She looked up at Jeff, then to me. "I've got so many wisecracks rolling around in my head, I can't think of which one to pick."

"Yeah, too easy," Jeff said, twirling noodles on his fork. He had to turn his head so his good eye could see what he was doing. "We should go ahead and let him off the hook."

Bev nodded. "Chad, you deserve to take some time off. You have the right, and it's the right thing to do. We'll be just fine, you know that."

"Ditto," Jeff said with his mouth full.

"Thanks guys. I was thinking that when I get back, though, I should look for a job. Right now, we need cash comin' in."

Bev shrugged. "Might be a good idea. I've been thinkin' maybe we should work on opening up at night."

I shrugged too. "You never know."

"While you're gone, I'm gonna do some door-to-door visits. Find out if people even know we're here and ask if they'd come for dinner. There's houses down Route 42 and up and down 19. You would think somebody would give us a try, just for the hell of it. We get trail riders and commuters, but nobody local."

"Sounds like a plan," I agreed.

"Meanwhile, Mumma is all set to be here for breakfast while you're gone. And Trish will help."

"If we can find a big enough cattle prod," Jeff smirked.

"Where is she, by the way?" I asked.

"In her ... ah ... *your* trailer," Bev answered.

Peyton finally spoke without looking up from her plate. "She doesn't like me."

"Or *anybody* with money, class, or intelligence," Jeff added. "Gets along with us just fine, though."

"How sad is that?" Bev said, rolling her eyes. "Just wait 'til she finds out she might get a roommate. I didn't tell you about that, did I?"

"No," I answered. "What gives?"

"I'll find out more tomorrow when Mumma gets here. My sisters might be moving in with us. My oldest sister, Brenda, has moved in with Daddy and Mumma. She's married and lives ... *lived* in Blacksburg. She has a good job at Virginia Tech, but the marriage is on the rocks."

"Abuse?" I asked.

"Not physical. Verbal and offensive. Abuse, just the same."

"It's what comes before physical," Peyton sighed. "Been there."

Bev looked at Peyton and nodded. "Her job is an hour drive from Mumma's, even longer from here. But she can work from home. Problem is, cell service at Mumma's is sketchy, so Brenda's been goin' to coffee shops and such. Might be better to live here. What do we get, one or two bars?"

"She can get four bars down the hill," Jeff said. "Remember

Chad? When Vicki got lost on the trail? I had four bars down there. And Mr. Bryson said it was for Marvin, so he could stay in touch."

"That trail rider that broke his leg?" I added. "I had four bars when I called 9-1-1."

Bev smiled. "I can see it now. Brenda sitting in the middle of the trail workin'."

"On mute when a rider comes through," I mumbled, my mouth full.

"Well, anyway, I wanted her to have the option. I hate the idea of her movin' back in with her husband if she doesn't have to. I don't like him."

"So she'd move in with Trish?" I asked.

"I don't know. Move in with me and Jeff or move in with Trish. Hell, I'm 'bout ready to kick Trish to the curb."

"What about your other sister?" I asked.

"Blair? She lives in Roanoke, alone, and hardly makes enough to get by. Works in the office at a hotel and handles payroll, billing … stuff like that. Well, her boss … her *married* boss … is making advances. And more and more he is letting her know she can easily be replaced."

"If she quits," Peyton interjected, "he'll give a poor reference."

"Seems like a job like that would make enough to live on," I said.

"It would," Peyton jumped in again, "if you were male. Do I sound … biased?"

"Oh no," I said mockingly, "not at *all*. And I apologize for bein' a guy."

"Same here," Jeff said. "And yeah, it ain't right … and nuthin' we can do about it."

"See why I love you two?" Bev quipped. "I can't think of any other men outside my family that I respect."

"Thank you," I said. "Not a high bar, though. So where would Blair live?"

"She has friends, and she can stay at Mumma's, depending on what Brenda does."

"And here," Jeff added, "dependin' on what we do with Trish. Or we can set up cots in the shop."

"I'm gonna push my luck here," Peyton started, "but you might have more problems than you can fix. I don't mean to be negative about it."

An uneasy silence followed that as the reality of Peyton's words sunk in.

CHAPTER 20

The Princeton Post Office opened Tuesday morning at 8:30 a.m. Peyton and I were there at 8:15. The tracking app told us her backpack was inside. The indifference and zombie slowness of the clerk was irritating, but Peyton put a positive spin on it.

"Just add it to the list of what we are leaving behind," she chirped, as we made our way back to Tree Fork. "All of this," she went on, pointing at the buildings we passed, "is fake. We, on the other hand, will enter a world of realness. Everything natural, pure, untainted, noble …and yet … indifferent."

"Wow," I said. "I'm in the presence of the master. I'll have to change my trail name to Grasshopper." I looked over to catch the grin on her face.

"I'm getting in touch with my inner Thoreau."

"Thoreau," I repeated, searching my brain. "That's the guy that lived in the woods … for fun."

"Ah," she said, delighted. "I will cast upon you more Thoreau than you can stand."

"Bring it on!" I exclaimed.

She licked her finger and held up an imaginary deck of index cards. She held a card up, shook her head, tossed it. "No." She held up another. It was getting hard to drive and watch her at the same time. She tossed another. "No."

She looked at another. "This one: *'Go confidently in the direction of your dreams! Live the life you've imagined.'"*

Turning to me, "How does that sound, WannaBe?"

"Nailed it. I like this guy."

She smiled. "You're gonna get so tired of me and Thoreau."

When we got back, Peyton began packing and repacking her new backpack. Apparently, there was only one right way to do it. For me, I stuffed mine full and called it good.

"Now unpack it," she ordered. I did as instructed. She picked through each item. "So ... you're not taking a change of socks?"

"Oops."

"Toilet paper?"

"Oops. Meant to add that."

"Where's your new headlamp?"

"In the bag in my truck. And my sleeping pad, come to think of it."

With our packs ready, Bev followed us to Daleville, Virginia. I parked my truck at the Holiday Inn and explained our plans to the clerk. Bev drove us back to Pearisburg. That leg took an hour and a half to drive.

It would take us a week to walk back.

Bev dropped us off where I met Trip and Slip. She hugged us both and drove off. I watched her little red car disappear behind a curve, then looked up at the ridge we would hike. Lost in thought, I listened to Peyton's footsteps in the gravel behind me.

"Peyton?" I asked, gazing up.

"Yeah?"

"Give me a minute?"

"Sure."

In my mind I watched myself ... lifted up over the mountains and back to Princeton, landing inside Mom's trailer. The living room was dark, except for the flicker of light from the TV. The volume was turned off because Mom couldn't follow what was said. Dirty pots and dishes covered the counter. The smell of poop everywhere. The days between yesterday and tomorrow endless. Mom between life and death ... but neither. A broken clock on the wall, where the hour and minute hands stood still, accurately showing the passage of time.

The disease took her personality. She didn't know who I was, so we each lived with a stranger. We both napped a lot just for something to do. I would've drowned myself in whiskey if I could've afforded it. And over the years, the walls seemed to come in closer, the ceiling lower, until it felt like a coffin.

Until one day ... *this day*.

I burst out of it. I flew back over the mountains and landed where the Appalachian Trail crossed Route 460.

I looked over at Peyton, leaning on her trekking poles. I nodded, put my hands through my seatbelt wrist straps, passed her, and started up the trail.

The crest was 1,315 feet up. The trail switch-backed to get there. In just a few hundred yards my legs started burning. It would start feeling better, right? No. And I breathed heavier.

What the hell?

I was once a first-string linebacker. This can't be!

I stopped and turned around. Thankfully, Peyton didn't look like she was doing much better.

"Break?" I begged.

She trudged up to me, breathing just as heavy. "Well, if you insist." She giggled. "I forgot … this part is hard."

"*This* part? What is *this* part!"

"Towns are down … at the bottom," she said, between breaths. "And we're heavy with provisions. First thing you do is go up … and … it's a bitch. Coming down into town … your pack is much lighter."

"Oh, well … if you put it *that way*."

She walked past me. "You follow me. You're walking too fast."

"Yes, Master."

Her slower pace was much better. It made a big difference. The view was better, too. Her long, slim legs were toned and watching them was pure pleasure. She wore baggy shorts, knee- high socks, and boots. Her top was a sports bra under a loose T-shirt. She was all woman, and I couldn't help what I was feeling.

Fortunately, when hiking, you're mostly looking down. Almost straight down, stepping in between rocks, gaps, and tree roots. I let her get ahead enough so she wasn't as much in view. I wasn't loving the walk, but I wasn't hating it as much as before. I lost track of time.

At a turn in the trail, she waited for me. I caught up.

"I think we're at the top," she announced.

I looked around, couldn't tell. "No view?"

"Rarely is." She turned to continue.

The trail was better, mostly straight and much flatter. For another hour the only thing in my head was where, and how, to place each step.

We slowed down and took breaks. New hikers can't log big miles. Eight to ten a day was about right. For us, since we started late, six miles was perfect because it got us to a shelter.

The shelter was small, three-sided, and vacant. We sat on the front edge, unbuckled our packs, and let them fall on the floor behind us. We sat there with our feet dangling just above the ground. There was still light, but it was cloudy. Nothing but trees all around and above. It was quiet. No sounds of civilization.

"This is nice," I said. "But I'm glad you're here for company."

"A little bit scary," she offered.

"You've never hiked alone?"

"Oh sure, it just takes some getting used to."

"Time for a Thoreau quote?" I guessed.

She thought for a minute. *"Breathe the air, drink the drink, taste the fruit, and resign yourself to the influence of the earth."*

"Good one," I nodded. Actually, it felt perfect.

"Yeah, I think … as you get comfortable out here … you find yourself. Your *true self*. At least, that's what I hope."

I shrugged. "Know what surprises me? I miss my friends … and my place. Crazy, right?"

"Yeah, I miss my friends. My lavish lifestyle. I even miss my husband, crazy as it sounds."

I nodded, did not comment.

After a while we fixed ramen noodles for dinner. We hung the rest of our food up on a tree limb. We rolled out our sleeping pads side by side with our heads at the front. It started to drizzle, but the roof overhang gave another four feet of cover.

With the next morning came rain, dripping off the leaves and forming little rivers that ran down gullies on the ground. And it was a little chilly. My fleece blanket was warm, but I had to lay it diagonally to reach head to toe. I pulled the blanket over my head and waited for Peyton to wake up. Except, she wasn't asleep.

"You awake?" she asked.

I didn't answer, figured I'd mess with her a bit.

"You're awake," she stated. I didn't answer. She poked me.

"Go away," I complained.

"Time to get up."

"Not happenin'."

"Get up," she ordered.

"It's rainin'," I whined.

"Don't be a wuss."

"Leave me alone."

She poked me again, harder. I sat up and rubbed my eyes, "I did a lot of reading about the trail. Hiking in rain like this, everything gets wet."

"Come to think of it," she replied, "your pack doesn't have a rain cover."

"Maybe my tarp will work?"

"Hope so."

We heated water for tea, then cooked oatmeal and raisins. There was plenty of water dripping off the roof for washing the pot and cups. We took turns walking up the hill to the three-sided outhouse. The open side faced away from the shelter, an obvious choice. We packed up and headed into the downpour.

Within minutes my shoes filled with water, my shirt and shorts stuck to my skin, and droplets dripped off the bill of my baseball hat. But the worst was the trickle of rain down the middle of my back. And the slippery trail. The noise drowned out all other sounds. You couldn't even hear yourself think.

Peyton hiked ahead, her pace slow and every step deliberate. Her trekking poles were more out to the side for balance. I wondered if she was having fun. For me, it was okay. This was the escape I asked for.

I was walking away from my prison.

We trudged through the rain, no shelter for a break. So we stopped now and then and munched on granola bars. Just to add to the fun, the trail turned off the crest and headed downhill. It was like walking in a stream.

Volunteers maintain the Appalachian Trail, and you could tell where they tried to steer runoff away from the path. But water goes where it wants, and foot traffic wore a perfect funnel. The trail switch-backed down the hill.

Out of nowhere a car horn beeped. It was faint, distant, hardly loud enough to hear over the rain that pelted tree leaves. A little while later, around four o'clock, we came to a shelter. Three hikers were there, all guys. We joined them and claimed a place for our packs. Peyton and I toweled off and changed into dry clothes. For her, I held up my blanket as a privacy screen. For me, she just sat with the guys and looked the other way.

It felt good to be dry.

As expected, the guys were friendly and easy to talk to. They were SoBos, south bounders, making good time. Even if Peyton had wanted to turn around and join them, she couldn't have kept up.

But it made me realize how easy it would be for her to come

across hiking partners. You could tell they liked talking to her. I mostly sat silent and listened to their stories.

When we woke up the next morning, the three guys were gone. But the rain was still with us. After breakfast, we changed out of our dry clothes and into our damp clothes and headed back down the trail. Part of me was glad about the wet clothes. I didn't want a week of blissful hiking to give me a false impression.

Every now and then I thought about Jeff and Bev but tried not to. I hoped they were doin' okay — knew they were doin' okay. There was hope for the diner and the campground, but I didn't want to think about any of that.

So instead, I gave all my attention to walking. Right foot, place it just to the right to avoid a rock. Left foot, a little longer stride to clear a root. Right foot, fine. Left foot, more than usual weight on my hiking sticks. Over and over and over. It was a mental exercise, but it helped me from dwelling on worries back home.

Around lunchtime the rain finally got tired of abusing us, but that didn't stop the trees from dripping as much water as the rain. We came downhill to a country road, crossed it, and started uphill again. It was a nice change. You use different muscles going up or down. Or maybe you use the same muscles, just differently.

For some reason the folks that cut this part of the trail didn't think it was necessary to do much switch-backing. It just went up … and up … and up.

Getting to the top, we were rewarded with another shelter. It was planned, of course, by Peyton. She had kept our pace up and we logged twelve miles.

The shelter was much like the last one, except there was a porch under the front overhang. And the roof was tin instead of shingles. We dropped our backpacks, sat on the edge of the porch, and let our legs dangle over the end. We were still catching our breath.

"One thing I like about hiking," I began, "is when we stop hiking."

Peyton nodded. "Yeah."

"Why are we hiking?" I asked.

"We're putting distance between past and future," she said, flatly.

"Thoreau?"

She shook her head. "Peyton Carter."

It felt like I was prodding, so I shut up.

But then she perked up. "Jeff and Bev told me about you and your mom. I never did say I was sorry to hear that."

"Thanks."

"So, *you're* putting some distance from those days?" she asked.

"I'm putting distance 'tween me and the prison I lived in. I wanted to live outside the walls instead of inside. Gosh, I read so many books about the AT, dreamin' about bein' out here."

She smiled. "And here you are."

"Thanks to you, Peyton. I doubt I would have done this if you hadn't come along. Probably would've just let it go . . ."

"So here we both are." She smiled again.

"Oh, that's another thing. You would've thought I'd've learned something, readin' all those books. I just can't believe how much I don't know."

"It's really very simple. You put one foot in front of the other … then the back foot goes to the front." She had her hands out, palms down, showing how to walk.

"And you know where the shelters are, distances, time, and probably keeping tabs on calories burned, far as I know."

She nodded. "I *am* keeping tabs on hydration. *You're* not drinking enough."

"See what I mean? It's so nice hiking with a grownup."

"Watch yourself, youngster." She smiled, and I laughed.

"Know what's weird?" she added. "I hiked this trail some twenty years ago, right out of college, and I recognize some of it. I mean, not most of it, especially in the rain. But little pieces, like a rock on the edge of the trail ... or a root you have to step over. Little pieces of the path I remember."

"So how old were you when you got out of college?"

"Twenty-two." Her eyes got big. "Uh-oh."

"So now I know your age." I grinned, couldn't help myself. "Let's see ... twenty-two ... plus twenty ... carry the one."

"There's no 'one' to carry," she mimicked, but still smiling. "Twenty-two plus twenty is forty-two. But I said *some* twenty years ago — not exactly twenty."

I watched her squirm, crossed my arms, and kept on grinning.

She rolled her eyes. "I'm forty-two years and twenty-six months old."

"Forty-four, plus."

"Just forty-four. The 'plus' is implied."

I laughed. "This is fun. I hope I'm not ... you know ... crossing a line."

She waved me off. "It's okay. We're good. But you're still going to make a reference to my age now and then."

"Oh yeah, for sure." I paused. "But ... can I be straight with you for a minute?"

She nodded and held out a hand, palm up.

"The thing about past and future," I continued. "I met you in your past — all done up, dressed up, and driving a nice car."

"The one with no title. A symbol of the 'fake' of my life," she interjected.

"Right, okay. Thing is, who you are *now* is much better — no makeup, no fancy clothes, you can take a joke. You're just better ... and prettier. Those three guys yesterday? They were, like, leaning in and talking faster than normal. They were into you. Not rude or nuthin', but ... you know?"

"Yeah, I noticed."

"So maybe it's okay to be in between the past and future. Maybe we should hike in the present."

She smiled. "Okay, from now on we'll *'put a little distance between cause and effect.'*"

"Another Thoreau?"

She shook her head. "Jimmy Buffett."

We ate ramen noodles and tea for dinner again, and more water. Then we hung our food in a tree like before and talked until 'hiker midnight.' Sunset — or darkness — is hiker midnight. It's when you go to bed.

The next day, and the next, were the same. Hike along the crest, down the side, cross a road, then hike up the next ridge and along that crest. Then stop. So far no falls, sprains, pulled muscles, or blisters. And making about twelve miles a day. Not bad.

We met lots of super nice people. Some were coming from the other way. Some passed us from behind. We usually stopped and shared information about what, and who, was ahead or behind. It reminded me of an ant trail where all the ants going one way stop and talk to all the ants going the other way.

One of the hikers we met, an old guy with bright-white hair and spindly legs, explained it to me.

"The Appalachian Trail is a village," he said, "two thousand miles long and two feet wide. Groups form and then splinter apart, then new groups form. You can lose track of someone in Virginia and meet back up with them in Vermont. Wherever you are on the trail, you're connected to all of it."

I tested him. "Ever meet two guys named Trip and Slip?"

He nodded. "Yes, up in Pennsylvania somewhere. Nice chaps. Slip turned an ankle and had to get off."

"Amazing," I nodded. "This really is a village."

The next day, Peyton was at the turn of a switch-back and waiting for me to catch up. This was totally normal. But when I got closer, I saw the problem. Two really big guys coming downhill with only Peyton in their sight ... 'til I walked up. I could hear their anxious comments.

"My, oh, my!" one of them smirked.

"What do we have here?" from the other.

Seeing me, their wide grins melted. We all came together and said our hellos. Their conversation seemed insincere to me.

I turned and looked back down the trail, then back to them. "Dependin' on the wind, you guys might get a whiff of poop the next hundred yards." I turned to Peyton. "Your damn brother had to step off the trail. Said he had to ... ah ... get a load off his mind."

Peyton caught on right away. She faced the two hikers. "Diarrhea. Probably from the spring down from the next shelter."

"Serves him right," I muttered, as if angry. "He never purifies his water."

I walked past the guys as if in an argument.

"Hey!" She exclaimed, sliding past the two guys. "Who do you think you are bad-mouthing my brother!"

"He's a dumb ass!" I yelled over my shoulder.

"Oh yeah? Well, who's the one that … don't you walk away from me. I'm talking to you!"

We kept fussin' all the way up to the crest. Then we stopped, too out of breath to laugh, so we just leaned on our poles and grinned at each other.

"Nice," she smiled. "I don't think they were really … a problem."

"Probably not," I shrugged. "Just gave me a … I dunno."

"Glad you were there."

We caught our breath and hiked on.

A little while later I was so deep in thought I almost ran into her back.

"Daydreaming?" she asked.

"Yeah, thinkin' about Jeff and Bev. I miss 'em. Hell, I miss even you."

She looked at me as if studying my face.

"No, wait!" I blurted. "I don't mean even you … I meant, even though you're still here. I miss you and you're not even gone yet."

She nodded. "Same here."

"Not to worry," I said. "You'll run into some hiker peeps."

And we did. The next day we came across some college kids

that had decided to take off the fall semester to hike. There were three of them — a guy and two girls.

The guy was skinny, medium height, good looking and energetic. His trail name was Starbuck, given on his first day when he showed up with a Starbuck's coffee.

One girl, a tall, broad-shouldered redhead, was Big Red. She didn't talk much but when she did, she spoke with authority. I took her to be the leader.

The other girl was Cookie Monster, named from the homemade cookies her mom put in the care packages that were mailed to post offices along the way. She was cute as a button, had long blond hair, was short and very athletic.

None of them had heard of Fakahwee so I got to tell the story. It got a good laugh and brought us together as a hiker family. They loved to start a fire every night and stay up past hiker midnight. We talked, laughed, shared stories.

It was like medicine for me.

And I could tell it was the same for Peyton. Among hikers, there is no hierarchy of race, gender, wealth, or age.

But Peyton was the only one with a thru-hike under her belt — and that earned qualified respect.

Sixteen miles out from Daleville, we all had a decision to make. Do it in two eight-mile days or one sixteen-mile day.

One of the reasons for choosing the latter — showers. Another reason — we were all running out of food. Peyton called ahead to make reservations.

The next morning the five of us got up early and got going. We hiked hard all day, consuming the last of our provisions as we went. The Appalachian Trail hits Daleville right at the I-81 exit, so at dusk we came out of the woods to face the noise, the lights, and the smells of the little town.

It was a short walk across the interstate and up Route 11 to the Cracker Barrel restaurant. We dropped our packs outside and walked in. There wasn't enough room on the table for all the food we ordered.

The hotel was right across the street. The girls got a room, us guys got a room, and we split the cost of the two rooms five ways. I can't imagine how much hot water we used for showers.

The next day was Wednesday, September 9th.

My truck came in handy getting everyone to the stores and post office. Cookie Monster picked up her care package and the homemade cookies were pulled out right away. They weren't for saving. They were for eating right then and there.

Coming into a town wasn't just for food. It meant getting laundry done, phones charged, a Wi-Fi connection, mail drops, and gorging on all forms of calories. It felt great to be helpful by carting everyone around in my pickup truck. The last stop was getting them back to the trail.

As the other three gathered around, Peyton and I embraced in a long hug. It was just short of a tearful goodbye.

"I'm going to miss you," she shared, as we stepped back.

I nodded. "Me too."

I watched the four of them walk into the woods and just stood there as they went out of sight. Memories of the week flooded through my head.

The hike didn't make up for all those years of caring for Mom. Not even close. It made me want to hike even more. At the same time, it made me appreciate the things I had back home — like indoor plumbing, if nothing else.

But more important — *my friends*. And a piece of property that no one could tell me to leave.

I turned and walked to my truck. Home was only two hours away. I kinda wished it would take longer.

CHAPTER 21

Even before pulling in, I noticed Carolyn and Vicki's RV so that was good news. As I pulled up to the gate, though, a very large Great Pyrenees came running up on the other side barking at me. It wasn't Bear, and it was bigger.

What to do? And what the hell?

Bev came out of the diner and headed my way. It was good to see her, and now there was *more* of her. Her oversized T-shirt stretched over her belly. She walked up smiling.

"Oh my God! Look at you!" she exclaimed. "You've lost weight!" She put her hand on my arm and kept looking at me as if wondering where all the pounds went. "Now I know what to do after the baby comes to get my figure back."

She was speaking louder than normal to be heard over the barking dog.

"What is *that*?" I asked, pointing to the dog.

"That's T-Rex, but we call him Rex. Isn't he gorgeous?"

I nodded. "He's a beast."

"Yeah, he's the big one."

"There's *more*?"

She nodded. "Leave your truck here. Jeff said to introduce them to you proper."

I turned off my truck and followed her into the diner. She hugged my arm as we went in. "Missed you," she smiled.

Everything looked the same inside. No customers, just as I feared.

"Jeff's out back." She pointed and walked into the back room. I followed, planning to walk straight out the back door, but stopped. To the left, against the wall, a commercial-grade washer and dryer.

"What is that?" I asked.

Bev stopped and turned around. "Oh, yeah. They showed up the day after you left. Obviously a gift from Peyton. She okay?"

"She's great! So much to tell you about."

"Here too. *So* much it's going to blow your mind. Anyway, this truck pulls in, two guys get out, and unload these things. They've been running nonstop ever since."

"Washin' what?"

"Our stuff, Mumma's, Erma's. All the campers' stuff. The RVs all have washers and dryers but can't handle blankets and throw rugs. So there was some serious catching up to do."

I stared at them and nodded absently. "Yeah, Carolyn said I'd be glad I did ... get them."

"Oh yeah! Big jump in everybody's standard of living. You wouldn't believe it. And also a source of income. Miss B had this pamphlet from one of the campgrounds they go to that had all the prices for laundry services — changing sheets, replacing towels, clothes washing. She put all the campers on a schedule for laundry services. None of them really need it right now, but she wanted us to get the practice in. For when more campers start coming in."

I took a picture of Bev with the washer and dryer and sent it to Peyton with a thank-you note.

"We don't charge Erma for using them," I said, not a question.

"Course not," she replied, heading out the door. I followed.

Jeff was cooking hamburgers over wood coals instead of propane. Another change. He looked better and seemed to move around better.

"He's here!" Bev exclaimed, triumphantly.

Jeff looked up and turned to get a better view with his good eye. "Where's the rest of him?" he chided, sizing me up and down.

I walked up and we fist-bumped. I felt like huggin' him, so I did.

Several trail riders were sitting around, some waiting for their orders. We were all on the outside of the fence. Rex had come over, still on the inside of the fence and still barking. Then another Pyr about the size of Bear came up and joined in.

"That's Gracie," Bev said, answering the question I was about to ask. "She's the mumma of the big dogs."

"There's *more*?"

"One more."

Another showed up, almost as big as Rex. "That's Tank." They were all barking, but you could tell they were harmless. Their big, fluffy white tails were wagging.

Two trail riders came up the hill. As they got closer, each gave us the peace sign. But it wasn't a peace sign. It was their order.

"Four more burgers!" Jeff said, reaching into a cooler. He pulled out a Tupperware container.

"And one for me," I added. "Um … make it two."

Jeff nodded and looked over to Bev. "Bev, honey, can you take over? I need to introduce Chad to the gang." He handed her the spatula and walked toward the gate.

We opened the gate and went in to greet the dogs. They gathered around me, tails wagging and sniffing me everywhere.

I stroked their thick, soft white fur.

"So they live here now?" I asked, hoping the answer was "yes."

"It's up to you. Right now, it's a foster situation."

"We're equal partners. You and Bev have majority vote."

He nodded. "Still, this one needs a unanimous vote, don't ya think?"

"Whatever, got my vote."

I rubbed Tank's head. Rex moved in for his turn. Bear waddled up followed by Barkley, the puppy. Still a puppy but now much larger. They joined in and huddled around me.

"So Barkley runs free in here?"

"He sleeps with Carolyn and Vicki but yeah, during the day he runs with the big dogs."

Bear was walking over to the gate. Jeff let him out. Bear liked to mooch handouts from the trail riders. Jeff walked back to me and my pack of white fur.

"Gracie is the mom of the other two. She's the oldest and she's the alpha. Barkley spends most of his time with Bear — in training, guarding the chickens. The big boy, Rex, he guards the front gate. His brother, Tank, patrols down at the bottom. And Gracie runs up and down this side. All of that, of course, is what *they* decided. No input from us. None needed."

"So … how do we run a campground with all these dogs?" I wondered out loud.

"I actually fretted about that, as if I didn't know this breed."

Jeff got down on one knee and petted the circle of fur. "They lived on a farm in Nebraska, see, and these are actual working dogs. They're lovable, but not pets. The couple that owned them ran a full-fledged farm, but as they got older they couldn't handle all the work. So over time they pared down to one of them pick-your-own-strawberries, hayrides in the fall, pet-the-goats-and donkeys type farms. Carolyn said they had a gate, like we do, and the visitors drove in and parked and walked around.

"The dogs adapted. They didn't run out the gate and got used to strangers comin' and goin'. But they still patrolled the fence line. A Pyr is mostly on duty at night."

As we petted them, wisps of white fur floated in the air.

"Anyway," Jeff continued, "the husband had a stroke. He recovered some, but they decided to give up the farm and move into town closer to their kids. That's when Carolyn and Vicki got Barkley, back in July. The farm couple had sold most of their livestock and were looking for someone that could adopt Gracie, Tank, and Rex. Keep 'em together, you know, happy, cared for, and useful. Carolyn wished them luck and promised to run it by us when she saw us.

"Well, she and Vicki got back here and the next day I ended up in the hospital. That's when Carolyn called up the couple and said if the Pyrs were still available, she had just the place for them. Obviously, Carolyn had made a good impression on them and they were very happy to hear from her."

"Explains why they left so quickly," I figured.

"Yeah."

"And didn't ask us."

"I asked Carolyn about that straight up. She said she already knew our answer, and we had enough on our plate. Also, it was only a foster thing unless we decided to keep them — which, of course, she figured."

"So how's it working out?"

"We voided the gate codes and met all the workers and delivery people at the gate to let 'em in. Didn't take long, though. The dogs figured it out. Hell, Erma came along and let herself in the gate here instead of the entrance gate. Didn't know about the new dogs. They didn't even bark at her — knew she was part of the flock. Gotta say, it feels a lot safer in here."

"I guess so, with four-and-a-half guard dogs."

"Nope. Other breeds are guard dogs. These are guardians. Whole different level."

"You might have just named the campground," I quipped.

"Yeah? What?"

"Guardian Campground."

He nodded. "Might work."

Bear came back in, and Jeff and I went out to join the trail riders. Bev had my burgers ready and I chowed down. Some of the riders puttered off. The most recent were still eating. Jeff fussed with the firepit in case more riders showed up.

Bev sat next to me so we were facing the same way. I was looking at the ATVs. She was watching Jeff. "He's such a beautiful man," she said.

"He's looking better," I noted.

"Yeah, not in as much pain. His ribs are a little sore, but his butt is healing. Keeps asking me to kiss it — make it better."

I laughed. "That's Jeff. How's his eye?"

She breathed in deep, then exhaled. "Too early to tell …"

We both fell silent.

Jeff walked over to the trail riders and got into a conversation.

Bev kept watching him.

"Burger business dropped now that school's back in. Biscuits-to-go is spotty. Walk-in dining … zip."

I leaned back and crossed my arms. "Goodbye carefree days of walkin' in the woods. Hello disappointing work conversations."

"Oh! Sausage apple biscuits are a hit. People love 'em. I think Bo got the word out that they bring employees in on time. We sometimes sell them to business owners by the dozen."

I nodded, and we fell quiet for a minute.

"How's Trish?" I asked.

"She's gone," she answered sharply, facing away from me.

"Might be a good thing."

"She took the money in the cash register with her."

"Geez. When?"

"Wednesday, the day after you left. Such a dumbass. It'd been rainin' all day, so no trail riders. Would've been more if she'd waited for good weather."

"I walked in that rain. All. Day. Long. *How much?*"

"A few hundred, so it could have been worse. Still, she stole from us, literally from the hand that fed her. I am so angry … and hurt."

Some trail riders were getting ready to leave. The engine noise interrupted our conversation. We waved goodbye to them.

Jeff picked up a bus seat and walked over and sat down. Bev

waited for the trail riders to get down the hill.

She looked at Jeff. "Tellin' Chad about Trish."

"I called the sheriff," she continued. "Told him I wanted her arrested and I would press charges. He said if he did that, it would go on her record. Said I'd never see the money. Just make it worse for her and do me no good. Then he said — if and when I see her again — tell her if she wanted the money that bad, I'd've given it to her. And that I forgive her."

I looked at Bev and thought about it. "Smart man."

Bev nodded. "It's all true. With all the anger I feel, I still love her ... or ... care for her. No, I *love* her. But my heart aches."

Jeff smiled. "See why I love this woman? She's an angel. Did 'ya tell him about the other dumb hick?"

Bev looked at him, smiled, then looked at me. "Rusty." "This is a good one," Jeff chuckled. He stood up and added a log to the firepit.

"Where'd all the wood come from?" I asked.

He sat back down. "Rusty cuts it and brings it up here."

"Ohhh good," I said, as sarcastically as possible.

Bev sat up straight, took a deep breath like before. "It was Wednesday. Wednesday afternoon. The rain was letting up. I decided to go into town for groceries. On the way, I saw Rusty thumbing on the side of the road, so I picked him up. He was headed for the interstate cuz that's where he was livin' ... under the bridge."

I looked at Jeff. He just shrugged and rolled his eye.

I looked back at Bev. She was shaking her head. "Don't know how to make this long story short. He'd been living with his brother Todd, in Todd's trailer in Princeton. I knew that. What I did *not* know was his brother, a few months back, moved to Florida with a friend. The lot rent was way past due and Rusty didn't have the money or a job. The trailer-park people said to pay up or he was trespassing. And they cut the power.

"Then his truck broke down while goin' up the hill on 19 heading toward Bluefield. It was towed. He didn't go to where they towed it cuz he had no money. So … no job, no truck, no place to live. I dropped him off, got on the interstate, called Jeff to tell him about it. Jeff said to turn around, pick up Rusty, and meet him at the trailer park. So we met at the trailer park and negotiated a reduced rent payoff. Jeff wrote the check."

"Money from my work for Carolyn," Jeff added.

Bev nodded. "Anyway, we towed the trailer here and parked it down the hill."

"Got his truck back, too," Jeff said, grinning. "Went to the shop, paid for the tow and the gas they put in it. That's what was wrong with it — it was just out of gas."

"So *he's* livin' down the hill?" I hoped not.

"Well … yes," Bev answered. "But not in Todd's trailer.

Told him that trailer was ours now."

"So he's in *my* trailer!"

"No, no." Bev held up her hands. "Jeff? A little help?"

"While we were at the trailer park," Jeff said, "I noticed two campers off to the side of the lot, both sittin' cockeyed, neither in good shape. I asked about them and the manager said they were abandoned. I offered to haul them away. He said he couldn't afford to pay me, and he couldn't sell 'em because of no titles. But if they went missin', it'd be no sweat off his back.

"Me and Rusty came back the next day, brought 'em here."

"You did all that with one eye?" I asked.

"Weren't too hard, 'cept for backin' up."

"So Rusty's *here*?"

"Yes."

I didn't reply.

"Pending your approval," he added.

I didn't reply.

"Chad, he's the father of my firstborn." Jeff was givin' it his all.

I couldn't reply right away. I wanted to say *"No! No way!"* But the look on their faces was pitiful.

"You guys are killin' me. I do *not* like him."

Bev reached over and touched my arm. "Remember the Rusty I was telling you about on the way back from Grammy's house?"

"I can't say no to you two," I complained. "Just not seein' the four of us sittin' around all chummy."

"Me neither," Jeff added, quickly.

"Or me," Bev added. "And listen … he's on a short leash. We told him this is temporary. He has to get a job, has to keep to himself, and no visitors. He can party elsewhere."

"And pay you back for his truck and trailer?"

They both shook their heads. Bev answered. "We'll never see that money, you know that. Besides, we're keepin' his brother's trailer."

"So what's Rusty livin' in?"

"Of the two campers," Jeff explained, "one is halfway livable. We got it pushed into the woods at the bottom, parked and level."

"He's really happy with it," Bev said. "Says it's much better than sleepin' under a road. And get this, JB is talkin' about Rusty doing some work around here."

"To do what?" I demanded. "Whatever it is, I'll do it. Hell, *I need a job.*"

"Just yesterday JB noticed Rusty down there puttering around his camper," Bev said. "They got to talking about growin' stuff — flowers, grass seeding, soil. JB came away very impressed."

"He knows all that stuff?" I asked.

"His parents live on what they grow or hunt," she replied. "They're very poor but self-sufficient. They sell flowers to a local florist and veggies to local stores. So yeah, Rusty knows a lot about growin' things."

"And he can't live with them, his parents?"

"That would be worse than livin' under a bridge. Let's leave it at that."

"I guess that leaves me out," I said. "But workin' for JB, he *could* pay you back."

"Maybe." She shrugged. "But getting him back on his feet … that'd be a good thing."

They were right. It was the right thing to do. They were taking the high road, so I nodded. "Does he know how to peel apples?"

She smiled. "Oh yeah."

"What if his brother comes back, lookin' for his trailer?"

She tilted her head to the side. "The way I see it, Todd left knowing his lot rent was overdue. Probably doesn't have a title. If he comes back and wants it, fine. He can pay us for the lot rent we paid *and* pay us for our lot rent."

"And pay someone to come get it," Jeff added. "Don't see that happenin'.""

"So we got three trailers —" I started, "— no, four if you count the one Rusty's in. I'm smellin' some rent money."

Jeff leaned forward in his seat. "One vacant, which is yours. One nice trailer, ready soon. The little camper — needs work. And the one Rusty is in. Bev, tell him about your sisters."

She nodded and faced me. "I was tellin' you about my sisters. It's lookin' more and more like both will be moving here."

"Would they live in one trailer?" I asked. "Or one each?"

"Probably one each. They don't get along that well."

I laughed. "So that leaves the little worn-out camper."

"I might have an idea about that one," she began.

"Good grief. Maybe I should leave for another week — see how many dogs and campers are here when I get back! So, what about the little worn-out camper?"

"The lady you told us about … you know, the one with the little boy? She lives in her car."

"She came back?"

"Yes. Saturday. Saturday afternoon. She asked for you, and I told her you'd be back in a few days. Told her she was welcome to stay, but inside the fence would be better. She was quick to agree, so things must've changed for her."

"Almost changed her mind when the dogs came runnin' up," Jeff said, grinning. "But once she saw how gentle they were with her son, she was fine."

"Poor little guy," Bev chuckled. "He kept throwin' sticks for them to fetch. Could not convince him Great Pyrenees don't fetch. He finally ran out of sticks, though."

"What's her name?" I asked.

Bev shook her head. "Wouldn't tell us. Kept to herself, and it started to get to me, ya know? Accepted our offer to park here … but acted like she didn't trust us."

"I remember. I was done with her."

"Same here. It drove me to doing something stupid. I was coming out the back door that night, Saturday. I left the door open and told her to lock up when she was done using the restrooms. And told her she was welcome to do her laundry. It got me some trust."

"I assume you weren't robbed for the second time last week," I goaded.

"Oh, hell no. She did her laundry, had some pie, wrote it all down on an order slip, and left the cash on the counter. She came in for breakfast Sunday morning, too, same time as Marvin.

"Come winter, I would like for there to be a place she can sleep. I'm *hoping* we can get the little camper fixed up."

"Did the dogs bother her?"

"No. That's what really helped make her feel comfortable. She said Gracie stayed right next to the front passenger door all night. That's where her son sleeps, in the front passenger seat. Said they both slept like a baby."

"She been back since then?"

"Sunday night, but not since then."

"Okay. So, we'll see how that goes," I nodded.

They both nodded but then fell silent. There was concern in their expressions, far as I could tell. "What?"

They just looked at me.

"There's more?"

Jeff spoke up. "Want a beer?"

"Naw. No…wait. Do I *need* one?"

"I'll get us a beer."

He got up and limped into the diner. Bev looked away.

We waited.

Jeff came back and handed me a beer. There was no "victory" tap of the bottles.

I studied their faces again. "Bad news?" *We were doing so good.*

"Can we stop now?" I asked. Bev shook her head. "No."

"What?" I begged. "Is Snake back?"

"No," Bev replied. "But his car is."

CHAPTER 22

Crap!" I grimaced.

Bev turned in her seat to face me. "The GPS thing was still on his car and Mr. Bryson got an alert on his phone app. It was set to go off if Snake got within a hundred miles. Mr. Bryson called Sheriff Bailey and he pulled the car over on the interstate. It was three men, middle aged, from Cleveland. All had prior arrests but no outstanding warrants. The men were cordial and respectful. They had a rental agreement to live in Snake's house."

"Damn," I growled. My stomach started doing flips. "Wonder who owns the car."

"Dunno."

"I wonder who owns the house."

"Dunno."

"Wonder if we're in danger?"

"Dunno."

"We should tell our camper friends."

"Did that."

"How'd they take it?"

"It varied. Vicki, of course, was gung-ho about it. Fun fact — they all have guns."

"Great, just … great."

I looked over to Jeff. He pulled up his shirt. His gun was tucked in the waistband of his shorts. I hadn't noticed.

"Oh damn," I said. "A shoot-out at the campground."

They didn't reply.

"I'm scared," I admitted, honestly.

That got a nod from both of them.

"Marvin knows about it," Bev said, encouragingly.

"We got six hundred pounds of Pyrs," Jeff added.

"We have the sheriff, and Mr. Bryson," Bev continued. "Everything I just said is from Mr. Bryson. I haven't heard from Sheriff Bailey, yet.

"And, oh … when the men got to the house, the GPS signal went dead. Getting pulled over must have tipped them off."

I grumbled. "This is bad."

We sat in silence for a few minutes.

I sat my beer on the seat, put both hands on my face, and closed my eyes. Then I rested my hands on my knees and looked down.

Then I continued. "I really, *really* think the hanging was believable.

"Snake coming after Jeff was stupid and would come across that way no matter what spin he put on it. I was a total wuss, so I was not a threat to them … and anyway, not even the one he was coming for in the first place. Marvin took him down … but Snake would have no clue who Marvin is.

"Mr. Bryson had a hood on. So did Piper. Mr. Miller did not have a hood and he introduced himself … so they know who he is. I'm sure Mr. Bryson is in touch with him. All the committee members were fake but, I think, believable.

"So … if I was one of the three men, I might have a grudge against Mr. Miller. But he wasn't the leader. I think Mr. Bryson, the hooded leader, and his hooded female assistant would be their main problem."

Jeff piped in, "*Everything* about our place is dangerous to them. Marvin is here, hooded people … a local neighborhood watch."

"And now," Bev deliberated, "their corrupt sheriff is exposed. "I'm feeling a little better."

"Maybe Snake hid something in the house," Jeff offered. "And they came down to get it. But why come down in Snake's car?"

We had no answer to that.

"Maybe we'll learn more from Sheriff Bailey," I said.

Bev nodded. "He'll say, 'Ongoing investigation.' … if he does, hold me back."

"Well, is that it for the bad news?" I asked. "Or were you just breaking me in for the *really* bad news?"

Bev held up her hand, her thumb and index finger almost touching.

"A little problem?" I guessed.

She spread her thumb and finger wider and wider apart.

I picked up my beer and took a swig. "Okay, hit me."

"This one could be worse," she suggested.

"Just to put a positive spin on it …" Jeff shrugged.

She gave him a look and turned back to me. "I guess it was Friday. Was it Friday, Jeff?"

He nodded, nursing his beer.

"I went out and canvased door to door to see if anyone knew we were here. And to hand out apple sausage biscuit coupons. I kept getting dirty looks … people barely opening the door … like a little girl was gonna … what … cast a spell on 'em? Couldn't figure it out."

She looked down and pushed loose dirt around under her flip-flops. "Finally, I got to this nice old lady just down off Route 42. Sweet little lady — all frail and bent over — invited me in. She already knew my name and all about the diner. Her name is April. April Post. She went about fixin' hot tea for us … and pulled out some lemon cookies. It was so genteel. Little teacups and saucer plates. I couldn't help but hold out my pinky finger when I was sippin'."

"This is the short version?" Jeff grinned.

"Oh, hush up," she countered, smiling. "There were pictures of her back in the day with bell bottom jeans and a tie-dyed T-shirt. A real hippie!"

From the smile on Bev's face, I could tell she was seeing that picture in her mind's eye.

"So, she starts out sayin' this is gonna get her kicked off the Christmas party list, but felt she had to 'splain some things. It's about the church just down from us. The preacher is a worn-out, retired minister livin' on what the church pays him. The annual budget for the church is mostly covered by one lady: Miss Bixley.

"Miss Bixley runs the show. She tells the preacher what to say and what not to say cuz he is, as Miss Post put it, 'bought and paid for.' And Miss Bixley has a grip on the congregation as well, and with that, influence over neighbors and relatives."

"You're not gonna believe the next part," Jeff interjected.

"Miss Bixley has a list," Bev continued, "of all her 'flock,' as

Miss Post put it. She spends all weekdays going down the list, says the same thing every call: 'Hello, been thinkin' about you, worried about you, how are you?'

"Next, 'what she's been doing, in spite of her many ailments, but she 'ain't complainin' or makin' a fuss.'

"Next, the weather.

"And last — most important — gossip about who is doin' who or what or whatever. Miss Post said you can expect a call every few weeks."

"And now that Bev is done chewin' the bark off the tree…" Jeff interrupted, again.

Bev waved him off.

"She doesn't like us," Bev announced. "She doesn't think anyone else should either. So now it's common knowledge around town: Avoid the Lighthouse Diner."

I stared at her in disbelief. Could not wrap my head around it. "W–why?" I argued.

Bev started to answer but stopped.

"Why?" I demanded.

"Oh … let me count the ways," she said. "First, Miss Post said Miss Bixley didn't like Jim — Jeff's dad — for startin' his junkyard business just down from the church."

"I remember him talkin' about her," Jeff nodded. "She didn't like him 'bringin' down the neighborhood.'"

I objected. "Bringin' down *this* neighborhood?"

"Right," Bev continued, "and carry the grudge to the next generation. Crazy, right?"

I shook my head in disbelief.

"Next guess — me, an unwed mother."

"Can't even comment," I growled. "I'm getting angry."

Bev smiled. "Next guess is even better — and remember, this is Miss Post being really open and honest about it. She was as disgusted about it as me. So next guess is an unwed mother with two older, good-looking, desirable bachelors. A *threesome*."

"That one's my fave," Jeff smiled. A look from Bev, "Not."

"Miss Post thinks that one comes from when we were gettin' the diner ready — me running around with the two of you. And nothing around here goes unnoticed.

"As time went by, more possibilities got added. Multiple times the law came in — with lights and sirens. Then add same sex couples, mixed couples, and blacks … and Erma's trailer catching fire. Very suspicious, you know."

"So what are we missing?" Jeff mocked. "Gays? Immigrants? Aliens?"

"Miss Post gave me her best guess and I have to agree. It is: Every martyr needs a dragon to slay. Gives Miss Bixley power."

"Don't suppose Miss Post had any solutions to offer?" I was hoping.

"No, just the problem."

"Actually, that's a lot of help," Jeff added. "Seriously, imagine us sittin' here for months and months, lookin' out the windows, wonderin' why no one is comin' in?"

"He's right," Bev said. "It should have occurred to us something was off."

"It's only been, what … three weeks? We knew it would take some time gettin' started," I countered.

Bev listed it out. "I started advertising early, and I mean every free option I could think of. It brought in the commuters, people outside Miss Bixley's tentacles. And the trail riders. The first ones passed the 'Opening Soon' sign and came in before we were even open! So it's not like there isn't business out there."

"Can't believe one person could do so much damn harm," I complained.

"I know," Bev agreed. "Miss Post was surprised to hear we're getting no business. She felt really bad about it. She can't get around and depends on friends for transportation. Could not have asked for a ride here, ya know."

Jeff nodded. "True."

"I gave her my number. Told her to call me if she needs anything. Poor thing. Said the only thing she can ask for is a visit now and then. You can bet I'm going to — as often as possible."

"Bev," I said, seriously. "You're the brains of this business. Please tell me you have some ideas."

"Well," she said, looking to the side. "I'm guessing people would be willing to drive further for dinner than breakfast. But that would mean getting a liquor license, and you know how Mumma and I feel about that. Maybe catering? But the drive is a problem. And that wouldn't do anything to utilize the diner."

"Take the seats out and open a roller rink," Jeff offered. "A very small roller-skating rink."

"I know you're just bein' silly," Bev began, "but you might be on to something. Rent it out."

"Like what?" I cried in frustration. We all fell quiet, thinking.

"Office space," Jeff suggested. "Said it, don't like it."

"Retail store. Another bad idea." Bev frowned.

"Barber shop, salon," I took a stab at it. "All these ideas are about strangers comin' *into our home*. The diner is where we get together at night and eat and talk and laugh. It's what I missed most when I was hiking."

We were so wrapped up in our problem we didn't hear the truck pull in. We didn't hear anyone come in the diner, walk in the back room, and appear at the back door. We saw him at the same time, stood up at the same time. Can't help but to stand when Bo Schmitz appears. He had to duck to come out the door.

"Bo!" Bev exclaimed, delighted. "Come over and sit a spell. You already met Chad, right?"

He nodded to me, turned to Jeff, and extended his massive hand. "Bo."

"Jeff." They shook hands.

"Sorry to hear about the fight," Bo said, earnestly. "How's it goin'?" He was looking Jeff over, especially the eye patch.

"Thanks," Jeff said. "I'm gettin' better."

Bo nodded. I could see the concern in his eyes. "Heard some good came of it, you and Bev gettin' hitched."

Jeff smiled. "I'm happy as a calf in clover 'bout that."

Bo looked over Jeff's shoulder. "You have *got* to let me pet these gorgeous dogs."

Jeff led Bo through the gate. By that time all the dogs had gathered. Bo got down on his knees and rubbed them all. So the giant man was surrounded by the giant dogs. The proportion was perfect. Bo giggled like a little kid.

"Heard about this breed," he said, then laughed. "Seen one at a distance, long ago. I got a border collie now. Poor thing is gettin' long in the tooth. When he's gone, this will be my next dog. How much this big one weigh?"

"About 180 pounds," Jeff answered, proudly.

"Way more than my Sparky," Bo smiled while rubbing on Rex. "Oh yeah … Sparky is gonna be so mad at me when I get home. He'll know I been cheatin' on him."

Good thing we had nothing better to do. Bo just kept rubbing the dogs. I came in, Jeff went back out and sat next to Bev. I mostly rubbed on Barkley since he was too low to get equal attention.

Eventually, the dogs started wandering off one by one. They had their self-assigned duties to perform. Bo got up and brushed off his overalls.

"Come show me your place," he urged.

We walked down as far as the four boulders so he could get a sense of the slightly sloped upper part and steep lower section. I got my first look at the new trailers but didn't see Rusty anywhere. Bo was impressed with the whole layout.

I explained JB's agreement to build the campground on his dime and turn it over to us when he was paid back. I quoted all the dollar amounts. I wanted him to know. I also wanted his opinion. He nodded in approval of everything.

"So this JB guy has the cash to do all the improvements," Bo said. "He gets his own personal campground for him and his friends. And he gets his money back first. That's fair. You get an up-and-running campground once he's paid. Bet you didn't know you had a gold mine under all the junk cars, did ya?"

He raised a hand to pat me on the back. I couldn't help but flinch.

"I was just buyin' it to keep Jeff from bein' kicked off his land," I admitted.

He smiled. "That's karma. Good karma. Once JB is paid off, you'll be set. Low overhead, minimum expenses, and geez … talk about a debt-to-income ratio. Wow."

"Bo, you talk like a financial genius."

"Aw, I'm just a West Virginia hick."

"Not buyin' it," I said. We wandered back to Jeff and Bev.

"Don't suppose you got any of them famous apple pies?" Bo asked Bev.

"Sorry, we don't. Can't make 'em fast enough," Bev explained. Then she pointed at me and grinned. "Havin' some issues with my apple peelin' production department."

Bo reeled back with a hearty laugh. "Well, as soon as you get that issue figured out, you'll be on your way."

"Want a burger?" I asked, changing the subject.

"Naw, I'm good. Whatcha got goin' on back here? Havin' a cookout? I see all the bus seats sittin' around and a firepit goin'. Y'all close the diner for the day?"

"No," Bev replied. "An ATV trail is down the bottom of the hill. Trail riders come up and we serve burgers and chips. Been doing it since before we were open."

Bo's chin dropped. His beard slid down even farther. His eyes got big. He walked over to where the rider path came up the hill, then looked back at us, then walked back up. "That's like … business out of nowhere! You kids are gonna break out in money."

"More money comes in from back here than the diner," Bev explained. "We sell biscuits first thing in the morning to the commuters, but we have no walk-in customers."

Bo tilted his head. "How long you been in business?"

"About three weeks."

Bo stared at her for a second. "Takes a new business some time to get up and runnin' ... sometimes a year or more. Probably should've planned for it. I don't mean that unkindly."

Bev nodded. "I know, but the diner was just sittin' here. Came with the property. Got a jump-start from one of the campers rentin' a campsite for a year lease. No payroll, just us and Mumma. We don't need much."

"Well, all that is good." Bo held on to the straps of his bibs. "Trouble is the bills keep comin' every month even if the money don't. It's hard, I know."

Exasperated, Bev gave him a short version of her conversation with Miss Post.

"Wow." Bo frowned. "Now that's a new one. As if things ain't hard enough 'round here."

"We were just talking about what to do with the space," I added, "when you walked in."

He stood there, thinking, then turned toward the door. "Let's get a visual on it."

We followed obediently.

Still with his hands on his bib straps, Bo walked around the diner, deep in thought. I could tell we were watching a pro.

"The windows face south," he began, looking out. "Good light, nice and bright. Floors ... are tile. Easy to clean ... and need to be cleaned."

He kept walking around. "Booths are in good condition. Restrooms ... not much done to make it cozy in here. No pictures on the walls. Cake stand is a nice touch."

"So far we were thinkin' office space or something," Bev said. "We could still use the grill for cookin'."

Bo shook his head vigorously. "No. When the campground gets up and running, you're going to need this space. Half for dining, half for RV stuff — extension cords, water hoses, batteries. T-shirts and ball caps with your logo on them."

He kept walking around and ended up next to the bathrooms. "A product display rack here, so you can't see in the restrooms when the door opens. Not good, the way it is now."

"I know, right?" Bev agreed. "It always nagged me, but I never thought about doing something about it. We could've put up a screen."

Bo wandered to the front door. He pointed outside. "Soon as things take off, add a patio outside. Put table and chairs out there, with colorful umbrellas. Run string lights. Later, add a rail. Then later, a trellis. Eventually, add an addition … to handle all the business you'll get."

"I'm standing in an empty diner," Bev said, desperately.

He nodded. "Plan for success, not failure."

"Between now and then, Bo, we need cash flow."

He walked back to where we were standing, then around some more while thinking. He stopped. "Birthday parties."

We looked at each other and back to him, waiting for what the hell birthday parties had to do with anything.

Bo laid it all out for us. "Kids have birthday parties and go to birthday parties. It don't take long to go through the rent- a-clown, rent-a-juggler, rent-a-pony ride, rent-an-inflatable slide options. The parents try to outdo each other, or at least come up with something different.

"The church lady cut off the church crowd. Doubt she can get to everybody. Offer birthday parties. Do it right … and do it cheap."

"We can make the cakes," Bev announced, eagerly.

"Right," Bo nodded. "Full service: cups, plates, party favors, balloons, and snacks. The older the kids get, the less the parents want to deal with the hassle. Or cleanup."

"I guess that could bring in some cash," she replied, hesitantly.

Bo waved his finger back and forth. "Not for profit. For exposure. It's a two-step strategy. Know any teachers? They can't give out kids' names, but they can spread the word."

Bev shook her head.

"Yes, you do," Jeff offered. "Erma."

"Erma," Bo repeated, eyes widened. "Erma Randolph?"

Jeff nodded.

"I had her in fifth grade," Bo said. "She's still alive?"

"Lives next door," Jeff replied.

"You should see her trailer," I added. "She's retired. Her and her friends feed the hungry kids 'round here. She is full-time food distribution."

"I'll go over there next," he stated. "I haven't even thought of her in years. She was my favorite. Hard as nails but she set me straight. That's when I started sprouting up and gettin' too big for my britches. I owe her."

He paused, looked out the window, shook his head. "I owe her."

He turned to us. "Just a suggestion … get the birthday parties going and advertise that the proceeds go to her efforts."

"For karma," I guessed.

He nodded, dead serious.

"Fabulous idea," Bev cried.

Bo started rubbing his hands together. "Now, we need a theme. It's the Lighthouse Diner, so, maybe little lighthouse toys with your logo on them. If they're cheap enough the kids can each take one home."

"I've got a lot of research to do, but this gives me hope." Bev looked happy.

While they were talking, I got to thinking about how we were getting around the church lady, and how to get to all those people in the church. Then it hit me.

"Bingo Night!" I shouted. Heads turned. Smiles appeared.

"Oh gosh," Bev exclaimed, "Mumma's church has those. Why didn't I think of that!"

Bo nodded. "Something to do that doesn't include dancing, drinking, or gambling. Now we're getting past the church lady … and into the congregation. Brilliant."

"Small entry fee. Refreshments served." Then Jeff added, "And proceeds to Erma."

"Big ups having the proceeds go to Miss Randolph," Bo nodded. "Can't call her Erma, she's Miss Randolph to me."

At that Bev started rubbing her hands together. "Oh my, this is going to be epic!"

"You're just at the tip of the iceberg," Bo began. "You can offer to host out your diner for club meetings … even bring in guest speakers. A flea market in the parking lot. Get yourself up to speed on everything going on in the neighborhood."

"So much to do," Bev gushed. "So much opportunity out there.

Thank you, Bo."

"And thank you from me," I added, sincerely. "Now I have a job."

"You could peel apples," Bev said, poking me on the arm.

"Well … that's why I'm here," Bo said, carefully sitting on a barstool.

"You're gonna peel my apples?" I asked.

"Yep. I'd like to."

At that comment, Bev walked over and sat at a booth. Jeff sat across from her. I took a barstool.

"I own a strip mall," Bo began, "up in Berkley. Half empty when I bought it, and now it's half full. That's progress, right?"

We laughed politely.

"Behind the mall, a bakery. It was part of the purchase, and it pretty much runs itself. They mostly make loaf bread and sell to country stores, restaurants, gas station stores, local mom and pop's. For the past … let's see … five or six months it's been losing money. The big-brand bakeries are starting to creep in on our hard-to-reach customers. It's all about distribution, ya know.

"I've been payin' salaries out of my own pocket. Can't keep that up much longer." He stroked his beard, thinking.

"Thing is … the employees are a tight-knit group of families that live in the area. It would be disastrous if it closed down. Whole families out of work.

"My proposal to you … is of little value to you. Has two parts. One, let me make Miss Baker's Blue Ribbon County Fair Apple Pies."

"Honest, Bo," Bev piped up. "I don't think you could make

them as good as we can. I'm positive we're not making them as good as Grammy."

"I agree. But it would still be a flour and lard crust, and her recipe and it would have the name and logo on the box."

"We just have the name," Bev clarified. "Not a logo."

"True, but you should. And have it copyrighted and registered."

"Your bakery can make homemade crusts?" I asked.

"Not now. But they could — and would — if it meant keeping their jobs. And they know how to bake. They're second and third generation. And they have the ovens. How many do you have?"

Bev lifted a hand and one finger. "One … oven. And we would profit … how?"

"The bakery would pay you — or your grandmother — royalties for the name. And you could still bake your own pies if you want. Or the bakery could supply you *your* pies. And all the other types of pies."

"That'd be weird," she said.

"I know," Bo said, with no change in his expression. "But I saw the oven you got. You don't have the capacity to fill the demand."

We all nodded at that.

"Let's go to that other part," Bev suggested.

"Right. The other part is that the bakery would put the Miss Baker brand on their loaf bread. No change in the recipe, just the bag it comes in. The brand would save the factory. Miss Baker and the county fair are … well, not famous … but recognizable. I have no way to know if it would work."

"Wouldn't be honest," Bev shook her head, looking down. "Miss Baker's loaf bread."

"No, it wouldn't," Bo agreed. "Just like all the other products out there with a famous face on the cover ... or the words 'organic' or '*low*' this or '*diet*' that."

For a minute, Bev kept looking down. Then she looked up and faced Bo. "You're not asking this for yourself," she said softly.

"I'm glad you know that," he nodded.

She looked at me. "Your thoughts?"

"I would ask the smartest businessperson in the room what they would do," I answered. Then I looked from her to Bo.

He sat up straighter and stroked his beard. "If I were you, I would design a logo. I would think long and hard about it. My advice is to do what works the best for you.

"In the meantime, I will continue funding the payroll ... as long as I can."

Bev smiled and shook her head. "I marvel at how you look at things."

"I'm just a simple hillbilly," he countered.

She smirked. "Yeah, right."

"My business model is simple: Do the best I can and be content I did the best I could. That said, I'm going next door to see if my favorite teacher is home."

He ducked as he went out the door.

Jeff began, "Those employees are not our problem —"

"They are now," Bev smiled, reluctantly.

"Yeah, I know."

"Before you put me to work, mind if I bring my truck in?" I asked.

"If you must," Bev kidded, lifting her phone. "Let me activate your code."

"And put my stuff away?"

"If you must."

"And walk down to see the new trailers?"

"You're pushing it. Now go!"

It was no problem getting past Rex. He watched the gate open, stepped aside as I drove in, watched the gate close, resumed his march up and down the fence.

I tossed my pack in the office door and walked down the hill to where it got steeper. I got to the largest trailer. It wasn't a camper, but a mobile home, and obviously the one that Rusty had lived in. As I got closer, the door opened. Rusty came out. He was carrying a cardboard box. He looked about the same — short and thin but worn out. He seemed surprised to see me.

"Oh! Ah, hi, I'm Rusty."

I nodded. "Chad."

"Just gettin' some of my stuff," he said, as if needing to explain. "Look, man. I…I'm *real* sorry about Jeff."

"Me too." I couldn't bring myself to be nice about it.

I walked past him and entered the trailer. It was bigger than Mom's trailer. A ratty futon was the main piece of furniture in the living area. There was a coffee table, one of the legs was a piece of lumber. That and everything else, to me, looked usable as firewood. Mounted on the back wall was a medium-sized flat screen. Good luck picking up a signal, I thought.

"This is like Bev's," I noticed. "A bedroom on each end."

"Uh, yes sir," Rusty said from outside. I had never been called "sir" before. I came out and shut the door.

"Bev was tellin' me about the trailers," I explained. "Thought I'd check 'em out."

We walked over to the next one, obviously the unlivable one. It was leaning so far it looked like it might flip over. "Not too good," I stated. We kept going.

"Mine's next," Rusty said. "I … I mean … not mine. Yours."

It was tucked into the woods, closest to where the trail riders came up. I looked at it and tried to figure out how they got it so far into the trees.

"Mind if I come in?" I asked.

"Sure, uh … yeah, okay."

I stepped in. It was small and very clean. Everything in a camper is built in, so there is no furniture. Nothing worked because he wasn't hooked up to anything.

"Nice setup," I commented.

"Oh yeah, this is heaven," Rusty answered, still outside.

"Bev said you were sleeping under the interstate." I stepped out.

"Miserable," he admitted. "Sleepin' on concrete … out of the rain, though. Soooo much better here. I really appreciate this … really."

I had figured I would never forgive him for the harm done to Jeff. But he was so pitiful and dirty, his head down as if ashamed. It's hard to hold a grudge against someone so broken.

"Later," I said, walking past him.

He nodded, looking away.

About ten steps up the hill, I turned around and looked back at him. "You got any clean clothes in there?"

"Oh, yes. Yes, sir. I ... I do."

I took a deep breath. I wasn't so much thinking as feeling. "My apartment is above the shop. Go up and get a shower. And change into some clean clothes." Probably sounded like an order. Probably was.

"Okay ... yes, sir. Thank ya."

Getting back to the diner, Jeff and Bev were still seated across from each other in the second booth. Bev was anxiously writing in her notebook and turning to a new page as I entered.

They were so wrapped up in their conversation they didn't look up.

"Balloons," Bev noted, scribbling away. "How much are helium tanks?"

Jeff shook his head. "Don't know."

I took a seat on a barstool and listened. There were things to do and things to buy. We would have to spend money — to throw parties that didn't make money, to get people to come in and dine, for meals that don't make much money. And then pay for the food, the supplies, the light bill. I wondered and feared. How long would it be before the three of us would have to give up and get jobs?

Bev looked up. "Did you see Rusty down there?"

"Yeah. I told him to come up to my place and take a shower."

She nodded. "Okay. We can get him to peel apples. I got stuff for you to do."

"Works for me."

"Oh, and ... there was something else Miss Post told me. I forgot to tell you."

I rolled my eyes. "So I need to stay seated?"

"Might be a good idea," she replied, glancing over at Jeff. "Turns out the rapist guy was a visitor ... someone we knew."

"A pal," Jeff added.

"Right ... and how did that come about?" I asked.

"Miss Bixley," Bev replied. "She refers to us as 'those kids down the road and their visitors.' Always includes 'visitors.' Sez we knew him."

"Not true," I stated.

"Prove it," Jeff challenged, lifting a hand.

"Hell, we took him down. It's in black and white in the newspaper article about it. It said ... how was it worded again?"

"Apprehended by local residents," Bev recited. "Sheriff Bailey kept our names out of it. And the picture — the picture I took — shows the sheriff walkin' him off in handcuffs."

"And that newspaper right now," Jeff added, "is sittin' on the bottom of a bird cage. Current news is 'those kids and their visitors.'"

I shook my head in disbelief. "Can't make something true by keep lying about it!"

Bev shrugged. "Well, if nobody calls you on it, then the lie is the only thing out there."

"Now are we done with the bad news?" I begged.

The rest of the evening was spent shopping for bingo and birthday stuff and getting signs made to post in stores. Bev was very organized and very thorough. I was impressed. It gave me hope for the diner.

We stopped off at her mom's house to pick up leftover

spaghetti, and then the grocery store for French bread and a bottle of wine. That evening, the three of us dined like upper class.

As I sopped up the last of my spaghetti sauce with the bread, I told them about my hike.

"The biggest thing I learned," I began, "was how important it was to have water, food, and shelter. That's all you had to think about. The trip was like … rebooting your brain."

I waited for Jeff's dig about my brain, but it didn't come.

"What, no comment?"

"Not if you're gonna drop it in my lap like that." He grinned. "Waay too easy."

"I get it," Bev said, "getting back to nature and all."

"If you were on the trail today," Jeff noted, "you'd be having ramen noodles tonight instead of Miss Bishop's spaghetti."

I nodded. "Right and, crazy thing is, enjoyin' them just as much. But if I was on the trail, and somehow *had* this meal, I'd be in heaven."

"If you were on the trail and could have anything delivered, what would it be?" Bev asked.

"Steak," I replied, quickly. "I was craving steak, probably for the protein. Also, I can't remember the last time I had one."

"Next time we have something to celebrate," Bev nodded, "we'll have steak."

I dug my wallet out and pulled out a piece of paper. "That reminds me. I have a list of things to mail to Peyton for her next post office pickup. Will you teach me how to bake cookies?"

We talked into the night, as usual, but not with as much laughter. There were obstacles to overcome and drug dealers to worry about. So we ended up going through stuff in Bev's notebook. We locked up earlier than most nights.

Getting down to the shop, I turned on the outside light, turned off the office lights, and took my backpack up the steps. I unpacked, fussed around the apartment a bit, undressed, and went to bed. I was sleepy from all the wine and pasta, but afraid. I listened for noises that weren't natural. Every now and then one of the dogs barked.

I got to thinking that maybe I would feel safer down in the woods. Hell, it works for Marvin. As time wore on, I tossed and turned. Crazy how hard it is to try to fall asleep. I got up, dressed, and collected my bed pad and blanket.

As quiet as possible, I came down the steps. I slowly opened the front door and peeped out. Couldn't see anyone out there. But as I looked down there was a very large Great Pyrenees below me. It was Tank, who's a little smaller than Rex. He was lyin' on his belly, front legs straight out, head up.

I opened the door wider and as I did, he sat up, turned, and looked up at me. From the outdoor light above me, I could see well enough to tell he was lookin' me in the eye. I got the sense he knew what I was thinking. The connection was so real I halfway expected him to just start talking.

"You here for me?" I asked.

He just kept looking at me. I rubbed his head. He liked that. Then he lay back down as before, but this time he put his head down as well. He was obviously there for the night. Amazing.

I turned off the outdoor light, walked back up the steps, and went to bed. Slept just fine.

CHAPTER 23

Mom used to say, "Things turn out the best for those who make the best of the way things turn out." Seems like making the best of things is all we ever do in West Virginia. For the rest of September, we did what we could.

Bev decided to accept Bo's offer to make Miss Baker's pies if, of course, Miss Baker went along with it. We doubted she would like having her name on pies and loaf bread, but she did. She even agreed to having her picture on them as well.

Bo said he would make the offer to the employees to take over ownership of the bakery. And of course, they accepted. A meeting was set up for Miss Baker to meet with the employees and pass along her recipe. Bev and I picked her up and drove to Beckley. Bo was there and he introduced us to the employees. They were your typical down-home, friendly, smiling folks, and they all seemed anxious to meet her. They were counting on her name and face to save their jobs. Or soon … their company.

Miss Baker walked up to Bo and handed him a large envelope. He took it, pulled out the picture, and chuckled. He turned it around to show us. We already knew what it was — an 8 x 10 glossy of her high school senior picture, with hair piled up tall on her head, a forced smile, and a look of innocence long since lost. You could hardly tell it was her.

Bo chose his words carefully. "Not exactly the face of a

seasoned county-fair contest winner." He looked down to her eye to eye.

She returned the look and said, "Bo, under all these wrinkles, *that's* who I am. You'll understand someday."

He nodded, turned, and passed the picture to the employees. "As you all know, my offer is to sell you folks the company for one dollar ... and one dollar per month for the next two years, contingent upon Miss Baker's approval that we ... I mean you ... can produce an award-winning apple pie!"

"Let's get busy!" cheered a voice from the back.

I was toting a bag of apples and Bev had a bag of spices and such. Everyone gathered around a long stainless-steel table and began. A machine would peel the apples, but slicing had to be done just right. *By hand.* Same for the notches. *No exceptions.*

As Miss Baker went through each step, folks were nodding. You could tell they knew what she was doing. And I think she was impressed with the questions and comments. There was unanimous agreement about the need for really, really, *really* cold water. I'll never know why.

Commercial ovens are different, so pies had to be cooked at different temperatures and times and the results compared. There was a lot of testing, nods, and opinions.

Everything tasted good to me.

Finally, Bo put ink to paper and handed the business over to the employees — now the owners.

We took Miss Baker home, and she talked about the day for the whole trip. She was tired, but very happy. We could have never guessed how it would play out.

One morning Jeff and I were sitting in the diner having breakfast. Marvin had just left, and Miss Bishop and Bev were in the back. A lady walked in, and two young boys followed. She passed by Jeff and me and ended up at the bar. Bev came out with her head down, busy with her phone. Startled, she looked up.

"Do we pick a seat?" the lady asked. "Or wait to be seated?" I've never seen Bev so stumped by a question.

"Um, how about this one?" she recovered, taking them to the third booth. She had to look for menus. Delivering them, she asked, "Something to drink?" The answer was "one coffee and two milks," but Bev didn't have an order pad.

She had to find one.

Miss Bishop came to the door, I guess to see if they were for real. The meals were delivered, eaten, and paid for. We watched in silence as the three left.

As the car drove out of sight, Bev turned and asked, "What just happened?"

A few days later I was driving home from a date, heading southbound on I-77. As I came over the bridge that crosses the trails, I saw a van parked off to the side. It looked to be exactly over the trail. They should have had their blinkers on but didn't. As I passed them, I could see figures standing between the van and the rail. I also glanced to the left and confirmed that the reflector tape was on the other side.

On a hunch I pulled over where the bridge ended. I ran back and made my way down the hill beside the bridge. It was dark and I couldn't see much. But I could see the van and figures beside it. Movement caught my eye as something was dropped over the side.

I crouched down and crept further. On the trail — more figures. And they were loading packages onto a UTV.

Not good, I thought.

Fear pumped my heart faster. I stayed low and scrambled back up the hill. At the top I broke into a sprint. I jumped in my truck and took off, watching my rearview mirror more than the road ahead.

Jeff and Bev were still up and sitting in the diner with all the lights on. Probably waiting to hear about my date. I ran in, my heart still pounding, and told them what I witnessed. It *had* to be something bad … and *had* to have something to do with the drug dealers.

"I'm calling the sheriff," Bev said. "Chad, he gave you his card when we visited Mr. Bryson. Still got it?"

I shook my head. "No clue what I did with it."

She dialed 9-1-1, put the phone on speakerphone, and set it on the table.

"9-1-1. What's your emergency?" came a female voice.

"We need to speak to Sheriff Bailey," Bev responded.

"Oh honey, I'm sure he's asleep. I can —"

"This is Beverly Bishop," she interrupted. "Wake him up, please."

"I doubt —"

"Wake him up. Tell him this is Bev at the Lighthouse Diner. Tell him it is urgent. He will be glad you did and not pleased with you if you don't."

A pause. "Stay on the line. I will —"

"No," Bev objected, "I will hang up and wait for his call. Make the call." Then she hung up.

The call came quickly. Sheriff Bailey was groggy, but all business. "Talk to me."

I leaned in and gave him my story. Meanwhile, Jeff pulled out his phone and started scrolling.

When I finished, the sheriff asked, "Describe the van." I did.

"I doubt you got the license plate."

"No sir."

"Do you think they saw you?"

"I could barely see them, so no. And I doubt they were even looking."

"If one of them knew you, knew your truck, do you think they might recognize it?"

"I don't see how. They would just see headlights comin', and taillights leavin'."

He paused. "Give me a minute." We could hear him put the phone down, footsteps, and a door close. After a minute, a toilet flushed in the background.

"Had to pee," he explained. "Now I can think better. Listen, these questions are about your safety. Chad, who knew you were out tonight?"

"Jeff, Bev, and the girl I had a date with up in Beckley."

"Jeff … Bev … did you tell anyone about Chad being out on a date tonight?

"My Mumma," Bev answered.

"No," from Jeff.

"Okay, good." A pause.

"Whatever they were doing, I'm going to assume they're done

and gone." Another pause.

"Colbert Mine!" Jeff exclaimed, looking at his phone.

"And?" the sheriff asked.

"It's abandoned, you know."

"Yes."

"It's right off the trail," Jeff began. "Whatever they're smugglin', they're takin' it to the mine. And the mine is way off the road. Bet that's where they're takin' stuff."

"I think you're on to something," the sheriff replied. "This obviously goes to the FBI. I'll let them take all the glory. Best if it doesn't hit any local papers ... for *your* sakes."

"If it does," Bev responded slyly, "tell 'em 'It's an ongoing investigation.'"

A chuckle came from the other end. "Copy that. Night, kids."

We were grinning at Bev. She shrugged and raised her arms. "Could *not* help sayin' that."

You would think things wouldn't turn out well with Rusty, but they did. He got a part-time job stocking shelves down at the Dollar General.

He worked on his little camper, too. At first, he smoothed out a path to the front door. Then later he lined rocks along each side. He cleared a small patch of ground around the camper and planted grass. It was the only grass anywhere on the property.

Then he placed flowers in pots, hung flowers from a pole, and planted more in the ground.

He brought firewood up to the diner for cooking the hamburgers. He took over feeding and tending to the chickens. He'd fetch eggs and bring them to Erma. He even helped her prep food.

One day he fixed the light for the old sign. He tied a rope to the light and the other end around his waist. Then he shimmied up to the crossbeam, pulled up the light, and wire nutted it like it was before. Then he bearhugged the pole and slid down. Now *that* was dangerous.

But we were the Lighthouse Diner again. We all got together and celebrated that night.

Bev wanted the small unlivable trailer available for the mystery lady and her son. Jeff and I towed it to his shop and worked on it. We pulled out the mattress, some cushions, curtains, and some *really* smelly stuff left in the little fridge. Then we cleaned it, added some paint, and it was done.

And wouldn't you know it, the mystery lady showed up that night. We had just finished dinner and doing what we usually did – – talking and laughing. It was our special time, even after bein' together all day.

The lady walked in, holding her son's hand. He gave a little wave. Bev immediately stood up. The lady seemed hesitant to close the gap between us. After a quick whisper to her son, she finally edged forward.

"Hungry?" Bev asked.

The lady shook her head, and hesitated. I turned in my seat and watched.

"Baby doing okay?" she asked.

Bev nodded.

More silence.

The lady took a deep breath, looked around, then turned back to us. "Um, could my son play with the dogs for a minute?"

Jeff jumped up and started toward the back. "Hey sport, wanna see what the dogs are barkin' at?"

"Sure!" he exclaimed. He followed Jeff.

On the way out the back, we could hear Jeff say, "I'm Jeff. What's your name?"

"Brent."

The lady rolled her eyes.

I got up, motioned for her to sit, and went to get a barstool. Bev took her seat. "I'm Bev, that's Chad, and the big guy is Jeff."

Still no smile. Just flat facts.

Another deep breath and, "I'm Stephanie ... Steph."

She sat down. I came back with a seat. Bev sat there with her hands on her lap. The mystery lady was looking out the window. I took the cue from Bev and just sat there too. I wasn't sure why she was playing hardball.

Finally, the lady spoke. "I need a favor."

"Name it," Bev said, flatly.

"I've come across as ... distant."

"Yep," Bev replied.

Another deep breath. "I'm in a situation ... and ... I'm asking if you could watch my son for a few days."

"We don't know you, Steph. And you don't know us."

"I know, I know. I'm asking you to trust me."

"Then tell us what's going on," Bev stated.

Steph shook her head. "I don't want to get you in trouble."

"Then tell us what would get us in trouble."

I chirped in. "We're guessing abusive husband." I looked at Bev, she nodded.

"No … no, not that. He's fine. We have joint custody." She looked out the window. "It's his two sons … from his previous marriage. They're bullies. They pick on my son. They make fun of him, shove him around, and play tricks on him. He's a little slow, by the way."

She looked back at Bev, put her hands on the table, palms up. "I've tried and tried to reason with my ex. Get him to understand. He just keeps saying, 'No big deal, a little roughhousing will toughen him up.'

"The last time I picked up Brent, on the way home he cried and cried, just bawled. He begged me not to take him back there again. It hit a nerve, Bev. I got home, packed some clothes, his meds and stuff, and took off."

I leaned in. "How would that get *us* into trouble?"

"I don't know … aiding and abetting? My ex could take me to court for kidnapping. I doubt he'd do that. But he might go after someone helping me. I wouldn't want to put that on anyone."

"Do you have a job?" Bev asked.

"I'm a textile broker. I connect companies that make fabrics with companies that make clothes, linens, curtains …"

Bev returned to her flat, no-nonsense tone. "And take care of a son at the same time?"

"Didn't think that through," Steph admitted. "Brent should be spending time with his father and his friends. Hell, he should be in preschool."

We didn't respond.

Steph pressed on. "You ever been bullied?"

Bev nodded. "My older brother picked on me. It was like you said. One time he locked me in a closet. I remember that."

"But your parents were there," Steph countered.

"Oh yeah. I remember the whoopin' he got. Never did that again."

Steph nodded. "You had a safety net. But getting bullied … with no sense of protection … it's horrible, Bev. It leaves a mark."

Bev put her hands on top of Steph's. "Steph, we got your back. But sleepin' in a car ain't right, is it?"

Steph's chin dropped to her chest. She shook her head. I got up to get tissues.

"We'll watch Brent for you," Bev said. "If he gets scared sleepin' by himself, we'll bring in Gracie."

Sure enough, I barely got back in time. Steph was crying.

Bev continued. "Jeff and Chad here have been working on a little camper. It's got heat and a little fridge. We'll pull it up behind the diner and have it ready when you get back."

"You'll need to buy a mattress," I added.

"I don't know what to say," Steph whimpered through wet eyes.

"Say you'll dine with us." Bev smiled for the first time in the conversation.

CHAPTER 24

About late September, the weather turned chilly. The days were pleasant, but the nights gave notice that summer was over and winter was coming. Bev's belly was growing. She had to run down to the Goodwill in Princeton and find some dresses that fit.

Jeff was feeling much better and almost healed … except for his eye. Surgery would fix it if we could afford it. Which we couldn't.

The trail-rider business dropped, and biscuit orders were spotty. Miss Bishop cut back to one day a week, and that was to bring in her laundry. Other than helping out with breakfast, I wasn't much useful. I started looking for a job.

Carolyn and Vicki would be staying for a few more weeks. They were having a lot of fun riding the trails. But it was time for JB and Miss B to head north to see the leaves turn in New England. Lou and Debbie would follow them, then break off to visit family.

We had a big feast — salad, steak, potato salad, asparagus, French bread, wine, and of course apple pie and ice cream.

Next morning JB came up to the diner in the golf cart. We were surprised because we had already said our goodbyes. He asked us to sit with him.

As we were getting seated, he started right in. "I'm afraid I have some bad news." His expression was dead serious. "I started the camp resort idea on the premise that all the campers we know would sign up for sites. This is exactly what they have been looking for and talking about for years. One by one they backed away from making a commitment. I am sure they will fall in love with the place once they see it, like we did. But now we're getting into winter, and they are heading south. I was a fool to make promises to you without getting promises to me in writing."

He let that sink in. It did.

"If you did get it in writing," Jeff offered, "you'd have empty promises and worthless paper."

JB nodded. "Bottom line is that I started with the money from our yearly rental to you, and the Ingram's as well. I spent that money on the gate, the site drawings, permits and such. Just the expenses, but nothing for my time. Come spring, I'm hoping we can get the others here to see the place and get things rolling.

"I think we'll get there. It'll just take longer than expected. I am so sorry."

None of us accepted his apology.

Bev managed a subdued "Okay ..."

He got up, turned, and said "I'll keep in touch" as he left.

Watching the door close, I blurted out, "I should've never bought this place!"

"Don't even go there!" Bev yelled. She sounded angry, but I knew it was just frustration. "You saved Jeff from ... what ... moving to Florida to live with his parents? Gave me the diner and something to live for! And ... it brought this gorgeous man into my life! And —"

"Easy, girl," Jeff cautioned.

"Hush," she ordered. "I'm in a huff."

She turned back to me. "And I'm the smart one, right? Spent days on social media to bring business in the front door! Comes in the back door instead! *You're* the one making things happen."

"She's right, bro," Jeff added. "You plow straight and to the end of the row."

Bev put her hands on her hips and sighed. "Chad, you are a good man. You have a good heart. Don't you realize how good karma follows you?"

I shook my head. "Not really. But what I do think is that I need to get a job. You and Jeff can keep up with the diner. The weather's been unusually mild so far … but sooner or later winter will close things down."

Jeff nodded. "He's right."

"Yeah," Bev agreed. Then she turned back to me. "But first, Chad, why don't you take one of those hikes you love so much?"

"Yeah," Jeff added. "Go poop in the woods for a few weeks."

"Really?" I smiled.

"I'll scour the internet," Bev promised, "and have a job waiting for you when you get back."

"I'll need a real sleeping bag this time," my mind flipping through pages of camping catalogs. "Cook stove, water purification, stuff …"

"Look at that." Jeff beamed. "You got him happy as a tick on a fat dog."

"Easy there." Bev scolded, then smiled. "You're gonna have to cover his workload."

"Oh, like that's a big deal? Hell, he's so lazy … if he had a third hand, he'd need another pocket to put it in."

Bev turned to me. "Does he ever run out of quips?"

"Nope."

I called Peyton. There was no answer, but she called back an hour later. She had reached Pennsylvania and was running into cold weather. She was thinking about pulling off and visiting her sister. She helped me plan my hike.

Around noon the two big campers lumbered up to the gate. I went out, opened the gate, and waved as JB and Miss B and then Lou and Debbie drove out.

Rex waited for the gate to close, then resumed his post. I was still there on the outside of the gate when a F550 pulled in towing a bulldozer. A large, nice-looking guy jumped out. He was maybe mid-forties. He was clean shaven, had a full head of salt and pepper hair, and a wide white smile.

"I'm Cody." He extended a big hand of stubby fingers. "Cody O'Brian." I braced for a strong handshake.

"Nice to meet you," I replied. "Chad. Chad Davis."

"Got a call from JB the other day," he continued, "waving me off the job."

I didn't know what to say.

"Wanna show me what you got?" he asked.

"Sure."

What would it hurt?

I opened the gate enough to go in. Rex was waiting to inspect the newcomer. He sniffed Cody, got a pat on the head, then waggled off to inspect the gate as it closed behind us.

Cody pulled out a crumpled piece of paper and looked over the upper sites. We walked around. He nodded, asked no questions.

When we got to the edge of the steep part, he looked down the hill, then at his paper, and shook his head. "Nope."

"Nope?" I repeated.

"Look," he replied, pointing at the paper. "He's got roads going down … and across. Too steep. Can't hardly do it in a car, much less a camper."

"Crap," I grumbled. "So we can't put anything down here."

"Oh no," he chuckled. "Put in switchbacks. From here, on the right — diagonal road over to the left, diagonal road left to right, and so forth."

"If it's too steep to make a 90-degree turn," I challenged, "how do you make an almost 180-degree turn?"

"From here, on the right," he explained "cut the road down and across over to the left … goes past the road below it. Keeps going onto a landing. Then you back down the lower road. Get to the other side, past the next lower road, onto a landing. Then you drive forward down that lower road. Back and forth."

I couldn't believe what I was hearing. "You expect people to back their campers two hundred yards … and keep from sliding off the edge?"

He looked down the hill with his arms crossed. "This isn't a campground."

"Not a campground?" I repeated.

"This is a trailer park," he replied. "What you put in down here, you only want to do it once."

"You can back a mobile home down the roads you're talking about?" I asked.

"Oh sure. Do it all the time."

I looked down the hill, disappointed.

"Goodbye campground."

"Hello trailer park," he encouraged.

"Kinda plannin' on a campground."

"Well," he replied thoughtfully, "things turn out best for those that make the best of how things turn out."

If he only knew ...

I apologized. "Sorry for your trouble, and I appreciate the information."

"Thing is," he said, "I came here to dig roads and make flat spots."

I reached into my pockets and pulled out empty liners.

"I had something else in mind," he began.

"Okay."

"I had this and next week or so scheduled for this job. Don't have any work lined up and need to stay busy. Then I remembered that my niece is looking for a place. She has one of those tiny houses on wheels. My offer is — I dig your roads and she gets a flat spot to park for say ... two years."

There were no dollar numbers to crunch, so all I could think to say was, "We won't have any utilities for a while. No tellin' when even."

He grinned. "Oh, she's off-grid. Solar with a bank of batteries, a small generator backup. Propane everything. Even has a composting toilet. And sits on a trailer frame."

"The sink water has to go somewhere," I guessed.

"Yeah, the gray-water tank. Let it out when it's rainin'."

"Sounds good to me."

He extended his hand. "Here's your contract."

Naturally, Jeff and Bev were outside the diner watching the dozer getting towed through the gate. As I walked up to them, Jeff pointed behind me. "Rex is waitin' for you to do somethin'."

I looked back. Rex was inside the fence looking in our direction. I had not closed the gate.

"Got it," Bev said, whipping out her phone. The gate closed and Rex resumed his duties.

We went inside and I explained everything Cody had told me. They sat there, stunned.

Bev spoke up first. "So ... our so-called RV resort is what ... twenty or so sites up here at the top?"

I nodded.

She stood up, started pacing with her arms crossed. She got to the far end of the diner, then came back. "So ... what do we do with the rest of the land?"

I shook my head. "Dunno. Cody said make it a trailer park."

She started walking in circles. "Wait! JB based his budget on utilities for *all* the land, right?"

We nodded.

"Well, if he refigured for just the top part, wouldn't his budget be less?"

We nodded again.

"With a smaller budget, he would need fewer contracts, right? Shorten the time frame, right? That would help, right?"

"I think you're on to something," I said. "I think JB is a good person, and he was upset with himself about letting us down. But he was figuring on the whole thing, like you said. I'll call him and see what he says."

I called JB and left a message.

CHAPTER 25

My hike started in Groseclose, Virginia. It is darn near further west than West Virginia. It took an hour to drive there. It would take ten or more days to walk back. I would need one post office care package and one side trip off the trail into a town.

Jeff dropped me off and I started walking on the morning of October 5th.

I knew to take it easy at first, thanks to Peyton. I couldn't believe how out of shape I was. At least it would level off, I just didn't know when. Then it hit me. This wasn't at *all* like hiking with Peyton. If nothing else, just having someone to share the misery, as it were.

With no one to talk to, it was like living in the trailer with Mom. Hiking was supposed to be my escape from all that. It got to where I was thinking of quitting. But then I made it to the top and the trail leveled off. Besides, I paid good money for the sleeping bag and stuff. And my care package was already on its way to Bastian, Virginia. Can't waste food.

So I kept walking and walking, hoping for a shelter to show up. Peyton had maps with shelters marked. I didn't. And one didn't show up.

At dusk I found a clearing, set up camp, and fixed dinner. I sat there wishing I was back at the diner with Jeff and Bev. Love those two to the moon and back.

The next day, and the day after, I just concentrated on putting one foot in front of the other. I tried not to think about anything else. It helped. I became more and more aware of the sights, sounds, and smells of nature. What I wasn't thinking about was prejudice, violence, lies, hypocrisy, and abuse — all the ills of society.

On the fourth day I got to Bastian, Virginia. It was a Thursday so the post office was open. I picked up my care package and walked down Route 52 to the trail. Luckily, I came up on a shelter right away, so I stopped and rested. I decided to experience something I only read about that hikers do — a zero day. I spent the entire next day at the shelter barefoot, to give my feet some healing time.

The following Tuesday I was coming down into Pearisburg, totally out of food. No worries, though. Crossing the bridge over New River, I could see Jeff — and my truck — parked exactly where I had met Trip and Slip. Now I was the hiker and Jeff was the Trail Angel.

We bearhugged, sat on the tailgate, and I started consuming energy bars and trail mix. And water. I hadn't peed since the day before and it was dark yellow.

First, of course, was a Jeffism — "Do hikers know they don't *have* to?"

"We breathe, drink, and resign ourselves to the influence of the earth," I answered. Couldn't believe I was quoting Thoreau.

He gave a huff. "Your engine is runnin' but ain't nobody drivin'."

He smiled, reached over, and rubbed my shoulder.

I smiled too. "Everything okay back at the ranch?"

"Oh. My. God!" he bellowed. "Remember how much stuff happened last time you went hiking?"

"What, we got *more* Pyrs?"

"No. Well … Barkley. Carolyn and Vicki rolled out and left Barkley with us. They felt bad about it, but they couldn't handle him chewin' on the furniture. They knew he'd be fine with us. They'll take him back once he grows out of it."

"Well, if *that's* all that happened …" I challenged.

He laughed. "Right. So much to tell you. Let's see … small stuff first. On two days, two sit-down customers. Can you believe it? Havin' real people in the diner? Bev started frettin' about her looks. Check this out."

He pulled out his phone, swiped, and showed me. I looked. "Okay." It was a picture of Bev.

He looked at it himself. "She cut her hair short. What a difference. She is smokin' hot!"

"Okaaay." I hadn't noticed the hair.

He looked one more time and put his phone away.

"Got some appointments on the calendar for hosting birthday parties, too. I'm hoping Bo is right about 'em gettin' the word out."

"Me too," I nodded. "I think it will."

A car was coming. Jeff waited for it to pass. "Oh, speakin' of gettin' the word out, word on the street is that Lighthouse Diner has a hamburger on the menu called Road Kill Biscuit. Best burger in the state."

I just waited for the punchline.

"Rusty came up the hill with a load of wood for the fire pit one day, really proud that it was all hickory. Then he went in the diner and made himself some burgers mixed with venison. Had a bottle full of a sauce he'd made. Well, I'm telln' ya … best burger ever!

Full of flavor with just a little kick! He had to keep makin' 'em cuz everyone wanted one!"

"So business out the back door just keeps getting better," I guessed.

He gave a thumbs up. "We had a bingo night last Saturday. Good turnout. Bev went and picked up that lady, April Post. The one that told us about Miss Bixley. Erma was there, too. The posters said half the cover charge went to the winners and half to Erma for feedin' the poor.

"We served tea, lemonade, and water, and Miss Bishop brought home-baked cookies. They went fast as deviled eggs at a church picnic. And get this — Miss Post said some of the folks were church members. Can you believe it? And Erma said some of the folks were families she took food to.

"I mean, geez, Chad. Next thing you know the hoot owls will be flirtin' with the chickens."

I shook my head. "Crazy."

"Okay, next is the bakery. The pies and bread are just startin' to hit the shelves. The pies are labeled Miss Baker's Blue Ribbon County Fair Apple Pie, right? Her picture and a little blue ribbon are in the upper corner. The bread — same bread as before — doesn't say anything about a County Fair, but it does have Miss Baker's picture. And guess what's in the upper corner?"

"A little blue ribbon," I answered.

"Yep. It gets the message across."

"Love it."

"So does Miss Baker. And, oh, we get four pies delivered free every day from the bakery. Priced 'em at $16 per pie instead of $20 cuz they're not as scarce anymore. But they're free to us. So that's

$64 a day, times 30 if we sell 'em all … that's almost two thousand a month! That's real money!"

"Score!" I cheered. "That's great, Jeff. Bet Bev is happy. She's always worried about the money."

"As she should be, but, oh … get this. Unsold pies go to Erma, right? Every night. Just this mornin' one of her pies showed up on Craigslist for $8. So from now on, she's gonna have to cut them in small pieces and hand 'em out per person. Geez Louise, no good deed goes unpunished!"

All I could do was shake my head.

"And get this. Bev's got you a job waitin'. It's drivin' the truck for the bakery deliverin' bread and pies. And pickin' up old stock and bringin' it to Erma. It don't pay much, but heck, it's somethin' to do for now."

"Sounds great," I said, honestly. "A daily road trip. Bring in some money. Make myself useful. Is that all … or are you just breakin' me in for the bad news?"

"No." Jeff shrugged. "It's all good this time."

"Any word on Bev's sisters?"

"Oh yeah, I moved the trailer that used to belong to Rusty's brother, Todd. Moved it up to JB and Miss B's pad. They won't be back 'til next spring, so why not, you know? Brenda will be movin' into that one."

"And Blair?"

"She's stayin' in Roanoke. She turned in her notice to quit, you know, the boss hittin' on her and all. Turns out the hotel is owned by the guy's wife. The wife comes in to hire someone to replace Blair and figures out Blair has been doin' the work of the manager, bookkeeper, and front desk clerk. She also learned from the cleanin' ladies that her husband is hittin' on all the girls. So she sends him to a car wash place she owns and asks Blair to stay. Gave her a raise and a budget to hire a new front desk clerk.

"How's that for shootin' the stinger off a bee?"

"Wow, that's great!" I was thirsty. "Got any more water bottles in that cooler?"

He pulled one out and handed it over. "Here ya go. Wanna hear about the drug dealers?"

"So ready."

"Sheriff Bailey was real fuzzy about the details — no surprise there. The distribution to the abandoned mine was the missin' link for the FBI. A nationwide bust is goin' on, but bottom line is our local drug guys are gone."

"That's great news, Jeff."

"Yep, mostly."

"Hello? Mostly?"

Jeff took a really deep breath, and that told me something bad was coming.

"Sheriff Bailey is concerned about the sudden shortage of opioids," he began. "You need meds and help comin' off the addiction. He's sayin' hospitals will get caught off guard. Social services will be stretched, and he's even afraid there will be suicides. Said he's puttin' in a request for more overtime for his deputies. Said to stay alert.

"Said Trish is probably one of the victims hooked on the stuff. Bev is tryin' to track her down. Crazy how a good thing can lead to a bad thing."

"Oh, no. Maybe I should just come on home …"

"Up to you, but there's no real need. We got the Pyrs. And I'm gonna start walkin' the fence line to let 'em know I'm concerned."

"You really think they'll pick up on it?"

"Wouldn't be surprised if they already know. That is one smart breed. I can't help myself from givin' them hugs and rubs. Next to you and Bev, they are most precious to me.

"Anyway, Bev prepped a really great care package for you. Be a shame to let it go to waste. Stay gone a few more days and we'll probably solve world hunger."

"Well, if you put it that way ..."

"I was gonna hike up the trail with you a ways and carry the care package."

"Okay then." I beamed. "Let's go!"

As we started the trail, Jeff was impressed with how often the "AT" slash was painted on the trees. And he soon realized how much effort it takes to walk up a hill with a weight on your back. He needed breaks as much as I did.

At one of our breaks I said, "I've hiked this part. Can't believe how much of it is familiar. I don't remember payin' that much attention."

"Kinda all looks the same," he said.

"That's what I thought too the first time I was here."

We continued up. I was in front, and I could hear him behind me breathing harder.

At the next break, Jeff said, "Forgot to tell you about Bev's plans for the so-called RV resort."

"Okay." I leaned on the poles he made for me.

"You got Bev's sisters up against abuse and tyranny. You got mothers up against bullying." He was using his fingers to count. "You got Trish up against abuse and addiction."

"And ignorance," I added.

"True. You got poverty, prejudice, and … don't forget rape. I'm runnin' out of fingers." He looked at me eye to eye, dead serious. "Bev wants the steep part of the property to be a refuge for people in need. To give them support. To give them hope."

I thought about Steph and her son. Brenda. Rusty.

"We already got one started."

He agreed. "Know how we're gonna finance it?"

"I would *love* to know how we're gonna finance it!"

"No f'n clue. No way in hell. The idea is nuts. I love Bev's moral spunk, though."

"She serious about it?" I asked.

"Not really. Just a pipe dream."

Now it was my turn to take a deep breath. "Jeff, walkin' on this trail … you're surrounded by nature. Everything is pure and real. It resets your yardstick for measuring what is real and right … and possible. What Bev *wants* … all she can hope for … or rather all she has … is *hope*. But that's enough for now because hope is real. It has the power to break through barriers."

Jeff smiled. "She would probably call it faith. Her upbringin' and all."

I nodded. "I think we should honor her idea and support it, and not let the impossibility of it all pull her down."

"I agree."

Normally Jeff and me would end a serious conversation with a joke, but not this time.

Hiking uphill wasn't too steep, but then it started goin' downhill and the grade required switchbacks. Different leg muscles started to ache. At the bottom we came to a road, so we both stopped and dropped our packs.

Jeff was smiling as if amused. "This is Clendennin Road."

He chuckled, looking one way and then the other. "Never had a clue a trail came through here." He looked up at the mountain we came from, then pointed down the road. "This way goes back to Pearisburg. Hell, we hiked up, then down. I bet we're level with the town."

"Good place to head back," I concluded.

"Haven't got you up to the top," he countered.

"It's not far," I fibbed.

"Not true. But I'm done with this pack." He handed it over.

It was heavy as lead.

"What the *hell*! What you got in here?"

"Remember what you said you would want on the trail if you could have *anything*?"

"Vaguely."

"Steak," he answered. "You were talkin' about the trail and Bev asked you, and you said steak."

He reached down in his pack and pulled it out. It was huge. He smiled. "Left over from the party the other day. It was frozen when I pulled it out this morning. Should be thaw'd out by now."

He reached in the pack again. "These are potatoes wrapped in foil so you can cook them in the coals. And a baguette. And … wine. Bag wine, see? So you don't have to carry the bottle."

"What am I gonna do with all *this*?" I asked.

He grinned. "I dunno … set up a buffet table for the other hikers?"

"Wait a minute." I pointed my finger. "She asked what I would want *delivered*."

He faked remorse with his one eye looking down. "Bev would be *awful* hurt if she knew you objected to her efforts."

"Ouch. Below the belt. You will *not* tell her I complained."

"I'll report that you whined like a baby."

We both laughed. Then we hugged and he started down the road.

I hefted the packs as best I could, crossed the street, and walked into the woods.

CHAPTER 26

It was a tough climb to the top, so I was grateful for the chill in the air. The path leveled off. I'd be on the crest from then on.

I came up to the shelter Peyton and I came to, wasn't planning to stop. A guy was sitting on the front lip of the floor, wrapped in a sleeping bag. He looked like a monk — sitting upright, head covered, legs in lotus position. I waved, of course.

As it turned out, *he* was a *she*. The sleeping bag slipped off her head and a gorgeous girl appeared. Her short, strawberry- blond hair framed a round, pleasant face. Her eyes were small, as if squinting, but gave a permanent expression of a smile. She had a button of a nose, and her lips were framed by dimples. It was not the face of a glamorous movie star, but much better. It was a face I couldn't stop staring at.

It was … *love at first sight.*

"Just passing through?" she asked, her velvety voice adding perfection to her looks.

I stood there, glanced down the trail, and mentally scratched out wrong answers to her question. I knew I couldn't say "no" because it was obvious I was *just passing through*. The silence was getting awkward. Then it hit me — something wasn't right.

So I asked, "Something wrong?"

She looked up the trail I just came from. Then, "Can you stay?

Please?"

I turned and walked to her, dropping my packs and poles. "Are you hurt? What's the matter?"

She shook her head. "I'm not hurt … just exhausted. I've been hiking nonstop since yesterday, all night and today. I can't go any further."

I came closer. I'm sure there was a big question mark on my face. I watched her bright hazel eyes dart back and forth.

"There's this guy," she began. "He keeps popping up and hiking with the group I'm in. Or *was* in. He keeps making comments … inappropriate, suggestive … obnoxious hints about the two of us. Makes me sick just thinking about it. He's so f'n relentless, and I'm afraid he'll catch me here alone."

I hopped up and sat next to her. "So I'll stay."

She looked at me, tilting her head. "Just like that?"

"I think it's trail code or something," I answered, "to help each other out."

"Okay. But I still feel bad about it. How far were you planning to go?"

"I didn't have a goal. Just puttin' in some more miles. Now that I'm sitting, it feels *good* not walking."

"You're not a good liar, are you?" She waited for me to lock into her eyes. When I did, I was a deer in headlights.

"No, not really." I smiled.

She smiled back and extended her hand. "I'm Hope So." I shook her hand. It was so soft and warm. "Wanna Be." Our hands stayed together longer than usual.

"Well, now," she giggled, "Aren't we a pitiful pair? Hope So and Wanna Be. Two people longing for more. You can call me Hope, by the way. It's my real name. It's how I got my trail name. I don't really like it."

"I don't like mine either. Got it before I even started hiking. I set up a Trail Angel station and a hiker named me. He asked me if I was a hiker, and I said, 'No, but I wanna be.' So, Wanna Be is what I got."

She smiled, then breathed in so deep it was as if she was sucking all the oxygen out of the air. Her cheeks puffed as she exhaled. Then she took another deep breath.

"God," she exclaimed, "I can breathe again. I've been so tense thinking about the perv. His name is Trail King, by the way."

"Not short on confidence," I noted.

"Yeah, obviously named himself. Picture a spoiled, rich kid at a country club rubbing elbows with the elite and snubbing the staff."

"With a British accent," I added.

"Yeah, not like your voice. You sound like my favorite singer, John Prine."

"Never heard of him," I fibbed, "but … *Ain't it funny how an old broken bottle looks just like a diamond ring?*"

Her eyes got big, her jaw dropped. "That's him! You do know him! Tell me you play the guitar, and I will marry you."

My chuckle gave away my answer to the offer.

"No, wait. I take it back."

"No take-backs, Mrs. Hope Davis."

I was letting her know my last name.

She shook her head. "No, no. I am currently done with men. I … I can't flirt right now. Okay? *Please?*"

I nodded. "I get it, I get it. Seriously, Hope, I know."

"Thank you," she said, earnestly.

"If he does come by, can I take him on?"

"Oh, heck yes! Hell, I could probably take him on if I was mad enough. But neither of us could out-talk him. He will counter everything and twist what you say. He just keeps pushing."

"You had guys in your group, right?"

"Yes, and they helped me several times. They cornered him and told him to back off. So ... what's he do? Becomes the victim. Implies their threat of physical confrontation is unlawful. And he's never down for long. Pops back up like a whack-a-mole."

She fell silent. I wondered how a guy being a nuisance could drive her to walking herself to exhaustion.

"It must sound crazy," she mused, looking over at the trail, "that I would go to this extreme to get away from someone."

I thought about Peyton. "I know a lady that drove three days straight trying to get away from her husband. So I guess the effort speaks for itself."

She looked at me, a look of desperation on her face. "He would say things like, 'The other hikers wonder why we haven't hooked up by now, since we're so compatible.' So ... I think to myself, what other hikers? Let's do a survey, ask if anyone thinks we're compatible.

"Why would I have to prove something so *obvious*?"

She shook her head back and forth.

"One night," she continued softly, "the guys in the group ganged up on him and told him to get in his tent. It was hiker midnight and everyone was fed up with him. He did, but he kept saying something vulgar about having wet dreams about me. From inside his tent he started thumping on the fabric as if he was masturbating. And he was oohing and saying my name. It was disgusting! I felt violated to my core!" She had a look of total embarrassment.

I looked her straight in the eye, drawing a blank on what to say.

"It's things like that and a hundred more," she complained.

"And always toward me. What does that say about the other girls? That they aren't worth his noble attention? Not good enough? Not that they would want his abuse. Still, the message was clear."

I worded my response carefully. "I can't honestly say I get all of what you're sayin'. I wasn't there. But already, I want to *hurt* him. And I'm not the kind of person that wants to hurt anyone."

She nodded. "Okay … close enough. Thank you."

I remembered the steak and potatoes. It would be a great way to change the subject. "I'm gonna start a fire. A campfire is always comforting to watch."

"Good idea. It's almost as good as watching waves on a beach."

"I'll take your word for it," I said, standing up. "Never seen the beach in person."

"Really? Oh."

I got a fire going. We needed the hot coals for the potatoes. I smiled and imagined her surprise in getting steak and potatoes for a meal. It was gonna be great.

As I was tending the fire, Hope walked up to the outhouse. When she returned she was humming a Toby Keith song. I joined in, adding the lyrics. So she started singing too. Unlike me, she could carry a tune. It was big fun, and I could tell it made her feel better.

We sat on the picnic table and watched the fire.

"One more thing about the pervert," she mumbled, "so I can get it off my chest. We called him Yellow Blazer, by the way."

"I know the AT trail is white blazes, and blue is for side trails. What are yellow blazes?" I asked.

"Yellow blazes are the lines down the middle of a road.

Yellow blazers get off the trail and skip ahead … by car."

"Misses the whole point of hiking."

"Yeah, well, he couldn't keep up with the group, so we'd lose him for a few days. But then he'd show up, waiting for us at a shelter. He'd say he took a side trail or hiked at night and passed us. Always a lie, but we knew. But don't call him Yellow Blazer to his face. You'd get an endless tirade."

"Sounds like I'd lose an argument with him. I can never think of anything clever."

"No one can."

"Sorry. I wouldn't be much help."

"Just stay with me long enough to get off the trail. I was scared to death 'til you showed up."

"That's not right."

"No, but it is what it is. I was sitting here thinking, *what if he walked up?* It'd be just the two of us. Would he get … would I have to…" Her voice trailed off.

We sat and watched the fire burn. I felt sad for her and anger at him. I thought about the rapist that we took down. The guy coming after Peyton that Marvin confronted. Trish's boyfriend that Vicki ran off. And how scared I was. And now this guy … someone that would never back down.

I couldn't fight him, but I had an idea. And this time, I had no fear.

I got up and put more wood on the fire. The coals were getting good and hot, glowing just right. I turned and faced Hope. She was watching me.

"If he shows up," I promised, "I can deal with him."

She didn't answer, and I couldn't get a read on her.

I walked back to her. "Hungry?" I asked.

"Starving."

"I'll fix dinner."

She turned and pulled her pack closer. "I have some ramen noodles in here somewhere."

I picked up Jeff's pack, pulled out a potato, and handed it to her. Then I pulled out the other one.

"What's this?" she asked, turning it in her hand.

"A soon-to-be baked potato."

She stared at it with joy. "These will go great with —"

"With …" I interrupted while pulling out the paper-wrapped steak. I carefully unfolded my prize.

"What's *that*?" she asked, confused. "Is that … what I … *what*? Are you *kidding* me!" The big juicy steak hit the mark. "Nooooo! Look at all that protein!"

I carefully refolded the paper and set it down.

"You carried a steak in this far? How'd you do that?"

"It's a long story that I'm going to make even longer."

I reached into the pack and s-l-o-w-l-y pulled out the long loaf of French bread. Then handed it to her.

She took it, quickly tore off the wrapper, and bit a mouthful off the top. Then she looked at my pack and asked with her mouth full, "Got one in there for you? This one's mine."

"Thought you might share," I grinned.

She shook her head as she took another bite.

"Maybe we could work out a trade." I pulled out the wine bag. Her head went from shaking to nodding.

"That's … wine! I have *never* seen wine this far in on the trail. That is amazing! I can't believe all this. It must weigh a ton!"

I had to fess up about Jeff's surprise and helping me carry it. The potatoes took a while, so we finished off the bread while waiting. The wine lasted just long enough to finish the steak.

When our feast was consumed, Hope leaned back on her pack. "I can literally *feel* the protein seeping through my body."

"Feelin' better?" I asked.

"I need to pinch myself to see if I'm just dreaming all this."

"Same here. Let's put the past in the past where it belongs."

"Got that right." She started singing another John Prine song, and I joined in. It morphed into a challenge, each coming up with songs to see if the other knew the lyrics. With all the years spent with Mom, I was up to the task.

We talked about everything. She told me about growing up in Houston, Texas, where her parents still lived. She talked about high school, her sisters, and trips to the beach. She talked about college at Texas A&M. And her career as an insurance underwriter.

I followed with my past starting with Mom, buying the land, and starting the diner. I told her about Jeff and Bev, Carolyn and Vicki, Marvin, the rapist, Jeff and the fight, and the hanging.

Hope's only question: "Where is your property?"

"About two mountains over," I answered, pointing. "Tree Fork. I'm sure you've never heard of it."

She looked at me, but her eyes weren't focused on me. It was starting to get dark, so it was hard to tell.

"Are you … um … Chad?" she asked, hesitantly.

I was dumbstruck.

"I'll take that as a yes." She readjusted herself on the picnic table and gazed at the firepit. "Back in Virginia … Big Meadows, maybe? Not sure. I was in another group. We were camped for the night, all of us SoBos.

"A group of NoBos came in — a middle-aged lady, a guy named Starbuck, a tall redhead, and another girl. They were off to the side, talking around a campfire. I wandered over there. The lady — she was from New York — was talking about running from her husband. She landed in a place in West Virginia. She met two guys and a girl who were running a diner. They saved her from one of the goons her husband sent after her.

"One of the guys she met was Chad, and he hiked with her for a week. And that's when she met Starbuck and the other two girls."

"Big Red and Cookie Monster," I confirmed.

She looked at me and the reflection of the fire was dancing in her hazel eyes. "I ate one of your cookies."

"Oh sure," I said mischievously. "You run into a lady in Virginia that I ran into in West Virginia, and we just happen to meet *here*. Small world, right? I'm sure it happens all the time. But care-package cookies are for gobblin' down at the post office, not later. That part makes *no sense* at all!"

"They ate Cookie Monster's cookies in town. Saved your

cookies for the campfire. They offered me one, and I accepted."

"Wow, *you* ate one of *my* cookies."

"Quit messing around." She giggled. "The point is you helped *her*, and now you're helping *me*. You're a good man."

"Thanks. Come to think of it, you're saying she called me 'Chad,' not my trail name. What gives?"

"She was talking about the person she knew *off* the trail. Not *on* the trail."

I thought about it. "Come to think of it, we called each other by our names while hiking. At least until we met Starbuck and them. Can't believe you pieced it all together."

"It's what I do." She shrugged. "My job and all."

"Oh yeah, insurance undertaker," I teased.

"Insurance under*writer*."

"What ev."

She punched me on the arm. "I like you, Chad."

We talked past hiker midnight. We got into our sleeping bags and kept talking past midnight. Then she rolled over the other way, scooched closer to me, and we spooned.

"Hold me, Chad."

I pulled my arm out of the sleeping bag and cuddled her in.

Soon she was snoring softly.

I wanted to stay awake and listen, but I fell asleep.

The next morning we decided it would be a zero day. Hope was still weak from her overnight hike, and I had plenty of food left. We talked all day. We covered religion, politics, secrets … everything.

I told her about the boulders, and the energy there that Marvin could feel, but I couldn't. And his comment that some questions don't have answers.

"I think I know what he means," Hope responded. "But I wouldn't word it that way. For me it's not the lack of answers, it's the abundance of questions. There is so much we want to know, but we're only human. What we don't know, we call mystical … or miraculous … or magical. As if it's something special. It's not special, in my opinion. It's just more of what we don't understand. "That's one reason why I want to live in a log cabin someday."

"So do I!" I blurted out. "Tell me why."

"Because the logs have energy, grown from the earth."

I told her about Miss Baker's house. I had not covered that part yet. We made plans on building one someday — flirting playfully. But I stopped short of telling her exactly where we could build it.

"What's the matter?" she asked suddenly. I guess she could read the look on my face.

I turned to the side, thinking.

"Look at me," she pleaded.

I tried but couldn't. "Hope?"

"Yes?"

I had to just say it. "I'm falling for you but … Hope, I'm just a dumb hick. I'll be drivin' a bread truck when I get back. You're out of my league. Sooner or later this dream is …"

"Hush," she whispered. "I'm falling for you too. So we can stop skirting around what's happening, okay? We're coming off this mountain together. We're going to see where this goes. And I have a feeling it's going far."

I hugged her and fought back tears. When I pulled back, I saw tears running down her cheeks. I kissed each cheek, then put my tear-drenched lips on hers. A shiver ran down to my toes.

When we parted, she was grinning.

"I'd jump your bones," she teased, "if I wasn't so stinky. God, I sound like a hussy."

I smiled. "I'd let you if … if … I can't think of any reason not to."

"Then stop thinking." She squeezed my face with one hand.

We both smiled, and took a long time gazing into each other's eyes. It felt like our inner souls were talking to each other. So from then on, things were different. From that moment on we were a couple.

Conversations were more open. If we disagreed about something, we said so. We laughed more often, touched more often, and kissed constantly. We talked about things in the future we would be doing together.

The next morning was chilly, especially with the shelter under a thick canopy of trees. I poked my head out of my sleeping bag and the brisk air helped wake me up. I was taking in the view of where the sun peeked through the trees.

I knew it was him at first glance.

He was walking up the trail and making as much noise as progress. Hope had described him as a country-club snob. I would describe him as a California surfer — short blond hair, clean-shaven, and wearing colorful clothes. He had on a bright orange button-down shirt, plaid dress shorts, and sandals. *Hiking in sandals?* And with a small backpack. You could tell it wasn't digging into his shoulders. He had come up from the south, so he must have jumped ahead of Hope and backtracked.

Hope heard him too. She peeked out of her sleeping bag, then ducked back in. "Oh God. No."

I leaned over her cocoon. "Listen, Hope, follow my lead.

Whatever you do, *do not speak*. Not a word."

She let out a muffled "okay."

He walked past us, waved, but then stopped.

"Wait!" he commanded. "I would recognize that backpack anywhere! Hope So! Hope So!"

She didn't budge. I reached down into the bottom of my sleeping bag, found my pants, and put them on.

"I know it's you, Hope So! You're about a day ahead of our group!"

A quiet, "Oh crap" came from her sleeping bag. Slowly, she poked out her head.

"Thaaat's more like it!" he crowed, triumphantly. He walked toward us from the trail.

I couldn't speak. I felt it was our best defense. But I had to do *something*. I reached down for my knife, whipped it out, and jammed it hard into the wood floor. The *thunk* sound it made was even better than I had expected.

He flinched, but then so did Hope.

"Whoa there, bud!" he responded. "That's aggressive. Not cool! Not cool at all! Hope So, you *know* this guy? Obviously not for long. He's not part of our group. You feel safe around him? This is not acceptable. Everybody knows that."

She leaned over toward me. "Nice," she whispered. "He's off

his game."

I nodded.

"Hope So! Really?" he bellowed.

She didn't say a word.

He looked to me. "What's your name?"

I didn't answer.

"I'm Trail King," he announced, unfazed. "Or King Trail, as some people call me!"

Hope whispered again, now closer. "We call him Asshole."

I smiled.

"I know this trail," he continued, "like the back of my hand. Hiked it both ways. I love this trail, and frankly, it loves me. It's the best trail … the *best*, none better. It's the most famous! It's the longest!"

"Not," Hope whispered.

"The highest! People don't know that."

Another whisper. "No."

"The longest!"

"Still *not*."

"Most dangerous!"

An annoyed whisper. "Nada."

He dropped his pack but stayed on the other side of the picnic table. He put a foot up on the seat and addressed me.

"Look," he began confidently, "Hope So and I have been hiking together a long time. Hundreds of miles, hundreds. Hope So, have you told him about us?"

No answer.

"We're SoBos. That's trail talk for south bounders. Started up in Maine …"

"Doubt it," she whispered.

"Hush," I returned, trying not to move my lips.

On he went about how he kept the group together. Kept them safe. How I was welcome to join the group, but aggressive behavior would not be tolerated. Not legal, even.

"Pissant," Hope whispered. He wouldn't stop talking, and she didn't stop whispering. "Clown. Fraud. Liar. Wish I could hurt him … somehow."

The guy j-u-s-t k-e-p-t talking.

Then, in a normal voice that she knew he could hear, she said to me, "Scooch back, I need some room."

I did as requested, reluctantly.

She gathered the sleeping bag snug around her neck. After all, she was just wearing a thin sleep shirt. Awkwardly, she stood up and pivoted around to face me. Trail King was talking but stopped to watch what she was up to. She looked back at him, then to me, smiled, and dropped the sleeping bag down to her waist.

I was getting a nice view. Trail King was not.

Whoa!" he yelled. "Hey! Hope So! Hope So!"

He started to come toward us, but I jumped out of my bag and grabbed the knife handle. It stopped him cold.

Hope pulled the sleeping bag back up, sat down, and started getting dressed inside it. Like me, she slept with her clothes inside to keep them warm.

Trail King started talking again.

Hope and I went about breaking camp. He just kept talking.

We just kept ignoring him.

"Okay, look," he offered. "There's a town down the hill. We can meet there. Maybe stop and get some lunch. Hope So, I know you're trying your best to get to the end. I'll help you. Bring your new friend if you like. We can work this out."

He put his pack on and headed back the way he came.

Hope watched him, smiled at me, gave me a very big kiss, then breathed a sigh of relief. "He's gone. I'm *so* happy."

I wasn't. "Hope, he's mental. He's dangerous."

Her eyes bulged and her shoulders slumped. "Oh no, you're right. He wants me … now *even more*. And he knows you and your knife are in his way. Crap. We should hike north, away from him."

I shook my head. "You were both north of here. He just came up from the south. He leapfrogged you, so he really is yellow blazing. He'll catch us either way."

She nodded. "Then we *have* to get off this trail. But which side? East or west? Either way is steep going down."

"West. Toward my place. Find a road and phone reception. I can call Jeff and he can pick us up."

"Okay. Let's go!"

We hiked north along the ridge, searching for a place on the left. But everywhere we looked was a sheer cliff. So we kept going. This was taking too long.

Then we heard him yelling. A ways back, but coming toward us.

We looked around, agreed on a rock formation off to the left, and ran there. There wasn't enough room for us and our packs, so we tossed them off the side. It made more noise than we expected.

His yelling must have drowned out the noise. He got closer, hollering, "Bastards! I tried to be nice! Think you can fool me? We'll see about that! You don't know who you're dealing with!"

We laid flat as possible, hoping we were hidden by the rocks. His threats got closer and closer. We tried to melt into the ground. The ranting passed us and continued up the trail.

I chanced a peek. There was no pack on his back. He had a pole in one hand, and a handgun in the other. I cringed and looked at Hope. She read my face.

"What?" she mouthed.

"A gun." She closed her eyes and shook her head.

The yelling faded in the distance. We jumped up and looked over the edge. Our packs were down below. We started down, hanging onto tree branches and planting our feet against rocks or tree roots. We finally made it to our packs.

"We can't get down with these on," Hope realized. She rummaged through hers and pulled out her phone. "Think he could see them from up there?"

"Doubt it." I pulled out my phone as well. "Doubt he would even come off the trail in those sandals … but let's throw them down a little further."

We tossed our backpacks and they didn't stop tumbling end over end until they hit a tree. We climbed down to them again and threw them down further. As we watched them tumble, we froze.

The yelling was coming back. Our heads spun around looking for a place to hide. We each found a tree and laid flat behind it. The yelling wasn't as constant as before. He'd lost us and he knew it. We'd hear an occasional "Fuck!"

His voice faded into the distance again. We got up and carefully made our way down to our packs.

"Hate to leave my pack," Hope murmured, still in a whisper. She pulled her trail map out from a side pocket. "My map might help. It shows roads."

"We'll find our packs." I pulled energy bars from mine.

"No big loss, really," she said. "Most of it will be tossed. It smells so bad. I'm off the trail for good, anyway. He ruined it … ruined it forever."

"There's some stuff worth comin' back for. When we're ready, and with help."

"And guns?"

"With a gun, Jeff, and four hunkin' big dogs."

We said goodbye to our backpacks.

We had the time, the energy, and good sense to take it slow. After an hour the grade wasn't as steep. The further we went, the better it got. But we stayed cautious.

"You okay?" I kept asking

"I'm good," she'd answer.

We continued heading straight downhill, but the lower we got straight down wasn't always in the same direction. I could tell we were getting lost. We stopped and checked our phones for a signal.

"Zero bars," I complained.

"Ditto. You okay? You look distracted."

"No. I'm good." But then a grin crept across my face.

"What? Fess up."

"I think my brain took a picture of you dropping your sleeping bag. Keeps popping up in my head."

"*Like* what you saw?" she teased. "Think this scrawny bod will work for you … for the rest of your life?"

I looked her in the eye. "Normally, I would not have a comeback to a question like that. But my friend Jeff, when he was in the hospital, told me exactly what I should say right now.

"That bod would look good in a wedding dress."

She jerked back and her eyes bulged. "Is that a proposal?"

At that, my mind went blank, but hesitation was not an option. "Yes."

"Really???" Her joy was contagious.

"Yes!"

She jumped into my arms and knocked me down. We celebrated with a long, passionate kiss.

Sitting back up, she flipped from passionate to serious. "Look," she began, "we met just hours ago. But we both feel the chemistry. We'll give it time, okay? We have to try."

I shook my head. "I can't believe this is happening. I'm afraid it's all a dream and I'm gonna wake up."

She nodded. "Me too. Let's go!"

We continued downhill, now much easier, but couldn't see through the trees far enough to know in what direction. And we had to push through the underbrush. I was in front guiding us through.

I stopped, looked back at Hope, and put my finger to my lips. She shrugged and raised her arms, palms up.

I motioned to slowly get down on the ground. When we both did, I whispered in her ear. "It's him, up ahead."

She mouthed "shit" without a sound. We crawled forward under the brush on our bellies.

A road was below us, and a camper — the kind you drive — was parked off to the side. It was old, dirty, and dented. And there he was. And *another* guy. They were arguing, but we couldn't make out what they were saying. Trail King had binoculars, and he was scanning the woods with them. We ducked as his sweep passed over us. He let his binoculars down and argued some more.

"What the hell," I whispered. "What's *with* this guy?"

"Classic narcissist," Hope hissed. "Doesn't handle rejection well."

They got in the camper and drove off. Trail King was the passenger.

"So *that's* how he does it! He gets chauffeured around in a camper!" She pulled out her phone. "One bar."

I pulled mine out. Two bars. Then a third bar.

"What the hell," I decided, "I'll call him and FaceTime." I dialed Jeff's number. "C'mon, Jeff, answer."

Hope snuggled in close to me, "Come on, Jeff."

Jeff wasn't looking at his phone when he answered.

"Hey bro, we haven't solved world hunger yet, so you can keep on poopin' in the —" He was turning his head and got to his good eye.

I could see on my screen that Hope and I filled the frame cheek to cheek.

He noticed. "Um … hello."

"Jeff," I announced, sporting a shit-eatin' grin. "This is Hope. Hope, Jeff."

It was funny, Jeff bein' speechless.

Hope turned, kissed me on the cheek, then nestled back against me again.

His eye bulged. He turned his head away. "Bev? Honey?"

We heard a distant reply.

"Bev! Honey! Please come! It's Chad!"

From over his shoulder Bev appeared from the back of the diner. You could see that she was pregnant.

Hope turned to me. "You didn't tell me she was pregnant."

I shrugged. "Oops."

Jeff gave his phone to Bev. Her face filled the screen. "Hey Chad. Um … hello."

Hope turned and gave me another kiss.

Bev screamed.

"That's Hope," Jeff said, calmly.

"What? Hope, you're gorgeous! How did this … how did you … is this *for real*?"

Hope kissed me again.

Bev screamed again. "Oh Hope! Chad is such a nice guy. You will *love* him! He's the best!"

The screen started to shake up and down as Bev shouted for joy.

Jeff's face came back on. "She's lookin' up your location on her phone." He smiled.

We couldn't see Bev anymore, but we could hear her loud and clear. "Look Jeff, look! They're here! See? Run and fetch them! Hurry!"

Jeff smiled. "Chad, I'm on my way. Hope, we look forward to meetin' you."

"Jeff," I said. "Can't explain why, but I need to tell you before

I lose the signal. Bring my truck, your gun, and Bear."

"On it," he confirmed.

Bev's face appeared. "Hope, we're gonna have a big dinner here tonight. Can't wait to meet you!"

"Bev?" Hope asked, "When are you due, honey?"

"Around Christmas! We just found out it's a girl! Gonna name her Carol. Like, Christmas Carol!"

"A baby," Hope purred, turning to me. "I want one."

I grinned, "Guess I better get started on that log cabin."

Bev's joyous squeal echoed out through the hills of my beloved West Virginia home.

ABOUT THE AUTHOR

Award-winning author David Major returned to his roots to write a story about the landlocked, third-world country known as West Virginia. The character of its people, the grandeur of its hills, and the unique challenges of the area beg to be told.

David lives in Glen Allen, Virginia. He has three daughters and four grandchildren.

He *did have* a beloved Great Pyrenees, Teddy Bear. While he may be gone, he lives in this story as a fourth main character. Teddy shows that a dog knows who *is* a friend, who *is not*, and what to do about it. After reading the story, you will know Teddy personally.